For Scott Allie
For his determination

Remember, Democracy never lasts long. It soon wastes, exhausts, and murders itself.

—JOHN ADAMS

AD JUST MENT DAY

People still talk about some do-gooder. A good scout, the one in every crowd. Some altar boy, some teacher's pet walks into the Southeast Precinct, looking both ways, whispering with one hand cupped beside his mouth. Past dark o'clock, it's midnight o'clock, when in walks the kid with his hood up, head down, wearing sunglasses, no less. He's nobody's Stevie Wonder. No white cane, no dog. Whisper-asks can he talk to somebody in charge. Asks the desk sergeant on duty. Whispers, "I want to report a crime's supposed to happen."

The desk sergeant's being, "Got some ID?"

Wearing a ball cap with the brim pulled low, his hood pulled up on top of the ball cap. Only his nose and mouth showing, this party pooper, concerned citizen, sweating dark patches through the back of his sweatshirt, he's all, "It's not me telling you, okay?" Shaking his head. "Not in public, either."

So Mr. Desk Sergeant, he calls somebody. Makes a big performance of pressing a button, picking up his telephone and touch-toning, never taking his eyes off this kid in the sunglasses, sergeant asking can a detective come down to the lobby and take a statement. Yeah, a possible tip. Sergeant looks at the kid's hands he can't see on account of they're shoved in the front pockets of his hoodie, not a good sign. Sergeant always head nodding. Pointing with his chin, like, "Want to keep your hands where I can see them?"

The kid obliging, but shifting his weight from foot to foot like he forgot to take a leak for the past hundred years. Craning around like he's expecting somebody to walk in off the street behind him. Kid's all, "I can't be exposed here like this."

This kid, his arms hang straight while he's hyperactive from the waist down, like he's in Riverdance, or like he's doing porn, the same way a porn star keeps that camera-side arm slack, pulled back, paralyzed, while his hips buck, like that one arm is attempting to flee the scene in understandable humiliation.

Sergeant on duty being, "Empty your pockets." Waving this goody-two-shoes in the direction of a metal detection tunnel deal same as at any airport.

This Eagle Scout extricates his wallet and phone and puts them in the plastic bowl. After a long hesitation, his sunglasses. The regular Homeland Security routine. The kid's eyes twitchy. Blue eyes under worried-together eyebrows. Making a face that will give him wrinkles one day.

In the police station there's a sound, like a pop, like a shot, like a gun going off only muffled, maybe outside. Kid jumps. Most definitely a gunshot.

Detective's like, "You high, son?"

Kid's got this look like he's just seen the wrong person naked riding a bicycle from behind. His voice falls off a cliff, going shrill all the way to the bottom, he says, "Can I have my wallet back?"

Detective's all, "First things first." The detective goes, "You here about the upcoming assassinations?"

And the kid's like, "You guys know already?"

The detective asks who else has the kid told.

And this useful member of society, this kid, he says, "Just my folks."

The detective gives back the kid's wallet, his keys and sunglasses and telephone, and asks, can the kid call or text his folks and persuade them to come here, to the precinct right this moment?

The detective smiles. "If you got a minute, I can answer all your questions." He jerks his head toward the camera on the ceiling. "Not here." Detective leads this kid, America's newest hero, down a concrete hallway, down a fire stairs, through a couple of metal doors marked Authorized Persons Only. Leads the kid to a metal door. Unlocks it with a key. Throws the door open.

This kid's folks, they text they're coming down to help him. They text not to be scared. Inside the metal door it's dark and stinks. A backed-up toilet stink. Kid follows the detective. His folks text they're in the lobby.

Here's the best part. Detective flips on the lights. This snitch, the tattletale sees piled in the center of the room a heap of bloody clothes. Next he sees the hands attached to each sleeve. It's only clothes and shoes and hands because the heads and faces have been obliterated. A distant voice, muffled from another room, says, "The only quality that truly unites us is our desire to be united . . ."

It's then our altar boy turns to the detective for help and sees nothing except the muzzle aimed point-blank at his own face.

Soon as the locating service scans for pipes and buried electrical cables he gives the go-ahead to dig. Spencer's Rental trucks over the backhoe, their one with the largest bucket.

The job's just half-dug when sauntering across the practice fields comes somebody too old to be a student. Somebody tenured. Some busybody in those India-print, cotton drawstring pants. Leather sandals and socks. Wearing a sweatshirt printed with the words "This Is What a Feminist Looks Like." Something rolled up and tucked under his arm. He's got the usual gray beard and eyeglasses. Once he's yelling-close, gray beard raises his arm and waves. Shouts, "Nice day for it."

Yes, and a ponytail. Sauntering across the soccer pitch. Bald except for the gray ponytail hanging halfway down his back. Sparkling in the sunshine, an earring. One dazzle-bright diamond earring.

Specifications call for excavating a rectangle three hundred by thirty feet. Twelve deep, with the bottom leveled and layered with two feet of impervious clay. On top of that, a seamless barrier of polyethylene sheeting to retard possible leakage into the water table. This site, here, a minimum of five hundred yards from any potable well or open water course. These are the same specs they're using nationally, the same specs as a holding pond at a mill, only minus the compressed clay hardpan the EPA would normally require.

Rolled up under the gray beard's arm? It's a yoga mat. He goes, "What are you gentlemen undertaking, here?" A professor slumming it among the proles.

Rufus goes, "Campus improvement." How he says this without laughing, who knows, but he's all, "Long-term underground parking for faculty."

Naylor laughs, only he puts a fist to his mouth and pretends it's a cough. Ostermann gives him a harsh look.

Professor is all, "Call me Brolly. Dr. Brolly." He offers a handshake nobody accepts, not at first. Naylor looks at Weise. Rufus hefts his clipboard and flips through the thick stack of paper it holds. Professor's hand hovers until Ostermann shakes it.

Rufus shuffles his pages, being, "Brolly . . . Brolly . . ." His fingertip traces down some list, and Rufus goes, "You teach something called 'The Arrogant Legacy of Privileged Euro-Colonial Cultural Imperialism'?"

Professor nods to indicate the clipboard, him being all, "May I ask to what you're referencing?"

Not missing a beat, Rufus comes right back with, "Environmental impact study."

Naylor and Weise both guffaw. Total jackasses. They turn their backs to everybody until they can regain a professional composure. They're still snickering until Ostermann goes, "Don't be dicks!"

Professor red-faced behind his beard. He shifts his yoga mat from under one arm to under the other, going, "I only ask because I serve on the university Committee Against Wounding the Earth."

Consulting his lists, Rufus is all, "Vice chairperson, it says here."

Naylor excuses himself to go inform the backhoe operator of the need to slope the west side of the excavation seeing how that's the side the dump trucks will be filling it from. Nobody wants it to slump under that kind of weight. Weise leans on his shovel, nodding to get Prof's attention, going, "Nice sweatshirt."

Arm up, sleeve pulled back to show a wristwatch, Prof makes a big show of checking the time. Being, like, "I'd still like to know what you people intend."

Nose still stuck in his paperwork, Rufus goes, "Your office still in Prince Lucien Campbell Hall? Sixth floor?"

Prof looks rattled.

Weise goes, "That a real diamond?" Stuck through Prof's left ear, so perfect.

The soccer grass runs right to the edge of the dig. Under that shows a little margin of dark-brown topsoil. Below that is a yea-wide stripe of subsoil, with under that ancient history, dinosaur deep. The bell tower over by the Administration Building begins to toll four o'clock.

Prof goes down on one knee, right at the edge of the hole. Nothing but raw dirt going down deeper than a swimming pool. Deeper than a basement. Dirt and worms. The steep sides clawed with stripes from the teeth on the bucket. Little clods bust loose and roll to the bottom.

Kneeling there, the professor leans out over the drop. Contemplating what he can't understand, he could be looking for fossils. Dumb as a hog led to slaughter, not recognizing the obvious, but trying to identify some last trace of a vanished civilization. Whatever the case, he's getting a good long, lingering look at everything pitch dark he's spent his entire life pretending doesn't exist.

The bits of breakfast cereal clung to his skin like fruit-flavored scabs. He peeled off a red-flavored one and ate it. It left a ghost on his arm like a tiny, round, red tattoo. Like he was turning into a rainbow-colored leopard.

That morning Nick wakes up in bed with spilled Froot Loops sticking to his back. Little circle stains in rainbow colors, like Life Savers printed on his sheets. He reaches his phone off the floor to try and reconstruct his evening before.

"Reward offered for information," it reads. A text that came through a few minutes after midnight. He tries to return the text, but it's a blocked number.

He's not out of bed before the phone rings. The Caller ID says: Private. Nick thumbs the screen and is, like, "Talk to me."

A voice goes, "Nicolas?" A male voice, but not Walter's. Not his dad, either. Raspy and wheezing, but cultured. Nobody Nick knows calls him Nicolas.

He lies, "No, this is Nick's friend." He needs to piss. On the phone, he's all, "Nick's stepped out."

The telephone man is, "Allow me to introduce myself." Rasping, "My name is Talbott Reynolds. By any chance do you happen to know the whereabouts of a Miss Shasta Sanchez?" Wheezing, "That most captivating and lovely of creatures."

Nick lies again. "Can't help you."

Over the phone, "You are acquainted with the enchanting Miss Sanchez?"

And Nick's all, "Nope."

"Have you recently been contacted by either the police or one Walter Baines?" asks this Talbott person.

Nick's getting the picture. Walter. Walt, the screw-up. The lame helpless loser. Every overdose or car crash, it went this way without fail. The time Walter did bath salts and tried to eat his hand, it was Nick who had to take him to Emergency. Or worse, when he tried to drill that hot Satanist. Not bothering to hide the anger in his voice, Nick goes, "Never heard of him."

The voice over the phone sounds echo-y. As if calling from a hole somewhere, this Talbott says, "Be assured I am an exceedingly well-off individual who would pay greatly for any assistance you might offer."

Nick's fingers feel among the bedsheets until they come across something round. A ten milligram Flexeril by the size of it. By reflex he brings it to his mouth without looking and chews it without water. If this phone call is a drug deal, Nick frets he might get dragged into it. The events of last night continue to be a little foggy in his head. He's waited too long, long enough for somebody to triangulate the signal from his phone. Time enough for somebody to be knocking at his door. He gets all, "Let me take a message for Nick."

"Tell him," the voice says, this Talbott, "not to go to the police." After only the slightest of hesitations, "Assure him that everything will be resolved in a few days."

Already feeling his muscles loosen and relax, Nick goes, "What's Shasta wrapped up in, this time?"

The voice, this well-heeled geezer, Talbott, he's asking, "May I have your name?"

Only Nick ends the call. He slips out of bed and squints to see through the bedroom curtains. Nobody stands at his door, not yet. He pulls a green-flavored Froot Loop off his arm and chews it, thinking. Before anything else, he swipes and thumbs to deactivate the GPS on his phone. As an added safety measure he snaps open the back and slips out the battery.

Rows of folding chairs are set up, even so there's people left standing along the edges and across the back. In that big-box sporting goods place, the one with the waterfalls and trout stream for indoors fly-fishing, only it's after hours so the waterfall's shut off and the stream is just dry fiberglass pools with the trout tucked away in tanks behind the scenes. Like Mother Nature's gone home for the night, there's no soundtrack of songbirds or recorded trumpeting bull elk.

Bing and Esteban check out the crowd, mostly a bumper crop of Bubba types. A smattering of Jamals. An army of lone wolves. Across the audience is that one douche from the gym, Colton-something, sitting with his significant other, Peggy or Polly. Facing the crowd is some man asking, "By a show of hands, who knows why people crop the ears of dogs?"

Before anybody can answer or even raise a hand, he gets revved up about how ancient shepherds cropped the ears of their puppies. To prevent infections. To prevent wolves from taking hold during fights. Shepherds used the same scissors they sheared their sheep with. They grilled the snipped bits, cooked them up and fed them to the same dogs to make them fierce, no shit.

Sporting-goods guy, he asks the crowd, "How many of you know ancient Assyrian law?" He gets no takers. Charging forward, he's all, "The Babylonian Code of Hammurabi punished law breakers by slicing off their ears?" For extra credit, he goes on how King Henry VIII punished sixteenth-century vagrants by cropping their ears. That, and American law allowed folks' ears to be lopped off as punishment for sedition or moral offenses as late as 1839.

Making his point, he goes, "It shouldn't surprise you none that since the beginning of warfare, mercenaries have collected ears to exchange for their pay."

Bing puts up his hand, going, "Sounds bloody."

Sporting-goods guy shakes his head, going, "Not . . . ," he points up an index finger to make folks wait, "if your target is dead."

The chief advantage of taking scalps, he goes, is they're lightweight. Easy to harvest and transport. The downside is they're messy. The same goes for hearts. Claiming a heart is slow going. Ears, on the other hand, ears are ideal. The left ear, to be specific.

Ears are portable in large numbers. Easy to conceal. A hundred ears hardly strains a paper shopping bag. That amounts to three hundred thousand possible votes, practically being your own political party.

Sporting-goods guy, he turns his head sideways to everybody and goes, "Grab hold."

He means his ear. Esteban looks around. Nobody's grabbing so finally he steps forward and grabs the man's ear. It feels warm and stretchy. The man says, "Give it a good tug." He drills them on the regulations: Only the left ear counts. The *left*. Only ears on the list. Random DNA testing will be utilized, and if you're found to have submitted an ear not on the list then you're facing the death penalty. Ears may not be exchanged or sold, and only the person harvesting the ear may submit it for voting credit.

Sporting-goods guy yaks on about bullfighters. About ears being the body's heat radiators.

Esteban standing there, he's holding onto the guy's ear like it's cash money.

Plus, the guy goes, ears are durable. "Even with a head shot the ear—you might have to hunt for it—but the ear will remain intact." To Esteban still tugging on his ear, he goes, "You may resume your seat."

The way the sporting-goods guy explains it an ear is mostly, the outside part, the pinna, is composed of cartilage of the elastic type. That, and the outer perichondrium, which supplies blood and lymph. As easy to slice as a tire.

The best method, he goes, is to slice downward from the helix junction to the lobe.

He goes, "If you can slash a tire, you can harvest an ear."

Sporting-goods guy gets to maintaining how folks need a straight edge, fixed four-inch blade with a full tang, no fancy leather handle or bone or wood, but an easy-to-grip polymer. Such is his job: Selling stuff. "What you want is high-carbon stainless steel." No partial-tang knives. Partial-tang knives tend to break. Folding blades break. "A man can harvest all the targets he wants, but if his knife breaks what's the reward?"

Sporting-goods guy is all, "The day comes, people will use their kitchen shears—but how are they going to head home and cut up a chicken with the same tool they took ears?"

Loud, too loud, Esteban goes, "Amen!" Folks laugh.

This, this being Esteban's brain storm, them becoming warrior kings and all. His thinking is most men won't team up. Men, they're freelancers, like in olden days, those knights for hire. Your typical man, he'll try to hit a target and harvest the ear, himself. Alternating tasks requires him to constantly shift gears. Slowing him down. The solution, Esteban goes, is for labor specialization. Bing's a crack shot, Bing is, so he'll put down the target while Esteban does the harvesting. Together, they're a hit-and-harvest duo. Together they can establish the foundation of a glorious dynasty to last forever. Their kids and their kids' kids' kids will be crowned royalty.

The Adjustment being one last shot at doing something useful with their lives.

Theirs was just like Nat Turner's rebellion or John Brown's raid. A legacy. Come the New Crusades, the One-Day Crusade, and they'll claim something comparable to the knights who'd been awarded estates. But a power set to outlast both land and money. Become royal blood. With a shopping bag crammed full of ears they'll take their place in history. Esteban and Bing and their descendants will control a most mighty nation for the centuries to come.

Back in his chair Esteban removed a tissue and tube of cocoa butter from his coat pocket. He was a sleek apex predator now. If he was going to give up a lifetime of getting hand-me-downs and leftovers, he'd need to get that man's waxy ear stink off his fingers.

Shasta didn't turn around. She was accustomed to college boys trailing her through the halls between classes, eye-raping her French vanilla curves, ear-raping her with their shouts of, "Let's mount Shasta!" These rambunctious douche bags shouting, "How'd you like to summit Shasta?"

They'd pull at her dreads and shout, "Shasta, let me get below your tree line!"

At this she turned. She hoped it was Walt. It sounded like Walt's voice. But when she looked it was a burner type whose breath smelled like a torched party bowl of cheap kush. He lunged at her, his tongue out and lips pursed, trying to steal a kiss.

The stoner went, "I'll miss you, Shasta."

Confused, she was all, "But I'm not going away!" She sidestepped as he tried to swat her bottom.

Then she realized that he was leaving. This sad burner dude, he was going to die.

All the college boys were going to die painful, awful, horrible deaths.

The poor guy. They were all to be pitied.

Here at the University of Oregon, no matter how intense the teasing grew, she didn't take it seriously. These boys, even those who tried to pinch her yoga pants, she knew for a fact they acted out simply because they were terrified.

Dr. Brolly who taught Patterns in Politics had explained as much.

For all in-coming freshmen, he'd led a module examining a book by some German braincase. The smarty-pants academic, Gunnar Heinsohn, theorized that all major political upheavals in history were due to an excess of young males. A "youth bulge," the savvy kraut called it. Teaching the concept left Professor Brolly breathless with excitement. The basic idea held that if at least thirty percent of a population consisted of males between the ages of fifteen and twenty-nine—watch out!

Such surplus young men, if they were somewhat educated and well fed, they yearned for status and would create havoc in pursuit of it. Gunnar held that starving people don't strive for recognition. Likewise, illiterate boys will never recognize how history ignores them. But if the youth bulge is fed, well fed and schooled, they'll become a pack of ravenous, attention-seeking wolves.

For his favorite example, Dr. Brolly cited Spain in 1484. That year the Pope, Innocent VIII, declared that any form of birth control would be punished by death, and the size of the average Spanish family jumped from two children to seven. Only the first-born male would inherit family assets. Female children expected little at the time. But extra male children craved status, power, recognition, and social position. It was this surge of young men who called themselves *secundones*—in English, "secondaries." It was these men who spilled into the New World with Christopher Columbus's second expedition and became the legions of conquistadores who enslaved and pillaged the innocent Maya and Aztecs.

If Wikipedia was to be trusted, Gunnar Heinsohn had been born in Poland in 1943, which officially made him super geriatric. To Shasta, even with his shaggy blond hair and cool euro name he was only medium hot.

Throughout history, Dr. Brolly lectured, similar bulges of rambunctious youthful men had toppled governments and triggered wars. Eighteenth-century France experienced a population surge that increased the demand for food. Prices rose, citizens revolted, and the frustrated young people overthrew the Louis XVI aristocracy and lopped off Marie Antoinette's bejeweled head. Same deal with the Bolshevik Revolution. It was set in motion by a flood of extraneous sons from the countryside who had no farmlands to inherit. In the 1930s, Japan experienced a youth bulge that spurred the invasion of Nanking. In turn, Mao's revolution was powered by a male youth bulge in China.

Shasta had absorbed every detail. Clearly, every bad event in human history had been caused by a surplus of cute, young boyfriend material.

According to the Council on Foreign Relations, between 1970 and 1999, some eighty percent of civil conflicts occurred in nations where sixty percent of the population was younger than thirty years old! At present there were sixty-seven countries with so-called youth bulges, and sixty of them were suffering social upheaval and internal violence.

As if in league with Brolly, Ms. Pettigrove, who taught Generalities of Gender, lectured that every conflict that culls the male populous increases the social value of men. In turn, this catalyzes a rebirth of the patriarchy. With fewer men to choose from, women go boy crazy and toe the line for anything wearing pants.

It didn't take much brain power to realize why the male student body at the University of Oregon strutted about, brash and loud, but secretly terrified. The United States was only days away from ratifying a declaration of war with the Middle East. That region was enduring its own burgeoning bulge of young males, while the United States was struggling with the hyperactivity and status demands of the Millennial generation—arguably the biggest boy bulge in world history.

In Miss Lanahan's class, Biology of Animal Dynamics, she showed them a video about animal rights filmed by PETA or somebody. It showed a poultry farm where super-cute, newly hatched chicks were checked for their gender. The baby hens were placed under warming lamps and given food and water. The baby roosters, they got dropped down a dark chute. They piled up in a Dumpster, so deep they formed a fluffy, seething mass, each chick struggling to stay alive. A forklift carried the Dumpster into a barren farm field and poured it out. There, the male chicks, alive and dead alike, were plowed under as organic fertilizer.

The young men in the class had howled with laughter as the teeming, peeping flood of Easter cuties spilled from the Dumpster. The tiny yellow balls of fluff stumbled, terrified and cold, across the bare dirt. In a twinkling, giant tractor tires and thrashing farm machinery pulverized every adorable new life.

The boys laughed, Shasta knew, not because it was funny but because the chicks were themselves.

How could these teenagers focus on learning collage in Art or ballroom dancing in Phys Ed when, with the stroke of a government pen, their lives were about to be over?

Everyone knew it. Their eighteenth birthday had been a death sentence.

This was how politicians had always dealt with the burden of surplus men. It made Shasta sad, really. Really sad. These loud-mouthed jocks and stoners and nerds, they were dead men walking. As soon as the declaration of war was ratified it was so long male Millennials, hello newly robust patriarchy.

The boys who trailed the hallways behind Shasta, trying to snap her bra straps and peppering her with sexually suggestive invectives, they were all registered for military service. Most of them would be shipped off to be bullet-raped by enemy combatants.

So whenever Shasta started to take umbrage at their harassment, she considered how most of them would soon be bulldozed beneath arid dunes with like numbers of boisterous and extraneous Middle Eastern boys. She'd scamper through her course work while her male peers would be conscripted. Their muscles and pimples would be mangled under tank treads and blasted into screaming pieces by landmines just like the buried-alive, just-hatched baby roosters whose only crime had been being born the wrong gender.

She would go on to earn her degree in social work, just the beginning of a rich, long life.

And she'd always remember to wear a poppy pinned to her lapel every Remembrance Day.

Behind her a voice hissed, "Shasta . . ."

She turned, ready to upbraid some new accoster, but she was wrong. Here was Nick. A one-time boyfriend. Nick, who'd dropped out at the end of first semester, reasoning that he didn't need Physics and Calculus II for a successful future career as shattered, bloodied cannon fodder. It was nice to see him.

To judge from the wan half-smile on his face, he was happy to see her as well. Before the moment could turn into anything sticky and romantic, he asked her, "Have you seen Walter lately?"

Walt was her current boyfriend. He'd also dropped out of school. He worked at Starbucks, earning a few dollars and trying to enjoy the precious smidgen of life left to him. No, she hadn't seen him. Not since the day before when he'd been ranting about some grassroots mass murder conspiracy.

"First off," went Nick, "if the police ask, you haven't seen me." He took her hand and pulled her toward an empty storage space underneath the school's south stairs. He was being all, "Shasta, sugar, we need to talk." He reached out and brushed the dreads away from her face. "Honestly, I'm not going to date-rape you."

Shasta allowed herself to be pulled in.

Gregory Piper had received a second callback. His agent was thrilled. The part he was reading for was a character named Talbott Reynolds. A fictional monarch who ruled a near-future utopia of warriors and maidens, Talbott existed above corruption. The character was an immortal, a political saint of sorts. A principal role in some television pilot in preproduction.

It went without saying the project sounded like utter crap. Another character cut from whole cardboard. Piper sighed to himself. Regardless, it was a shop window. Face time. He hadn't worked, not a single television commercial or cartoon voiceover, nothing, for almost a year, and he was seriously underwater on his condo.

If need be he'd surrender his career to sad independent productions. Pilots that never got picked up by a network. He'd kowtow to film school auteurs funded with legalized marijuana money, who didn't know a key light from a lens filter. Thus he'd always find himself re-blocking every scene and advising the cameraman, teaching the director how to imply a counter narrative through placement of the principal actors.

Granted, today's hiring crew looked to be a notch below even the usual Hollywood outsider types. The men who shook his hand abraded his palm with their calluses. They smelled of sweat. They drank cans of beer at a folding table as they loudly argued the merits of each actor. Their fingernails were rimmed with dirt, and no surgeon had injected dermal fillers or stretched the skin to erase the creases in their unsmiling, sun-damaged faces.

The casting director was named Clem. Just "Clem." His knuckles were brown with scabs of dried blood, and he looked more like a shop steward. Clem shook Piper's manicured hand and gave him the audition script. He'd liked Piper's performance as Ronald Reagan, the time he'd played him in a cable network documentary about the president being shot. Clem pumped his hand and gushed, "You were great, the way you grabbed your guts and kept not-dying for two hours."

A man with a broken nose and mutilated cauliflower ears like cabbages stuck to either side of his bald head stepped up and introduced himself as the cinematographer. His name was LaManly. Nobody gave a last name. LaManly had a dees-n-dohs accent and a swastika tattooed on the side of his thick neck. LaManly looked Piper up and down and muttered, "Sweet threads."

The casting call had dictated for applicants to wear a suit and tie as befitted the leader of the free world. Combed hair, shined shoes. Piper took this to heart and broke out his best Savile Row single-breasted. A quick assessment of the competition assured him he might get the role based on his suit, alone. The others here to read were romantic leads past their prime. Handsome men who'd skated on their lantern jaws and jutting brows. They were wooden actors who specialized in wooden characters: judges, lawyers, family doctors.

When someone called his name, Piper took his mark before the video camera. A poster stood on a tripod beside it. The handwritten lines ran like a list under the heading "Read the Below." An assistant director put his eye to the viewfinder as if checking the focus. With one hand, he directed Piper to move sideways a half-step. The man wore a plaid flannel shirt, unbuttoned, and as he bent over the viewfinder the shirt fell open to reveal a stained wife-beater T-shirt and a shoulder holster containing a pistol.

The assistant director pointed a stubby index finger, making his hand like a fleshy gun, and signaled to begin. The thuggish crew sat at a nearby table and watched him on monitors.

"Fellow citizens," Piper began, channeling his best Reagan, "I speak to you as the head of your new government." The secret to doing Reagan was to keep a slight burr in his voice. "Throughout history, power has been earned." Another Reagan rule was that the silence between words was as important, perhaps even more important, than the words themselves.

"Historically, power was awarded," Piper continued, "to those who demonstrated it. None but the best warriors were crowned."

Piper lowered his chin almost imperceptibly. "Now politics has degraded power to a popularity contest." By gazing up, his pupils half hidden under his tilted-down brow, he implied disdain. The menacing disapproval of a caveman whose eyes were so deep set as to be lost.

The small group of actors awaiting their turn could learn a valuable lesson. Piper had played Lear. He'd played Moses.

"Until today," he lectured, "modern leaders have pandered for their position instead of fighting to earn it." He paused, letting the words take root.

"Since the beginning of the Industrial Revolution," Piper said. It was a tricky segue. A better writer would've made a smoother transition, but an actor who knew his craft could always fix the flaws in bad writing. Often by simply repeating the opening phrase, thus: "Since the beginning of the Industrial Revolution, global forces have imposed a great standardization on humanity."

Without breaking eye contact with the camera, Piper could sense the repetition was a success. The casting director nodded and jotted a note in his script. Two other men, a producer and the screenwriter, exchanged smiles and cocked eyebrows. No feet were bouncing with impatience. No one drummed his fingertips on the table. Even the director ceased chewing the doughnut he'd been stuffing into his mouth,

Piper continued, "In our lifetime we've lived under the tyranny of standardized time zones, standardized measurements for temperature and distance, required codes of behavior and approved methods of expression . . ." There was no ellipse here, but Piper added it so the subsequent passage would have greater effect. ". . . these universal conventions have robbed us of our lives."

Here he smiled to indicate a new segue. Piper watched the digital counter on the camera. They wanted this brought home in four minutes, and he would hit that mark exactly.

"The heroic acts of today have freed us from the tyranny of longstanding conventions." He drawled each word, stretched it, savored it, to give the message a Roosevelt-fireside-chat jovialness. "From today forward, the people who run our nation are proven heroes."

Piper's inflection turned patronizing, pure Hyde Park smug, dismissive of any fears his audience might harbor. To land the speech, he punched it up with JFK bombast.

"These new leaders are the warriors who have delivered us all," he half-shouted. "For generations to come, these liberators will steer our nation's new course of freedom."

These words, Piper knew they didn't need to make sense. They only needed to evoke a positive emotional reaction.

"From this great day," he decreed. His voice sounded as if it issued from a granite mouth on Mount Rushmore. It seemed to echo across time like the Gettysburg Address.

"From this great day we reject the leveling and dumbing-down imposed by global standards, and we devote our lives . . ." Piper paused as if overcome with emotion. "To the restoration of our identity and our sovereignty."

A decent actor stays true to the script.

A great actor knows when to improvise and drive home a point the writer has overlooked. Going off script would either scuttle this job or clinch it.

Giving the camera an LBJ glower, Piper adlibbed. "Before we can create anything of lasting value, we must first create ourselves."

Still gazing squarely into the lens, he added, "I thank you."

Four minutes, exactly.

The room erupted with applause. The rough-hewn crewmembers rose to stand, whistling and stomping booted feet. Even Piper's competition, his fellow actors who'd been sitting on the sidelines awaiting their turns to read, even they begrudgingly applauded his triumph.

The knuckle-dragging casting director, Clem, lurched forward, his meaty face wreathed with a smile. He slapped Piper on the back, saying, "Your bit about 'creating ourselves' . . . sheer brilliance." He thrust forward a sheet of printed paper, saying, "Before you leave your mark," indicating the masking tape on the floor, "would you read this into the camera as well?"

With rough, scarred fingers Clem offered a white index card. Written on it was a single sentence. Piper read the words and handed it back. He fixed the camera with a stern gaze and delivered the line:

"Do not seek it out," Piper proclaimed. "The list does not exist."

From off-camera the director said, "Next line."

Piper read, "A smile is your best bulletproof vest!" A still photographer hovered in his peripheral vision, snapping pictures.

The director ordered, "Keeping rolling. Next line."

Piper narrowed his eyes and gave the camera a sage look before reading, "The divine wages a constant battle to prove itself to us."

Minus a context, he performed his best. Reading, "Those who demand peace are the people who already hold power."

They made him repeat the list of jingoistic slogans until he knew them by heart and was no longer reading. He was reciting. Without pause, a gofer handed him a large blue-black book. It was roughly the size of a coffee table album, the type usually filled with glossy artwork. The cover was blank save for the title in gilded lettering. *Adjustment Day* by Talbott Reynolds. His character. The photographer snapped pictures of him holding the book open, taken from every angle and distance.

No one applauded but a sense of their deep, nodding approval filled the room. Before Piper could leave his mark, the director told him to read from the first page.

Piper studied the text. Printed across the top of the page in a large typeface was, "Declaration of Interdependence."

There were no protesters. The National Mall, stretching from the Capitol Building to the Washington Monument, it should've been filled with protesters. Milling, chanting, sign-waving hippy-dippy hordes. Millions of antiwar demonstrators. The phones in his office, the office of Senator Holbrook Daniels on the fifth floor of the Hart Senate Office Building, the phones should be ringing off the hook. The phones were silent. None of the millions of furious emails his staff had expected were appearing in his senatorial inbox.

No, the only sign of activity was a small crew of construction workers. From his high window, Senator Daniels watched them excavating a wide trench. It was roughly the dimensions of two Olympic-sized swimming pools placed end-to-end. The work was taking place on the lawn between First Avenue and the Capitol steps.

The stupid blue-collar slobs doing the digging, the senator almost pitied them. He settled into a leather desk chair in his air-conditioned, public-financed inner sanctum. If they weren't going off to die soon, their sons would be. Their sons and grandsons or nephews. Their apprentices and their journeymen. The surplus males of a generation.

With the vote on the National War Resolution only days away, angry and frightened Americans should've been beating down his door. None were. Not only was his office silent, but every office in the building seemed as hushed as a church. His assistants and pages had checked with the switchboard and the IT guys. The phones and servers were working.

His best guess was that Americans were too fractured along the fault lines of personal identity politics. It seemed that no one cared about others being compelled to gird their loins and perish. Recent politics had effectively branded young men as an internal enemy—perpetrators of rape culture, school shooters, and neo-Nazis—and media-frightened Americans were glad to see these bad apples culled.

The mass media had done its state-instructed job to demonize draft-age men, greasing the skids for their induction.

Before the end of this week, elected federal officials would vote unanimously to reinstate the military draft and commit two million young men to fighting a war in North Africa. Likewise, the leaders of a dozen countries in West Africa and the Middle East would pit an equal number of young men against the Americans.

Grim but true, rumor had it that this would be the fastest world war in history. Once the combatants were mustered along the battle front, a thermonuclear strike would eradicate everyone involved. A nonexistent terrorist group would be blamed for the nuke, and the warring nations could withdraw with no loss of face. The war would be declared a "draw."

Yet another war to end all wars.

From his office window, Daniels marveled at how fast the pit was being dug. In D.C. public works projects lasted for years while the parties involved lined their pockets with taxpayer money. Whatever motivated the crew just across Constitution Avenue, it had to be something beyond the monetary. Even as he watched, the earth-moving equipment sunk deeper, almost out of sight, as the mound of dirt grew taller along one edge of the vast hole.

The plans for this war had been unfolding since the first of the Millennial generation had been born. The Census Bureau had recognized that the Millennials would be the largest demographic in national history. They'd be healthy and well educated, and eventually they'd all want respect and power. The dynamic had played itself out in countries like Rwanda and Ivory Coast, where surplus young men had sparked civil wars until the national infrastructure had been destroyed and the entire population reduced to grinding poverty.

For a time, American officials had kept the lid on this human powder keg by dosing the boys with Ritalin. After that, peace came in the form of endless online gaming and pornography—all covertly supplied by government contractors. Despite those efforts this generation was waking up to its mortality. They wanted more than drugged, time-wasting numbness.

Unless the United States could resolve a sizable portion of its restless bad-boy problem, this nation would be doomed to the same misery as Haiti and Nigeria. America's version of the Arab Spring was just around the next corner.

Today, the Millennial males were already committing skyrocketing rates of violent crime in places like Chicago, Philadelphia, and Baltimore. They were hacking into state secrets so it was vital to implement the new war and purge the youth bulge. If the public ever caught wind of this plan, it might lead to a revolution. Families fighting to save their sons. Men fighting to save themselves.

As far as their loved ones need know, these young men would die heroes. They'd venture into battle like their forefathers and sacrifice their lives for the comfort and security of their fellow Americans back home.

The senator looked down on the workmen digging away in the afternoon sun. Sweating in the humid Potomac summer. He smirked, considering how in a few weeks there would be a sizable surplus of women. Feminism would fade out, and ladies would have to play nice or risk dying alone and being devoured by their cats. Less social upheaval, more available babes. For Senator Daniels and men like him, the war resolution was a win-win.

Far below him, the laborers swarmed like ants. Like obedient drones doing the bidding of their master.

At last the reality of their project dawned on the senator. It was obvious. They were preemptively building a memorial to the soldiers who'd be dead by Halloween. This was someone's extremely efficient idea. Rising from that ominous pit would be a white-marble confection of Greco-Roman statues and columns, the usual emotionally cathartic frou-frou. It made sense to begin construction now, even before the war was declared. The faster the dead could be honored, the faster they could be forgotten.

Here was an expedited shrine. Being erected even before the college students and pizza delivery boys and skateboarders received their draft notices. Proactively, their names were already being chiseled into marble plaques to honor the dead.

Now the world made perfect, logical sense. And slowly, between the softness of his leather chair, the lull of the air conditioning, and the unassailed silence of his office, Senator Holbrook Daniels drifted to sleep.

Frankie's dad told him that sometimes firemen need to burn down a bad house on purpose in order to save a good neighborhood. A type of back-burn, they called it when fighting forest fires.

The father and son had been driving around in the white Fire Marshall car with the special sticker on the back window and the red light on the dashboard, except the light wasn't switched on. They drove past spray-painted houses, houses with wood nailed over the gone windows, houses where only a basement was left, like a swimming pool filled with weeds and trees growing inside.

They drove to Frankie's old school from before he started remote learning on the computer in their kitchen at home. After the day that Frankie's dad called the Last Straw. After a bunch of kids dogpiled him at lunch. After they took turns stomping his head against the lunchroom floor, something Frankie couldn't remember, even after the teachers had shown them the lunchroom video and the camera movies some kids had posted on World Star Hip Hop.

Today, same as before, his dad brought a Super Soaker, the deluxe model with the bigger tank, made to shoot longer and farther.

Firemen have a special key, his dad showed him. It opens every door. Another special key shuts off the security alarm. He told Frankie not to mind about the security videos. The high-up cameras watched them go down every hallway, walking past Frankie's old locker, past the spot where nobody did anything besides videotape him getting his face stomped. Any trace of blood had been scrubbed away.

Same as usual, his dad worked the pump action on the Super Soaker, spraying every bulletin board hung with paper. Hosing every school spirit banner, with that service station smell. As they strolled the hallways, Frankie's dad squirt-gunned the smell of filling the lawnmower and cleaning paintbrushes. He sprayed the ceiling tiles until they were so saturated they warped and sagged.

This was his secret recipe of Styrofoam ground down to just its little white balls, dissolved in gasoline with Vaseline stirred in to make it thick, to make it sticky so when he sprayed the gunk on the ceiling it never dripped, and when he sprayed it on window glass it didn't run down.

He'd added some paint thinner as a surfactant, his dad explained, to break the surface tension so the ooze wouldn't bead up but would coat everything more evenly.

It was summer vacation so Frankie knew no hamsters or goldfish lived in any classroom.

His dad took aim and soaked a security camera that was spying on them.

After the day of the lunchroom beat-down Frankie couldn't remember, his dad never looked at him. If his dad looked in his direction all he saw was the scar that now ran down the side of Frankie's face. A red line shaped like the curved edge of a Nike basketball shoe where the cheek skin had torn. Even now walking down the empty summer hallway lined with lockers but no padlocks, Frankie could feel his dad sneak looks at the scar. Frankie's dad never smiled at him, not after that day. He scowled, but he was scowling at the scar. The ghost of that final last stomp. The last day in public school.

Lining the halls, big posters showed smiling kids from every place on the planet. Holding hands under a rainbow with covering the rainbow the words "Love Comes in Every Color."

His dad hosed the poster. Doing so, the look on his dad's face was worse than any scar. From his expression, he wanted to be spraying this fire juice into the eyes and mouths of those kids who'd left their footprints on Frankie for the rest of his life.

The whole time Frankie's dad super-soakered the school walls, he yelled stuff like, "Eat it, cultural Marxism!" And, "Get fucked, vibrant ethnic diversity!"

His dad hosed the poster until it sagged and slid down the wet wall. By then the soaker was empty and he pitched it a long ways, almost all the way to the school office.

"In a little bit, kid," said Frankie's father, "I'm going to do you a solid one."

Frankie couldn't picture that. The kids who'd kicked his ass, they still went here. None of them had been sent home. But it helped to know that after today nobody would go here.

"Maybe they caught us off-guard once," his dad said, "but we'll get our revenge."

Frankie followed his dad into a bathroom and waited while he washed his hands.

His dad said, "Nobody is going to shit on this family, ever again."

Before they went out to the car, his dad took out his phone and placed a call. He said, "Hello, may I speak to your news director?" With one hand he dug in his pants pocket. "This is Fire Marshall Benjamin Hugh. We're currently responding to reports that the Golden Park Elementary School is ablaze." From his pocket he withdrew a book of matches. He ended the call and placed another.

"Hello, may I speak to the City Desk?" Frankie's father held the matches out to his son. Frankie took them. Waiting, his father turned away from the phone and said, "Today is just practice. Just to see how many show up."

Into the phone, he said, "I've gotten word that arsonists have struck another local school." He listened. "It's Golden Park Elementary."

Frankie stood by, holding the matches, just as he'd stood by at Madison Middle School and Immaculate Heart and the three schools before. Frankie figured this would be the last school, and that his dad had only burned the others so this one wouldn't look special. When his dad was finished with the last phone call, then Frankie knew what came next.

In his heart, Frankie knew that the bad parts of the world would have to be burned away to save the best parts.

"Frankie, you . . . ," his dad knelt in front of him and took both of Frankie's small hands in his own, saying, "Son, these dipshits will pay you tribute for the rest of your life!" He let fall one of the small hands and reached up to stroke the scar on the side of Frankie's innocent, trusting face. "My boy. You will grow to become a king! And your sons will be princes!" He lifted the one small hand he still held and put it to his own lips.

As a special treat, his father let Frankie light the match.

After that they went outside to count how many reporters and cameramen would show up. At first it was only a couple television crews, but now every station came, plus some foreigners in town for the serial arson story. The newspaper sent a team. Even a helicopter. Radio stations sent people. Frankie's dad took notes and strategized his clearest angles and best shots, to see how easy his work would be when the actual day came.

Only then did Frankie's dad dial 9-1-1.

Before everything you've read so far in this book . . . before this book was a book, it was the dream of Walter Baines.

Back in the world you still know . . . back in Before Times, here's how Walter had always dreamed of doing it.

On Shasta's twenty-fifth birthday he'd suggest taking a bus, the bus going uphill, the one that most days carries her mom and the other housecleaners to work. He'd wear his lucky Lamborghini scarf even if it's so old it's turning back into dirty wool.

The two of them would catch the last bus of the night, following the route past that house. Not the house Mrs. Shasta cleans but the one with Scarlett O'Hara columns lining the front porch and the rooflines and lightning rods and red-brick chimneys rising above the ancestral oak trees. It's the house Shasta has always gawked at the way a dog eyeballs a squirrel, like that pile of bricks and ivy is her pornography. One stop past the house in question Walter would step off the bus and walk back to where the windows would be dark. When she pulled away, he'd get her, tight, around one wrist and tug, gently, saying, "It's a surprise," leading her past a statue that creeps him out.

It's a monkey made out of that metal where if you touched it on a cold day you'd be touching it forever, and anyone who touched you would stick as would people who touched them until everyone in the world would be trapped together like Ice-nine in Vonnegut. The little statue brings to mind a little monkey dressed as a clown, maybe to ride a horse only with his face painted white. Like in Japan.

Walter would cross the damp grass, beyond the Kabuki-faced monkey-clown statuette, past the little yellow sign for the alarm company.

To mark the occasion, Walter would pull out his lucky pipe and tamp the bowl full of Hindu Kush. Ever the gentleman, he'd offer Shasta the first hit.

He'd pat his hip pocket to double check for a bulge, a round bulge like old-school Kennedy half dollars, like pirate doubloons or chocolate gelt—in reality only gold foil-wrapped condoms his ma distributes wholesale. His fingertips would trace the outline of something else, coiled, a larger circle, a loop of something tucked deep in his back pocket.

Walter would lead her, shivering, onto the porch, where and when she'd hide behind a column, standing sideways-skinny in the shadows, blocked from the street. She'd be trusting him but be ready to run. Then and there, he'd say, "Let me go get your birthday present," and he'd disappear around the side of the house.

She'll cower there, hearing crickets chirp and the hiss of in-ground sprinklers. Smelling this and that. The nighttime air carries swimming pool chlorine and the vanilla fabric softener of billowing steam from some dryer vent. A private security patrol will cruise by playing its searchlight over the hedges. Since her finger-painting days, this house has stood here, filled with history, never changing, a place where she could never imagine feeling afraid. Here and now she's hugging herself behind a column, looking on her phone for a taxi, surfing the Neighborhood Watch sites to see if anyone's reported two prowlers.

The front door creaks open. As if by itself, the paneled, white-painted door will swing aside on its brass hinges. Nightmare slow. Before she can bolt down the steps, comes a whisper from the darkness inside the front hallway, Walter's voice whispering, "Happy Birthday, Shasta."

Walter will edge his head out until the porch light puts a white mask on his face, wave a hand for her to come inside. He'll whisper, "It's okay."

She'll stand there between the fear she feels and what she wants most: the end of all fear.

He'll say, "Hurry."

She'll give the empty, dark street one last look and step inside.

He'll shut the door. The two of them will kiss until her eyes adjust so she can look around in the half-light. Take note of the brass chandelier holding a forest of fake candles above their heads. Check out the stairway curving down, out of the darkness. The carved, leather-scented wood of everything. From somewhere, Walter will hear a clock ticking, loud against the silence. Little smears of light will bounce off a swinging, polished silver pendulum. Flicker in shades of blue off the mirror above a fireplace.

The thing about Shasta is the taste of her mouth. In his experience a girl can be beautiful with all the tits in the world, long legs and a button nose, but a bad-tasting mouth makes her only as good as porn. Shasta, the inside of her mouth reminds him of high-fructose corn syrup, like soaking Maraschino cherries stewed with red #5 and gelatin until her tongue has the mouth-feel of a Hostess fruit pie flaking sugar like a baby snake shedding its sweet, dead, sweet skin. Until every French kiss is him deep-throating a semi-molten, sugar-coated snake, like a little garter snake or a garden variety brown boa. Like Walter's mouth is locked overnight in a delicious combination reptile house and Danish pastry shop.

She'll whisper about the alarm system, and he'll point upward. Her gaze will follow his arm to a camera mounted high on one wall. When and where he'll give her a silent thumbs-up, A-Okay. He'll explain that he hacked the system. Before they even boarded the bus, Walter deactivated everything, remotely. He found a window unlocked in the back. He'd been planning this for weeks. No one will ever know they were here.

As irrefutable evidence that he's more than a slack-jawed, single-digit brain cell burner, he'll explain about network enumeration and exploitation. Walter will boast about his genius cryptographic keys while leading her toward the stairs.

Shasta will be heel dragging, whispering about homeowners with shotguns. About stand-your-ground laws.

If anyone catches them, Walter will promise to lie. He'll swear that he lured her here to strangle her. He's a serial killer. He's got victims buried in shallow graves all over the American West. He'll pretend to a jury that he'd told her this was his house. He'd planned to eat Froot Loops out of the bowl he'd make from her skull. Using her blood, he'd write Helter Skelter on the glass door of the Sub-Zero wine cooler. As an almost-butchered woman, she'll get off scot free.

Walter will say that he's already snooped around. No one's home. He'll reach into his back pocket and show her the coil of thin wire. It's ready for when the police frisk him: A garrote, for strangling her, with a small wooden peg attached to either end so he can pull it tight. It's her get-out-of-jail-free card. Seeing condoms and a murder weapon will be all the insurance policy she'll need. She can relax.

Sex is sex, but sex plus danger is great. The looming threat of being serial killed or getting jail time will bring down her juices faster than green M&M's. The both of them a tangled knot, he'll go at it until they're half dead. They'll christen every room. If there's a safe, behind a painting or a secret panel in the wall, Walter will find it. He'll press his ear near the dial and listen to the tumblers spin. Before she says not to, he'll throw the handle and open the heavy door, taking only enough cash for two first-class one-way tickets to Denver.

In Denver, he'll take her on another bus ride to where big houses sit far apart. He'll show her on his phone how he reverse-engineered the security monitoring software, how easy, and she'll follow him around the sides of a house until they find a window unlatched.

Before here and now, she's only known him as some baked chode. A hammered nobody who can only afford ditch weed shake full of seeds and stems. He lives in his ma's basement, where the plumbing growls like a stomach like the sound of an impending bad smell. Shasta likes him okay, but not so much that she'd marry him.

By Denver, she's bought into his secret Robin Hood bad-boy side. The way he can open doors—abracadabra—and human traffic the two of them into rich, forbidden worlds. After they make love on a bearskin rug and throw the goopy condom into a roaring fire in a stone fireplace under a crystal chandelier, after they drink stolen wine and she washes the glasses and puts everything back, then he'll locate another safe. This one, hidden under the false bottom of a seemingly empty bathroom cabinet, he'll have it open in a flash and withdraw just the money they need to fly to Chicago.

That bad-boy Walter will completely win her over. Chicago will be a repeat of Denver. Minneapolis will take them to Seattle. As a sign of her newfound awe and respect, she starts referring to his junk as the Penis de Milo. In Minneapolis she slips up and calls him "daddy." Seattle leads to San Francisco, where they'll sneak past the doorman at some art deco skyscraper that they'll just happen to be passing one night. He'll hack the elevator code and ride to the penthouse. Using his phone, he'll show her the view from every security camera to prove nobody's home. While Shasta stands lookout near the elevator, he'll trip the locks, then hurry her inside. He'll remind her of the back-up scenario. Him: Serial killer. Her: Victim. The two of them, outlaws. The next day they'll be strolling along a dock in Sausalito where he targets a yacht. They take it out into the bay, not sailing, he's not that much of a show-off. He'll use the motor and spend a sunny day on the water. On the deck, catching some rays, she'll say, "Show me, again." Then and there he'll pull the coiled wire out of his pocket and demonstrate how easily it fits around her neck. Just to give her peace of mind.

A locker will yield an array of bikinis all in perfect Size Shasta. He's neither a tit man nor a leg man so she's his physical ideal, stretched out on a deckchair, sucking down Durban Poison until her skin burns the color of deep dish chili cheese Pepperoni Stix. That same evening, he'll moor the yacht and look for a new safe, this one hidden by a spice rack camouflaged behind a panel in the galley. The money he finds will get them both down to San Diego.

Still they're trespassers in paradise. She might be having a ball, touring the glamorous life with Mr. Douche Danger. But she'll never marry him, and he knows that.

As long as her vacation time holds out, they'll hop from San Diego to New Orleans to Miami. In a waterfront villa, they'll be making love. In a canopy bed beside big windows that look out on the ocean under a full moon. Not a minute after they've taken each other to Heaven and back, the bedroom doors will burst open. Uniformed men train their side arms on Shasta. The lights blaze bright, and she screams, clutching damp sheets over her naked body. Not like Walter practiced, not exactly, she screams, "He's a serial killer," meaning him. She screams, "He told me he lived here." So much for her acting skills. She says, "He planned to strangulate me!"

A voice among the uniforms yells, "Police!" Commands, "Put your hands where we can see them!"

This is how it ends, their cross-country crime spree. Bonnie and Clyde without the body count. With the spit still wet on each other, he'll climb out of bed and find his pants. He'll show the police his driver's license. Keeping his hands in the air, his pecker still stuck out so hard it shines, still waving the filled condom like a little white flag, he'll cross the room to an elegant antique French desk.

She'll still be in bed, openly weeping, saying, "Thank God, thank you! He calls this love, but he plans to destroy me!"

The police won't allow Walter to actually open the desk drawer so he'll direct an officer to do so. Revealed within, lying on top in plain sight, will be a deed of property ownership. On it, notarized and duly recorded in all public records will be the same name as on the driver's license. His name. Where and when, in the elegant intonations of a landed aristocrat, he'll explain, smiling, naked, "Officers, I own this house."

In the bed, the weeping will stop. Shasta's voice will ask, "Huh?" The two of them had been drinking red wine, and the edge of her glass will have left a thin, red Salvador Dali mustache curving up from the corners of her mouth.

He'll explain. He owned everything. In Denver, in Seattle, every house is his. He knew the codes, the combinations to the safes. The cash he took was his own. He left the windows unlocked and tipped doormen to look the other way. Even the yacht and the bikinis. Secretly, Walter dialed 9-1-1 to bring the cops at this, the perfect moment.

Blithely, he'll pull off the condom and cast it side. Not only is he a brash bad-boy douche bag with the stealth and cunning to skate through life and show a girl a good time, he's also rich. He'll be the same old Walter she liked before, only loaded. The regular him, but with so much more to love.

With the police officers looking on, their guns lowered, him still naked, her naked, he'll kneel on the floor near his pants. He'll reach into the pocket where the garrote is hidden and bring out a ring. He'll ask, "Will you marry me?"

A big diamond ring.

There and then, a crew of caterers will arrive with chocolate-dipped strawberries and Mountain Dew–flavored Doritos with garlic popcorn and extra ranch dressing on the side. He'll fire up a big, juicy party bowl packed with New Purple Power, and even the cops will greedily partake. For the honeymoon him and Shasta will live happily ever after on a tropical isle he owns, reforested with fields of White Rhino. Either there or maybe under a geodesic dome terrarium sunk on the bottom of the ocean with self-contained, recycling everything, surrounded by an ever-changing galaxy of colorful tropical sea life.

Whatever the case, this is how he'll propose.

There's not enough of him, not yet, to constitute anyone's everything. What he has to do is, first, make a shit-ton of money.

Tweed O'Neill and her crew beat the first engine company to the raging school inferno. Of course, the Fire Marshall was already on the scene. Other television news crews were soon to follow, aligning their satellite hook-ups, each angling for the best view of the blaze. It was the city's fourth school to go up in flames recently. Every outlet worked from the same press releases, but this time Tweed had brought a secret weapon.

Enter Dr. Ramantha Steiger-DeSoto, a senior professor in Gender Studies at the university. The lady doctor was a well-spoken, camera-friendly egghead with her own unique spin on serial arson.

Tweed had texted the doctor from the television studio, and the two met up at the crime scene as flames leapt high into the sky. With the gymnasium collapsing slowly behind them, sending up bright geysers of sparks and embers, Tweed blocked out the interview. She and the doctor stood at a safe distance as the cameraman adjusted his focus and the sound technician wired a microphone to the lapel of the doctor's Ann Taylor trench coat.

Through her earpiece Tweed could hear the anchors discussing the fire. In a moment they'd throw the audience to her, live, on location. She eyed her competition. None had brought anything new to the story. They were merely passing the Fire Marshall from set-up to set-up, and he was giving each outlet the same list of official facts.

The doctor appeared unfazed by the bright camera lights and the billowing, acrid smoke. Someone had suggested a rumored propane tank, possibly related to the school's kiln, was liable to explode at any instant. Nevertheless Dr. Steiger-DeSoto looked determined to voice her theory about recent events. Standing tall, almost a head taller than Tweed, her frizzy blonde hair was tied up in a sensible bun. She looked every inch the no-nonsense sociologist who stood ready to enlighten the television viewers.

The cameraman shouldered his steady cam and signaled 3-2-1 with his fingers, finally pointing to indicate they'd gone live.

"Tweed O'Neill here at the scene of yet another three-alarm fire," Tweed began. "Marking the destruction of a fourth local school this summer."

The cameraman widened the shot to include both women.

"With me tonight is Dr. Ramantha Steiger-DeSoto to present insight into the motive for these recent fires." Tweed turned to the elegant academic. She tossed, "Your thoughts, doctor?"

The doctor wasn't fazed by the attention. "Thank you, Tweed." She faced the camera full-on. "Federal criminal profiling shows the average arsonist to be a white male between the ages of seventeen and twenty-six. For this man, the act of fire setting is sexual in nature . . ."

As if on cue the rumored propane tank exploded deep within the building, a concussive boom-BOOM that elicited a deep moan from the crowd present.

The doctor continued, "For the pyrophiliac, the act of spraying liquid accelerant equates to expressing his sexual ejaculate in a symbolic degrading rape of the structure . . ."

Collapsing fire and sex meant ratings gold, but Tweed worried that the doctor's language was too highbrow. She tried to redirect. "But who . . . ?"

The doctor nodded sagely. "Self-isolating men. Right-wing

adherents poisoned by the toxic masculinity of the so-called Men Going Their Own Way movement. These are your culprits."

Tweed tried to lighten the tone. "So Maureen Dowd was right?" she joked. "That having men around is just too high a price to pay for sperm?"

The doctor smiled weakly. "For generations popular culture has been promoting the idea that all men will eventually attain high-status positions in society. Globally, today's young males have been raised to feel entitled to power and admiration as a birthright."

Tweed knew the station was coming up on a hard break. To cap the segment, she asked, "Doctor, how can we best deal with today's troubled young men?"

Backed by the hellish glare of flames, the doctor proclaimed, "Men in general need to accept their diminished status in the world." Against a backdrop of smoke and shouting, she added, "The impending war, for example, will be an excellent opportunity for them to earn the acclaim they crave."

Tweed tossed to commercial. "Thank you, doctor. This is Tweed O'Neill at the pointless destruction of another community landmark."

The cameraman signaled the feed had cut.

The doctor fumbled with her clip-on mic. Suddenly pensive, she asked, "What's he doing?" She glared at something in the middle distance.

Tweed's gaze followed hers. Both women looked at the Fire Marshall. Tweed's impression was that he was taking a head count. His attention seemed to settle for a moment on each of the journalists present, and he seemed to be checking them off a list he held. His eyes met hers. His hand holding a pen drew a line through something on the paper held in his opposite hand.

Only now did Tweed notice the little boy. A grade school–aged child with a strange discolored mark running down one side of his face. Then the reality struck her: It was so cute. The District Fire Marshall had brought his own little son to watch Daddy at work.

Watching the two Tweed made a mental note to spin that touching father-and-son moment into a feel-good story she could peddle to network programmers.

For Garret Dawson it was the coffee filters. In the kitchen, working the Mr. Coffee, he found they were almost out of filters, again. Another five hundred pots of coffee gone, another year, more than a year.

He was growing old. Garret had realized that fact when he made it a habit to look at something—a houseplant, a clock, a book—before looking at his wife, Roxanne. If he was attending a party and talking to a pretty young woman, somebody's teenaged daughter, for instance . . . or even watching a beautiful woman read the news on cable television . . . and he looked from her smooth face directly at Roxanne, it was too jarring. In her day his wife had been beautiful, but she was no longer young. Thus he needed a buffer between looking at someone youthful and looking at her. An ashtray or a pipe wrench, something not-human.

At the same time he noticed her looking from handsome actors in movies, focusing on her popcorn before directing her attention at him. It might've been his imagination. A projection based on his own behavior. But it reminded him that he was also getting older. The Talbott book put it so well:

> Beautiful people become powerful because they recognize the nature of power, early, and fear losing it. People beautiful in their youth learn to transfer power by investing it in subsequent forms. They trade their youth for education. Their education they invest in developing contacts and expertise in a skill. Their money they invest in redundant forms of power, back-up resources.

That is why an expiring form of money is crucial.
Power passed from generation to generation in the
abstract form of wealth leads to privilege and corruption.
Money must not be hoarded for its own sake but must be
continually employed for a fruitful purpose.

The coffee filters were the last straw. At the machine shop, Leon had come at him with some cockamamie plan to seize control of the government and reshape the nation. It sounded bogus, but at this point anything sounded better than buying another five hundred coffee filters and watching them count down his final years. He poured ground coffee into the last filter and filled the machine with water. He flipped the switch to start brewing. Calling out to Roxanne in the other room, he said, "Coffee ready in a sec." He added, "I'm going out for a minute."

He'd give Leon a call. Meet him down by the tavern. Find out if this harebrained scheme was a for-real proposition. Leon had given him the blue-black book, which said:

> *Imagine there's no God. There is no Heaven or*
> *Hell. There is only your son and his son and*
> *his son, and the world you leave for them.*

Roxanne called from the dining room, asking where he was headed.

As he pulled on his coat, he checked the pockets for his keys and phone. He stepped into the doorway, where she sat at the dinner table, some kind of tax forms spread out in front of her. He answered, "We need coffee filters."

After a long pull of silence, not looking up, she asked, "Already?" Garret could hear the defeat in her voice. Life was going by just as quick for her. Another reason to explore some radical options.

Leaning over, he whispered, "I got it handled." And he kissed her on the forehead.

There had been the age of religion when cities were dominated by their cathedral or mosque. The domes and spires had dwarfed every structure that cowered around them. Then had come the age of commerce, and the skyscrapers of business and fluted columns of banks had dwarfed the churches. Factories outgrew even the largest mosques, and warehouses overshadowed temples. Most recently had begun the age of government when the buildings regulating civic life had exploded on the horizon. These were vast monoliths containing a power that religion and commerce could only dream of wielding. These were opulent vessels for protecting and showcasing the might of lawgivers and judges.

In the final weeks before the Adjustment, it was into these great fortresses that ordinary people ventured, pretending to be awed, wandering around as if they were merely sightseers. They snapped photographs and pretended to be lost so they could wander into restricted areas and claim innocence when they were apprehended and asked to leave. They mapped possible escape routes they would need to bar. And they determined the locations that would give them the most-clear lines of fire.

And as they marveled beneath the chandeliers and craned their necks to see the glory of the murals and the gilded ribs of the lofty domes, they knew that food had built this. Food that could've been eaten. Food that had been taken from them. And security had built these marbled stairways, security that could've been theirs. And their lives had been siphoned away so that these walls could be paneled with polished mahogany, and rosewood, stuff shipped from around the world to add to the comfort and pleasure of the ruling elite. These hillbillies and rubes with their slack-jawed, hang-dog expressions, they pretended respect, and they acted out admiration for these grand statehouses and the grand potentates who orchestrated their lives from within.

They whispered one to the other. They mapped with video. They began to see themselves doing the cold task they had set their minds on doing.

And all knew the truth: Hoard food and it rots. Hoard money and you rot. Hoard power and the government rots.

Instead of every stupid person having one vote, the smartest, bravest, most-bold would have one hundred or three hundred or one thousand votes while the weak and lazy had none. No longer would the most productive be slaves to the idle. The idle would be made to work.

On tip-toe they trickled into the halls of power. Stately edifices their sweat had erected and to which they'd for too long sent themselves by proxy. They came as witnesses to survey the noble settings where their lives would either begin or end.

When they gazed up into the soaring granite vaults or down at the acres of polished marble they felt tiny and weak. But when they crammed into the spectators gallery, elbow to elbow, knee to knee, forming a single mass, and they surveyed the thin numbers of the duly elected, they felt invincible.

They bridled at being grouped into small herds and herded by elderly tour guides who dictated by rote the politically approved meaning of each flag and statue. They dared to picture the great chandeliers shot to pieces. They pictured the galleries with every painting slashed and all the statuary toppled in a jumble to suggest a mass grave of stone heads and severed fingers.

They closed their eyes to better envision the tall windows of the statehouse or courthouse shattered and sparrows building nests in the rotunda's gilded cornices and niches.

The media labeled this surge of the curious as an uptick in patriotism. A reengagement of citizens with their nation. And on that count the media was correct, but not in the way they assumed. The media depicted the people as pilgrims supplicating themselves before their betters. And the media foresaw a growing future of peace and cooperation, and on this count they were also correct but not in the way they'd anticipated.

For their part, these newcomers kept their eyes lowered and

feigned timidity. In keeping with their low position as plain people they stepped aside in deference as even the lowliest usher or interns charged through their ranks.

In the last days, the tourists flooded into every building of government. Then, as if a switch had been flipped, the gawkers had ceased. The halls were empty except for those who did business. They exchanged nods and shook hands with the guards on duty. Those in uniform and those in street clothes agreeing with their eyes about what needed to happen. All parties in conspiracy toward the one day they'd act together.

None but the security guard treated these people with respect because only the guards and peace officers recognized from whence the real power of the nation arose.

For now, crouched in the storage space underneath the south stairs, Nick said, "I don't know. I used to love the police." They leaned against a wall of boxes crammed with old band uniforms. Gold braid showed through where the cardboard had split. Brass buttons glowed like treasure in the dim light.

Shasta's legs were cramping. Most likely they were breathing asbestos and cancerous chalk dust. Talcum powder was chalk, and talc caused cervical cancer. The world teetered on the brink of war, but Shasta liked it here. Thigh-to-thigh with Nick. Talking felt real. Nothing important ever happened over a telephone.

The truth, Nick said, used to be easy to find. The truth was inside the newspaper until it printed an obituary for Nick's dad. It said, "A beloved husband and father, the deceased died as a result of a cerebral hemorrhoid . . ." The web picked up the typo and it ran as a humor piece on hundreds of news sites. Even becoming a meme, typically a picture of Ronald Reagan or Gore Vidal bracketed with the words *Died of a* . . . along the top margin of the picture, and running along the bottom, . . . *cerebral hemorrhoid!!*

The word everyone was looking for was *hemorrhage*; Nick's father had been mowing the lawn when an aneurysm in his brain had burst. Just that one word, and the newspaper couldn't get it right.

Shasta took pity on him. She tried to explain.

Dr. Brolly in Methods of the Media, he'd explained how modern print journalism, daily newspaper reporting, what we think of when we think of objective, that balanced truth was killed by Craigslist. Craigslist and Monster and Backpage and eBay. Newspaper profits had always come from the sale of classified ads. Those pages and pages of puppies for sale, apartments for rent, used cars, jobs, and SWM seeking SWF, those had been the foundation upon which rested the massive edifice of the Fourth Estate.

All of those ads for garage sales and yard sales and seal-point Siamese kittens, those people seeking to buy WWII souvenirs or Fiestaware or split, seasoned firewood, those were the underpinnings of the oldest political dynasties. At a nickel or a dollar per word, those pages had been the goldmine that had financed the high culture. The editorials and book reviews and investigative reporting that was awarded Pulitzer Prizes. According to Dr. Brolly, our brightest, most-erudite observations owed their existence to poor people trying to unload vintage Avon cologne bottles and unwanted timeshares.

"Movies exist," Dr. Brolly told every class, every year, "because movies enable theaters to charge you five dollars for popcorn." His point was that worthless popcorn supported the glittering world of movie stars and the Academy Awards. In the same way single, worthless words printed for a few dollars per day had supported the colossal newspaper empires.

With the passing of newspapers the credibility of everything came into question. No one was dictating or arguing effectively, defining quality from crap, truth from lies. Without a gatekeeper, an arbiter, everything had equal value.

Dr. Brolly had made them read *The Sibling Society* by Robert Bly. The book said modern society had lost its traditional hierarchy. Be it the patriarch or the matriarch, mothers and fathers had been reduced to the same status as their children. No one wanted to be an adult, and people were friends, peers, equals, rather than teachers and students. Reduced to siblings.

This flattening of the social hierarchy, Brolly predicted, would lead to populism. Instead of a few enlightened sages, vast numbers of people swayed by emotion and greed would seize the reins of power.

Below the stairs, Nick interrupted, "You know he's stoned all the time?"

Shasta asked, "Robert Bly?"

Nick shook his head. "Dr. Brolly." And told about seeing a transdermal patch stuck to his back, where his T-shirt pulled out of his pants. Brolly wore the same T-shirt every May 1st. It was white except for under the arms and had the words "Parlor Pinko" printed on the front in red. It meant he was a fag, people said. The patch was Fentanyl. Other days he wore "Limousine Liberal" or "Champagne Socialist."

Every kid at the University of Oregon could recognize a Fentanyl patch or a Percocet seen from outer space.

Crouched in the dusty space under the stairs, Nick counted on his fingers the things he'd put his faith in. Santa Claus, the Easter Bunny, the Tooth Fairy, religion, the daily *Oregonian*, the government, Dr. Brolly, and the police. In school, history changed, geography changed. The moment after you passed a test, the facts you'd learned were obsolete. Now he didn't know what to trust. He wanted to check his telephone messages but didn't want to risk installing the battery and activating any form of locating device.

Shasta checked her phone. No word from Walter. Neither had his mom texted back. She wondered if just a girlfriend could file a missing persons report. It sounded lame. The truth always did. But she offered, "Maybe we all need to start trusting ourselves."

To make matters worse, she added, "Maybe you need to trust yourself."

Nick scowled at her until she looked away. His voice got intense. "Tell me," he demanded, "everything Walter knew about this big conspiracy."

After Piper had read for the part, the casting committee had dismissed the other actors. The job seemed as good as his. Still the committee conferred. To assure themselves, they'd given him fragments to read. Platitudes, really. For instance, "We must discard past measurements and invent for ourselves what a minute is . . ." These were handwritten on cue cards and held near the camera. An actor's job was to make the unreal believable. To spin imaginary straw into tangible gold.

"Moments," Piper read, "are the building blocks of our lives. And our lifetimes must not be measured in weekends. Our time on Earth must not be judged by wages earned and taxes paid."

A crewmember replaced the cue card, and Piper read, "This is Talbott Reynolds, absolute monarch appointed by the Council of Tribes."

The director, the man, Rufus, asked for another take. "This is Talbott Reynolds," Piper intoned, "absolute monarch appointed by the Council of Tribes."

The casting committee put their heads together in conference. The director asked for another take. A lighter tone, more jovial this go-round.

Piper put a smile in his voice. "This is Talbott Reynolds," he lifted his brow slightly to give his face a more-open appeal, "absolute monarch appointed by the Council of Tribes."

They changed the cards and had him read, "Article Seven of the Declaration of Interdependence."

Hoard food and it rots. Hoard money and you rot.
Hoard power and the nation rots.

They rewound the recording and watched his delivery a second and third time. They nodded as if in mutual agreement. They replaced the cue card with another, saying, "You are not going to get loved by being lovable!!"

Nodding, the director said, "With the double exclamation." He added, "Please."

"We neglect our own destiny," the next card said, "while we impose an arbitrary destiny upon others. Doing so we ruin both our own lives and theirs."

To Piper it was all gobbledygook, but he delivered each speech with solemn dignity. He read, "Each of us must pursue his or her own destiny and allow others to pursue theirs." He read, "Out of respect, we must not dictate the progress or the goals of others."

A hulking brute who smelled of gun smoke, like fireworks and gasoline, approached and used a folded paper napkin to delicately dab the sweat from Piper's forehead.

The crew replaced the card with another. Again, "This is Talbott Reynolds, the absolute monarch appointed by the Council of Tribes." The take was ruined when his stomach growled.

This time, the director ordered Piper to read the capitalized letters as if they were capitalized.

Piper winged it, "This is Talbott Reynolds, aristocrat supreme, head honcho, grand wizard, the absolute monarch . . ." He dragged it out forever.

In the same way the people came to pay special homage to the final days of their government, they gathered for long, last looks at other relics. They stood in crowds supervising television crews broadcasting from crime scenes. And the reporters were inwardly flattered and felt themselves to be celebrated. And the reporters felt smug in what seemed to be proof of their respected authority in the world. Likewise, the crowds flocked to what they knew to be the farewell lectures by esteemed academics, and those much-lauded laureates took such attentive mobs to be a compliment. And these professors felt the future, for the first time in many years, might be an improvement. And both the journalists and the lecturers were mistaken.

For schooling had given the people very little in exchange for their money. And the media had given nothing in exchange for the people's time and attention.

And now when the crowds came to witness them, it was with bitterness and pity. Others watched with morbid curiosity and sadness, the way they might look upon the last passenger pigeon in existence. For the people knew these were the final days of such institutions, and an event would soon occur that would divide the present from the future. They studied the twilight of such professions so they might describe them to their children, someday.

With nostalgia the people stared at the hollow power of the statesman, the journalist, and the professor, and the people silently bid them farewell.

From outside Prince Lucien Campbell Hall, to Jamal standing on the quad, the venerable old building looked like the model for Poe's House of Usher. Of quaint and antique design, it towered into the Stygian nighttime sky. A mellow rainbow of green and gold glowed through one distant set of stained-glass windows, and a thread of smoke spiraled up from only one crumbling chimneypot to suggest but a single late-night occupant.

Jamal motioned for Keishaun to go first, and the two men pushed past the stout, heavily carved oaken door, its iron hinges crusted red with rust. As they made their way inside, fallen plaster crunched under their tread. The flutter of bat wings reeled through the shadows above their baseball caps. Mounted at intervals along the walls, the elaborate gilded sconces of a bygone epoch threw off weak illumination, flickering and pallid as gas lamps.

The two navigated the warren of narrow hallways. The steep-pitched flights of stairs. They braved the grim attic odors of dust and soot. The stone and timber of the great structure held a silence so complete it made Jamal's hungry ears hallucinate. In the silence he heard words, spoken words, a hushed jumble of faint voices like rushing water, like an audience of phantoms whispering in those dank apartments.

One cluster of fetid rooms gave way to another jumbled hodgepodge of rank, ruined stalls and scholastic carrels. Shelves of books, their leather spines furred with mold, stretched out of sight. A metronome sound of dripping water ticked off the moments, and damp had blackened the building's elegant velvet hangings. A nightmare of branching corridors led them past musty, cavernous lecture halls where Jamal would swear the souls of lost Humanities majors still thirsted for revenge. Demanded vengeance. As they ought to, he reflected. Generations had been taught the worst brands of social engineering; they'd been drilled and tested until these institutional lies had replaced any rational thinking of their own. The ghosts that inhabited Prince Lucien Campbell Hall wouldn't rest until Jamal and Keishaun had found the answer they sought tonight.

The pair lurched from one ruined level up to the next, until a single note struck on a piano caught their attention. A series of notes followed. This, Chopin's Nocturne in E-flat major, led them to an unlocked office. Beyond that lay a moldering suite of rooms, and in the furthestmost they found their objective.

Here was an inner sanctum, a plush oasis high in the building, where some great man's staff of lackeys had left for the day. Here the walls were impressively paneled in Circassian rosewood, and a fire crackled softly below an elaborately carved overmantel of Italian marble, richly detailed with cavorting putti and heraldic iconography. A setting not atypical for learned senior professors at the University of Oregon. Streaming rays of moonlight lit the rich stained-glass windows, scattering ghostly colors that further decorated the arabesque patterns of the room's elegant oriental carpet.

Modern touches included a framed poster of Che Guevara hung above the fireplace. An American flag, also framed, had been hung upside-down above the professor's antique desk. One edge of the flag looked eaten away, blackened with singe, from some long-ago attempt to burn it in riotous protest. Arrayed upon the desktop were various rare volumes and costly bibelots. What caught Jamal's eye was a signed sepia-tone photograph of Emma Goldman mounted on a small bejeweled easel. Near it rested a razor-sharp letter opener of ancient Moorish design.

The great man himself dozed in a leather wingback chair, an open copy of *Rules for Radicals* lay against his chest, half hidden by his ratted, gray beard. Despite both the beard and the book, the slogan on his T-shirt was still legible. It read, "This Is What a Feminist Looks Like."

The legs of his cotton, drawstring pants were rolled up, and his pale, wrinkled feet were submerged in a shallow plastic tub of steaming water. Ready, beside the tub, a folded bath towel waited.

A crystal decanter of rich, amber sherry sat on a small, priceless table beside him. An empty, thimble-sized glass held a golden trace of his last round.

Jamal and Keishaun crept into the room, admiring its historical finery. Knowing these luxuries had been built with the sweat and failed dreams of uncountable liberal-arts students. The strains of Chopin issued from a shimmering, onyx-hued record album that revolved slowly on some ancient heirloom gramophone.

The esteemed scholar, Dr. Emmet Brolly, blinked awake. "To what do I owe this pleasure?" he asked, his rheumy eyes fixated, openly captivated by Keishaun's closely fitted slacks.

Too cowed to speak, the students shifted their weight uncomfortably and stared down at their worn tennis shoes. Abruptly Jamal looked up and stammered, "Sir, do you remember Walter Baines?"

A beat later, feeling naked under the brilliant man's leer, Keishaun insisted, "We think he's in trouble."

The doctor knitted his brow. Slowly he closed his book and set it aside. "What brand of trouble?"

Jamal looked to Keishaun, and they regarded each other with worried eyes. To Brolly, Jamal said, "It's some list . . ."

To clarify, Keishaun added, "A list on the Internet." He explained the rumor and what little Walter had known. It seemed simple: If you thought a person was a threat to society you could post his or her name on a certain website. If no one agreed with your nomination the name would disappear within a few hours. But if several people supported the nomination the name would linger to attract more possible votes. The more votes a person got, the more danger he or she was facing.

Jamal interjected, "It's like an unpopularity contest!"

His hysterical outburst made them all cringe. No one spoke as the burning logs in the fireplace softly popped and sighed.

At last, Dr. Brolly laughed. His was a deep hearty chortle, dismissive, and scented with sherry. It displayed every one of his marijuana-stained teeth. As a freethinking scholar and molder of young minds, it was clear he'd faced many such witch hunts in his long career. As if to calm himself, he reached for the decanter and poured his small glass full. After sipping it, he regarded the amber liquid and smiled wryly. "Yes, my children," he said. "There has always been a list!"

Jamal and Keishaun hung on his words. Eyes wide. Their souls filled with dread.

The doctor gestured grandly with the tiny glass. "Sit," he bade them.

The two young listeners sat cross-legged on the carpet, at his feet.

Brolly spoke down to them. "There has *always* been a list. Oh, how human beings love their lists!" He smiled patronizingly. "From the Ten Commandments to the Hollywood Black List. From Nixon's Enemies List to Schindler's List to the *New York Times* Bestseller List. From Santa Claus's list to God's list separating the sheep from the goats." He went on to describe genealogies as lists, taxonomies, inventories. He finished his glass of sherry, poured another, drank that and poured another. "Our much-flaunted Bill of Rights is a list! As was Martin Luther's Ninety-Five Theses nailed to the cathedral door during the festival of Fasching!"

When Jamal and Keishaun looked at him with blank expressions, he bellowed, "If you two had read your Lewis Hyde and Victor Turner—instead of smoking bath salts and playing Pokémon Go—you'd know of what I speak!"

Slipping easily into a lecture he'd delivered countless times, he declared, "Power-reversal rituals!"

Jamal and Keishaun steeled themselves for a long-winded, didactic sermon.

Brolly's dissertation gushed forth: Most civil societies perpetuated their status quo by practicing these rituals. For a short period each year, sometimes seasonally, the lowest-ranking citizens were granted power over their superiors. In modern societies this still occurred at Halloween, the juncture between summer and autumn and supposedly between the living and the dead. On the night of October 31, powerless children donned the costumes of outsiders—of animals and the dead and outcast loners such as cowboys or hobos. Boys dressed as girls and girls as boys, and all of these alien others had the power to roam freely and demand tribute from property-owning upright members of society. If no tribute was paid the threat of Trick or Treat promised property damage.

"Why," the doctor sputtered, "by the 1920s so many homes were burned and so many tires slashed that newspapers colluded with insurance and confectionary companies to institute the ritual of giving away candy!" He marveled, "Picture it! The poor burned the homes of the rich! All offenses of the preceding year were revenged!"

Even Christmas caroling—heartwarming, traditional Christmas caroling—had been a blood sport. The poor congregated outside the homes of the wealthy and sang as a threat. Nothing but bribes of gold and rich food would dispatch them to the next house. Our practice of offering flowers at a funeral originated with an ancient ritual wherein the local poor would gather wildflowers and fragrant herbs. They would arrive at the dead man's casket and hand these gifts to the mourners in exchange for money and bread.

With obvious childlike enthusiasm, the doctor splashed his bare feet in the tub of water.

He declared, "The military is rife with traditional occasions when officers must obey their inferiors for a brief period." Aboard nuclear submarines every tour features a Hefe's Café night. Dinner is celebrated by the ship's officers decorating the mess as a fancy restaurant and then, themselves, cooking and serving the enlisted personnel a gourmet meal. Similarly, in antebellum America the power-reversal ritual was known as Saturnalia. At Christmastime a plantation owner would give his slaves gifts and allow them to travel short distances to visit relatives on neighboring plantations. All of the slaves were given several days of freedom. They received all the apple brandy they could drink and all the pork they could eat. As reported by Frederick Douglass, the slaves would eat, drink, and carouse until they were sick. Every year, this sickness of excess left them miserable. It convinced the slaves they were weak willed. They needed a master to control them and their base impulses. After a few days of bingeing on everything, they were happy to return to being slaves.

This far along, the doctor's lecture was long and liquored and indulgent.

"For the Amish," Brolly droned on, "it's their curious practice of *Rumspringa*. A word which translates to *running or jumping around*. At the cusp of adulthood, Amish adolescents are allowed to enjoy the fruits of the outside world. Like the slave enjoying Saturnalia, the Amish youngsters inevitably overindulge in drugs, in sex, in tedious minimum-wage lifestyles. After they make themselves miserable," Brolly crowed, "they're only too happy to return to the plain and simple Amish life."

Jamal looked at his wristwatch. Keishaun resisted the urge to check his text messages. Clearly the professor was on a roll.

The doctor paused to catch his breath. With liquor shining on his lips, and the rambling wisps of his long gray hair that had escaped his ponytail, he looked like nothing less than a wizard. Some jabbering heretic. Fixing his small audience with a gleaming eye, he asked, "Do you know why this country, supposedly the wisest, most successful human experiment, does *not* practice a power-reversal ritual?"

When neither of the two young men spoke, the doctor shouted, "Karneval!" He bellowed, "Fasching!"

The latter was a word derived from the German term for "last call." It was the equivalent of modern Mardi Gras, a final carnal indulgence before the hardships and self-denial of Lent. In seventeenth-century Bavaria the power-reverse ritual allowed peasants to eat and party and sometimes copulate in the churches and cathedrals while the celebratory parades featured monks and priests riding on wagons—the equivalent of our parade floats—while throwing feces at the onlookers. The profane became sacred and the sacred, profane. But only for a short time.

Nevertheless, it was within this lawless window that Martin Luther made his move. He posted his objections to the Catholic Church. And in doing so he founded Protestantism.

"You'll agree that the United States is nothing if not a Protestant nation?" Brolly asked, adding, "At least at its founding."

Because the Protestant religions had been created during a power-reversal ritual, those religions have always been wary of such a practice.

Brolly nodded, knowingly. "The Pope, His Holiness, will continue to wash and kiss the feet of the poor on Holy Thursday, but the Protestants will never risk the same vulnerability."

That was the fatal flaw of this great country, he surmised. It never allowed the weakest, the poorest and most disenfranchised to enjoy even an hour of ritualized power. Yes, we had castrated versions like Halloween and Christmas caroling for children, but there was nothing to exhaust the adult underclasses and leave them contented to remain poor for another year.

Jamal allowed a respectful amount of time to pass before he tried to redirect. "So the list?"

Desperate, Keishaun begged. "Is it real?"

Drowsy and a little soused, Dr. Brolly tut-tutted. He lifted a pale hand and toyed with a few strands of his wild hair. "As a cultural anthropologist I've long heard of this fabled list." He assured them, "And it is an urban myth. A complete fantasy."

The two students couldn't help but look crestfallen. They'd come here asking about Walter, trying to discover if the professor could help them. He could not or would not. This was a dead end.

As if sensing their disappointment, Dr. Brolly stirred. Perhaps to appease them, maybe just to flirt, he asked, "This mythical list?" Strictly from an anthropological standpoint, he asked, "What happens if a nominee gets too many votes?"

His eyes downcast, Keishaun edged forward until he knelt at Brolly's feet. The water in the plastic tub had long ceased to steam. Keishaun reached for the folded towel. "It's like this," he began, and gently lifted one pale foot from the tepid water, dried it with the towel and let it rest on the carpet. The student repeated the process with the other foot before bringing each foot to his mouth and kissing the cold, wrinkled skin.

Dr. Emmet Brolly stared, his hairy jaws agape, dumbfounded.

Having done that, Keishaun reached one hand around to the small of his own back. From his waistband he produced a snub-nosed revolver and fired a single shot into the professor's slack-jawed expression.

No footsteps came running. The desolate building was deserted. Jamal ventured, "No pun intended, but you've jumped the gun."

Brolly sprawled in his chair, blood filling the ragged crater that had replaced his face. Blood sputtered in the opening exposed at the top of his blasted windpipe. He wasn't boring anyone, not anymore. The entire array of his research and education was splattered on the walnut paneling in back of his chair. His hands trembled for a moment. Then the blood stopped flowing down his gray beard, and he was officially dead.

Keishaun stashed the gun back in his waistband. "In a few days it won't matter." He motioned for Jamal to fetch the fanciful letter opener from the desk. He asked, "What's his value up to?"

Jamal was studying his phone, scrolling through a long list of names. He kept scrolling. The list got longer every day as people submitted their last-minute nominations. At last he said, "You're not going to believe this . . ."

Keishaun froze. "Tell me!"

Jamal looked up from the screen, beaming. "*Sixteen hundred votes . . .*"

His friend gasped. That practically made them their own political party. Keishaun covered his own mouth with both hands and whisper-shrieked with joy.

As Jamal used the letter opener to carve away the dead man's ear, he sighed, "Thank God Walter told us."

Keishaun shrugged helplessly. Blushing a little, weakly he offered, "Poor Walt." He yanked up the hem of the dead man's T-shirt to expose an adhesive patch on the skin beneath. Peeling off the patch and slapping it onto the side of his own neck, he savored the instant rush of Fentanyl.

Jamal handed over the ear, its diamond still sparkling in the lobe. The two young men bumped fists over the mutilated remains of Dr. Emmet Brolly, they slapped high-fives. Before leaving, Keishaun went to the framed flag, that half-charred relic from some long-forgotten protest or demonstration. He took it down, regarded it with reverence, and rehung it right-side up.

Jamal leaned down to pick up the Alinsky book. Coolly assessing its pages, he said, "The time for pretty words has expired." And he gently consigned the fragile paper to the hungry flames of the fireplace.

Piper's voice rasped. His throat hoarse and dry, he felt exhausted. After they'd dismissed the other actors, the casting team had kept him reading random lines. What had begun as an audition was becoming a marathon, as if they were testing his endurance. Clem or Naylor, or whoever the casting director was, he'd grimace and say, "They're not convinced you're man enough." As if baiting Piper, he'd say, "The part calls for lots more gumption."

They'd put up another cue card filled with gibberish, and Piper would be hell-bent not to read:

Caucasia is at war with Gaysia. Caucasia has always been
at war with Gaysia.

Their stack of unread cards still stood thick as an old-school telephone book. Someone would hold up another, and Piper would read aloud:

The fires consuming our cities have been sparked
by loyalist forces of the old regime.

They'd hold up card after card.

The world wants a unified field theory. A single thing,
one something that explains everything—give it to them.

The measure of a man is not what he does for wages
but what he does for leisure.

A grand military processional will retake the decimated city of Portland!

The joy of fiction is that it only needs to smell true.

Gibberish it was. Utter and complete balderdash invented by hack writers for a series that would never get picked up by any network. However Piper delivered each line with vigor and gusto. He knew the knot of his tie had sagged away from his collar button. And that strands of his hair had come unglued and begun to fall across his forehead. But he did not give up. His bloodshot eyes burned, but he was not giving up. Even as the casting director, Rufus or Colton or Brach, put up a new cue card.

———

Before this book was a book . . . before the digging of the burial pits . . . there was just Walter's big plan to get rich.

Walking the streets of New York City, he'd pulled up some porn on his phone. Just still images to peruse until his 'nads filled up. Just so the blood went down to his junk, and he was thinking with the fearless brains below his waist. A hard dick was never scared. Porn did to him what spinach did to Popeye or rage did to the Incredible Hulk. Putting him in a state where he could Where's Waldo the ceiling of the Sistine Chapel and never find God because the butts of all the angels are so infinitely fuckable.

Porn made of Walter a ruthless wolf pack of one. On his phone he'd Googled:

Ted Bundy
Wayne Williams
Dean Corll
Richard Ramirez
Angelo Buono
David Berkowitz

Toe the line. Follow the straight and narrow, and no one cares if you live or die. Walter can starve to death or stumble into traffic and get mowed flat. He can ship out to some combat zone and get bayonet-raped. He's nobody's little baby, not anymore. Nobody gives a crap whether he lives or dies. But kill off a few of his fellow nobodies, and society will move Heaven and earth to keep track of him. A billion taxpayers will provide for his food and shelter for the rest of his life. Dress him in clean clothes. Stop eating, and they'll shove a tube down his throat and pump him full of food, a treatment he hasn't enjoyed since he was a fetus.

Until then he walked the streets of New York, a predator in the land of spring lambs.

All they'd taught him in school could only get a person so far, or else his algebra instructor would be flying on a private jet drinking champagne out of a slipper. What they teach more or less gets everyone to the same place. They say you need to become a thing—a lawyer or bookkeeper or lion tamer to barter bits of your thing for other somethings. In place of one thing, Walter wants to be everything. But to rise above the fray he'll need a mentor. Some billionaire so-and-so to take him under his billionaire wing and show him the ropes on money reproducing itself like rabbits, on insider trading and leveraging commodity futures, the bloodless world of corporate takeovers and funds piling up in some tax haven in some bank account numbered to infinity.

Today, Walter had told himself he could do this. First, he'd done his homework. Had read the financial pages to identify some George Soros or Koch brother. A big-name hedge-fund mogul or investment tsar. He'd strolled through the pages of *Town and Country* magazine and the Fortune 500 Who's Who. Found himself some King Midas who pulls the strings and spins straw into gold.

The way Walter saw it, he hadn't been slacking. He'd been biding his time, conserving his resources, waiting for his one main chance. He'd made a list of what he'd believed in:

Santa Claus
Catholic God
Baptist God
Buddhist God
Pagan God
Satan
The Easter Bunny and the Tooth Fairy
The Seattle Sonics and the Oklahoma Outlaws
Gary Hart and Walter Mondale and Al Gore
Circumcision

To date he'd believed in democracy and Manifest Destiny. He'd believed in capitalism and moral relativity and Social Marxism. If he could put his faith in them, he could believe in anything. Maybe believing in those ridiculous abstractions was an exercise in believing, period.

His only faith, these days his only religion, was Shasta. He'd dipped two fingers into his pants pocket. Pinched out a pink blob. Like a marshmallow only smaller. An earplug. One afternoon in Tools of Industrial Design Shasta had shut down the drill press. She'd pinched the pink foam plugs from her ears and set them aside. While she'd gone to make a call Walter had stolen one, and now on the streets of New York he lifted the earplug to his nose and sniffed. Huffed the sweet ecology of Shasta's skin and brains.

Granted, maybe his dad hadn't been a world heavyweight douche sufficient to score him a big trust fund, but Walter could remedy that. If a dad can have more than one kid, why can't a kid have more than one old man? And if a parent can adopt a kid, why couldn't Walter adopt a new parent? A rich one. Somebody to slip the silver spoon between his hillbilly redneck white-trash lips. Him, the him walking the streets with a concealed weapon, about to become the son some Croesus never knew he had.

Cherry-pick some T. Boone Pickens. Like fantasy football only with his own family lineage.

Money being the purest soul of everything, the form everything takes before reincarnating as something else. Walter made of himself that original Walter, before opinions and education and caution came pouring into him. The Walter that watching porn turned him into.

There on some Madison Avenue he'd be, Walter's new old man, with his hard-boiled oil-painting face and his head for figures. Maybe not the rich Top Hat guy from Monopoly in striped pants and tailcoat, but patriarch enough. And if Walter could pick up a stray dog on the street, then this should be easy. He kept telling himself, "Hostile takeover." *Hostile* takeover. Looked at from the right angle, it would be a compliment, he'd told himself as he'd Mark David Chapman'd to New York City and put a midtown hotel room on his credit card so he could Mark David Chapman the crowded streets, hoping to cross paths with his new old man. The father who didn't know he was, not yet.

On his phone he'd Googled: Chapman's list of approved people to kill.

Johnny Carson
Marlon Brando
Walter Cronkite
George C. Scott
Jacqueline Kennedy Onassis
John Lennon
Elizabeth Taylor

Thinking with his porn brains Walter had lurked the streets with his list, trench coat pockets bulging, on the lookout for one of several potential fathers. Beggars couldn't be choosers. Some of his prospective mentors not even men, but lady stock brokers or real estate wheeler-dealers, just so long as they could school him in their money-making hoodoo. Walter pounded the pavement, on roving stakeout, the list on his phone, complete with photographs and suggested likely locations for hunting down financiers. He'd always thought: Shasta. Thinking: Shasta's facial expression when he showed up at her dorm room, in style, driving a private jet with a string of polo ponies to spirit her away, complete with Beyoncé as her new maid of honor. On his phone he'd Googled: Charles Manson's death list.

Steve McQueen
Richard Burton
Tom Jones
Frank Sinatra
Elizabeth Taylor

With the roll of duct tape in his coat pocket, he'd walked along Wall Street. He'd walked up Lexington Avenue to Bloomingdale's, eyes peeled, not certain how he'd handle an actual close encounter. Blood-hounding billionaires in their natural habitat. Could be he'd trail his new old man for block after block until they'd get caught at a red light, standing on the corner of 57th Street, waiting for the Walk signal. He'd sidle up beside this Michael Bloomberg and ask, "Aren't you Warren Buffett?"

His aristocratic, patriarchal skin would look as pale and brittle-dry as old rolling papers. He'd give Walter the moldy stink eye, and Walter would counter by saying, "It might interest you to know I have a Glock 15," boldly displaying the bulge in his coat pocket.

That would capture the man's attention. There and then Walter told him to hail a cab, and they'd both climbed inside. Walter had told the cabbie an address in Queens, a spot several blocks from where he'd stashed his rental car. The two of them had rode there in shared silence, Walter's bulge pressed into the man's kidneys, him Walter's ticket to a life where he wouldn't have to cram all of his living into Saturday nights. To steel his resolve Walter had surfed more porn. He'd pulled out a pack of skunkweed resin-infused chewing gum and offered the driver a stick. The cabbie had taken it, not really sure what it was. Walt had offered this Bernard Arnault a stick, but he'd refused it so Walter popped the gum into his own mouth and began to chew. He'd said, "I'm not going to hurt you."

This Amancio Ortega, he'd asked, "For not hurting me you need a gun?"

Walter had said, "I only need to borrow your brain a couple days."

With the architectural grandeur of New York going by on every side, this Karl Albrecht had asked, "Was there not lint on that gum?"

Walter had asked back, "What?"

"Pocket lint," he'd informed Walter. "On the gum you so generously offered me." Lifting both hands palm-up, he'd addressed the roof of the cab, beseeching, "At my age, with the precious little of life I have remaining me, why should I trust this young ruffian who so generously offers me cheap candy coated in filth?"

Walter had felt the hairy threads of something between his teeth. His cheeks had burned with shame, but he wouldn't want to make the man right by spitting the gum out the window. Instead, he'd said, "You're crazy. This gum is great!" That's when he'd needed to pull out his phone but didn't want his new old man to see him getting his porn refill.

The cab driver had spat his gum out the window. Walter had told them both, "This gum is delicious!"

So the cabby wouldn't see his rented ride, they'd disembark early. Then, when it was just Walter and the man walking through Queens, when Walter had arrived at the rental car and opened the trunk, he'd nodded for this Carlos Slim to climb inside. Walter had promised him, "One week, tops."

Walt had pulled up the photos of Shasta on his phone. Held the screen for his new old man to see. Scrolling through the photos of Shasta smiling and Shasta asleep and Shasta ignoring him, Walter had said, "This is my motive."

The man's eyes had gone to the inside trunk release lever. Walter let them, just so long as the man climbed in. Let him think he can jump out at the first traffic light. He'd sighed, this Ingvar Kamprad. His shoulders had slumped, and he'd muttered, "One week, Mister Terrorist tells me!" Curled next to the spare tire in Walter's trunk he'd scrambled to offer his wristwatch, his phone and wallet, but Walter had refused them. Giving it a second thought, Walter had taken the man's phone so he could deactivate its GPS. Walter had said, "You don't fully comprehend my motives." Had said, "I don't want your money."

Walter had said, "I'm not any terrorist," and he'd slammed the trunk lid.

Once the trunk was locked shut Walter had spat out the scary chewing gum. In his coat pocket he'd found the one-hitter and sucked his lungs full, holding the smoke, letting his mind wander. Poor Elizabeth Taylor, he'd thought. Twice targeted. Hadn't she also been the target for the elaborate car-crash murder plot in J. G. Ballard's novel *Crash*? Where they plotted to drive off an overpass—called a flyover in England—and symbolically rape her limousine by crushing her to death with their sedan? Or were so many plots to kill her actually the ultimate measure of her movie stardom?

Through the closed trunk lid, Walter had said he was sorry about what went on, about the Holocaust and all, but this wasn't going to be like that. Walter wasn't prejudiced since he'd made a diorama about the Final Solution in middle school. It had been his rebuttal to hateful online Holocaust deniers, complete with incense smoke rising ominously from the Lego building-block chimneys. Sandalwood incense because it was all his Wal-Mart carried. He'd had a Tonka toy bulldozer bulldozing naked Barbies into a dirt hole to hide them from advancing Allied liberation forces. A worthy effort, that diorama, but one that got him sent to the counselor's office to watch a video about being a wrong-headed cultural douche bag. Since then he'd always strove to make a special blood-and-guts, balls-out effort to practice sensitivity in regard to other differently religious people.

When he'd put the one-hitter back in his pocket he'd felt the coil of wire. The garrote.

The truth was he didn't have any gun. The gun in his coat was in actuality a sizable baggie of California Ultraviolet. That, and the duct tape he'd forgotten to use. He'd whisper-told the locked trunk, "Nobody's going to gas you."

Only then did Walter risk another porn refill. All along he hadn't known anything. Hadn't yet seen the whole picture.

This entire abduction would go so easy, so quiet and painless and easy that he should've known something was terribly wrong.

The trunk had said back from the inside, "Who's to gas?" Had said, "Me? I'm Lutheran, Mister Terrorist." Then and there, from the metal inside had come muffled peals of triumphant laughter.

Sixty days out the list was frozen. Nominees with insufficient support were expunged. Those that remained had their reward values fixed. These measures would ensure players couldn't identify, nominate, and up-vote one another. Once Adjustment Day commenced the list would be taken down. The list would not exist.

They'd made Piper say it repeatedly. Each time with exactly the same intonation, as if he were a robot.

"Adjustment Day is upon us," he dutifully recited.

Again, "Adjustment Day is upon us."

"I repeat, Adjustment Day is upon us."

He'd produced the words until they'd stopped sounding like words. Each sentence formed a mantra or a drum beat. To prevent lisping, he'd worked to control the hissing sibilant sounds of the three evenly spaced S's. Every take was perfect, but the assistant director had stood beside the camera and pointed a finger at him to deliver another.

Piper had asked for a bottle of water. Someone dug through the crushed ice in a Styrofoam cooler, but the closest they had was lite beer. The taping had begun anew.

Repeating, "Adjustment Day is upon us."

Repeating, "The list does not exist."

Repeating, "The first casualty of any war is God."

Repeating, "If a man can face reality at the age of twenty-five, at sixty he can dictate it."

The casting director, Clem or Rufus or Naylor, studied his clipboard, nodding. He looked up. "Great job," he said. "Now we need everything in Spanish."

Piper couldn't afford to take offense. He needed the work. Finally Clem promised to be in touch with Piper's agent regarding the terms of a contract. The casting board members had each come forward to shake his hand in their rough, stained hands. Each paying his respect with a gruff "Thank you." The cinematographer, Colton, had pressed a manila envelope onto him and escorted him to the parking lot. Once Piper had climbed into his car, with no one in sight, he'd torn open the envelope. Inside was a banded stack of one hundred hundred-dollar bills. Whether this was a retainer or a bribe, Piper had no idea. Everything about the afternoon had felt the way he'd imagined shooting a porn movie would feel. Printed on the paper band was "$10,000."

At his workstation Charlie positioned a rubber bumper cushion in the hydraulic press. Atop it he aligned a steel mounting flange, and through these he ran a bolt. His foot stepped on the pedal. The press hissed and stamped the parts together, and Charlie added the locknut and torqued it to specifications. He released the pedal, removed the finished axle stop, and tossed it into the wire-mesh bin labeled with the part number. He reached for another rubber bumper, another steel flange, another bolt. What had once been tedious, now every repetition filled him with joy. Every task counted down toward the future, and for the first time since he was a little boy Charlie looked forward to the future like Christmas Eve.

The impossible had happened. Garret Dawson had said, "You." He'd jerked his thumb for Charlie to come over. Garret Dawson, the king of the factory floor.

That's how fast Charlie's life had been saved.

This man had selected him out of all the loud, bullying, bullshit artists in the factory. It was flattering. Charlie felt anointed, like in the Bible. Visited, like by an angel. Like he hadn't even been alive until Garret Dawson had walked up to him after their shift ended and informed Charlie that he wasn't like everyone else, and Charlie had a destiny far beyond assembly work.

Nobody, no teacher or priest or sports coach had ever flat-out told Charlie he could help rule the world.

Charlie was a man. Twenty-seven years old. A man working on an assembly line who had three warning letters in his file and if he punched the clock late he'd receive a fourth letter and be fired. And his job was shit. And he hated himself for clinging to such a shit job. Since school, he'd come to expect so little from life. Nothing special, just to be treated with courtesy and politeness by the world. Wanted people to see him and not fear him, not admire him but just to see him. He wanted to be recognized so people would think twice before badgering or insulting him.

Now he had been chosen for a team. The most exclusive team in human history. And if his team did well they might pool their victories. And if that number was sizable, they might be the leading body of lawmakers in the new nation. And the nation they would lead would lead the world. And this future made it hard to sleep at night.

The day of the invitation Garret Dawson had shown him the list, on Dawson's phone, shown him where to find it, the web address. Dawson had seen in him something heroic and predicted Charlie could do his part on Adjustment Day. Charlie, Dawson proclaimed, had the stuff of men throughout time who'd taken action to radically improve their society in a single day.

This from Garret Dawson, himself, who hadn't punched the time clock late in seventeen years and had never gotten a single letter of warning in his file. Dawson who was living proof that hard work had dignity. Him with a wife and kids, he had everything to lose, Garret Dawson had staked everything on inviting Charlie to join.

Not that Charlie would disappoint such trust. The man had told only Charlie, of all the line workers at KML Industries, the man had sought out Charlie, watched from a distance, seen Charlie's quiet, self-withheld way of conducting himself. He'd sensed rightly that Charlie could keep the secret, wouldn't brag about it and endanger the enterprise. He'd picked out the latent strength and untapped potential in Charlie. What no one had ever recognized, not even Charlie's old man, Garret Dawson had zeroed right in on.

By careful observation the man knew Charlie would buy the

necessary weapon. Charlie would do his practice shooting on moving targets. He'd prove to be an asset come Adjustment Day and as a member of the ruling class for decades to come.

At the risk of sounding astrological, Dawson had talked about the Saturn cycle of people's lives, and how Charlie's had begun at age twenty-seven, and by the time Charlie turned thirty-one he'd be unrecognizable to himself. Dawson, he spoke to Charlie about human brain physiology. He cited studies that prove the last major changes in the human brain occur around the age of thirty-one. That's the year when a man's experience and his education merge to create something greater than the two elements. If a man could live beyond twenty-seven—the death year for so many rock stars—then his greatest ambitions stood to come true by the age of thirty-one.

How Dawson saw it, nature hadn't gifted him a big problem-solving brain so he could punch in and spend his life putting widgets together. The two of them, him and Charlie, were the end result of millennia of smart choices and backbreaking work. Dawson called it comical, how the evolutionary culmination of every genius and muscle-bound savage was standing here. Here at KML Industries, Charlie and his brethren were equipped for the worst shit that fate had ever thrown at any man, yet here they were worried sick about getting fired, and prayed to spend the next four decades threading nuts onto bolts.

Their ancestors, Dawson said, were watching and didn't give a rat's ass how many gadgets Charlie pieced together in an hour, eight hours, fifty years. Everyone in the hereafter wanted to see Charlie display the same courage they'd bequeathed him. They'd given their lives for him and expected Charlie to do the same for the future.

Garret Dawson likened the lineage of their ancestors to the line of power he was inviting Charlie to join. The younger man was all ears as Dawson had described the system. How each line of power radiated from a member of the Council of Tribes. Those seven members had created the list. They'd chosen the first round of soldiers to enroll, cherry-picking only the steady, the able, and the resolute. And each of those chosen had invited a single soldier. And this method allowed each line of power to be traced back to its founder on the council. And the failure of one soldier would be the failure of everyone in that lineage. While the success of each would be the success of his lineage.

By this time a secret network of the chosen was cast. Ordinary men doing their jobs. Normal people. Quiet and drawing no attention, they continued to raise their families and pay their taxes and treat others with a knowing dignity, full in the knowledge that soon they'd be unleashed to resolve all the flaws contained in society.

It was Charlie's next move that worried him. He wanted to enlist his brother-in-law. To bring him into the lineage. At every family get-together the two of them sat hunched in front of the television. To keep the peace, they spent their lives not talking. Thanksgiving or Christmas, every holiday was an echo chamber with certain family members squawking like parrots, repeating each other's approved opinions about the world. To risk a conflicting idea would be dropping a turd in the happiness punchbowl, so Charlie and his brother-in-law hunkered down. They kept their heads low and didn't draw any fire. They gobbled the turkey or Easter ham and pretended this wasn't their lives disappearing into the past.

Charlie knew his brother-in-law would be an excellent asset on Adjustment Day. Charlie just wasn't certain the man could keep his trap shut, and if Charlie's sister found out that would end everything. She certainly couldn't keep a secret. Besides, she was among the parrots who said the world had to stay a certain way, and she'd live and die trying to earn gold stars from teachers who wanted to earn gold stars from teachers who yearned for gold stars.

Her mouth would get them all killed. Rumor, more than rumor, lineage protocol decreed that if anyone snitched that player would be terminated. Worse yet, the player who'd enlisted that player would be terminated. That meant Charlie and his sister and his brother-in-law all would get targeted before Adjustment Day with no legacy and no dynasty for any of them, and his family would be forever left out of the sphere of national power, and Garret

Dawson, poor Dawson, would feel stupid because he'd enrolled a dipshit loser who'd betrayed the cause. Dawson, who'd watched Charlie and measured his character and staked his own life on the belief that Charlie was solid and worth trusting with a role in the glorious new future, Garret Dawson and the entire lineage would falter a step while other lines of power stretched longer.

A few of the lines of power had stuttered and lost momentum this way. Someone had narced and two men had had to be put a stop to, but the third man back had chosen once more and the line had moved forward. Other lines had moved forward without a misstep and those lines stretched for hundreds and those lines would take the most targets.

But for that to happen Charlie had to fulfill his first duty. His first test. Even now Garret Dawson watched him from across the way. Charlie put a rubber bumper into the press. Inserted a flange and a bolt. Compressed the assembly and secured it with a nut.

Living in a castle didn't make a man a king. Not anymore than flying in a private jet made him an astronaut. Or flexing muscles made him strong. Nor did having a trophy wife make a man a winner. All his life Charlie had sought the trappings of power, never realizing that only power is power.

Only courage is courage. Only actions counted. The book said that. Garret Dawson had also given Charlie the famous book.

Now Charlie needed to invite the next member to his lineage.

Other lines were growing by the day, by the hour, but Charlie's was stuck. Stalled. To choose a snitch would get him killed. To not choose would cripple the lineage, the very progression of men who'd put their trust in him. Worse, if he couldn't take this one big risk, how would he ever perform on Adjustment Day?

With its blue-black cover the book stood out like a shaved head. Too large to be hidden in a pocket. With its title embossed in gold, it badged the men carrying it on the street and reading it on the bus. Branded them heroes. Here was reading as a covert act of revolution carried out in plain sight but recognized as such only by other men with the book.

If, for instance, a patrolman stopped a man for speeding and saw the book resting on the seat beside the driver, no ticket was issued. If a woman noticed a man reading the book and asked about it, when the man refused to describe it he was instantly more attractive in her eyes.

As Dr. Brolly had explained it, every youth bulge had a text. It had a book to justify the actions its men must take. The Conquistadors had the Bible. Mao's army had his book of quotations. The Nazis had *Mein Kampf* just as American radicals had Saul Alinsky.

Parents and teachers were thrilled to see boys pick up a book. Boys and young men who'd never willingly finished a book, they were poring over these pages for hours at a stretch.

Only men who'd been invited into a lineage were given copies. Only among such men could it be discussed until all who'd read it knew the words by heart.

To read it in public served as an openly brazen political act. Each blue-black cover was a dog whistle. A status indicator. Reading it was an ideological advertisement to the like-minded.

No library had a copy. No bookstore sold it, this book by Talbott Reynolds.

It jumped to catch the eye. Made the holder a hero among those who knew the plan. Readers carried it to catch the eye of fellow travelers. The badge of its blue-black cover displayed their numbers and bolstered their confidence. It declared that the bravest among the bravest among the brave had chosen its bearer as an equal. And men carried the book every day, everywhere, as they'd carry a flag into battle.

The same as all the most important books it made sense only to the faithful. Like the Quran or the *Book of Mormon* or *The Communist Manifesto*, if a nonbeliever were ever to open a copy she would be puzzled, frustrated, and quickly dismiss the text and set it aside. An outsider could never finish the book while a convert could read it a million times from cover to cover and find fresh insight in every pass.

Those who carried it, they were tired of being consumers. They wanted to be consumed.

In lieu of choosing a vocation they had been chosen. Each of these men had received his calling. A conscription larger than the government's draft lottery.

Terrence's mother finally caught him. He was in bed, reading. He'd been reading the blue-black book since his last hospital stay, since her father had delivered it via a sympathetic nurse who'd agreed not to tell Terrence's mother. His father had never appeared in person, not in Terrence's hospital room, but he'd written an inscription on the title page: "For my son. In a few days the world will be a very different place. Be strong."

Within the book, certain passages were underlined. Terrence knew enough to hide the book by Talbott Reynolds from his mother. He'd smuggled it home when he was discharged. The staff physicians hadn't found anything wrong, nothing to explain his seizures. They never did. To play it safe they'd simply increased all of his dosages of Zoloft, prednisone, beta-adrenergic blocking agents, and colloidal silver.

Whatever his father's intention, the book became Terrence's bible. He read it upon waking each day because dawn was the only time he could. After he took his morning round of meds his mind clouded and he had hardly the concentration needed to follow the storyline of a television cartoon.

Today, for example, he'd been reading:

A happy past cripples people. They cling to it with nowhere better to go. Nothing to improve upon.

When he dredged his memory, the only detail he could retrieve about his father was Brylcreem. The smell of Brylcreem, like a combination of lanolin and old typewriter ribbons. The way his father would pull the point of a comb through Terrence's hair to create a part along one side. To duplicate his father's own haircut, on Sundays before they went to pay a call on God. No face did Terrence salvage. No nothing else. Just the Brylcreem smell and the scratch of that comb along his scalp was all he could recover.

That comb drawing a line like this pencil had. Like a plow. It thrilled Terrence to imagine his father underlining these words with long, steady strokes. Carefully, thoughtfully choosing them especially for him, his son. Each passage was a revelation. In the page margin next to many, in the same stern handwriting as in the inscription, his father had written, "Tell Terry." Proof the man was looking out for him, hovering in the margins. The next highlighted passage read:

> Consider that no one wants you to discover your full potential. The weak do not want to be around the strong. The stagnant can't bear the company of the vigorously growing.

He whispered the words to himself, trying to repeat them into his memory.

> Pain and sickness will always befall men. Choose yours, be it the pain from manual labor or the sickness of overexertion. Schedule it. Savor it. Use your pain so it will not use you.

There was no warning. Perhaps he'd forgotten to lock the door. Either that or his mother had stealthily used her key while he was absorbed in the book. The door swung aside, and there she stood bearing his breakfast tray with its perfectly coddled egg, whole-wheat toast, and halved grapefruit. Her eyes seized upon the book and blazed, but only for a moment. Then her eyebrows relaxed. Her eyes narrowed with hostile suspicion, and she asked, "What are you reading?"

Of course she knew. The Talbott book was a sensation hotly debated on television and the Internet. Like all mystical texts, from *The Celestine Prophecy* to *Jonathan Livingston Seagull*, those who liked it revered it. Those who didn't despised it. His mother fell into the camp of the latter. She bent to set the tray on his bedside table, slyly eyeing the open pages.

When he didn't respond, she forced a smile and said, "Got you a pink grapefruit, today!"

In bed, the first rays of dawn illuminating the words, silently Terrence read:

> The weak want you to forgo your destiny
> just as they've shirked theirs.

She must've known whence it came. Who'd given it to him. For years she'd kept his father at bay, telling the nurses, telling Terrence that his father was a bigoted, race-baiting psycho obsessed with micro-aggressioning the transgendered and rape-culturing tipsy coeds. Ever since Terrence had begun having his mysterious seizures, she'd been his caretaker and only daily human contact.

She motioned for him to scooch over so she could sit on the edge of his bed, her hips pressing against his blanketed thigh. She leaned close, puffing the pillow beside his head. Doing so she snuck a look at the open pages. Aloud, she read:

> We must allow each individual to persevere
> or to perish as he chooses.

A scowl twisted her mouth. "Garbage," she declared. Her disgusted tone, shame-raping him. One of her hands gripped the edge of the cover and she pulled gently. "Give it so you can eat."

When he held tight and refused to look up from the page,

she asked, "What are you hiding?" With another less gentle tug at the book she said, "You'd think I was planning to burn the damned thing!"

Seeing he was determined, she sat back. Coolly assessing him, the bedclothes, the book, her face was flat, expressionless. A mask of cunning. She changed tacks. Inching herself closer, she leaned over him. She reached to press one cool palm against his forehead. Saying, "Your eyes look glassy," she stroked his cheeks. "You feel warm." Brushing some hair back from his temples, she said, "You're close to having another seizure, aren't you?"

This is how it always started. She'd pet his face. She'd coo. His mother would look deep into his eyes, telling him he looked pale, his skin felt clammy. She'd croon and purr, "My poor, sick baby . . . My fragile, sick boy . . ." And sweat would begin to pour down Terrence's face. His eyes would lose focus. She'd prompt, "Your ears are ringing, aren't they?" And his ears would ring.

Next, like a curse, she'd summon the headaches, migraines, chills, and they'd all manifest in him.

This time, as she ran her fingers through his hair and called forth the fits and spasms that would land him back in the hospital, this time Terrence kept his eyes on the open page. Reading:

> The black thug conducts gang violence and the
> homosexual indulges in promiscuity because both
> acts demonstrate political identity. Remove the
> outside observer and you eliminate the impetus
> for the behavior.

Her voice loaded with scorn, she baited him. "Do you know what sensible people are calling that book?" When he didn't bite, she snapped, "They're calling it the 'new *Mein Kampf*'!"

Terrence felt the threat of a seizure pass. The trance broke. His breathing steadied and grew deep. His heart no longer raced.

When she saw her ministrations weren't having their usual

effect, his mother sat back. Once again, she asked, "What are you so ashamed of?" When he didn't respond, she asked, "You didn't have another nocturnal emission, did you?" Her hands dug at the sheets and blankets as she demanded, "Let's see your catheter!"

To protect himself, Terrence strained to roll away from her. Hugging the book to his chest he protested, "Mother! I'm nineteen years old, and I'm tired of wearing a catheter!"

She'd found the collection bag, a clear-plastic balloon swollen with his nighttime output. Holding the collection bag aloft, she shook it for emphasis, sloshing and horrible. "We can dispense with the catheter," she railed, "when someone quits wetting his bed!"

The bedwetting was only an excuse, Terrence knew. Year by year for as long as he could recall she'd measured the output of his bladder and bowels and logged the results. To what end, he'd never questioned, not before reading the Talbott book.

His mother dropped the weighty collection bag and made a sudden, violent grab, snarling, "Give it!"

Terrence clung tightly as she latched onto the spine and fought to drag it from his grasp.

She slid off the bed, squatting low, her feet planted on the floor, pulling with her full weight. With one hand she gripped the book. With her free hand she reached for something Terrence couldn't see. She battled half-heartedly as she focused on some task blocked from his vision by the edge of the bed.

"Your father," she hissed, "he doesn't know how sick and weak you are!"

Terrence's eyes fell upon the current page. There, the words said:

> What you resist persists. Direct opposition
> only strengthens your opponent.

Triumphantly, she lifted her free hand into the air. Somehow she'd managed to snatch the long tube that looped from his catheter, and she'd wrapped a length of it around her fist. If he didn't relinquish his father's gift it was clear she meant to yank the tubing cruelly. She had him by the tackle.

"Hand it over," she growled.

Terrence pleaded, "Mother, no!" But his steadfast grip didn't loosen on the binding. The blankets had fallen away, revealing his pale, hairless legs and arms, the rest of him attired in only a white cotton T-shirt and briefs.

She gave the tube a warning pull. The full length of it jumped and went taut where it entered the front of his tented underpants.

Terrence could already feel the ominous tug and cried out, "Mother, don't!" His voice cracked, "You'll pull it off!" Still he held tight to his treasure.

One hand still pulling at the contested volume, his mother used the other to give a ferocious jerk. The catheter sprang free, the long tube cracking like a bullwhip. Spraying hot urine across his breakfast tray. Dissolving his precious day's worth of benzodiazepine. Urine drizzled onto Terrence's coddled egg and lightly buttered whole-wheat toast with the crusts meticulously cut off.

A pain ripped through, not just his tender junk but Terrence's entire urinary tract, an agony that made his hands spasm and release their grip. The book slipped away, and his mother fell backward. The catheter flailed in the air, jetting its salty, amber contents. The blue-black book came into violent contact with the edge of the breakfast tray, knocking it from the night table. The tumbling plate sent eggs and marmalade flying.

As she tumbled, the heavy book so quickly released struck her boldly across the face. The impact made a dull thwack, followed by his mother's guttural moan of suffering.

His mother sprawled backward, resting on her elbows. Steaming yellow waste still shot from the tubing that had a mere instant before been lodged deep in her son's urethra. Under the putrid rain of this hellish fountain she shrieked, "See what you made me do!"

The book's impact had broken her nose, laying it sideways

against one cheek. A froth of blood and mucus poured from her nostrils, making her words sputter. The room was a shambles, littered with urine, blood, and bacon. The wallpaper, dappled with orange juice and partially dissolved serotonin reuptake inhibitors.

With one hand, Terrence gripped his wounded manhood in anguish. The trauma had almost turned him inside out. While the shame and rage burned in his tear-stained cheeks, his opposite hand flew to his mouth and he fell to sucking the thumb feverishly. That's when a voice came to him, a voice he chose to believe was his father's. It bade, "Be strong."

At this, he swung his thin legs off the side of the bed. Despite his mother's curses and sobs, he lowered his bare feet to the carpet and took a wobbly step toward the bathroom. Ignoring the shouts that followed him, he staggered toward the toilet. His hands fumbled with his shorts as a voice screamed, "For Christ's sake, put up the seat!"

He left it down. Straddling the bowl, his legs spread wide apart like the legs of Atlas, for the first time in his life Terrence Weston took his first standing leak.

We've all watched the little ritual. When you go to pay with a fifty-dollar bill at the store, or a hundred, the cashier always holds it up. She looks at the light shining through and squints to see the watermark. The cashier whips out a felt-tipped pen and swipes it across the face of the bill. Because a lazy counterfeiter will use well-worn paper made from wood pulp, the pen contains a solution of iodine that reacts with the starch in cellulose and leaves a black stain. Real currency is printed on rag paper made from cotton or linen fibers. It's more like fabric than paper. That's why real money survives the washing machine. On real currency the iodine pen leaves no mark.

Masie would be the first to admit she was a geek about money.

She studied the feel of security threads woven into bills. She loved watermarks and color-change inks.

That's how come Masie worked late at the printer, tonight. She knew printing, and she knew money, but this contract job was something new. A special order. A new process.

She lifted one of the unprinted sheets. Even the term *printing* was inaccurate. This process was more like exposing photographic paper to light, like developing a picture.

Each sheet measured an arm's length wide. Slippery and shiny, more stiff than paper. Her instructions were to place each sheet in a jig. She'd then place a template on the sheet, a kind of stencil. And she'd switch on an ultraviolet light and allow it to shine on the template and sheet for one minute. She'd remove the sheet and run it through a cutter that divided the film into thirty-six, stiff, thin . . . coupons, they had to be.

It was a promotional gimmick, Masie guessed. As the customer had explained, the finished coupons would have a six-week lifespan. After fifty-odd days the pattern on them would fade to nothing.

The way the customer had explained it, this was a new technology originally developed for creating self-erasing, top-secret military documents. It used nanoparticles of gold or silver sandwiched within a thin gel sheet. When the particles were exposed to ultraviolet light they bonded in the pattern of the exposed area. Thus, they bonded to create the patterns allowed by the stencil. Sheets impregnated with gold particles were red, and the exposed areas became blue where they filled with the bonded particles. Sheets impregnated with silver particles looked yellow, and the exposed patterns of particles turned violet.

Masie lifted a stack of the finished coupons. The colors were vivid red-and-blue or yellow-and-violet, patterned with convoluted details similar to paper currency. A lacy border, intricate background crosshatching. A picture of a pompous man dominated one side. The caption identified him as Talbott Reynolds.

"Absolute Monarch Appointed by the Council of Tribes," the caption read. He looked familiar, as if he could've been an actor she'd seen on forgettable television commercials.

On the opposite side of the red coupons a slogan read: "Money Is Better Burnt Than Spent on Folly."

On the yellow coupons, the slogan was: "Hoarded Food Rots. Hoarded Money Rots Man. Hoarded Power Rots Mankind."

It wasn't visible, not yet, but the tiny particles were already beginning to break their bonds and drift apart. The coupons might be legible now, but in six weeks they'd appear blank.

It was built-in obsolescence. Talking to herself, Masie muttered, "Ezra Pound would've loved this!"

She counted the cut-out coupons, banded them with paper in stacks of one hundred, and packed them in boxes for shipment to the customer. When the crew switched duties, she ran the printer—actually it was a vacuum frame that sucked the air out and made sure the template was tight against the sheet of film. This way the images were crisp and sharp, although only short-lived.

As a money geek, she'd studied how the poet Ezra Pound had advocated for a vegetable-based currency. As some form of money that would quickly rot, it would force holders to spend it or invest it as soon as possible. No one could pile up great fortunes in cash, and money wouldn't outlast people. It would be as perishable as a loaf of bread or a passing hour of labor. Masie knew it was radical thinking like this that attracted Pound to Fascism, particularly to Mussolini, particularly to the money theorist Silvio Gesell. Gesell urged that all large denomination currency have an expiration date so that it could not be hoarded by the rich while the poor starved for employment. In Pound's dream, banks and rich men could never enslave a nation with the power of its own monetary units.

These crazy ideas had landed him in prisons and mental hospitals for much of his life.

To Masie, the ideas didn't sound so insane. To her money ought to be a gateway like Superman's telephone booth that allowed transformation. Money was agar, aether, undifferentiated stuff that had to take a new form quickly or perish.

As she packed a carton with stacks of red bills, Masie wondered about their purpose. What forward-thinking advertising agency was behind this? Whatever their use, it had to be soon. Within weeks they'd be worthless. They could still be restored using another burst of ultraviolet light, but only the original creators would have the template. Whoever owned the stencil owned the means of producing more.

The shipping labels showed the boxes were headed to cities throughout the nation. Most likely hers wasn't the only shop producing them. Whatever the Council of Tribes was, it wouldn't be a secret for much longer.

The list had been a joke. A listicle. Click bait. The most easily consumed form of information in the post-information age of churnalism. No one knew who first posted it. Late-night talk-show wags joked that they weren't hated as much as other talk-show wags. Others saw it as a way to rebrand themselves as villains or victims. For hate is a form of passionate attachment, and to be despised seems better than to be unknown.

Thus people who felt neglected, they nominated themselves and were hurt not to be seconded. Hate took the place of love as our measurement of popularity. For it takes everything to be loved. To be loved is to serve as a slave. Hate demonstrates a complete freedom from pleasing others. Like wildfire almost everyone alive was nominated, but few received the votes they needed to sustain any rank. Those who remained were public figures who'd betrayed huge groups of followers. The staggering vote totals went to media figures, actors, journalists. By far the most hate went to teachers and professors who'd been exposed for teaching students *what* to think in place of *how* to think.

However the greatest tallies of rage were heaped upon political figures. Those preening public servants who constantly created bigger problems and offered themselves as the only solution.

Visitors to the site marveled over the skyrocketing scores. They scrolled through the list of America's Least Wanted and looked for the ones nearest themselves. This pornography of public hatred.

The names of ordinary people dropped away even as the votes snowballed for the famous. New distractions presented themselves, and most people forgot the list. Dismissed it as they had the Tamagotchi . . . the Beanie Babies . . . pogs.

But in obscurity the list continued to swell. The remaining names ticked upward into the millions of votes. And no one gave a thought to the list except for the mysterious team that had created it. Visitors downloaded copies of the final version. And just as mysteriously as the list had once appeared, suddenly it was gone.

The list did not exist.

Charlie was determined not to look, not at first.

And then he'd looked, and he wasn't going to look anymore, but then he looked some more. And what he'd dreaded most had come true. Both their names were on the list.

He noted the date on which each name had been posted. The first had been posted only a day before the second. Neither of the two had enough votes to stay on the list past the three-week mark. Every day Charlie checked, and every day he prayed both names would just drop off the list for lack of votes.

Just hours before the threshold, both names had racked up too many votes. They were both targets. Both were going to die.

The two weren't in Charlie's region, but they'd be targets for some lineage. And it was completely unethical, but he drove around all day Sunday until he found a phone booth so isolated no one would overhear his conversation. The booth stood at the edge of a pay parking lot near the train station. Charlie bought latex gloves to prevent leaving his fingerprints on the buttons, and he dumped out the Mason jar where he collected spare change and picked out all the quarters. He wore sunglasses and a baseball cap with the brim pulled low. He parked a ways from the phone booth and walked around block after block, always making sure nobody was following him. And as surreptitiously as sliding into the door of a dirty book store, he side-stepped into the phone booth.

His pockets loaded with quarters, the weight of these quarters tugging his pants low on his hips, Charlie stuffed his hands in the latex gloves and dialed a long-distance number he knew by heart.

The phone rang at the opposite end, and Charlie prayed for someone to pick up.

"Hello?" A man's voice.

Charlie said, "Dad?"

His father asked, "Charlie?" Away from the phone, he shouted, "Honey, pick up the extension. It's the dropout calling!"

Charlie scanned the surrounding parking lot. Into the receiver he asked, "How soon can you and Mom get to Canada?"

A click was followed by his mother's voice. "You're in Canada?"

"No," Charlie insisted. "You and Dad need to get to Canada, fast!"

His father chuckled. "With the big war coming, it's *you* who needs to do the draft dodging!"

His mother added, "If you were still in college and hitting the books, Charlie, you wouldn't be eligible for getting drafted."

Charlie didn't want to argue, but he didn't want to tip his hand, either. "Mom, that was Vietnam. This is different." His nervous fingers went back to his pants pocket, from pocket to phone, and continued to drop quarter, quarter, quarter into the slot. Each coin set off a bell. Between and behind their words, the bell kept tolling.

He couldn't say as much, but they were both on the list. Even if he told them the full situation they'd run to the police and the police would most likely kill them for knowing. After that, the police or someone would kill Charlie for telling them. Their only hope was to flee the country. Because even if they hid out, stayed at home, whatever, someone, someday would target them.

Charlie tried to reason with them. He asked, "Dad, if you and I were in a lifeboat with my son, and I could only save you or him, who do you think I should save?"

His mother gasped, "Charlie! You have a son?" She sounded shocked and delighted.

"Theoretically, Mom," he replied. "Should I save you or my kid?"

To Charlie, the coming slaughter would elevate him and all his descendants to the status of royalty. But it would also kill his parents. A conundrum. They were both professors at a junior college, they dabbled in local city and county politics, there were a dozen reasons for people wanting them rubbed out. But, still, they were his mom and dad. It was difficult to weigh the love he felt for them against the love he'd feel someday for his future sons and grandsons. His love for them was conflicted. His love for his unborn sons was unqualified.

"So," he approached the issue from a new direction, "if I get drafted, do you want me to kill people?"

Without hesitation, his father said, "To save our nation, yes."

The bell rang and rang.

As he fed the phone quarters, Charlie asked, "What if I die?"

His mother said, "God forbid!"

Another quarter rang the bell.

Charlie asked, "And if it meant saving our country, would you want me to kill someone's parents?"

His fingers sweating inside the latex glove, his hand went to his pocket and found it empty. He'd run out of quarters. The bells had stopped.

After a pause, his father said, "Yes, if that's your mission."

To clarify, Charlie asked, "You'd want me to murder someone's mom and dad?"

His mother asked, "What's that sound?" She asked, "Are you crying?"

Yes, he was crying. Charlie was crying. He sniffed as tears washed down his cheeks.

His father asked, "Is this about drugs? Charlie boy, are you high?"

Before they'd be cut off, Charlie choked out the words, "I love you guys."

His father said, "Then why the big boo-hooing?"

And that's when the connection went dead.

Gregory Piper watched television, waiting for a final decision on his audition. Television was better than the Internet. If he ran across himself on television it was by accident and it could still send a frisson of chemical euphoria into his bloodstream. Surfing the web it was too easy to search himself and build a lifetime out of watching video of his work and perusing still images of himself. Too *Sunset Boulevard*. On the Internet, a person could spend a lifetime in egomaniacal self-worship.

Sitting on the couch, he considered the cash. The ten thousand dollars. Considered whether he ought to mention it to his agent or not. His hand squeezed the remote, bouncing between channels. On one, the actor John Wayne appeared, and he ambled into the center of a white space and fixed the camera with his trademark glower. Clearly this was a sequence digitally lifted from some classic film and inserted into a new context. The Duke whipped off his Stetson and dashed the hat against the dusty leg of his chaps. "Shucks, pilgrim," he drawled. "I ain't made it to the toilet this time . . ."

Piper clicked the remote and the image froze.

It was a commercial to sell absorbent underpants.

He watched in shock. Clearly the actor's estate was willing to license Wayne's image for anything. This was something few actors foresaw. How their residual celluloid self could be computer manipulated to serve as a slave, a digital zombie beyond death. The actor Robin Williams had been among the first to draft a will forbidding electronic misuse of his image. A star with less foresight, a digitalized Audrey Hepburn continued to work, shilling for Galaxy Chocolates. Fred Astaire sold vacuum cleaners. Marilyn Monroe hawked Snickers candy bars.

Like ghosts, Piper thought.

An ear worm, like a song, echoed in his head.

"Adjustment Day is upon us," he repeated to himself as he watched the television. He'd been asked to recite that line so often he'd probably never vanquish it from his head.

The envelope of cash was stashed in his kitchen, in a cabinet, stuffed inside an empty cereal box. He would spend some on a lawyer. Would finally write his own Last Will and Testament. He'd make sure no one could harness his image after his death. That demise being peaceful and painless and in the distant, distant future, he supposed.

Back in Before Times . . . in the world you want to think is still real . . . Walter had driven west through Illinois. He'd ranted that the greatest proof of love's power is that it couldn't be reduced to words. Love isn't a scientific experiment that could be replicated. No man has to be a rocket surgeon to recognize love. It's like that poem about ignorant armies that clash by night. *That* poem. Where there's no joy or cure for pain.

While his kidnapped new old man had listened or slept or died in the trunk of the car, Walter had described Shasta. Every detail about Shasta.

He'd surmised that love is a mission a man goes on every day. A mission a man never completes until death. In that way, true love is a suicide mission.

Dawson was determined not to look. But then he'd looked, and he wasn't going to look anymore, but then he looked some more. And that's when he saw the name on the list.

The name had already racked up an impressive tally. It wouldn't be Dawson's lineage, but some lineage was going to earn big votes on this target. Futile as it seemed, Dawson knew he'd still have to make an effort. Someday Roxanne would ask if he'd made an effort, and he'd have to explain. Tell her how he'd tried.

Dawson bought a throwaway phone at the 7-Eleven and took it to the center span of the Morrison Bridge, a place where no one would overhear. Not over the sound of traffic. He dialed a number from memory. As it rang on the other end, he looked down on the dark water of the Willamette River and prayed the number was still valid. It had been a long time.

"Hello?" A boy's voice.

Dawson asked, "Quentin?"

His son asked, "Dad?" Music blared in the background. "Dad, I can barely hear you."

Dawson shouted, "Turn down your music!"

Against the music, his son shouted, "Is Mom okay?"

Dawson shouted, "Your mother is fine, but you need to get your ass to Canada!" Out here in public, shouting like this was risky. Cars passed, but the bridge's sidewalk was empty.

His son shouted, "If you mean the war, I'm joining up. Dr. Steiger-DeSoto says it's my duty as a pan-gendered individual to show the world that courage knows no gender!"

Whatever his kid had just announced, Dawson wasn't certain. In response, he shouted, "There won't *be* a war!"

His son shouted, "Dr. Steiger-DeSoto says the war is necessary to preserve human rights!"

It was Dawson shouting, "I'm trying to save your life!"

His son shouted, "Dr. Steiger-DeSoto says I'm not a child anymore!"

Dawson shouted, "Turn down your stereo!"

Against the music, his son shouted, "Dr. Steiger-DeSoto says I'm her most promising grad student and that I should start thinking for myself!"

Dawson risked everything. If he told and Quentin went to the police, they'd both be killed. Roxanne would be alone in the coming new world. No one would benefit. Still, Dawson told. "Your name is on a list to be killed!"

His son laughed. Laughed and laughed. "Dad," he said, catching his breath, "I know! Isn't it great!"

Dawson didn't understand.

"I even voted for myself!" laughed his son. "It's nothing." He sighed. "Dad, don't worry. It's like . . . it's like the new Facebook!"

Dawson tried to explain the truth. A beep interrupted.

His son said, "Dad?"

The beep interrupted.

His son said, "Dad, Dr. Steiger-DeSoto is on the other line."

The beep interrupted.

His son said, "Dad, I love you. See you after the war!" And the connection went dead.

And Dawson thought of the quote from the Talbott book:

We must kill those who would have us kill one another.

And Dawson let the phone slip from his fingers and drop to disappear with hardly a splash into the deepest point in the river's deep water.

Jamal called his mom to tell her he wouldn't make it for dinner on Sunday. He called from a hotel suite in Albany. Eating around him, perched on various chairs and sofas as well as seated on the floor, the group of them eating room service, his fellow teammates awaited their turn on the phone. Not his whole lineage, just a segment of his squad. They were silently drinking wine and beer from the minibar. They were listening as each took the phone and called his family. He wanted to share the secret. To tell his mama about the Declaration of Interdependence and how it promised a homeland where no race would live under another like an occupying army. Each race would call the shots in its own homeland and no minority would be called out by the hostile stares of the majority. Like-minded could dictate their own culture. Children wouldn't be schooled to serve as human colonies of an alien cultural imperialism.

On the phone, she demanded, "What do you mean you're not stopping by?"

He wanted to tell her about his lineage. For the first time in human history each line of power wasn't going to be based on blood and marriage alliances. Jamal looked at the man who'd invited him, then at the man he had invited. This cohort was only a small segment of a lineage that crisscrossed the nation, tonight. These men, eating room-service pizza, eating club sandwiches and sliders, and pretending not to eavesdrop, their brotherhood was based on mutual respect and trust and admiration. Here he was one link in this chain of men, none of whom were his enemy. Every one of which expected him to be nothing less than a hero.

He wanted to read to her from the Talbott book, the passage that went:

> The last thing a black man wants to be
> is another fake white man.
> The last thing a homosexual wants to be
> is another imitation heterosexual.
> The last thing a white man wants to be
> is another phony paragon.

On the phone, his mama asked, "Jamal?" Not all screechy like before, she asked, "What aren't you telling me?"

If he told her anything, she'd rush down and insinuate herself. That was her way.

Tonight, on the last night of the old regime, the lines of power were assembling outside statehouses and courthouses. Those invited by the invited by the invited in lineages linked by trust, they met their fellows for the first time and gasped in happy awe at their own numbers. Tribes chosen from the best, not the weakest, they gathered to wait outside of city halls and all the places where elected traitors would return the coming morning.

If a target's vote count was astronomical, a team might be dispatched to lie in ambush outside the target's home. Otherwise they camped in ready groups, no one mentioning their task. The time for practicing and planning had passed. Their coming actions had to be as automatic as putting on their pants before their shoes.

Most were quiet, saving everything for the next day's work.

To his eyes the group in the hotel suite looked like that painting, that church painting showing Christ and his homeboys chowing down. That *Last Supper* picture. Only with them passing a phone so, man by man, each could call home and make his good-byes. Not to explain himself, but to make his peace.

They were an army of lone wolves.

For Jamal the idea of power didn't translate into sex and drugs. As he saw it, those short-term pleasures were the distractions men sought when they had no real power. To wield power, real power, meant a peace of mind and satisfaction beyond the numbness and dumbness that the bong and the whore could provide.

Power meant access to anything and everything. Meaning a man wouldn't need to hustle and hoard. It meant a life unencumbered by back-up plans. Alternate routes. Second choices.

The Talbott book stated it so well:

> Each group must inhabit a homeland where it
> constitutes the norm. Otherwise either self-destroying
> self-hatred or other-attacking self-aggrandizing
> occurs. Drinking, drugs, and toxic sexual behaviors
> arise when cultures are compelled to share public
> space. No culture should be held to the expectations
> and subjected to the withering gaze of another.

Young people in their own nation state, they'd be released from the college-prep standards of the alien European culture that sought to standardize every human being regardless of his natural talents and inclinations. The currently imposed one-size-fits-all code of human behavior. Power meant Jamal not having to present himself as an imperfect copy of someone he'd never wanted to be in the first place.

His lineage had rejected the proscribed, standardized everything of laws and schools. That chutes-and-ladders game of rules and taxes where it took forever to climb, but only one misstep sent a man into poverty or prison.

Jamal sensed how others were waiting to make their calls. He listened to his mother's worried breathing and the kitchen noise behind her. He wanted to tell her that after tomorrow the world would be different. Through him, her life would be improved and noble. They'd, all of them, be as close to royalty as the Declaration of Interdependence allowed.

Everyone's success depended on everyone. And due to that, none wanted to disappoint such high expectations. Each strove to be worthy of the honor bestowed upon him by his comrades. By his tribe.

Jamal wanted to tell his mama everything. He wanted to say he loved her, but everybody would hear. Instead, he asked, "Feed my dog?"

She sounded relieved. "You want I should feed Bouncer?"

He could hear her deciding. Like she wanted to yell and tell him to drag his ass home and feed his own damned dog, but like she didn't want to yell if this might be their last talk on Earth. He exchanged looks with the man he'd invited. A man who knew how Jamal's mama could get. Finally, he asked, "Please?"

Something he'd never heard he heard now. Over the phone his mama started to cry. So even with his team listening, he said, "I love you, Mama." He sniffed. He couldn't help it. "Just feed my dog, okay?"

His mama sniffed. Hushed so he could barely hear, she said, "Okay." Her voice, scared.

Jamal ended the call and handed the phone to the next man.

Among those who waited for the dawn were the former journalists. They bided these last few hours outside what remained of the major newspapers. They loitered on the sidewalks around the television headquarters. Honing their resolve was the knowledge that the few journalists who'd retained their careers did so by inflating lies to terrify and enrage the public trust. Telling the truth wasn't sufficient power.

As consolation the remaining journalists convinced themselves that no absolute truths existed. This new untruth they propagated as the new truth. The entertainment value, the ability to titillate or provoke, came to be the litmus test of any new truth.

Their goal now was to shape people's minds and warp information to that purpose. Honest reportage, which people in a democracy needed as badly as they needed to breathe, ceased to be a priority for the Fourth Estate. Those journalists who couldn't be corrupted, they were discarded.

They tested each other with photos displayed on their phones. Each a smiling head shot of a distinguished man or woman with neatly styled hair and a gleaming smile. Gray hair or dyed. Wearing a necktie or pearl necklace. And the challenge was to name the person and give his or her vote tally from the list. Or to recognize that the photo was an innocent who'd never appeared on the list and wasn't deemed a target.

These were the hollow-cheeked, flinty-eyed former newshounds who gathered outside radio stations and cable networks, ready to return objectivity to the public airways.

On that same night, Esteban and Bing bid a dozen of their closest friends attend a potluck. Supping from paper plates loaded with mulligatawny and mole de pollo, the local segment of their lineage finalized their list of targets. Despite their weeks of drilling, apprehension hung in the air like the pungent curry.

As the assembled men ate, Esteban read aloud from the Talbott book:

> It's living among heterosexuals that makes the homosexual feel abnormal. Only among whites do blacks feel inadequate. And only among homosexuals and blacks do whites feel threatened and guilty. No group should be blighted by the intellectual expectations and the moral yardstick of another.

Standing in the center of the group, the book open in his hands, he read:

> Art should not be social engineering. Art that seeks to repair people must be rooted from society.

The next line, Bing knew by heart:

> Bearing that in mind, we must allow each man to decide upon his own happiness.

Before he was with Esteban, tiny Bing had been embroiled in an unhealthy relationship with his pimp. Despite Audrey Hepburn being his lifetime idol, Bing's life had been a far cry from that depicted in *Breakfast at Tiffany's*: swanky nightclubs and jumping out the top of super-sized birthday cakes to the vociferous applause of mobs of love-struck Shriners. No, in actuality when Bing's former pimp spoke, he was all the time, "These dicks ain't going to suck themselves, bitch!"

So when Esteban had made his play, the tiny, younger man listened. The older, sophisticated Cuban had invited him to take up arms in their lineage of power, and Bing recognized an improved circumstance when he saw it.

Closing the Talbott book and carefully setting it aside, Esteban proclaimed, "Queer bodies have always been the shock troops in Western civilization."

When inner cities had rotted down to the charred skeletons of their once-elegant housing stock, he said, it was queer bodies that had brought back those crime-ridden neighborhoods. Queer homesteaders had no children to risk in the failed school systems. Strong queer backs and bright queer minds had nothing except their own lives to risk! Those intrepid pioneers had settled the harsh wilderness of decayed Savannah and the derelict wastelands of Baltimore and Detroit. Those queer settlers had arrested the death spiral of each local tax base. With queer resolve they'd tamed the lawless urban frontier. With queer sweat equity they'd boosted the land values.

Here and there, hushed cries of "Amen, brother" punctuated Esteban's fevered delivery.

"When nobody else dared," he called out, "it was queer courage that nailed the roofs back on those houses! It was queer determination that repaired the dry rot and made the ghetto into a safe investment for white bankers."

He described how rising property values had attracted a spate of heterosexuals. Improved schools and close proximity to city services had brought many more. Clearly, Esteban had merely started to build his case.

He looked from listener to listener, letting a stretch of quiet pass before he redirected.

"For better or worse—" he jabbed a plastic fork forward for emphasis "—queer bodies have always been the advance guard in emerging politics, too!"

Citing recent scholarly writings as proof, he described how Malcolm X had gone on the down low, servicing the wealthy white men he'd later return to rob. "But do we celebrate the subversive queer energy of the man?" he demanded. "That hero who sought to subvert power by any means possible?"

A general chorus of "No!" and "Hell, no!" went up from the small crowd.

"Don't even get me started on James Baldwin!" Esteban wailed. "The man . . . the prophet . . . the poet laureate who wrote the liturgy of his entire race, and his people won't celebrate his queer spirit!"

Not only did Esteban stew a mean chicken marsala, but he was holding forth with a pep talk the power of which Bing had never heard.

Food and drinks went ignored and people set down their spicy meals and raised their hands and swayed together in their show of unity. Tiny Bing could only grin; he was proud to witness the rhetorical might of his man.

"Not so helpful, but just as historic and just as ignored," wailed Esteban, "was another little queer boy!"

Teasing his listeners, he described a child wildly in love with a classmate who rejected him. This same boy had grown to become a decorated soldier before finding himself impoverished. His youth had opened the doors and wallets of wealthy male admirers, and the young man soon found himself leading a political party. And not long after, helming an entire country.

"Arguably the most powerful leader of the twentieth century." Esteban spat the words in disdain. "And nobody will speak of how his queer heart brought him to greatness."

This demagogue, this lovelorn mustachioed gigolo had built an entourage of like-minded queer leaders and launched a style of visual imagery that continues to be emulated to this day. But when the radical queerness of his political movement was exposed and ridiculed by the world press, that same leader called for the wholesale execution of his entire queer power structure.

"In one night," Esteban ranted, "they were summarily executed and the man himself was the only survivor, forced to hide his queer shame and suffer it to his suicide."

His audience hung on Esteban's every astonishing utterance.

"That man," he swore, "in all his queer power and cowardice, was none other than—" He looked to Bing.

The younger man offered, "Not Adolf Hitler!"

Esteban nodded in wordless affirmation.

Here his audience gasped. The boy whom little Adolf had loved in grammar school, he revealed, was Ludwig Wittgenstein, a talented Jew who would mature to become a kind of anti-Hitler, a brilliant philosopher and teacher unafraid to conceal his queer self. Inventor of Wittgenstein's Duck-Rabbit. As for the night when so many of Hitler's compatriots were slaughtered, that was the legendary Night of the Long Knives when the Nazi Party purged itself of its founding queer members.

Unspooling before the spellbound potluckers was a history heretofore forbidden to their ears.

"Yes," Esteban forged onward, "even in the noble Women's Movement . . ."

After the work of Betty Freidan, after the labor of the 1960s, and the blood spilled by a generation of queer women, the leaders had evicted their queer sisters in an effort to make liberation more palatable to mainstream, middle-class women. Heterosexual women. History would always repeat this pattern: Queer foot soldiers blazing the path and being dismissed once the heavy lifting was complete.

Already being distributed among them—among all the tribes and lineages—was a book. Because all great doings require their manifesto. Every copy of this book was bound in the richest blue-black and bore its title and the name of the author on the cover in gilded lettering. Be it *The Communist Manifesto*, the Bible, the Koran, *The Feminine Mystique,* or Saul Alinsky.

"Consider every hipster," Esteban sighed. One hand fluttered to demonstrate how words now failed. He shook his head as if perplexed. "They're covered with tattoos and riddled with piercings, but few of them know the name Jean Genet. And none know of the Urban Aboriginal culture of 1970s queer San Francisco that revived the primitive arts of body modification!"

He allowed the energy in the room to settle. Every one of them felt the burden of failure. The steadfast manner in which history had refused to celebrate or even acknowledge the events of queer history. Many sniffed back tears. Their feast of unity began to feel like a funeral. Esteban snuck a glance at Bing to reassure him that all was not lost.

"Beginning tomorrow," he said in a soft growl, "history will no longer ignore us." His voice rising, he continued, "Our lineage of power will prove itself! We will harvest many targets, many more than any other lineage!" He shouted to be heard over the rumbling agreement around him.

Bing took up the rallying cry. "We will prove our queer power and earn the right to control the nation . . . that controls the world!"

Lost were any further individual words as the lusty huzzahs of all filled the loft.

Charlie and his fellows bowed their heads and prayed for the souls of men who had never found their destiny. They invoked the dead and invited those ancestors to join them. And the war parties swelled with the living and the not. As Garret Dawson had invited Charlie did Charlie eventually invite Martin who'd invited Patrick who'd invited Michael who'd invited Trevor until their lineage stretched from ocean to ocean and city to city. And on that night the great chieftain lines were complete.

Theirs was a tailgate party, the air scented with charcoal and bar-beque sauce. Rough men attired in brimmed caps and camouflage-print hunting ensembles.

Above them reared the statehouse, the way all grandiose edi-fices are designed to make the people outside feel powerless and those showcased within feel omnipotent. The bloated, useless shape of its marble dome, it was a citadel to be taken. The new

Bastille. Garret Dawson glared up at it like the ridiculous stage set it was. His pale blue eyes filled with contempt.

The marble dome, washed with floodlights, appeared so like a full moon frozen on the horizon. Like Moloch fed on slaughtered children yet always hungry. It loomed above them. No police officers asked their business. No one gave them a second glance.

Tomorrow they'd no longer be men who measured their time by red traffic lights and their pleasure by pints of microbrews.

Charlie put two fingertips into his mouth and called for silence with a long, deafening whistle. Dawson was about to speak.

Not a tall man, but built strong and made lean by a lifetime on the shop floor, Dawson modestly accepted the crowd's silent attention.

"The queers . . . ," said he, and he faltered.

Beginning with a new breath, he repeated, "The queers became artists because nothing they could do in public came naturally."

From their first awareness, he explained, they'd had to study and mimic behavior instinctual to all others. To survive they needed to observe and remember, and in doing so they'd served as the scholars, artists, and clerics of civilization.

Likewise the blacks had raised families. To survive they'd built careers and businesses. Blacks had established churches and fought as soldiers and set themselves as moral paragons of virtue that outshone their white counterparts.

"But identity politics," Dawson continued, "has reduced the homosexual to nothing but his sexual preference. It has reduced the black to only his skin. And each has become a caricature of his former dignified self."

Men like Dawson and Charlie had not left their drill presses and lathes in order to rescue the gays and blacks. Their lines had formed to battle the same corrupt identity politics that were now forcing the white races into one monstrous stereotype.

Theirs was perhaps the meanest of all caricatures.

Instead of being salt-of-the-Earth machinists and carpenters, they were being compelled by modern politics to rally under one flag as goose-stepping Nazi NASCAR storm troopers.

Gays had been coerced into a two-dimensional identity that had reduced them to hypersexual behavior, and that behavior had decimated their numbers. Blacks had been told they were powerless unless they became thugs, so that anything that could be construed as disrespect led to them murdering one another in staggering numbers.

"White men," Dawson vowed, "will not be stampeded into adopting a similar self-image."

On the contrary, the actions they took, the actions of all the lineages would destroy the ideological slavery of current politics and replace it with a world where proven heroes would steer the course.

Veiled by the smoke of grilling meats, the men prayed to be worthy of the myriad creatures that had died to bring them life. They surrendered themselves to their destiny and asked for the strength to fulfill their labors.

As they'd called upon their forefathers, they reached out to their sons yet to be born and recruited them to lend their strength.

Late that same evening, Senator Holbrook Daniels dismissed his usual contingent of bodyguards and jogged alone along the National Mall. His trim physique filled him with a secret pride. Indoor desk work and lightweight resistance training had left him a spry specimen of masculinity, and he reflected on his privileged status among the Washington elite. He'd easily live to be one hundred.

It was a sweet deal, being a United States senator. Tomorrow promised a free haircut in the senatorial barbershop, followed by a hefty luncheon bill he could ignore in any of the city's finest eateries. An endless stream of wide-eyed congressional pages were waiting to be groomed as interns, even as sexy college-aged interns were being marshaled for his sexual pleasure. And—lest he forget—there was the war resolution to rubber stamp.

Two million surplus men, undistinguished young men, tomorrow he needed to resolve their lives with a stroke of his pen. It was all in a day's work.

A tough job, he chuckled to himself, but somebody had to do it!

As he jogged through the darkness, the night breeze carried the aroma of barbequed pork. Flames flickered orange from a line of grills. As the senator passed, a grim company of working-class men fell silent and watched him. Bottles of beer looked small in their hairy fists. One bearded ruffian craned his neck and emitted a thunderous belch. Their silent gaze unnerved Daniels, so much so that he almost stumbled over the edge of a seemingly bottomless pit.

There, sunk in the lawn at the foot of the Capitol steps, yawned the huge excavation he'd watched grow from his office window. Another stride, and Daniels would've tumbled into its depths. That no one had fenced it off with barricades, it was insane. Such a hazard. He sensed the beer drinkers' eyes on him, and Daniels turned to confront them.

Self-conscious and suddenly feeling vulnerable, he wanted to tell them they were trespassing. The mall was closed to cookouts and alcohol. But something in their cold eyes made him hold his tongue. Many of them held cameras and filmed him. Others swilled beer. The steaks hissed and spat, dripping gobbets of hot fat that sent up geysers of bright sparks. Men glared sullenly at him as they lifted ribs and drumsticks to their mouths. Their huge teeth made a horrible sound, gnawing against the bones and stripping away the gristle.

In his futile anger, the senator stood at the lip of the deep hole and pointed into its emptiness, shouting, "When will this be filled?" When no one responded, he shouted, "This is a hazard!" An oafish brute broke wind. Determined to have the final word, Senator Daniels shrieked, "Someone could get killed!"

He wasn't on CNN. Without the acoustics of a marble chamber, without a bank of microphones and amplifiers, his voice sounded frail and shrill in the open-air darkness.

Several of the roughnecks looked from him to something nearby. He followed their pointed glance.

There, neatly stacked along one edge of the abyss, were bags of something. Piled as neatly as bricks, white canvas bags formed a wall almost as tall as the men. Daniels squinted to read the labels printed on the bags. In the flickering light of scorching grease, and through the dense smoke of burning flesh, the labels were almost illegible.

As a car passed along First Avenue, its headlights swept the scene. For an instant, they were all illuminated: the senator, the beer drinkers, their ragged hole, and the bagged supplies staged beside it.

In that moment, the senator could read the labels.

Quicklime, the words said.

An inexplicable frisson of terror pricked the hair on the back of his neck. It took all of his lean, gym-trained muscles, all of his self-discipline to turn away from the scene and begin running. Putting distance between him and the mob with every stride, Daniels boiled with confusion and rage. Tomorrow, he swore to himself, he'd make a few telephone calls.

Tomorrow heads would roll, damn it, and that dirty, dangerous hole would be filled!

His telephone woke Gregory Piper before dawn. According to the screen it was his agent calling, but Piper knew better. He'd pick up, and it would be a young voice, entry-level young, an assistant telling him, "Hold for a call from Mr. Leventhal, please." A loud click would indicate he'd been put on hold, to wait while his agent finished another call. Or two. Piper knew where he stood in the pecking order.

He looked at the bedside clock. Five-thirty, Pacific Standard

Time. It wasn't even banker's hours in New York. Over the phone a voice asked, "Gregory?"

Piper sat upright in bed, stunned to hear his agent. It was dark outside. He could hardly hear the freeway.

The voice continued, "Have you seen the television?"

Using his free hand, Piper dug among the sheets and blankets for the remote control. "Which channel?"

His agent snapped, "Any of them." He added, "All of them!"

Piper found the remote and switched on the television near the foot of the bed. Filling the screen was himself, wearing his blue Savile Row single-breasted suit. Looking directly into the camera, he said, "This is Talbott Reynolds . . ."

Piper switched channels, and there he was once more, saying, ". . . absolute monarch . . ."

Piper tried a new channel, and he was there again, saying, ". . . appointed by the Council of Tribes."

Over the phone, his agent demanded, "Did you sign *anything*?" Without waiting for an answer, he said, "We're still waiting on those contracts."

Between every televised glimpse of himself, Piper found no sports, no music videos, no advertisements. On a fourth television station, he was saying, "*El dia de ajustamiento esta sobre nosotros.*"

He considered the envelope of cash and if accepting it had implied a contractual agreement. It was stupid, but he hadn't mentioned the money to anyone. If he could avoid the tax obligation he would. On a new television channel he was proclaiming, "Before creating anything of lasting value . . ."

That was his improvised line. Now the beer-swilling, cruller-munching production crew, they'd have to give him a writing credit on the project.

Another channel showed him saying, ". . . we must first create ourselves."

The clock-radio on his bedside table went off, but instead of a morning traffic report, it was his voice saying, ". . . we must first create ourselves."

Over the phone, his agent stormed. "We've already issued a cease and desist!"

The doorbell chimed.

On television, dignified and handsome, delivering his best Ronald Reagan tinged with his best JFK, Piper declared, "Adjustment Day is upon us."

The phone held between his hunched shoulder and his ear, Piper rose from the bed and found his bathrobe. The doorbell chimed, again, as he tied the belt.

The television repeated, "Adjustment Day is upon us." To anyone except him this would look like a repetition of the last take, but Piper heard the slight variation in how he stressed each word.

In his ear, his agent swore, "It's on the radio and all over the web!" Over the phone's tiny speaker came the layers of sound, each offset by a microsecond. "Adjustment Day is upon us." An entire choir comprised of Talbott Reynolds. The synchronized voices resonating like a chant.

"Adjustment Day is upon us."

Piper crossed his living room and squinted through the peephole on his front door.

From the bedroom television. Over his phone. From neighboring apartments, the words came. "Adjustment Day is upon us."

At his door stood the man with the cauliflower ears and neck tattoo of a swastika. Piper wracked his memory for a name. The low-rent cinematographer. Into the phone, he said, "They're here." It was dawn with the light rising behind the visitor. Edging toward morning rush hour, the noise of the 101 grew louder.

His agent asked, "Who's here?"

The chorus of words seemed to fade and blur. "Adjustment Day is upon us." Becoming audio wallpaper. A new normal. White noise, like the freeway. Room tone.

Piper opened the door. He had the name, "You're LaManly, right?"

His phone demanded, "Who's LaManly?"

From every direction, "The list does not exist."

The man, LaManly, reached into his jacket and produced a pistol. Without a word he leveled it at Piper's chest.

From a neighbor's window, "The list does not exist."

As much as the impact, the noise of the gunshot rocked Piper back on his bare heels. His bathrobe billowed open, revealing white undershirt. Grayed chest hair. He dropped the phone but didn't collapse. Not at first.

His own voice, rich and echoing now from his own telephone, began to repeat, "The first casualty in any war is God." Echoing from the television in the next room. His field of vision began to narrow until he was looking down a long, dark tunnel to where the gunman was walking away, following the sidewalk to a car parked at the curb. A rushing sound louder than the freeway roared in his ears. Near the car the man muttered, "Damn," and slapped himself on the forehead with the butt of his palm. With fast steps he hurried back to the apartment doorway. He reached in, grabbing the doorknob, and pulled the door closed behind him. The knob rattled as if he were testing to make certain it was locked. Outside the closed door, his rapid footsteps faded into the distance. A voice, Piper's voice, proclaimed:

**May each man strive to be hated. Nothing turns a man
into a monster faster than the need to be loved.**

This left the actor alone in his living room. His own voice, recorded, duplicated, overdubbed, immortal, the voice of Talbott Reynolds, continued on and on, even as Gregory Piper sank to his knees and bled out on the rug in front of his own image on television.

The Senate majority leader took the final vote, and it was unanimous. As he announced passage of the War Resolution Act a voice shouted from the spectator's gallery.

"Friends, Romans, Countrymen," a man shouted, "lend me your ears." It was Charlie in a moment for all the history books of the new future. Those borrowed words, words Charlie's lineage had deliberated over. Words that would become as famous as Nathan Hale's.

The majority leader gaveled for silence. He called for the Captain of the Guard to remove the disruptive young man. The guard took no action. In the gallery a second man stood and shouldered a Dragunov sniper rifle and the red pinprick of its laser sight found the center of the senator's forehead. The triggerman was Garret Dawson.

That same year, grouse hunting season never opened.

Nick had lived through worse. At first he worried the police were after him. He caught a whiff of smoke and went to look out the window. Flames rolled up the brick sides of an Urban Outfitters down the block. No sirens wailed. More worrisome, no one stood in the street to watch. What scared Nick most was the fact that nobody was looting.

He dialed emergency but couldn't get a signal. Not as much as a recorded message.

He'd spent the last few nights hiding in the coffee shop where Shasta had worked last. They'd made the mistake of giving her keys and the alarm code before eventually firing her. He'd escaped his place with nothing but his stash and the clothes on his back. He'd eaten all the chocolate-dipped biscotti and was mildly curious when the morning manager would arrive to evict him. That's when he'd smelled the smoke. The wind was driving the fire in his direction.

Nick foamed some milk and mixed in a dozen shots of espresso and some vanilla syrup and called it breakfast. Nobody had messed with the cans of spray whipped cream so he worked each nozzle to huff the nitrous off the top. He checked the sell dates on the grilled chicken ciabattas. He washed his face at the bathroom sink and finger-combed his hair. When he looked next the fire had jumped to Baskin-Robbins. Considering how much stock he'd eaten and all the places he'd left his fingerprints, he wasn't unhappy to see the inferno bearing down. Just this teeny bit fucked up, he'd started to feel safe again.

Anyway, it was around time for the marijuana dispensaries to open up. That would do until First Methodist at lunchtime, the Narcotics Anonymous meeting, the primo place to score.

Then the first van arrived at the curb. Outside the front window a second van screeched to a halt. The first was hefting a satellite dish and aligning it with the sky. A familiar woman took her place in front of a camera and began to narrate the fire scene. A circus like this should've drawn a crowd of the curious. That was the scary part. No one gathered to watch. No cars slowed to rubberneck. There were no cars, period. The street was otherwise empty.

Another news crew arrived and set up to broadcast. As did a fourth. A wall of newscasters stationed themselves in front of the blaze.

Nick's ass vibrated. The back pocket of his jeans. His phone, with a call coming in. Keeping his eyes on the fire scene, he put the phone to his ear and asked, "Walter?" With no immediate reply, he tried, "Shasta?" A man's voice said, "Adjustment Day is upon us." An automated robo call.

The caller ID read "Private." The voice repeated, "Adjustment Day is upon—," but Nick hung up. Already the phone was vibrating with a call from the same private number.

Last on the scene were the emergency responders. A police squad car, followed by a single engine company. Without unrolling hoses or tapping hydrants the firefighters and officers positioned themselves in a perimeter outside the filming. Cameras swiveled to watch them. Nick studied it all through the coffee-shop window. In some recess of his brain he knew what was about to occur. Instead of watching content being made, he was watching history being made. This was just like that batshit story that Walter had been trying to sell him. That was it. More than ever, he had to find his buddy. Walter would explain what was going down.

Because just like Walter had predicted, the police officers drew their service revolvers. The firefighters unbuckled their slickers and shouldered rifles. And just as Walter said it would happen, this unlikely firing squad let loose with a July Fourth flurry of blasts, as brief as a string of firecrackers, filling the air with drifting gusts of white brimstone smoke. And before the last echo had died away the uniformed men were wading among the fallen journalists.

Seizing each by a fistful of perfectly coiffed hair, they lifted each head. Following close behind, a man holding something bright was dragging a burlap sack. At each head he brought his bright tool down with a single stroke. A knife, Nick realized. And the man reached back to drop something into his bag.

An ear. Walter said they'd take the ears. Ears smeared with pink makeup and powdered with talc. Ears with tiny transmitters still plugged into them.

The man with the knife had a name. Nick knew him from somewhere. No, not hacking off dead ears, but someplace regular. And repeating in Nick's head was a memory of a man's voice, this same man reciting, "Hi, my name is Clem . . ." Repeating, "I'm Clem, and I'm a junkie . . ."

Adjustment Day is a misnomer. Altering human history took little more than an hour.

The police stood aside. After years of being branded villains by politicians and the media, the police turned a blind eye as citizens lugged duffle bags into every statehouse, every courthouse, city hall, into every college administration building. That morning, the police knew the calls to report fires and murders were only bait, lures thrown out to draw the media into an ambush.

Every year voters and taxpayers were killed by criminals. Policemen were killed by criminals. This year crime would seek out the lawmakers.

Participating, here, in Adjustment Day would expunge all of Bing's and Esteban's criminal charges and warrants. It would eliminate Jamal's student debt.

Stray targets, of course, had to be stalked down emergency fire exits, across parking lots, underneath parked cars where they cowered, weeping. Others hid behind locked office doors that required breaking down with fire axes. Even with these stragglers the old regime would be eradicated by lunchtime.

The words of a former teacher came to mind. A while back, a professor had lectured Jamal. Professor Brolly talked about the culture of the Hellenistic Greeks, how the Greeks had valued comedy above all other theater. Their comedic plays had far outnumbered their tragedies because they believed that all human endeavors looked trivial and laughable to the gods who watched from on high. The gods found mankind endlessly funny.

But when Christian culture supplanted the Greeks, the Christians destroyed most of the comedies. Stories of tragedy reinforced the Christian viewpoint so the church preserved *Oedipus the King* and *Medea* and *Prometheus Bound* and eradicated all that did not celebrate the church's ideals of suffering and martyrdom.

For the ancient Greeks the absurd was closer to the profound than the tragic was. This occupied his mind as Jamal looked down like the gods of Olympus.

Below the railing of the spectator's gallery, the squealing, teeming carnival of the wounded and the blinded statesmen, this circus of wailing, flailing, rich and powerful, these gore-choked, gasping clowns were the pinnacle of human folly. Hilariously, they hunched forward and tried to gather armfuls of their own burst, stinking intestines. Their pale hands held together the brains spilling from shattered skulls. These were the same pencil-pushing bureaucrats who'd voted moments before to send him and all of his friends to be similarly resolved.

As Jamal picked off target after target, his every muzzle flash another old man, a thought flashed. The professor, Dr. Brolly, in Anthropology had explained a theory about pratfall humor. The gags wherein someone trips and falls suddenly. Those bits of clumsy physical comedy. According to anthropologists we laugh out of some prehistoric reflex.

When primitive man was prey, when he and his tribe ran in terror from a saber-toothed tiger or whatever, the man who fell would be eaten. For everyone else, his death would occur as a huge relief. According to Brolly all humor arises from escaping death.

For years Jamal had walked in constant terror. Before he was registered for . . . not *the draft*, he and his friends called it *registering for the death* . . . before the idea of another world war had ever appeared on the horizon . . . he'd known he'd die young. Nerve gas-raped in battle.

Instead, from today onward, he was the saber-toothed tiger.

The pain in Bing's trigger finger meant more to him than the bullet-shattered old men who crawled across the smeared marble floor below him. His rifle's blast bothered him more than their screams. The recoil of the rifle butt against his shoulder hurt him more than shot-to-shit political Brahmins who tried to claw past each other for another moment of life.

He and other members of his lineage stood in the gallery, a vantage point they'd occupied and filmed from for weeks. They knew every avenue of escape a target might take. They'd taken positions to shoot around any obstacle on the floor below.

The screams made it easy. The screaming made Bing hate them more, if that was possible, these old ladies and old men who couldn't tell the truth. Every statement they'd made was hedged and qualified and conditional. These screams constituted the first honest sound out of their mouths since adulthood.

What a sight: Rich old men pounding and pushing, climbing over one another to find safety.

They stampeded like panicked fat cats. Wrestled, piling themselves against locked exit doors. They huddled and wept beneath desks. For helmets they opened thick volumes of law and held those books cupped over their heads. It helped for Bing to envision the mass round-up and culling of wild animals. A video had circulated between members of his tribe. It showed footage of dolphins corralled in nets and clubbed as the seawater itself foamed into a bloody froth. That slippery, squirming mass of the dead and dying, it was harder for Bing to watch the beautiful dolphins die than it was to see the suited statesmen die. On the Internet he'd watched wild rabbits stampeded into pens, great leaping waves of rabbits heaving in one direction, then another, as men waded among them and crushed their skulls with metal hammers. Bing had watched the videos of kangaroos and baby seals. The culling of legislators was nothing compared to the clubbing of tiny baby harp seals.

The recoil of the rifle butt ramming his shoulder, that pain stoked Bing's anger and made him take aim at every sign of movement in the chamber below.

With the blessing of the police these skirmishes took place. For the police had already been sacrificed for political correctness. And the mass extermination of the young was prevented by forfeiting a comparatively tiny number of those already near death, who'd already raised their children and been feted.

The courtroom, the assembly chambers and on-location newscasts, the lecture halls, they stunk of gun smoke and spilled shit.

Not until the snipers gave the go-ahead did the harvesters venture among the dead. Here a seemingly dead body screamed at the knifepoint and a target was found to be playing opossum. Here Bing was summoned to come down from the gallery, and the target shrieked so cowardly that it was a pleasure to see him dead.

Things happened too fast to think. Something moved, and Charlie would squeeze off a shot. Transfixed. His eyes watched for motion. Movement across his retina. Something alive. Any motion seemed to bypass his brain, his conscience, and put him in a trance state the same as playing video games, same as a dog watching a squirrel or a cat waiting at a mouse hole, or like his own old man on a riverbank watched the same red-and-white fishing bobber afloat there in the water, waiting for a trout to take a bite.

The trance kept him from imagining what was no doubt happening to his mother and father at this same moment.

Any thinking he'd done a time ago. In the back of his mind, Charlie had mulled over his reasons for taking part. He'd lost faith in all the regular, gradual methods for self-improvement. After a lifetime of posting on blogs and videotaping his every move and emotion for social media, he was facing nothing less than identity fatigue. There were no more fresh starts. He'd established his brand so thoroughly. Documented himself for posterity. There was no frontier where the Internet hadn't already told the world all about him since he'd first learned to keyboard.

Adjustment Day would give him a fresh start. Whether it worked or not, it would be a radical shift. He'd be dead or in prison or a revolutionary hero, but any of those would be an improvement on the happy-sad, hopeful-fearful ordinary nobody the online world could watch getting older, getting taller, but never actually getting anywhere.

Suppressing hysterical laughter, he popped rich men and wealthy old women, only pausing to reload. Charlie went for kill shots to the back of the skull. An entrance wound at the top of the spine with the exit wound through the screaming mouth. Less clean-up that way. Protein is amazing shit, he knew, it was the glue that sticks to everything. Cut a body in half with an AK and your lineage will still have to scrape away all the scraps.

Welling up from deep inside him was something. A feeling.

Something enormous. The only word for it was *Glee*. For the first time in his life he didn't need to worry about the draft. He'd never given his future much thought because the draft or nuclear war had always loomed there. It was inevitable that after he turned eighteen he'd die. But here, for the first time he could see a future. From this point on he had some control.

All his life he'd been taught that men were protectors and guards, and that the most-noble destiny he could attain would be to die in order to preserve another person's life. If humor comes from anything, it arises from an immense feeling of relief. Charlie felt joy now because for once death was outside him.

The scene below him was ugly as ugly gets. Bloody as bloody gets. But it wasn't the worst that could happen.

According to the Talbott book, history would never know its greatest mistake because no one would be left to record it. The task at hand looked like a bloodbath, but it most certainly preempted a nuclear war. A global famine. A pandemic that wiped out billions.

All his life Charlie had been told that he and his kind were the evil patriarchal oppressors, the haters who'd colonized the globe and enslaved the gentle savages of Rousseau's paradise. Thank you, academics. Charlie could wear that. The worse-than-Hitler label. Today he'd give people the proof they were right.

It was like those news stories where they'd interview the neighbors and lifelong best friends of a serial killer, and everyone swore the killer was a regular, friendly, nicest-fellah-on-Earth. After Adjustment Day the world would know a new truth about Charliegoodguy144.

He was tired of learning history. He wanted to be it. Charlie wanted the history of the future to be him.

Senator Daniels lay still among his dead colleagues. He'd burrowed and wormed his body between the leaden corpses until their blood soaked through his custom-tailored suit. He'd been among the first to take cover, and the slaughtered had toppled, staggering and tumbling, and fallen beside and upon him. He'd felt the twitches and little kicks as the life had gone out of bodies. Their blood painted the hair flat to his head and gummed his eyes shut. Blood stuck his pants tight to the skin of his thin legs and webbed his fingers. His breaths were the quick, shallow sniffs of a rabbit playing dead. He lay face down atop his hands to hide their trembling.

The gunshots had stopped. The screams, also. Voices moved through the room, men's words and the grunts of exertion. The weight on his back lifted and was gone. The body beside him was pulled away. A hand gripped him around one upper arm, and Daniels felt himself being rolled face up. His breathing stopped as he let himself be dragged by one arm, a skidding distance across the stone floor slick with blood. The hand let go, and he let his arm fall limp, and he continued not to breathe. He lay frozen with shock but sweating off his mask of blood, fearful shivering would betray him.

Fingertips pinched his ear, and a jagged agony bit at his head where the top of the ear met his scalp. The senator screamed, tearing open his sticky eyelids and his lips pasted together.

The fingers had released their grip. A man stood over him, a savage wearing camouflage-patterned bib overalls and holding a hunting knife. A laborer from the barbeque the night before. His latex-gloved hand was smeared with red, but not barbecue sauce. His eyes met the senator's for a moment, green eyes, wide with surprise.

Daniels whisper-begged, "Please." Praying for pity, for the savage to move along and leave him among the dead. Tears sprang to his eyes and washed clean streaks down his face.

Instead, the man twisted his head toward other voices and called, "Got a live one!"

Discovered, Daniels struggled to sit up. Around him similar bloodied savages looked up from where they were wading among the dead. The heaps and drifts of bodies and half-bodies and headless bodies and desks smashed to scraps of wood. A nearby savage held something bloody between two fingers before tucking it into his hip pocket. This other man called back, "Put him with the left-overs." And with his own dripping hunting knife, the man pointed across the chamber.

There, a cluster of weeping men squatted against a wall. Bald and pot-bellied. Skeletal and stooped. Like him, they were old men drenched in other people's blood.

A third savage, a few steps away, was leaning over, sawing at someone with his knife. He lifted something small that trailed a thin coil of wire. The wire stretched down to lift a small box. When the coiled wire and the box fell away from the man's hand, Daniels realized it had been a hearing aid. What the man held was a sev-ered ear, which he stuffed into his back pocket.

The man who stood over Daniels smiled. It was a wicked, lopsided smile, but not without pity. "You remember that hole, outside?" He jerked his head toward the bloody group of survivors. "You guys' job . . ." With his knife he gestured broadly over the butchered. "You're going to pile this big mess into that hole. Got it?"

Daniels's fingers crept to his ear, to where the pain still burned. They felt the warm blood still streaming, still warm. Not dead.

"Now go," ordered the smiling savage. "Get with your friends."

Senator Daniels nodded slowly, before scrambling to his feet.

Back in Before Times . . . before the pits were being filled . . . driv-ing back to Portland, Oregon, Walter had taken turns with Talbott Reynolds, yelling out a game they'd invented to keep proving he was alive. At the wheel Walter would yell, "A-1 Steak Sauce."

From inside the trunk Talbott would yell, "Formula 409."

Walter would yell, "Seven-Up."

Talbott, he'd yell, "Chanel Number Five."

Walter, "WD-40."

A lull would fall over the car. Only the sound of Idaho had

rushed around them like a tunnel. Here were all Walter's dreams, of romancing Shasta with money, of rising above the economic mysteries that submerge most people, his dreams might be dead in the trunk. In his head had been the idea to turn around and hunt down an alternate mentor. Yes, to bury this dead one and locate a replacement.

Then a voice would yell out, "I could've had a V8!"

Joy. Everything in the world would make sense and wouldn't be just jumbled chaos. The dead were brought back to us. Jubilant, Walter would forget this was a rental and he'd put a match to a fatty.

This would eat up the miles until Talbott Reynolds would yell, "Enough!" From the depths of the trunk, he'd yell, "I hope you love the taste of fat, white Nazi dick . . . !"

They were tallied, the dumped-out sacks of ears. The ears dug from pockets. Black ears and white ears. Ears plugged with hearing aids. Ears dangling hoop earrings. Ears hairy with age and ears streaked with orange tanning spray.

In each statehouse, a Garret Dawson or a Jamal Spicer addressed the small, remaining group of trembling, bloodied leftovers. "You will remain," he read from the approved page of the Talbott book, "you survive to do the bidding of the voting lineages and conduct all necessary business." Those allowed to survive would bury the dead. "You neither propose or impose any new laws. You will serve as merely clerks." The men reading these lines in courthouses and college lecture halls said, "Your term will be for life, and if you fail at your duties a vote of the electorate can call for your execution."

The Talbott book made it sound simple. Only people who'd harvested targets on the list would get to vote. The tally of each target, combined, determined the number of votes each lineage was allotted. The reason being that only people with votes had made their sacrifice for the cause. This ensures that nobody hijacks the movement, because the people who racked up the most numbers will ally with each other and elect one of their own, and because only these people will have the gumption to hold on to power via the same action they took to attain it.

Officially, liberated assets are supposed to go to the new government, to offset the cost of establishing the correct system. And they go to compensate displaced persons forced to forfeit property due to relocation to the correct jurisdiction.

"Once the bodies are resolved," read each man to his captives, "your first item of governmental business is to institute the Homeland Relocation Act."

Back before this book was a book . . . on the ride back to Portland, Oregon . . . Talbott Reynolds had been locked in the car's trunk, always going, "You'd better get used to being some passed-around prison bitch getting your shithole sold for cigarettes!"

As he'd told it, Talbott had a surgically implanted tracking chip. Implanted he-wouldn't-say-where, but just under his skin. It gave off a GPS signal that the FBI would use to find him. Once the car stopped, it would only require an hour or two for agents to triangulate the chip's location.

He'd cited kidnapping laws going back to the Lindbergh baby. Saying, "You're going to learn all the subtle flavor differences between Nazi dick and black dick and Mestizo."

Even as Walter had marched him down the basement stairs of an abandoned house, and he'd strapped the old man to a heavy chair, some tiny device had been pinging their whereabouts. Any minute now the outside door would bust open, and he'd be busted, awaiting trial, convicted, sentenced to serve with not another moment of Shasta.

Game over, unless he could find and excise this homing device.

Cut it out of the old man's hide, wherever it was buried. Just one flick with a razorblade, a swipe with rubbing alcohol, a little digging, and it would be Walter's to crush under the heel of his shoe. Close the wound. Wounds. Death by a thousand paper cuts.

With this in mind, Walter had rounded up a bottle of rubbing alcohol. A razorblade. Bandages and Super Glue. Preparing for his treasure hunt.

He'd sliced the clothes off the old man, looking for a little scar to indicate where the chip was buried. Cutting the seams and peeling away the arms of the suit, the collar of the shirt, as if he were peeling an orange. Starting from the extremities, the wrists and ankles, and working his way inward. He'd find a lump on one forearm and ask, "Is this it?"

Talbott had tensed, going, "Find out."

Walter had swabbed on rubbing alcohol to clean the skin, then sunk in one corner of the razorblade. His fingers slippery, sliding, slimy with blood, him without latex gloves, his fingernails rimed with red, his eyes overflowing in sympathy, this not being any Walter who Walter had ever planned to be: somebody who tortures an old man strapped to a chair, razorblading a hole in one arm, picking carefully around the bigger veins and tendons.

The hunt had turned up a cyst. The search had to go on.

Walter had peeled back enough pant leg to discover a small hardness in the skin covering a wasted calf muscle. He'd looked up at the wincing, flinching, giggling Talbott and asked, "Is it here?"

Giggling Talbott, the crazy old geezer, clearly getting off on Walter's squeamish agony, he'd gone, "You'll be very popular in prison."

Forcing Walter to slosh on more alcohol. Rubbing to locate the little hardness under the skin. Trying to pinch it, to hold it in place as he sinks the razor blade next to it. Except the hardness slips. It migrates, sliding under the hairy skin, skin now greasy with blood. Forcing Walter's razorblade to chase after it, making a little incision longer, making it cut sideways to follow, finally striking pay dirt only to fish out another false alarm. A lump of fat.

Despite his new old man springing leaks all over, if Walter hit some spot in a certain way the blood would spout like so much ketchup-colored jizz. With a smell like mashing it with some babe who's been dead and buried in the ground for the past ten years.

Old Talbott, always shaking then with laughter, not holding still, tears streaming down his cheeks and every wrinkle in his face stretched tight. He'd squirmed against the belts holding his arms to the arms and his legs to the legs of the chair. The death by a thousand cuts wasn't killing, but it was paring away, flaying, whittling away the human part of Walter so that the next likely lump was less effort to excavate and the one after that took no effort to lance. The blood, at first so alarming, had faded to only an annoyance, and Walter's sympathy had soured to rage. After that he'd dug indiscriminately. The empathy burned out of him, Walter had dug to torture the old man for not telling him the chip's location from the start. Slicing him to strips of bait so the old man would tell. Would cry uncle. Only to have Talbott keep laughing, swearing at Walter's ineptness as the razorblade had to trench and explore across the man's scalp and down his back and Walter began splashing cold alcohol on cuts already opened to rinse them so he'd not cut them a second time, and Talbott's head had hung limp on his neck, his face pale and his laughter reduced to a hissing, like someone laughing in his sleep.

For fortitude, Walt had surfed porn on his phone. His favorite videos, the clips that featured only dead people fucking and giving blowjobs. Alive when they were filmed, but dead now. The fact that they could still excite him even from beyond the grave was the most proof of a human soul he'd ever found. Those carnal saints, their ancestral beauty had made it okay to slice up somebody who remained only flesh and blood.

Still, Walter's fingertips had found no chip. No diode. Only lumps of scar tissue. Just clumps of fat or warm cysts he'd had to pinch out and examine to be sure. Precancerous cell clusters. Calcified foreign objects. Bits of gravel or tiny cubes of safety glass, leftover souvenirs from a car or a bicycle crash a lifetime ago.

Walter had carved away the T-shirt and boxer shorts, rubbing his wet fingers in little circles, searching for that foreign anything that even now was relaying his location, this abandoned house, this bloody crime scene, him dripping with sweat, wincing in sympathy as he swiped the razor blade only to uncover a bolus of fat . . . an enlarged lymph node . . . something hard and firm, or an in-grown hair, the stink of a carbuncle bursting in his face, a boil he'd lanced by accident. His new old man flinching to make the blade go wrong, laughing, hysterical.

The police, tracing the ping, the silent distress call, the police every ping getting that much closer.

After Adjustment Day, the book was everywhere. To be seen without a copy of the blue-black book was to risk being reported. What came of that, no one was sure.

Despite it having broken her nose, Terrence's mother had allowed him to keep his copy. Urine and colloidal silver dappled the pages, but he could still read the notes his father had made for him. Among them was a list. On the final blank page, under the heading "My Dreams for You," his father had written:

Excellent Health and Strength
High Status
Wisdom
Courage
Becoming a Great Healer

In bed, Terrence continued to begin each day by reading. Today, for instance, the Talbott book decreed:

The American of the formerly united states was constantly held in check.

His schooling was comprised of the constant
repetition of the same narrative model. In the most
classic stories of American fiction, the ones most
promoted by critics and the school system, the same
fates befall each of three main characters. The meek
and obedient destroys himself. The most aggressive
and openly rebellious is murdered. And no one except
the often mute, yet always watchful character is left
behind to recount the story.
A suicide. A murder. A witness.

Always the suicide occurs first. This is a childlike innocent. In *One Flew Over the Cuckoo's Nest* it's the obedient son, Billy Bibbit, who's committed himself to a mental hospital in order to please his mother. After sex with a prostitute he kills himself rather than face his mother's disapproval.

The rebel is murdered next. In the same novel, the brash Irishman, Randle Patrick McMurphy, is smothered in his bed. The witness, the unspeaking Big Chief, breaks out of the heavily barred ward and escapes into the world to relate the story.

Likewise, in *The Great Gatsby*, the desperate Myrtle Wilson throws herself in front of a car. From the first time she enters the story Fitzgerald describes her as a suicide. Soon after, the new money Jay Gatsby is shot to death in his swimming pool. Following that, the narrator, Nick Carraway—sounds like "carry away"—escapes back to the Midwest and delivers the story's "take away" lesson.

This is not the only model, but it is the ideal for Americans, and the enduring success of any book is determined by how close the story hews to this pattern.

Often outspoken female characters aren't killed; instead, they're banished or shunned. In *Gone with the Wind*, the obedient Melanie Wilkes chooses to die, attempting to have a child she's been told will kill her, but wanting to please her husband with a large family. In the next turn, the bold Scarlett O'Hara is excommunicated from her community and her family, while the understated Rhett Butler takes his leave for Charleston, escaping the scene like Big Chief and Nick Carraway. The same variation takes place in *Valley of the Dolls* where the beautiful Jennifer North works constantly to please her mother but finally kills herself out of the fear that a tumor in her breast will destroy her beauty. The ambitious, outspoken Neely O'Hara—a fictional character who's chosen her stage name from an earlier fictional character—is soon discarded for her show-business transgressions. And the book ends on the placid, ethereal Anne Welles, the outsider, an escapee from a distant New England family not unlike Big Chief's tribe, as the most unscathed.

In *The Dead Poets Society*, a student commits suicide out of fear of his father's disapproval, a teacher is banished for being unorthodox, and an outsider is left as the witness.

Even a seemingly transgressive novel like *Fight Club* traced the same pattern. The most inventive aspect of *Fight Club* was how it collapsed all three of the archetypes. By killing himself, the martyr murders the rebel and by doing so creates an integrated passive/active voice that recounts the story as a new self-aware narrator.

Over and over, the lesson to Americans is not to be too passive or aggressive, but to pay attention and to avoid notice. To escape, to survive and tell the tale.

To believe Talbott, half the population of the formerly united states was always forced to live as the slaves of the other half. And this relationship shifted almost every four years. Voters were compelled to be slaves or tyrants, tyrants or slaves, depending on election results. Their literature was calibrated to keep people sane despite these wild reversals of power.

Terrence closed the book and held it in his lap. If merely to stay alive, that's what Terrence wanted to do: Escape this formula altogether. And that's why he knew he'd have to find another option. Something a lifetime of books and movies hadn't primed him to choose.

———

Half alive, Talbott had admitted to having no tracking device. It had all been a lie. It was a test to see how far Walter would go to achieve his goals. How mercilessly he could act.

Sputtering the words, breathless and bone pale, ashen lipped, the old man had said, "I'm so proud of you."

Walter, not the same Walter. Walter had turned into someone he didn't know, he was slick with the old man's blood. Stiff fingered.

His new old man had gasped, "I'm very proud of you." His eyelids had fluttered and he'd faltered as if ready to die, but he'd rallied. Fixing Walter with red-rimmed eyes, he'd said, "Listen closely." He'd said, "For I am agreed to teach you all the secrets of success." He'd swallowed hard and coughed to clear his throat. "Write this down," he'd ordered, "Write: 'Declaration of Interdependence.'"

And at the old man's urging Walter had rushed away to find a pen and a notebook.

Shasta checked the battery icon on her phone and pressed the switch to turn it off. The battery showed as mostly dead. She knew the feeling.

She watched Talbott Reynolds on television and tried to feel reassured. Not everyone was terrified. The man who delivered firewood, her professors who weren't shot dead and being buried in the pit on the soccer practice fields, most people appeared to be exuberant about the reshaping of society. None of the old solutions had done anything but make social problems worse. People seemed willing to try something radically different.

What the Talbott book referred to wasn't a wholly new concept. Leading political figures like Keith Ellison had long before called for separate homelands. In fact, Talbott's plan mimicked Ellison's by requiring Southern states to be united as a single nation, to be occupied exclusively by people of African descent. The remaining states would be reserved exclusively for citizens of European ancestry. With the exception of California—the Golden State would be set aside for a special purpose.

Strange newscasters appeared on television to replace those who'd been targeted. They explained how the national census and college applications provided the initial rolls for racial identification. To further refine the process, the data of Internet-based genetic testing services were subpoenaed. The Genetic Information Nondiscrimination Act was, no duh, suspended. The popularity of such testing had established a ready-made roster for identifying those citizens in each region who would need to be relocated and compensated.

Shasta didn't want to be caught in a dragnet. Blindsided by a skeleton in her genetic closet. To play it safe, she'd found a website that still took Bitcoin, and she'd submitted a saliva sample under a fake name. They were to send her the test results by text message, to a mobile phone she'd bought from a ragged hobo on Martin Luther King Boulevard. The stranger had asked for fifty dollars cash and didn't offer a charging cord. Fingerprints of dried blood suggested a violent past, but Shasta was quick to scrub them off with an antibacterial wipe at Safeway. The battery was half dead when she got it.

The waiting was worse than a pregnancy test. She tried to calm her nerves with the reminder that both of her parents were white. Both pairs of her grandparents were white. Still, the wait felt worse than some AIDS test.

In the new world decreed by the Declaration of Interdependence, a great many people were enduring the same ordeal. Others, interracial couples and families mostly, were making a beeline for the Canadian border and seeking refugee status. Others had self-exiled to Europe or Mexico, but the Talbott book decreed doing so meant forfeiting the bulk of their property and assets. It proposed like-for-like compensation only for citizens who willingly surrendered their homes and businesses and relocated to the appropriate homeland.

On television, Talbott Reynolds assuaged fears, repeating that the death squads had completed their work. Those who'd liberated the formerly united states would oversee the relocation process with only the force appropriate to any resistance they met.

As she carried the switched-off phone, trying to save the battery for the eventual text, Shasta wrestled with the idea of imminent racial separatism. No group was a monolith. Not even gays. Especially not gays. Queer identity cleaved faster than a cell dividing in the uterus. Resisting the urge to power up her phone, Shasta recalled the brilliant writer Zora Neale Hurston from Black History Month, who said African Americans come in

High yellow
Yellow
High brown
Vaseline brown
Seal brown
Low brown
Dark brown

Not to be outdone by the cream of the Harlem Renaissance, Shasta systematically broke down whiteness to the following scale:

Rice white
Buttermilk
Been-in-prison pale
Vampire
Peeled potato
Ecru
Grocery bag
Regular Barbie

As far as she knew she was no more ethnic than peeled potato.

There was no telling how much time had elapsed, but she couldn't resist any longer. She switched on the phone. It chimed with a new text.

Talbott, on television, over the radio, decreed temporary measures. All public employees must remain servants of the people. They must forget their dreams of early retirement. Yes, they'd postponed their dreams in exchange for security and the promise that one day the young would relieve them. But now the young had seized control and were giddy with power. Boys who'd never expected to attain drinking age—they'd been granted a future— and the last thing they wanted was to deliver mail or write parking tickets. So Talbott had called a temporary halt to retirements and sabbaticals and vacations in the public sector. Strictly as a short-term, stop-gap measure. For how long no one could say. Exempt were the police and military for they had aided the tribes.

For a period the nation continued to lurch forward, headless. The agencies whose purpose it was to deliver mail and to write parking tickets continued to deliver mail and to write parking tickets because they could rally no counterattack and because no one knew who the attackers had been in the first place and because no one wanted to draw the focus and become the next target.

The threat of repercussions prompted public employees to rethink any bad mood. It motivated with less carrot, all stick.

To preempt further violence, Talbott appeared on billboards, a beaming image of him, with the slogan:

A Smile Is Your Best Bulletproof Vest!

The same image and slogan appeared on posters and bus stops and in employee lunchrooms. People recognized it was a smile-or-be-shot edict, but what choice did they have?

It became not uncommon to see clerks in the post office grinning widely while beads of sweat blistered their foreheads. For their sole exit strategy was via a dirt hole filled with quicklime. Thus public employees constituted a new serf class, tied to their tasks. Held like chattels.

As per the Talbott book people were kept confused, living on the brink of chaos for so long that they'd be grateful to accept the terms of any new governing body. The word *grateful* falls short. Absent the constant threat of death, they were gleeful, joyous with relief. Willing to pledge allegiance to any new order so long as it kept the peace.

Money was no longer power. Merely a short-lived tool.

The dollar, Talbott declared, was dead, and the new currency had to flow downward through the members of each lineage. Through the members to their families and loved ones. Even so the new currency was short lived, fading to plastic film in fewer than a hundred days. And because money could not be hoarded it had to be traded for bread and wine, and because more bread and wine were needed more people were employed in raising wheat and growing grapes.

And always there was the possibility of a new list, this one directed at unpopular bus drivers and meter maids, and this spurred terrified smiles and a groveling humility among civil servants. Everyone else kept a low profile and for once were glad not to be government workers. To the Millennials of the youth bulge the street sweeper was just as guilty as the senator and just as ready to see the new generation marched off to war. Just as the French Reign of Terror had commenced by beheading royals, then expanded to severing the heads of clerics and clerks and servants, the danger existed that Adjustment Day would become an annual event.

From when it broke over the distant horizon, the figure looked like a haunt. Thin and shimmering in the desert heat, wavering, flickering like a flame, it grew taller with each step along the highway. It brought to mind abandoned animals. The dogs poor people took out to the countryside to dump, hoping household pets could fend for themselves. Starved a few days, those lap dogs and pedigreed mutts always resort to eating the shit of other animals. That shit, laced with the eggs of black flies, eggs ready to hatch out worms. The result being a dumped animal starves all the faster, eating more shit, hatching more mouths to feed, and finally finding a bush, a tree, a fence, but shade enough where a poor animal can collapse, panting, and die.

That's what the ghostly figure brought to mind.

Garret Dawson had only to turn his head to watch the stranger's progress. Former shop steward, prince of Caucasia's most-powerful lineage, he lay on the dusty roadside. With his top half under his truck, his hands twisted a bearing cap off the driveline U-joint. His legs stretched across the road's gravel shoulder, full in the hot sunshine, until his jeans felt steam-ironed to his legs and his toes felt baked inside his boots.

He picked the needle bearings from the cap and cleaned each in his mouth, spitting away the burnt grease. Peeking to see the stranger come another stretch closer. By feel, his fingers pressed the bearings back into their race. The differential input yoke was almost too hot to touch. His toolbox set half in the shade, socket sets and extensions just a long reach away.

The radio was playing, turned up so he could listen. That man, Talbott, was on. No music. No broadcast ballgames. The entirety of television and radio played nothing but Talbott Reynolds. New ruling potentate, most likely he lived in a castle, lucky sumbitch, waited on hand and foot by teenage virgins. The voice rattled in his tinny dash speakers:

Paradise isn't created by splendid architecture or dramatic scenery but by the quality of souls that populate the place.

The great man's voice echoed across the sand and sagebrush. In the time since Dawson had first heard his bearing burn out, not one car had gone past. His visitor he could see was something woman-y. Minus her dusty clothes, he figured she hadn't the booty to hide her back hole. And what the sun had done to her blistered skin, it had done twice over to her scorched hair. The wind had knotted the strands, and sweat had plastered it flat to her head with dust. Talbott's voice declared:

> If a man can face reality at the age of twenty-five, at sixty he can dictate it.

She didn't look like much, but just in case Dawson slipped off his wedding ring and stuffed it in a front pocket of his jeans. He rolled a needle bearing in his mouth, sucking off the scorched grease. He spat black.

Tucked deep in his pocket, his fingertips felt a slip of something. A sheet of paper. Wadded and soft with age, the paper listed the items he'd promised his wife, Roxanne, he'd bring home. Her handwriting would be illegible now, creased with wrinkles and washed with his sweat, but he knew the list by heart:

Coffee filters
AA batteries (for kitchen remote)
Avocados (not Hass)
Toilet paper
Peacock tongues

Life hadn't slowed any, he reckoned. Except now they measured their passing days in peacock tongues.

A heartbeat later the abandoned woman had staggered within spitting distance. She'd come to stand beside his rig, his tool box at her feet.

As she edged within hearing of the radio, the woman hesitated as if spooked by the voice. The radio preached:

> When they run, hunt them. Find the stragglers
> where they shelter. The shame they feel comes
> from squandering the authority built up
> for them by generations of fathers.

To Dawson's mind there were different degrees of sunburn. First was *Roofer's Tan*, from laying tarpaper and stapling shingles on plywood decking angled to offer a man like so much blistering steak for the sun to broil. The even darker shades included:

Castaway in a Lifeboat in the Open Ocean Liver-Colored
Hawaiian Tropic SPF #5 Bondi Beach Under-the-Ozone-Hole
  Suicide Red
Bain de Soleil Saint-Tropez Orange
Arnold Schwarzenegger Roll-On Pro-Tan Bronze
Demented Tucson Bag Lady Baked Brown

This stranger was none of the above. Her sunburn red had blistered and peeled away to reveal ovals of lily-white. Hers was the first sun exposure of a cosseted lifetime.

Dawson's lips, he figured, were black with grease, but hers where frosted white with flakes of dried skin. Her teeth looked straight and white as a movie star's.

It was common knowledge that many targets had sidestepped Adjustment Day. Mostly academics had managed to evade squads since schools of higher learning kept notoriously erratic schedules. Word was these fugitives were playing dress-up in rags and trying to pass themselves off as normals while they picked their way toward the Canadian border. Mexico didn't want them, but Canada hadn't closed the door entirely. Washington State Route 21 rolled north across the caliche scablands of eastern Washington State, straight to the border, but only a born idiot would hike it in hot weather.

If there was anything Dawson knew about academics, it was the fact that they weren't too bright.

The closest town back that ways was Kahlotus, a good twelve clicks. She stepped closer to his tool box and squatted down to see under the truck. "Hey mister," she drawled. Her voice sounded put-on, picked up from reruns of *Hee Haw* or *The Beverly Hillbillies*. "Hitch a ride?"

Dawson rolled to one side, facing her. He snaked the phone from his shirt pocket and framed her blistered face. If the stranger knew about face recognition software, she was too tired to care. He snapped a picture and texted it. To test her, he held out his hand, palm up. "You want to reach me that 7/8ths extra-deep socket on the offset extension?"

Her faded blue eyes went to the array of chromed tools in the box's top tray. Her eyes twitched over the hex nut drivers and snap wrenches.

Roxanne would've known the correct tool on sight.

Dawson rolled the needle bearing between his lips like a toothpick. To show his impatience, he snapped his grease-stained fingers.

Could be a heartbeat later, she slapped something hot metal into his hand, and when he brought it into sight it was a closed-end 5/8ths wrench.

His phone chimed. The database had her pegged. This starved wretch, crouched here, her feet flapping in torn basketball shoes, her legs and arms lost in baggy coveralls patched with duct tape, the tape curled up at the edges and black with grime, her name was Ramantha. She'd gone missing from the University of Oregon where she'd headed the Selected-Gender Pathways Department. But she was a dead academic walking. A small army of bounty hunters were closing in, fast. The nearest was only a little ways back, and here she'd wandered into Dawson's life. A windfall. Already doomed.

Her vote tally was a measly eleven hundred. It wasn't a dynasty, but he could make a small fortune by voting the way of the highest bidder every election. Whether he could murder her, and how, was another question.

Maybe she read this in his eyes. She said, "I suppose you're going to kill me?" Her voice had lost its yokel twang. It sounded cosmopolitan, cultured. Nowadays, cultured was bad. Cultured got you killed.

From the cab of the truck, Talbott lectured at full volume:

> Adjustment Day is not about vengeance. The
> hunter does not hate the elk. He holds great
> respect for his prey, but the hunter knows the
> animal must die for his own survival.

It struck Dawson as a shame. Looking at her, destitute like this, grit crusted around her cracked nostrils and caked in the corners of her mouth, her neck festering with mosquito bites and raw scratch marks, hidden under her unwashed stench and her clap-trap political ideology he could tell she had once been a pretty fine-looking young lady.

She twisted her neck to look back over one shoulder. Squinting, her eyes searched the horizon for pursuers. To no one in particular, she said, "It wasn't some run-of-the-mill panty raid . . ." Hoarse with misery, her voice was barely audible. "They had guns." The squads had left her alive, she said, and they'd ordered her to haul her dead coworkers to the burial pits. "My entire staff . . ."

Not a heartbeat later, her knees buckled and she dropped from squatting to kneeling defeated in the sharp gravel. With her head bowed, her hair dangled to hide her face. A human sacrifice. She'd dug a linoleum knife out of his tool box and offered it. "Take it," she said. "I'm begging." Her other hand drew the fried hair back to uncover her ear. "Cut it off, but take me to the border, please . . ." She knelt there in the dust as if too tired to run any farther. If he didn't target her, someone else would.

Torture or not, she wanted him to report her as dead. He'd pocket the votes, and she'd escape into Canada. What was left of her. It looked like a win-win.

Again Dawson snapped his fingers, but this time he pointed at the socket he wanted. The first bounty hunter was liable to catch up soon. "Samantha?" he said.

"Ramantha," she said, correcting him. She had that much pride left. She set aside the knife and retrieved the socket. She seemed to get the message.

Nobody was getting carved up, and nobody was going anywhere until he could get this driveline attached.

A regular notebook hadn't worked. In a world before The List . . . the world you think is so stable . . . Walter hadn't been able to write that fast. No one could've, not as fast as Talbott Reynolds had talked, crazed as he'd been. Giddy with blood loss from the razor nicks and diggings that had kept leaking blood, his head had lolled, and his eyelids had fluttered, woozy with the ecstasy of his pain. Still naked and strapped to a chair that stood in the puddle of the great man's own sweat and piss and blood, long strings of spit had looped from the corners of his mouth as he raved. A jabbering cadaver. An oracle delirious on an overdose of endorphins.

A notebook hadn't worked so Walter had traded it for a laptop computer. His fingers racing to keep abreast of Talbott's words. How this was going to make his fortune so he could propose to Shasta, Walter had no idea.

As he tapped the keys his fingertips left red fingerprints. Leaving the keyboard sticky. Spirals and whorls of Talbott's blood.

Talbott dictated, "The homosexual will always be an engine of wealth production because he does not suffer the expense of raising his own children." He paused to watch Walter. To be certain his words were not wasted. "The next generation of homosexuals," he continued, "is always borne and raised by heterosexuals before leaving to join its brethren. Thus the industry of the adult homosexual may accumulate while the industry of heterosexuals is siphoned away for childrearing costs, which ultimately benefit the homosexual community."

Walter completed the passage, repeating aloud, "Homosexual community," to indicate he'd caught up.

"Plus the time of the homosexual," Talbott lectured, "is not frittered away in child production and may be allocated to improving his skill set or simply laboring longer hours without the cost of neglecting a family . . ."

Walter keyboarded, echoing the final words aloud, ". . . the homosexual state will always enjoy a cost-free influx of new citizens."

To date, the rich man had advised Walter to present a pattern and allow other men to fulfill it. Walter was to set in motion a machine that no one would be able to stop. A machine that would run itself. That even Walter would not be able to stop.

How this would make him rich, Walter hadn't the foggiest. Like most writers he'd been too busy typing to think.

"In order to preserve the integrity of mutually exclusive hetero- and homosexual nation states," Talbott continued, "the heterosexual children born to lesbians and the homosexuals born to heterosexuals must be swapped . . ."

Walter completed the sentence aloud, ". . . in equal numbers."

Talbott had gasped. His mutilated torso had twisted against his bonds. "If an unequal number of persons must be exchanged . . ."

Speaking the words as he typed them, Walter had said, ". . . then a dowry or ransom will be paid to compensate the parents not receiving a child."

So it had gone, day after day. The old man had spewed words and Walter had faithfully collected them. The only other task, the only tangible task that Talbott had ordered him to carry out, was to build a website. Whenever the man had slept Walter had tinkered with the site, and it was almost complete.

Apropos of nothing, as if in a moment of delirium, the old man had fixed Walter with a manic grin and shouted, "A smile is your best bulletproof vest!"

Gibberish or not, Walter keyed the words into his document. Trusting, always faithful that the ramblings of this old coot were going somewhere. That he wasn't wasting his life documenting the dying words of a lunatic.

The website, for instance, the one Talbott had told him to build, it hardly seemed like a high-tech moneymaker.

It still hadn't launched, not yet. But Walter had built it exactly according to Talbott's instructions, right down to the stupid name. A nothing name. Nothing clever. This yammering, grimacing, demented old man had demanded the site be called simply The List.

The post office clerk reached under her side of the counter and retrieved a form. Form Number 346, Application for Resettlement in Appropriate Homeland. As she handed the paper across the counter to Gavyn, she smiled, licking her lips, and said, "Funny, but you don't look black."

Gavyn took the form, saying, "I'm not."

Her eyes lingered over his hair, such red hair, his wide jaw line, his broad chest, and she sighed. "What a crying shame."

What could he say? He'd done nothing wrong. He was simply following the new law. Gavyn told her thanks and took the form to a counter under the windows where he could fill it out. People stood in line waiting to mail packages. People waited to exchange small amounts of their old money for the new perishable skins money.

The first line of the form asked for his name. Gavyn Baker McInnes, he wrote.

He filled in his place of residence. His current homeland. His parents' names.

Under age, he wrote eighteen.

At Work Skills, he hesitated. He was an expert at many things, none of which he could enter on any official government form.

Under Highest Level of Education Attained, he wrote that he'd graduated from high school and gave the date. It had been yesterday.

Before Adjustment Day, before any talk of homelands and relocating populations accordingly, back in ninth grade Gavyn had learned a thing or two. For instance, he knew that teachers teach a lot of stuff, but only what they want a kid to know. The important things, he'd had to discover on his own.

He'd listened as his teacher, a woman who'd never been beyond North America, explained the whole of Europe and Asia. Gavyn had taken notes as another teacher, who'd never written so much as a short story, dissected Faulkner, Fitzgerald, and Donne. When he echoed back their pale misconceptions they praised him and pronounced him smart. Smart, yes, smart enough to know he still understood nothing and that his teachers were idiots. Nothing except his own hunt in the real world would ever educate him.

Under Reason for Relocation, again he hesitated.

Gavyn craved a happiness that would make his parents vomit to witness. He yearned for a love that would completely destroy their love for him. His life was an either/or proposition. He'd someday have to choose between his own happiness and theirs.

Under Criminal Record, he lied and wrote, "None." Officially that was true. He didn't want his relocation to be nixed for any reason.

He wondered what it felt like to wipe away someone's life to make room for your own. He'd trained himself not to want anything. Christmas and birthdays were the worst, occasions built around the wanting of things. When his parents had asked him to write his list for Santa Claus, Gavyn had had to consult his classmates. As if he were conducting an anthropological study, he'd survey boys about what would make them happy. Lego sets or Nintendo, whatever got the most votes, that's what he'd pretend to want. Unwrapping it, he'd have to pretend his delight. He couldn't allow himself to consider what he really wanted.

The next question asked: Have you sought professional mental health counseling?

He'd begun his secret life by shoplifting clothes. He'd walk through Sears and try on shirts, walking out wearing a new shirt underneath his old shirt. A coat underneath his coat. After Sears, he'd hit JC Penney or Nordstrom. He could never explain a shopping bag filled with leather jackets to his mother. The solution was to take his loot to the mall office and relinquish it at the Lost and Found, always filling out a card with his name and contact information. After three weeks, when no one appeared to claim these items no one had actually lost, the mall would phone to say they were his. Problem solved.

It was the perfect laundering scheme. But it couldn't keep pace with his stealing. The mall staff and his parents would only accept him discovering so many windfall bags of designer shoes and belts. Everything always his exact size. He was immensely proud of his skill at something he could never share with his parents.

Besides, owning the clothes wasn't the point. The joy was in finding the item and stalking it. Circling it. Waiting in a lustful trance. Ready to pounce. In the clutches of some impulse he couldn't control, he bided his time. Often the shirt wasn't anything he'd ever wear. He might even hate it, but again, the excitement wasn't about owning it forever.

If anything, owning the shirt or the jeans filled him with shame. They served as reminders of his werewolf side and how easily he could throw away his law-abiding life. To that end, Gavyn had begun to burn the plunder in the family's basement fireplace. On afternoons when his parents were still at work he'd hold a shirt at arm's length and play the flame of a match along the lurid paisley cloth. Burning the clothes was almost as enjoyable as stealing them. He'd lay flaming pants across the andirons and keep adding shirts and sweaters until they, all of them, were reduced to powdery gray ash.

His downfall had been a leather bomber jacket. Red leather. Oxblood. The satin lining had burned as had the knitted collar and cuffs, but the leather itself had given off black, stinking smoke, the smell of a strand of hair held in a candle flame. He'd been frantically fanning the smoldering pile when his mother had walked into the basement game room.

He told her everything. Okay, half of everything. The half he thought he understood. The shoplifting part. And she asked if he'd agree to see a counselor.

Enter Dr. Ashanti. Tuesday afternoons Gavyn took a bus to the basement office, downtown, part of the county's mental health services program. Payment was according to a sliding scale, but it still meant his mother had to pick up extra hours at work. He'd sit in the waiting room with other pimply boys his own age. Some accompanied by parents, most not.

For one hour every Tuesday, Gavyn sat listening as Dr. Ashanti explained that shoplifting was a pre-sexual impulse. Textbook words. In stalking clothes, Gavyn was practicing the skills of seduction. Followed by acquisition. Ending in divestiture of the desired object. It made sense.

What Gavyn should do with this impulse was another matter.

There in the basement office, the walls covered in corkboard squares, pushpins holding the corners of posters showing sail boats canted dramatically above captions like "Find the Wind That's Going Where You Want to Be," Gavyn eventually broke. He was slumped in a beanbag chair. The doctor sat in a swivel chair pulled away from his desk.

Gavyn was looking at a sand candle on the desk. He couldn't look at anyone's face when he finally said it. "I think I'm gay." In a whisper, in case the waiting-room kids could hear.

Ashanti's response was instant. "No," he shook his head, "you're not."

Stunned, Gavyn couldn't think of a rebuttal. The denial didn't resolve anything. Gavyn risked a look at him.

The doctor had steepled his fingertips together. "After talking to you so regularly, I can safely say this is a phase." He shut his eyes and snorted softly as if amused.

At the same time, Gavyn felt grateful and enraged. The one fear central to his self-identity, it was being flat-out denied.

Ashanti spoke with the certainty of a faith healer. "You're not homosexual."

All the extra hours his mother had worked. After all the money she'd paid to help resolve this crisis, the doctor was going to deny any issue existed. The money and time would be wasted, and Gavyn would be back at square one.

Dr. Ashanti glanced at the clock on his desk. The session still had twenty minutes remaining. "Don't you feel better?" he asked. His smug smirk and arched eyebrow seemed mocking.

Gavyn did not feel better. What happened next was less sex than it was a political act. Gavyn was taking part in a game of chicken. He slowly rolled himself out of the beanbag chair and made his way across the carpet. Ashanti didn't stop him. Not even when Gavyn knelt between his legs and found the man already erect. Gavyn undid the belt, the top button, and pulled down the zipper carefully, stealthily, as if his plan was simply to steal the man's pants.

Gavyn smirked. Ashanti's face had gone slack, his breathing shallow. His eyes met Gavyn's even as the high school freshman squeezed a fist around the erection that was like a third person in the room and slid back the foreskin to reveal its leaky purple mushroom. Gavyn closed his mouth around it and didn't flinch when the first jet of raw egg white, that hot syrup of sour cream, salt, and onions hit the back of his throat. Another surge splashed up into his sinuses and bubbled out his nostril.

He was no longer a virgin, at least not his throat. This felt less like a sexual act than like someone with a bad sinus infection had sneezed in his mouth.

He'd made the doctor wrong. Gavyn had proved he was smarter. He at least knew himself. The clock showed that eleven minutes remained in the session.

The doctor panted, boneless in his chair. Brown moles spotted his scrotum in profusion and wiry gray pubic hair exploded from around the base of his limp penis. His untucked dress shirt stretched to cover his round belly, and from this low angle the loose skin of his neck was gathered into a single fold that looked like a shaved vagina just above the knot of his tie.

As unappealing as the man looked, he was still Gavyn's first, and Gavyn knew he would always remember this moment. Victory or not, it felt more exciting than shoplifting, but only marginally.

In the weeks to come, his mother's extra work and money would be paying for something different. Tuesdays, Dr. Ashanti would vehemently deny Gavyn's preference and Gavyn would prove him wrong. Learning to vary the experience, pace it, plot it like a thrilling movie, and finally bring things to a climax within scant seconds of the session's end time.

Once more Gavyn grew to be an expert at a skill he could never share with his parents.

When he first heard about The List, he'd gone online and posted the name Dr. Anthony Ashanti. It seemed like a safe way to channel his hate. Everyone assumed the list was a joke.

When within a few hours seventeen hundred people had posted their votes to the name, Gavyn's eyes were opened. He began to grasp the man's patient load and the secret history of his long career. The waiting room outside his office filled with brooding teenagers suddenly took on a new meaning. A harem. There was no overestimating Ashanti's stamina.

Ashanti, apparently, had put the *rapist* in *therapist*.

Gavyn had long stopped his course of treatment by the time Adjustment Day resolved the doctor's life.

Under counseling, he wrote, "None."

The alley in back of First Methodist was crowded with tweakers. Everyone waiting for the doors to unlock and the regular meeting. People amped about getting glassed. Nick scoped out a talky kid and asked if he had any Vitamin V to sell.

"Shit was for *real*," marveled the kid, scratching and dancing.

Everyone knew someone from recovery who'd been a gunman.

"Dude tried to recruit me," another swore morosely. "Wish I'd listened. I'd be rich."

Nick countered, "I just need some Vitamin H."

The kid countered, "You got the new money?"

Nick knew what he meant; but, no, he didn't have any.

The church doors didn't unlock.

People were hungry. Drinking water was getting scarce. The social order was in chaos with no gasoline, and electricity browning out, people robbing people of their food, and whispers of people eating cats and dogs, and even people eating people. But Nick knew the magic bullet to make all this ape-shit disaster movie agony instantly A-Okay was a fat baggie of hydrocodone. Given a year's supply of Vicodin he needn't sweat finding food or a place to shit. He could ride out the misery.

The talky kid, him and all the tweakers, were dispersing. A few obviously headed for the next meeting, to see if they'd open the doors at Ecumenical Ministries. Walking his way was a guy with a dog, a black guy holding a dog by a leash with one hand and carrying a big blue-black book in his other. White fur covered the dog except a black spot around one eye, a pit mix sort of dog. From talking distance the guy said, "Nick."

Nick asked, "You holding?"

The guy shook his head and smiled. "Forget that shit." His name was Jamal, a regular at this meeting until he'd dropped out a couple months back. Everyone thought he was dead, but here he was. Jamal reached into one back pocket and brought out a handful of something. Like playing cards. Like a weirdly colored deck of cards. He offered the stack, saying, "Take these, I got plenty. But you need to spend them within a couple of weeks, okay?"

The cards were slippery, thin sheets of stiff plastic. Each showed the face of a man, like somebody's dad on television, a handsome face like an actor would have on a television commercial selling gold coins. Nick accepted the cards and fanned them to count how many. They were the new money he'd heard about. Nobody had any, not unless they worked for one of the vigilantes. Dropping to one knee, he stashed the cards in the top of his sock. Some he stuffed in his pockets. Plenty of hungry people around these days, it didn't pay to take chances.

Jamal nodded at the dog. "Bouncer and I are boarding a plane in a few days, headed for a new life." He meant in Blacktopia, the nation partitioned exclusively for anyone with a preponderance of sub-Saharan DNA. He said, "It's been an interesting experiment, but it's over."

He was referring to black people and white people living together, the whole united states thing, Nick figured.

Jamal asked, "In school, you ever read that *Grapes of Wrath* book?" He shook his head in disgust. "Those people running all over. Saying they need to strike back to fix the system. But they never do anything, just dig ditches for a nickel and give birth to dead babies." He spat on the ground. "That book's bullshit."

Nick kept one hand tucked in his pocket, touching his windfall. "Yeah, we read it."

Jamal asked, "What do you suppose was the sense of reading about those useless people?" He turned to address the dog, asking, "You ever wonder what that book was *really* teaching us?" To Nick he offered the blue-black book in his hand. "Talbott says it's okay to kill yourself with drugs. But he says there's no greater high to be gotten than killing your oppressors." A big diamond glinted in one of his earlobes.

Nick asked, "Did you kill Brolly?"

Jamal asked, "You ever hear of the Peabody Plantation?" He

turned and spoke to the dog. "We own it. Don't we, Bouncer? One entire valley of forests and farmland, and an impressive Greek Revival mansion set down in the center of it."

Nick guessed this was in some former state, what used to be Georgia or North Carolina. "You have people used to be slaves there?" He didn't mean anything harsh. Such a nowhere house just seemed like an odd choice for a one-time druggie. It was tough to imagine Jamal as a farmer.

Jamal dug in his pocket and offered up another handful of the money cards. "Take it. I can't spend it before it all expires." He offered the book and the new money in the same hand like a package deal. "It's the law. You'll get arrested for not carrying this book."

Nick took them both. Here was somebody, one among the many he'd never see again.

"Come on, dog," Jamal said. He tugged the leash and the pit followed. The two walked away.

Cash in hand, Nick sprinted in heart-racing, sweaty strides in the opposite direction. To score a mountain of Oxy or hydro and get so fluffed the state of the world wouldn't matter. To catch the talky kid before he sold his stash to someone else.

To Jamal, Adjustment Day was doing the opposite of that *Grapes of Wrath* book. The book people had to read for seventh-grade English. Where white people are bullied off their farm. A tractor runs over their house, and they do nothing. A loan officer or some such comes and tells them to move on, and this family does nothing. Yeah, they talk about getting guns and storming the bank to kill the bankers, but they never do it.

Instead this white family hauls ass to California where they get dumped on by the police and worked to death for small change. But they still do nothing. They keep talking about one day. Talking about taking up arms in some revolution against the rich man, and all along they do nothing except let their old folks die and get buried in unmarked graves. They let their kids starve. For hundreds of pages Jamal kept reading, expecting the revolution, and in the end it's just a dead baby dumped into a creek and some old dying old man getting to suck on some young girl's titty. The author, John Steinbeck, had been a pussy, too afraid to make anything happen. He'd abandoned his characters to suffer.

As had God.

Only a white man had the inflated self-worth to write that book, and only a white man would have the secret pride to read it.

It's only the white man who clings to his guilt. Guilt for Adam's fall. Guilt for Christ's sacrifice and for black African slavery. It was clear to Jamal that for whites their guilt constituted a uniquely white form of boasting. Their breast beating was a humblebrag always saying: We did this! We thwarted God in the Garden! We killed his son! We white people will do with other races and natural resources as we see fit!

Showing off disguised as a mea culpa.

For the white man, his guilt was his biggest badge of accomplishment. Only whites killed the planet with global warming so only whites could save it. Their boasting never let up.

It was the white racket: Creating problems so they could rescue everybody.

And while school forced kids to read that pathetic *Grapes* book . . . kids volunteered to read *The Fountainhead* by Ayn Rand. Kids yearned to be Howard Roark on the witness stand. Schools despised the fact that genius only touches a few men. Geniuses recognize the school teachers' mediocre campaign to teach mediocrity to the mediocre. And kids reject the idea of lifelong suffering and failure.

In *The Fountainhead*, somebody does what Steinbeck only talks about. That's why kids love Rand's book.

How Jamal saw Adjustment Day, it amounted to the happy ending that *Grapes* book failed to deliver.

And today, Jamal and three of his cohorts returned to the state house, victorious.

That's not to say Jamal didn't feel conflicted.

People ask what it felt like. Adjustment Day, that is. He told them that what he'd done felt like walking into the world's skuzziest bus station. Like walking into a stinking world of vomit-coated concrete floors and face-down winos. Like wading through this stink to find the Men's Room, a shithole of dripping pipes and backed-up drains. Sidestepping the puddles to get to a toilet, then sitting bare-assed on the still-warm, gooey toilet seat, breathing air that's nothing but accumulated farts. And then looking down and spotting something on the floor.

Like looking over, and there next to the filth-streaked toilet bowl, stuck to the crap-dappled, sperm-sprinkled concrete floor, there's an almost-pristine-looking 800 milligram Oxycontin.

To help, you tell yourself it's medicine. And by its very nature medicine kills germs. Somewhere some doctor had prescribed it. A scientist in a laboratory had made it, even if it's spotted with overspray from a bunch of diseased bus station perverts.

All that needs doing is to bend over and pry that pill off the floor. Only that one, quick, nasty job. Just pop that pill in your mouth and swallow it and everything will be all right. Better than all right, everything will be perfect. Like a perfection you can't even imagine.

That's how Adjustment Day occurred for Jamal in retrospect. And here he was returning to the scene of his . . . not crime, but triumph. In the statehouse, the janitors had scrubbed away the blood because they could imagine no other option. Somewhere the widows wept, but the dead were not Jamal's dead. The widows counted as nothing, not compared to the widows and mothers who'd be wailing if the war had been declared and his entire generation had been shipped to some bureaucrat-organized, offshore mass execution.

A man representing his lineage stood at the front of the great room. Everyone carried a copy of the blue-black book, and everyone smiled. It wasn't the law, but holding a copy of the book, everywhere public, all the time, was motivated by something more frightening than the law.

The bullet holes in the paintings couldn't be helped. Nor could the divots where ricochets had bounced off the marble columns and panels. Details that future tourists would marvel over and photograph. The few remaining senators scurried around the place, doing everyone's bidding. Those old men looked gaunt, eaten away on a cellular level. One man had a scar notched at the top of his ear. He approached, bowing and scraping, and placed a dossier on Jamal's desk, then backed away, still bowing.

The man at the lectern leaned into a microphone and announced, "Our first order of business . . ." The warmth of television cameras bathed them.

As directed, Jamal stood and held the Talbott book open in both hands and began to read aloud, "Act One, Article One of the Declaration of Interdependence . . ."

A hush fell over the room as he continued. Jamal risked a glance upward and searched among the faces in the spectators' balcony. Time stretched into forever. The silence waited. He searched among the faces for a particular woman. The waiting, watching faces. And there, standing where he'd stood on Adjustment Day, there the woman stood so high above him.

Only then did Jamal return to the book and resume reading, "All persons compelled to surrender real property and to relocate to an appropriate homeland must be compensated with an amount of property equal to or greater than that relinquished . . ."

Her smile beamed down upon him. Her eyes so proud, there stood his mother.

People had seen the new money on television: slightly stiff-feeling slips of plastic, too rigid to fold. The colors: vivid combinations of red-and-blue or yellow-and-violet. Officially, the order called them Talbotts, but everyone knew them as skins. Rumor was the first batches were refined from, somehow crafted from the stretched and bleached skin taken from targeted persons. People seemed to take a hysterical joy from the idea.

Instead of being backed by gold or the full faith of government or some such, this money was backed by death. The suggestion was always that failure to accept the new currency and honor its face value might result in the rejecter being targeted. Never was this stated, not overtly, but the message was always on television and billboards: Please Report Anyone Failing to Honor the Talbott. The bills held their face value for as long as a season, but faded faster in strong light and fastest in sunlight. A faded bill held less value as the markers along the edges became illegible. But even when the skin had faded to a slip of white-ish, slightly opaque plastic, not unlike a bleached and dried rectangle of parchment or lambskin, fueling the rumors each was a souvenir scalped from a television newscaster or college professor, even when the skins were anonymous white-ish cards, they still held a slight value. These faded blanks—most referred to them as *blanks*—could still be returned to the government for a small refund. Children collected them from trash bins, or the homeless gathered them from the gutter like aluminum cans and glass bottles for recycling. A hundred blanks were worth a five-Talbott note, thus they were the equivalent of an old-order nickel. Incentive sufficient to keep children recovering them.

The lineages that for so long had sunk themselves, deeper and deeper, man by man, like tap roots into society, they'd come to form long chains that permeated across all social groups. Now these channels of men were used to suffuse the new society with its currency.

The man above him, Garret Dawson, gave Charlie a cardboard box containing one hundred thousand Talbotts and told him to spend what he could and pass the balance to the man below him along with the same orders. Charlie bought a necktie and planned to keep the rest of the money, but the next day Garret came to him with another box, and a third on the third day. All along the Talbotts were fading infinitesimally, and Charlie was forced by good sense to begin passing them along to the next man who spent what he could and passed the balance to the next. In this way the money flowed down the length of each lineage, making those men wealthy beyond their dreams and making the people who knew them wealthy and the people who knew those people rich and those who knew those rich people became well off, and in this way the new economy began to float and stabilize itself.

The new money cascaded down. It bucketed from man to man.

Because the money could not be hoarded many tried to trade it for gold and diamonds, but those who held the gold and diamonds refused to sell, and thus gold and diamonds fell out of circulation and lost all value. They became like masterpiece paintings, items traded among the rich as signs of status, but they meant nothing to the majority of people. As the largest fortunes of the old times lost their wealth, because they could not use money to make money, and knew no other way to survive, their possessions came to the market.

Oh, and the women. They left Charlie breathless, the women who migrated to him in droves, young women, older women presenting their daughters, women who understood the value of their beauty and vitality in this market. To them Charlie, skinny Charlie, ridiculous Charlie who'd hardly finished high school and could only operate a drill press, these women who'd only ever snubbed him—that is, if they'd even realized he was alive—these days they fought among themselves merely to catch his eye.

Mondays and Tuesdays Charlie sat in a chair at the head of a table littered with photographs. The table had belonged to a medieval king, and the chair to a Renaissance count or whatnot, the names of neither Charlie could remember. Not that it mattered. Now the table and chair and the suits of armor clutching lances that lined the hallways and the flags that fluttered atop the turrets, they belonged to Charlie. A fire blazed, continually replenished with logs carried in by men on Charlie's payroll. While other men fanned him with peacock feathers, and others presented braised peacock tongues and peeled grapes, neither of which Charlie could bring himself to eat, and even with the expenses involved in the upkeep of such a household Charlie could not spend the new money as fast as the lineage required. Most of it passed on to the next man and the men beyond him.

Mondays and Tuesdays an agent in his employ brought a selection of women who'd been chosen, handpicked from the throngs who'd submitted detailed applications. Women with movie-star faces and porn-movie bodies, they sat in the outer rooms and assessed one another, and the agent escorted each, woman by woman, to the receiving hall where Charlie more or less held court.

Most Charlie dismissed with a glance and a polite "Thank you." Some he'd invite to come closer. Of the women some brought business propositions. Some wanted to be appointed to a position in the new government. Whatever the case, Charlie considered them all with the same intent.

Within a season the old order subsided. The new lineages became the knights crowned, dukes and lords who held their rewards by a single successful battle, and those who were family to them benefited, and those who learned to be of service to those fresh noble families, housed in ancient estates recently acquired, those who served them best, with labor, with food, with entertainment, they were the next most prosperous. And lastly, the persons who could offer no skill except their prowess at manipulating the old currency, restricting its flow and dolling it out for fees, that class of persons with their outdated field of expertise, they were left to wander in the street seeking out the blanks that they carried by the dirty paper sack-load, like once ears had been carried, to the counting stations.

Regardless of how the skins arrive at the counting houses, there they are cleaned, fitted under a stencil, and re-exposed to the ultraviolet light. Revitalized for another three months, these Talbotts reenter circulation at the top of the lineage chains.

People accepted the new currency with all its flaws because there was no other option. As stated in the blue-black book:

First make yourself despicable, then indispensable.

The replacement economy was like a balloon being filled with water from a spigot. As more money poured into it, the balloon swelled and hung heavier, but until it was filled no one could say how large it would grow or what shape it would ultimately assume.

If anyone asked Miss Josephine Peabody, the lost politicians were show-offs, showboating snake-oil fakirs whose summary executions they had coming. Good riddance and God bless. Rest in peace. No, the natural order, if one followed the classic models of beauty and governance, held that property owners alone should determine what was best for people, for only the owners had the proper vested interest. Planters in particular in the agrarian tradition of Jefferson, without the corrupting influence of the Jew and to a lesser extent the Catholic interests.

If anyone asked, that is, but no one had. No, it took Arabella coming up from the kitchen one morning to suggest Miss Josephine turn on the idiot box on account of the same man appearing on every channel. A loathsome habit, watching television before supper, but Arabella insisted, standing by Miss Josephine's chair while this man announced:

A house is not a homeland. This calls for the partitioning of the formerly united states in order to provide separate, distinct autonomous nations wherein each people can conduct their lives. It is wrong for one culture to impose itself upon another either by actions or expectations. Therefore each must exist free of the demands placed on it by the other.

Miss Josephine pointed the remote control like a scepter, to banish the man, but his image and pontificating persisted:

Each group must inhabit a homeland where that group
constitutes the norm. Otherwise either self-destroying,
self-hatred, or other-attacking self-aggrandizing
occurs. Drinking, drugs, and toxic sexual behav-
iors arise when cultures are compelled to share public
space. No culture should be held to the expectations
and subjected to the withering gaze of another.

Arabella wore her apron and twisted a dish towel between her hands. She asked, "What's it mean?" It didn't signify, Miss Josephine assured her and sent her back to shelling peas. Arabella didn't appear convinced, and left the room slow as molasses, walking backward so she could keep her eyes on the screen. There the man was speechifying:

Just as the genders are separated in most
athletic competitions so should the cultures
be removed each from the others so that one
culture might not always dominate.

The unhappy result of which being that Arabella's man, Lewis, felt it his duty to show himself into her sitting room doorway where he approached no closer than the threshold and tried to claim that Georgia was no longer a state of these United States, but had been given over along with Florida, Louisiana, Mississippi, and Alabama to create some sort of Martin Luther Kingdom designated to be inhabited by only blacks, and at this Miss Josephine wheeled herself to the door and shut it in his face.

Despite the evidence of her eyes and ears, the Peabody Plantation remained her property and her home. And before her clan owned it, the land had belonged to the Muscogee Creek and Yamacraw tribes. No gerrymandering tomfoolery would change matters.

Here she had stature. If she allowed herself to be uprooted and carted northward or out west, why, she'd be reduced to nothing more than a garden variety old lady, a spinster in possession of thirty-six full place settings of Crown Darby.

Some trees were too old and particular to tolerate transplanting. Lest Arabella and the others forget, Miss Josephine was the soul of the plantation. No one but her knew the idiosyncrasies of the well pump or how to drain the cistern. Only she knew the rotation of sorghum versus tobacco. Why, without her expertise the oil burner and the furnace fan would burn down the house within a year's time. Just let them, Arabella and her man, Lewis, and their boys, Chester and Lewis Jr., and their girl, little Luray, let them see. Let them try and run the place without her say-so.

Such knowledge was part and parcel her province and hers alone. To that effect they agreed it only fitting she take up residence in the attic of the main house, a narrow suite of dusty rooms, hardly space sufficient to contain the family treasures she insisted follow her into hiding. The tureens and swords, the oil paintings of Daddy and his people. But the attic would suffice only until such time that this moment's political madness should come to a cessation. At that point she would be reinstated as mistress with full reign.

Mornings, when Arabella brought up her tray, Miss Josephine asked, "Did you call around to the Ives and the Caldwells like I asked?"

Arabella left the tray and went to making the bed. "I called," she said, "but wasn't nobody left. They relocated."

If Arabella was to be believed anymore, every family of European descent had decamped Georgia.

When it came to stubborn, Miss Josephine could teach a mule a thing or two. She, herself, would not be so easily dislodged.

Lest anyone get other ideas, she crept out nights. Once the household was abed, she tiptoed her way down the attic stairs, tracing the backstairs to the kitchen. Nights she might make it her foray to loosen the pressure screw on the propane line, a defect only she knew how to repair. Other nights she'd bleed air into the water main until the pump lost its prime. This mischief amounted to not so much sabotage as merely gentle reminders that her mind was the mind of the home place. The anchorite and soul of the house. She alone could perform the secret rituals to restart the reverse osmosis filters; otherwise the house water was undrinkable.

Regardless of the Martin Luther Kingdom these people wanted to impose on Georgia, the plantation remained a money-making concern, and she was key to keeping it profitable.

Always on television and the radio was that man. Talbott whoever, preaching:

> Allow each culture its own courts of law. Allow each to evolve in isolation. For too long the differing strains of mankind have been blended into an increasingly blander pool. A culture of shared mediocrity that only serves as a broader field of consumers receptive to the same generic advertising and thus steered to desiring large amounts of a narrow spectrum of products. Cultures developed over millennia in relative isolation, in climates and conditions that prompted each to create its own imagery and rituals, all of these are being displaced by the global standard. To preserve the integrity of each, the cultures must be allotted living space away from the influence of other cultures.

Egged on by some misguided effort to be helpful, Arabella's man tromped up the attic stairs one afternoon to fetch her a book. Lewis offered it in both hands, saying, "Here's the way things are." When she wouldn't accept the gift, he placed it on the table beside her chair, and he took his leave.

It amounted to a large blue-black volume supposedly penned by that man Talbott. The television man. A hodgepodge of half-baked observations concerning the obvious, it was. Page after page of, for example:

> In-group crimes may only be dealt with within
> the same group. Gays decimate their own kind in
> huge numbers with disease. Blacks annihilate
> blacks in violent crimes. Whites would appear
> to be less a danger to fellow whites until we
> consider World War II, World War I, the American
> Civil War, the One Hundred Years War, etc.
> Therefore, the crimes of each group must be
> judged only by members within that group.

To a learned personage such as herself, this was clearly the work of the Jew, the Jew in league with the Papist, both parties attempting to agitate the preexisting negro situation and dispossess the region's Scots-Irish of their ancient birthright. The land had been a wilderness until the arrival of her ancestors, and it would revert to the same without them. Let Arabella and her people try and run the place without her. None but she could comprehend why certain sumps and hollows held water whole summers while others went dry.

That night, she tiptoed down to the cellar and loosened the lid on every other jar of preserves so the contents would spoil.

The morning that followed, Arabella brought up the breakfast tray and set it on the drinks table in front of the settee. She shook out the folded napkin and spread it over Miss Josephine's lap, saying, "The new law says you'll be rightly compensated . . ." Arabella poured the coffee and moved it within reach. She added, "It's not healthy, you alone in this attic day and night."

Miss Josephine would not budge. It went without saying that should she depart on foot or in a box, the land would wither, thank you very much.

Arabella surveyed her with soulful eyes. She'd been born and bred on the place. No doubt she looked to take over as the new mistress. Miss Josephine dismissed her with a curt, "Thank you, that will be all." Alone, she couldn't bring herself to eat. A thought haunted her: What if Arabella and her people sought to poison her? Who would know? Not the neighbors. The old families had relocated. To poison her and bury her . . . worse, feed her body to the hogs. That would be the perfect demise.

But how to defend herself? How could she prove herself so necessary that folks would continue to feed and look after her?

The next day, Arabella brought her breakfast tray and took the warming cover off the eggs. Pouring the coffee she said, "You should be glad it's not the homosexuals getting this place." As Arabella explained it, the state of California had been set aside to create a homeland for male and female sodomites. Arabella sighed and winced at the very idea.

The sordid details of this, Miss Josephine had no desire to know. But Arabella persisted, saying, "Folks should reside among their own kind . . . that's the idea." She watched as if waiting for a reaction. A corner of her mouth twitched. "Miss Josephine, you've got to appreciate that and move forward with your life."

Hiding her malice, Miss Josephine gave the woman a bright smile. "That will be all, Arabella."

Soon as she was alone, just as she had the day prior, she cut the eggs, fried ham steak, and toast into bite-sized pieces. Following that she carried the plate into the tiny attic bathroom and flushed the meal down the commode.

By nightfall she was ravenous. Her wheelchair had always been more of a convenience than a necessity, and after midnight she crept down to the kitchen and filled a shopping bag with as much canned tuna fish—awful stuff—canned milk, and Saltines as she could carry back upstairs.

If Arabella ever took note of the missing items she never mentioned it. Every morning she brought up the tray, and every afternoon she brought up supper. Every bite of which Miss Josephine put down the commode.

History books were filled with similar stories of the right-minded who went into hiding until the storm of tyranny had passed. Those individuals trapped by evil ideologies. Why, the nation of Israel had practically been founded on the diary of one, a sweet persecuted girl who'd sought refuge in just such an attic apartment!

Lord, no, Miss Josephine would not be run off. Hers was still the nation of Thomas Jefferson and her daddy, God rest his soul, and theirs were the Christian ideals for her to uphold. Why, if you asked her daddy it hadn't been until the 1890s and the flood of immigrants from the Baltic region that conditions had destabilized. In 1890 the nation had fewer than a half million Jews. By 1920 it had millions.

Nights, if it was raining, she'd venture out to spread rock salt in the garden. Or she'd sit in the dark and eat her purloined tuna fish. Reading the blue-black book. The last book she'd read in its entirety had been *To Kill a Mockingbird*, and that had been mistake enough for her, thank you. Who was this Mr. Talbott to go against her? No amount of political voodoo or civil-rights mumbo jumbo would persuade her.

Days, Lewis would tromp up the stairs to complain. He'd fret how the cellar stunk and was full of flies and the septic pump had quit on him. The garden had wilted and died almost overnight so now everything needed to be bought at the Piggly Wiggly. He showed her something like playing cards. Plastic cards colored red and yellow.

"It's the new money," he told her, "but it don't last." He described how folks had to work all the time because the money couldn't be saved. "Any money we earn we need to spend before it disappears."

If the coast was clear, Miss Josephine would accompany him downstairs and out back to the barn. There, she'd ask him to fetch this or that tool to be rid of him while she replaced a widget she'd stolen from the thresher or the tractor some nights before. He'd marvel as she brought each piece of machinery back to life.

One night she sat reading the Talbott book. Having flushed her dinner of pork side meat and wild rice. Eating Saltines and drinking tap water, she came across the line:

A bounty should be paid for information regarding any person living outside his appropriate homeland.

Not waiting to read another word, she snuck down and disabled the kitchen stove. She jimmied the gate on the hen house.

Morning brought Arabella with the breakfast tray and the news that they had no eggs on account of raccoons having killed every last hen. There was no bacon or oatmeal because the stove had quit on them. What she brought instead was toast with peanut butter. Miss Josephine put this, too, down the commode.

The next night she decommissioned the toaster.

She took the sheet-metal back off the clothes washer and stole out a gadget.

She disabled the television and the kitchen radio, hobbled the dishwasher.

Always preying upon her, eating at her was the fear that Arabella and Lewis might betray her for reward money. She needed to be more valuable to them than any bounty, more valuable alive than poisoned.

At Arabella's request she ventured forth the next day to tinker with the stove. She sent the woman to search for a screwdriver while she reattached the wire she'd loosened in the toaster.

"I see you fixed it," Arabella said, not smiling with the usual relief, her arms folded across her chest. With the day's plague of troubles banished, the woman gave Miss Josephine a lengthy half-eyed stare. She set the screwdriver on the kitchen table and said, "Funny ain't it, how things just bust." Her stare not letting up, she said, "If I didn't know better, I'd think we had a gremlin."

Miss Josephine pooh-poohed the idea. She laughed that Arabella and her people blamed everything on haunts.

Arabella didn't share the laugh. "You ailing?" she asked, something in her voice, not a helpful concern but a prying.

Miss Josephine made as if she hadn't heard.

"I only ask," the house servant said, "because the other day I heard your toilet, must've flushed fifteen, twenty times in a row."

Hearing that, Josephine resolved not to flush in the daytime. She could hold the day's food, set it aside in her sewing basket, and flush it late at night after Arabella and her man Lewis had retired to their own little house. She laughed and picked up the screwdriver off the table and began to totter off.

Behind her Arabella asked, "Where you headed?"

Not bothering to hide her annoyance, Miss Josephine answered, "To fix the washer." She gasped as if to suck the words back. Her mouth froze open.

At first, Arabella said nothing. Her not-talking filled up the kitchen. With elaborate slowness, in low-slung tones she asked, "The washer's broke?" A big, broad victory hung in her voice.

Miss Josephine turned to face her. She laughed to shake off the mood, saying, "Isn't it?"

Arabella said, "Search me." She sucked her teeth and cocked her head as if to study the old woman from a fresh angle.

Miss Josephine felt her cheeks burn. She let her eyes drift and shook her head as if stymied by the younger woman's forgetfulness. The stolen gadget hung heavy in the pocket of her housecoat. The screwdriver dropped from her hand and clattered on the linoleum floor.

Nick, Nick was smart, not book smart per se, but his parents' house used to get tagged by graffiti punks. No sooner than Nick's dad had the latest tag painted over or scrubbed away, but another late-night vandal would throw up some new masterpiece. Instead of installing a camera and trying to get the city to pay attention to the problem, Nick actually solved it.

One night, between taggers, he went out with his own can of spray paint. All down two sides of the house he wrote swastikas as tall as he could reach. He sprayed the words "Kill Queers" and "Niggers Suck." The whole job took less than a can of paint. Not that Nick was a Nazi, he just had a plan.

He went to bed. He didn't tell his father or mother.

The next morning their doorbell rang. A television crew was outside. The street was crowded with people taking pictures. His parents were confused and angry, but he could tell they didn't mind the sympathy. After being ignored for so long, dealing with the graffiti alone, they were glad that the problem now belonged to the entire city. The mayor of Portland called a press conference to condemn hate speech, and extra police patrols were added. No tagger punks would dare touch their house in the future and risk being accused of this hate mess. The media lauded his parents as brave, long-suffering heroes. And Nick never told them.

That's the kind of smart Nick was.

After the household was abed, Miss Josephine soundlessly descended the attic stairs. She needed no light. Every squeaky floorboard was an old friend. No shadow held any surprise for her to stumble over. Fifty-seven steps led down to the narrow kitchen door. She held one palm flat against it, pushing softly so the latch would not clack as her other hand turned the knob.

The door wouldn't budge. The knob turned, but something kept her from pushing it open. She braced the satin shoulder of her dressing gown against the wood and planted her bare feet a mite wider. Miss Josephine bore into the door with all of her weight until the old wood barked out a cracking sound. It was locked. The hinge pins, located on the outside.

Voices whispered in the breathing of the kitchen air conditioner. She fancied she could hear the measured heartbeat of the clock in the front hallway, but she wouldn't swear that what she actually heard wasn't her lifelong memory of hearing that clock. In the dark she heard people talking who'd been dead since she was a girl.

She lowered herself carefully until she sat on the lowest step, hugged her knees to her chest, and listened for anything, and when the first birds signaled the sunrise she retraced her footsteps back to bed.

Back in Before Times, Walter had closed his eyes to see better with his fingertips. His fingers had tapped and stabbed at the keys of his laptop. His fingers had danced out the words as Talbott spoke them.

> *A bounty would be paid for photographic*
> *evidence of anyone in public not*
> *carrying a copy of the Talbott book.*

Talbott had dictated and Walter had written:

> *A bounty would be paid for proof of any*
> *individual faking a disability.*

The old man had decreed:

> *A bounty would be paid for information regarding*
> *any person living outside his appropriate homeland.*

The website Walter had launched at Talbott's instruction was already proving to be a success. America's Least Wanted. People were logging on and registering the names of politicians, academics, and journalists. Hundreds of names. The registered names were racking up votes. Millions of votes. How this would make him rich, Walter couldn't begin to guess. He was an apprentice who couldn't yet see the big picture. He simply took notes as his new old man rambled on.

According to Talbott Reynolds the nation needed an aristocracy. The kings of Europe and Asia hadn't been voted into power. They'd spilled blood, and whoever spilled the most blood gained the most power. The Queen of England and the kings of Sweden and Spain stood atop a mountain of butchered men. Strapped to his chair, shellacked in a few drops of blood leaked from each of a double hundred small incisions, he ranted, "Why wait tables when a hail of bullets will be your coronation?"

Democracy was a short-lived aberration. He'd insisted that America needed a ruling class of men who'd seize power the way men had always seized power. Men who take action will become this new royalty. Learning a trade was fine. College wasn't for every man. But thirty years into framing houses or wiring buildings and what will become of your body? Once a man's knees or his back age, how will he earn his livelihood? Adjustment Day was about men joining forces.

Walter had looked up from his typing. "So this is like *Fight Club*?"

His new old man had shaken his head. He'd asked, "Are you referring to the novel?"

"What novel?" had asked Walter. His fingers poised above the keyboard.

Talbott had smirked. "Hardly." He'd said, "*Fight Club* was about empowering each man through a series of exercises." His ghastly face shined with its coating of blood. "*Fight Club* taught each man that he had capacity beyond his greatest concept of himself. Then, it set each man free to fulfill his destiny: to build a house, to write a book, to paint a self-portrait."

Walter could recall that much from the film.

Shaking his head dismissively, Talbott muttered, "Palahniuk. All of his work is about castration. Castration or abortion."

Adjustment Day, Talbott had explained, was to be a model for how men could form an army in order to attain permanent high status. It would draft them to take action before society drafted them. These men would kill on their own behalf, for their own benefit, rather than for the benefit of those who already held power and assets.

"What men want," he'd said, "is a structure for communion."

As Talbott had seen it, a demographic explosion of young men were becoming men, men with good educations, healthy and well fed, who'd been raised to expect a glorious future for themselves. No such future awaited them. The democracy of capitalism guaranteed that only the most banal men, the men with the most moderate intellect and most readily appealing looks and talents, would rise to notoriety. And these would only be a handful from among the millions.

Walter had waited, uncertain if this merited writing down. "What happens to the rest of us?"

Talbott had smiled and sighed. His eyes blink-blinked and drifted to consider the blood-flecked cement floor. "What happens is what always happens."

Going on, he'd claimed that the government had always known Pearl Harbor would be attacked by the Japanese. He'd insisted the government had known all along about the impending destruction of the World Trade Center. The battleships sunk had been practically obsolete. The Twin Towers were a necessary expenditure. In both cases, what the nation had really needed was a war to cull the impending generation of young men reaching adulthood. Such a war would cut down the labor pool and ensure a sizable wage to the survivors. It would throw the surplus men of many countries into combat and stimulate economies the world over.

"Most importantly," Talbott had said, "the conflict would create a shortage of men and preserve the patriarchy."

Walter hadn't wanted to buy that theory. He'd hesitated to contradict his mentor, but the police and the military would stomp out the sort of grassroots insurrection Talbott had described.

"Once the police had been sufficiently humiliated and blamed for crime . . . ," Talbott had replied. "Once the military realizes it's being led to slaughter . . ." Both would look the other way when Adjustment Day came to pass. Members of both might even join the attack, especially if it guaranteed that their descendants would hold power for generations to come.

A man might hesitate to kill if it meant only his own benefit, but if his action would crown his sons and, in turn, their sons and their sons as royalty in a new society, that man who had no option but to commit murder in someone else's war, that man would gladly create a meritocracy based on murder.

At this Talbott had fallen silent. His gaze had come to rest on the computer in Walter's lap. It was clear the discussion had been over for the time being when he'd pronounced:

> With the exception of members of the police
> and military, all retirement from public
> service is suspended until further notice.

And in full faith, still not comprehending where any of this was headed, Walter had dutifully typed out the words. As Talbott saw the situation the clerks and bureaucrats of the world had traded their unstable youth for security and routine, and now that would be all they'd ever have. It was too late for them to kite off to Tuscany and dabble at beings painters. It was too late for them to be anyone but themselves.

Mid-lecture, Talbott asked, "Have you read Flaubert's *Bouvard and Pécuchet*?" In the novel two clerks inherit a fortune and leave their jobs to dabble in art and literature, eventually realizing that they have no talent for leisure. In the end they return to their boring, steady, structured lives as clerks. The Baby Boomers would have to accept a similar fate. Under a new regime they'd be required to work and support the Millennial generation until a wholly new system was put in place.

Jamal wandered, awestruck, through the rooms of his new home. His pit bull, Bouncer, loped a few steps ahead, sniffing behind a chair, pawing at a cabinet door, as if to flush out whatever animals might be hiding there. Each room opened into a larger room, the walls lined with pictures of white people, lined with fireplaces and shelves packed tight with books. Bright sunlight lit up big, clean windows and white paint. He'd requisitioned the house from a long list of surrendered properties. Photographs posted on the Internet. Today marked the first time in his life he wasn't living under his mama's roof.

The paintings looking down, they'd been a lineage of the old world. The stuck-up faces of high and mighty dead folks. The paintings could go. The books he'd keep. With Adjustment Day past, what Jamal truly wanted to do was write, to be an author who put a world of symbols and images into people's minds with his careful, steady stream of words. The way Talbott had done. As Talbott had phrased it:

No man is an adult while his parents are alive.
Until they die he is merely a performance
to either please or punish them.

For too long the whites have acted as the
finger-wagging parents of blacks.

For even longer heterosexuals have acted as the
shaming parents of homosexuals.

To Jamal it seemed he'd always been expected to back down, to forever defer, step aside. He'd always played the submissive good guy because the only other role was to be a thug. Everything he'd done was meant to keep people happy. Killing people wasn't ideal but it was the first time he wasn't trying to make them all love him. It mostly felt strange—strange not bad—because he wasn't trying to please these people. It felt nice to just shoot them and not worry about whether or not it made them happy. That relief made Jamal happy.

Opposition seemed unlikely. The downtrodden had always

turned to church, and their numbers had swelled until a leader appeared to organize their power. This time, history's displaced, the disenfranchised had long ago laughed off the idea of God. Their churches had been colleges and government offices, and these days their preachers were buried in mass graves. The new peasantry might have advanced degrees and awards galore, but they had no churches to harbor and comfort them.

Smarter men might exist. Stronger men. But Jamal was the one who pulled the trigger so they would work for him.

Whoever the owners of this house had been, they'd long since relocated to the appropriate homeland. Traveled light, from the look of it. They'd left behind their furniture, even the clothes and shoes in the closets. Not that it mattered. From today on this would be his house, his land, his farm. Jamal's mother was installed in a house in town, nicer than anywhere she'd ever lived but not near as nice as his place. Three floors, from the look of it, with Greek temple columns out front, the only word that seemed fitting was *grand*. Just as he'd always imagined it would be. He opened doors to find only more rooms, more doors and staircases. Behind one door he found the kitchen. A woman his mama's age stood at the stove. She wore an old-time uniform, just a gray dress with a white apron tied over it. Her hair was netted tight to her head.

"Pardon me," he said. This could be a mix-up. She was black, too. Could be the website had allocated the property to two parties by mistake. His status in a lineage gave him higher rank, of course, but he didn't relish the idea of putting somebody out of a house she'd come to think of as home.

"I live on the place," she offered. The sound of boiling. "Me and my family look after things."

Bouncer nosed his way past Jamal and moseyed over to press his muzzle alongside the woman's thick legs.

When he didn't speak, she asked, "You the new owner?" She looked into the pan as she spoke, like whatever she was cooking, she hated it to the point of sadness.

He let out the breath he wasn't aware he'd been holding. Even the kitchen around her was a marvel, all knobs and drawers, hanging pots and copper sinks and machines and all of it his. It would take him months, might be years, to grow into such a place. It relieved him, the thought he wouldn't be living here alone. Bouncer left the woman and went to sniff and paw at a door, a narrow door with a brass knob. The dog whined. He sniffed at the keyhole.

The woman followed Jamal's eyes to the door. "It's locked," she said. "Been locked since we misplaced the key."

The dog continued to sniff along the crack running beneath it. One paw scratched at the wooden floor.

"Must be he smells mice," the woman said. She turned back to the pan she was minding on the stovetop. "Nothing up those stairs but the attic." Her voice was sing-song, featherweight, saying, "Nope, just one empty old attic."

Jamal went and collared the dog, dragging Bouncer away from the locked door. "Where are my manners," he said, and he offered her his free hand. "My name is Jamal Spicer."

She did a double-take, one eyebrow arched, looking him up and down, slow, as if for the first time. Her shoulders sagged and she shook her head as if to clear her vision. "You the one from the TV?"

From the first lineage is what she meant. The state media had been running little biographies to introduce people to the system of men who'd be running the new nation of Blacktopia. Each man in his tribe had read aloud from the Talbott book, and these readings rotated night and day. Seeing himself on television had made Jamal feel sick with the limited reality of himself, his crooked teeth and big ears, but getting recognized had begun to make him proud to be the man he turned out.

The woman wiped her hands in her apron and accepted his handshake. "Pleased to make your acquaintance," she said, her voice breathless with amazement. A smile relaxed her face. A glad smile, not like part of the uniform she was forced to wear. "My name's Arabella."

Folks here to cook and clean for him, it would seem he'd walked into a ready-made family. "Here's Bouncer," he said, shaking the dog by its collar. And Jamal returned her smile.

The wait stood as his only option. Gavyn had registered as a resident alien, gone to the post office and filled out the forms, declared his homosexuality and taken an oath to the same. The clerk who'd administered the oath fixed him with a stern look.

"You know you can't work," she'd warned, "not legally."

Gavyn had read as much in the Talbott book.

"You can't vote or operate a motor vehicle, either," the clerk had said.

Gavyn said, "I understand."

The clerk slipped a pamphlet from a packet of papers. She read, "Until relocation can be approved, resident aliens must report their current place of residence and any changes in said place to the appropriate authorities."

That meant his parents' house. Fat chance he could move out, not without a job or a driver's license. The Declaration of Interdependence guaranteed mutual respect between all races and sexualities, but respect was easier when each was isolated, snug in his own homeland. Gavyn was an outsider, stuck among heterosexuals. For how long, nobody could say.

To make matters worse, the clock was ticking. To be queer, at least until Adjustment Day, meant almost two decades of torture. Being called "Gay-vin" and getting pounded into lockers on a weekly basis, with parents who hadn't a clue about what a queer kid needed to know. But the payoff was turning eighteen. That birthday vaulted a person from being the weakest, most victimized member of society to the heights of becoming one of the most powerful.

Women knew this transformation. One day they're off-limits, horsey, coltish jail bait. Ignored. Dismissed. And the next day they're leading men around by the nose. Rich men. Powerful men. The most attractive men in the world are vying for a young woman's attention. It was a form of power that didn't last forever, but it was power. And it could be leveraged for money and education and access to people, eventually to a more-lasting form of power. Sure, someday he'd be a lawyer or an engineer, but for now Gavyn merely wanted to be beautiful and pull the focus every time he entered a room. After so long getting ridiculed and slammed into walls, he deserved his moment in the spotlight.

The window of youth opened at eighteen, and it had a shelf life. Gavyn loved his parents, but he couldn't wait to emigrate to a world where he'd be normal.

Until then he was more or less a hostage.

The holdup came in the form of the Compensation Clause. The Talbot book held that homosexuals accrue wealth and skills faster because they're not burdened with bearing and raising their young. Like the egg of a cuckoo, the homosexual child was born into a heterosexual home and fledged to join his homosexual family. Thus the heterosexual exhausted time and resources that ultimately benefited the homosexual world. A constant export of new adults from the white and black homelands to the homosexual represented a trade imbalance of the cruelest kind. Young, vital, fully schooled offspring were siphoned away to their appropriate homeland while their parents were left without compensation or support in their waning years.

It wasn't ideal, Gavyn understood that.

The Compensation Clause had been enacted to balance the situation. It stated that a homosexual adult raised by heterosexuals could emigrate only when a heterosexual raised by homosexuals was ready to emigrate. Somewhere, Gavyn prayed a kid was coming out as straight to his lesbian parents. That kid would, like Gavyn, get sent to the post office where a clerk would give him the forms Gavyn had just now filled out. That disapproving, cluck-clucking clerk would warn the straight kid not to seek employment or operate a vehicle or attempt to vote in any election. And that kid, the anti-Gavyn, would go back to his two mommies or two daddies or whatever the case might be, to pray for a phone call.

Senior year, they'd done a unit on Adjustment Day and the new nation states. The teachers who were left, the ones who weren't buried in the end zone of Franklin High School's football field, those teachers were giddy with praise for the lineages. To listen to them, the lineage guys were heroes. If it wasn't for the heroes, Gavyn's generation would've been marched off to die in the false flag war. Gavyn included, thanks to stupid equal civil stupid rights.

When his teachers hadn't been reading aloud from the Talbott book, they'd been lecturing that the men had been justified. Students held up camera phones and tried to catch anyone not carrying the blue-black book or not expressing love for the new order. The lineages were justified, as per the teachers, due to the fact that male babies used to have their genitals routinely mutilated and the courts of law were biased against men in child custody and no-fault divorce cases, and because the prisons were so filled with men that the male suicide rate was more than four times the female suicide rate.

Between lectures they'd watched an educational film: Bulldozers pushing great moldering heaps of something. This mess wasn't the usual slaughter of tiny baby roosters. Screaming flocks of seagulls wheeled in the air, circling the bulldozers and the garbage being buried. A gull dove to grab something, then flew past the camera. Pinched in one of the bird's talons was an ear. The mounds of gray, squashed stuff being ground beneath the bulldozer treads and bladed into the dirt, they were untold numbers of human ears.

When called upon, students were expected to know each article of the Talbott book by heart. For example:

> Bounty will be paid for information leading
> to the arrest of any person using any unit
> of currency other than the Talbott.

As an alien resident Gavyn wasn't eligible to earn bounty money.

In theory Gavyn should've been happy. Only nobody mentioned all the blood and how people could find bullet holes in the cafeteria wall behind where the targets were lined up. No duh, a homosexual homeland sounded great to Gavyn, but he felt conflicted. As if he'd met a young priest wearing a short-sleeved shirt, only the guy has sexy tattoos, only he's a priest, only his arms are astonishingly muscular, only the tattoos are full of swastikas. That kind of a mixed blessing.

Gavyn hadn't been asked to wear a pink triangle, but that didn't seem very far down the road. Only there wasn't much choice. This was the new real world so he was going home to sit and wait by the phone.

Back in the Before Times, Walter's fingers had slowed as if walking behind Talbott's voice. Walter's writing, the shadow of the old man's talk. He'd expounded on the idea of perishable money and how it would create a ferocious climate of earning and spending. Such money would be a medium instead of an asset, it would no longer keep human time and energy suspended in locked vaults.

It had been slow going. Whether from blood loss or age, the old man had rambled:

> The Principle of Fatal Contrarians holds that society
> has worked against the benefit of certain individuals
> for so long that those persons will never trust it.
> They will continue to position themselves against
> society regardless of its aims, even if those goals
> ultimately work in the contrarian's best interests.

Talbott had gasped awake. His head had lolled on his stringy neck, and the dried blood had crusted in his wrinkles, those furrows across his forehead, and the crow's-feet radiating from the corners of each eye. Flakes of red littered his shoulders as he dictated:

> People will celebrate beauty or genius but not
> when they occur in the same person. To find
> both qualities in one individual occurs as an
> injustice no one will tolerate. When it happens
> either one or both gifts must be destroyed.

Walter had checked on the list every hour. Names had appeared and vanished, and those that remained were collecting impressive votes. The politicians, especially. Talbott would nod off, his head flopped to one side, and Walter would toggle to The List website. With a snort, his new old man would jerk awake and announce:

> Drugs are popular because they give the user a window
> of madness or illness that can be scheduled. Unlike
> sickness, drugs can synchronize the infection,
> derangement, and recuperation of a group of people.

Pronouncement made, the old man had collapsed into another drooling stupor.

As for the list's purpose, Walter had no idea. It consisted of only names and numbers, names and numbers. As per Talbott's instructions, if someone posted a name and it didn't attract at least three thousand votes within a week Walter was to delete it. To guess by the pattern, the way the numbers seemed to double every day, then double the next, knowledge of the website was spreading by word of mouth.

On an impulse, Walter had entered the name of his least favorite professor. The man had failed him for refusing to accept every lecture as gospel. Walter had typed the name Dr. Emmet Brolly and hit Enter to post it. The list had automatically scrolled to show where the name occurred in the alphabetical order, sandwiched between a state senator and a cable news anchor.

Even as he'd watched, a single vote appeared beside Brolly's name. A two replaced the one. A three replaced the two.

No parents ever named their child Delicious Bastille. That's the name she chose for her immigration papers. A new homeland, a new name. Beginning on Adjustment Day, every emigrant took advantage of a fresh start. Aristides and Aristotles. Baccarats and Beauregards. And Delicious, who without question should not have worn buttermilk-yellow crepe muslin, not if she'd suspected it would rain, donning a skintight dress without a coat or wrap. No amount of elastic and underwire could improve upon the eye-popping curves of her body so she did without. Halfway from where she'd parked, the skies had opened up, every drop painting the pale fabric to her until the dress hid no more of her mocha skin than would a layer of melted butter.

Every lesbian eye snuck peeks at her. At the swelling breasts that seemed to lunge up, up, and away from Delicious Bastille's chest. The nipples, two obvious purple bull's-eyes beneath her clinging bodice. Strangers eye-raped the taut muscles of her tawny thighs, the savory cleft of her ample buttocks, all so clearly delineated through her rain-soaked skirt.

Let them stare, she told herself. Their stares had prevented her from looking around the restaurant. If she'd met their leering eyes, she'd never be able to hide her frustration and rage.

Here she sat, naked for all intents and purposes, picking half-heartedly at her salad. She kept her eyes fixed on only immediate objects: her glass of pinot noir, her bread plate, the single pink rose in the table's center. She shut out the buzzing dining room filled with gays and lesbians. Except here, they weren't gays and lesbians. In the complete absence of heterosexuals, the people seated at the tables around her amounted to mere men and women. Women and men.

To help avoid so many eyes, she focused on her dinner companion. Across the table sat a woman sporting a wild blaze of red hair. The post-relocation name she went by was Ginger Prestige, and she was the latest of many blind dates arranged for Delicious by the women in the aerospace corporation. None of her coworkers seemed able to tolerate an unmarried female in their ranks, so they were forever throwing Delicious together with single women named Calyx or Esteem. Delicious suspected that a single gal was a threat in the paired-up, domesticated world of middle-aged women's society.

The redhead lifted long fingers to toy with a dangling curl beside her face. She met Delicious's gaze and asked, "So you're an aerospace engineer?"

Delicious sipped from her glass of wine. She gave a modest nod.

The woman, Ginger, looked sheepishly at Delicious's transparent dress, which stretched taut to cover her tiny waist. The admiration shined in her blue eyes as she said, "What you're doing is so heroic."

What she referred to was the mission to Mars—a tent pole, nationwide campaign to unite the fledgling homeland and claim, at least symbolically claim, the entire planet of Mars in the name of the Oscar Wilde set. Delicious was one of the homeland's leading experts in rocketry, arguably the linchpin of the nation's race to put same-sex-oriented astronauts on the red planet.

Delicious had only taken a single sip of wine. To avoid temptation, she signaled for the waiter to take away her nearly full glass.

Ginger's long fingers and full lips invited fantasy. Delicious shuddered with a frisson of sensation as she imagined Ginger's freckled-pink face at work between her own cocoa thighs. The brilliant aerospace engineer caught herself and shook off the appealing vision. She'd been alone too long, trying to remain faithful. The fantasy said less about Ginger's sexiness than it did about how long Delicious had abstained from sex.

Ginger waved for the waiter to refill her own glass, saying, "I'm drinking for two." Of Delicious she asked, "What sign are you?"

Delicious rearranged the napkin spread atop her little lap, saying, "Late May."

Ginger smiled. "A Gemini."

When Delicious failed to engage, the redhead asked, "So as an aerospace guru, what do you think of the whole flying pyramid thing?"

Delicious had been celibate for five months. Twenty soul-crushing, lonely weeks had gone by since she'd entered this strange nation. She began fork-raping her salad greens in search of an artichoke heart. Lifting her eyes to request a glass of orange juice, another boring glass of orange juice when what she craved was a vodka martini, a vodka martini with three garlic-stuffed olives and a certain blond man's massive, rock-hard erection bringing her to a toe-curling climax . . . when she glanced up for a waiter she saw the blond man.

He sat in a narrow booth at the far edge of the room. A thin white man, skinny, with, at best, a tennis player's build, but in actuality hardly more than skin and bone. She recognized his blond hair, cut longer now and combed in a boyish spray across his wide, ivory forehead. He sat sideways to her so Delicious could see his full profile. Across from him ate a heavily muscled giant, a black man barely contained in a too-tight jersey pullover. The giant's jeans-clad legs were visible beneath the table, and Delicious watched as he wedged both meaty knees between the knees of the slender white man and slowly began forcing those boney knees apart.

The slightly built man pulled away, but the confines of the booth didn't allow room for him to fully escape contact, and Delicious watched as the predatory giant spread the unwilling man's scrawny legs. Blushing, holding back tears of humiliation, the slender blond seemed to sense Delicious watching and turned to meet her gaze.

She looked away. Her heart knocked against her ribs. Here a woman risked everything if she stared a moment too long at a man. She could be fired from her job, evicted from her home. The government could take custody of her children, and she'd be deported to a homeland, white or black, where no one thought it a perversion for women and men to be intimate.

If the redhead had noticed, she said nothing. She sipped her wine and ruminated about the baby-making race. Every hour heterosexuals were creating homosexuals. The homosexuals could never keep pace. They'd never provide matching numbers of heterosexual children to exchange, and that meant a steady backlog of homosexual children trapped in heterosexual homelands. Her office with the government tracked the numbers, she explained. In an attempt to balance the books, they were proposing a cash equivalent be paid for children who couldn't be traded for children. A kind of dowry would be paid to the heterosexual parents as compensation for their efforts and to help fund their old age. Called a "liberation fund," it amounted to hundreds of millions of dollars, but the monies could be raised through donations.

Delicious only half listened. It took every strength she possessed to not turn and look at the blond man. She sensed his eyes on her, on the soft curve of her breasts, and she gritted her teeth in her effort not to weep.

As the palace of San Simeon is to its isolated stretch of California coastline so is Maryhill castle to the Pacific Northwest. Each is the steel-reinforced concrete legacy of a wealthy tycoon sheathed in Old World architectural details and furnished with the treasures bought at fire-sale prices from impoverished royal families. Both edifices stand atop heights, overlooking the dramatic landscape for miles. Each was nicknamed by its respective builder as "the Ranch."

All magnificence appears as folly at first. As the Eiffel Tower dared to rise above Paris in 1887, the French cultural maven Victor Hugo condemned it as a hideous oil derrick that would deface the city. Likewise, as the Empire State Building was completed in 1931 and sat through the Depression without tenants, the people of New York began to deride their new landmark as the "Empty State Building." Time legitimizes the outrageous.

Maryhill, that improbable Italian palazzo, is no less impressive than its California rival because of its grim situation. A desert surrounds it, little aside from barren, wind-scoured scablands. Ornate bronze grills wrought in some Renaissance style bar the windows, making it as much a prison as a fortress, for accumulated within are Slavic thrones and crowns, Tsarist portraits and priceless porcelain looted from the Orient. And it was in this ready-made kingdom that Charlie established his household. His income amounted to the only source of Talbott dollars in the region so the destitute from miles around presented themselves at his door. Hat in hand, each asked to be taken into his patronage. The most comely among them, Charlie accepted as team wives, with the marginally more attractive made to serve in his household while the lesser would labor as field wives. To a woman, they were all to wear rippable bodices, and the men were to wear kilts or trews as the weather did dictate.

Charlie himself favored an overtunic densely embroidered in gold, worn to cover a linen shirt featuring commodious sleeves. Velvet-paned trunkhose adorned his lower limbs, the fabric made fast about his calves and ankles by a crisscrossing of leather thongs. For such a costume was in keeping with the nascent cultural identity of Caucasia.

Among the long list of arduous tasks was the renaming of everything. For every mountain and watercourse need be rechristened in accord with the emergent society. In addition did Charlie order the erection of a stout stone brewhouse for the manufacture of mead. As he did summon the waters of the mighty Columbia River—from henceforth to be referred to as the "Charlie Bourne"—he decreed that waters enough be piped and compelled upland as to provide for the farming of expansive fields. A grand enterprise did Charlie undertake to found, his palace was quickly the center of expanses of curly endive giving way to great swaths of sugar beets, cilantro, and a surplus of rutabagas.

In accord with the cultural values of Caucasia did common men roam the countryside attired in tunics and cassocks and capes, shod in boots or sandals dependent upon the season, while atop their heads sat headgear denoting their rank. Liveried were many in doublets featuring gored sleeves of flashing ruby-colored brocades. About their shoulders they carried the jewels plundered from no few museums and more, for pearls could be bought from the formerly well-off for the price of an egg, and gold had use to neither the starving nor the dead.

So Charlie and his courtiers did squire and bind to themselves the youngest and most lovely whom could be flushed out. And by the wearing of such raiment did Charlie and his fellow chieftains of Caucasia rediscover their noble heritage. And trussed in Venetian breeches did they grip pewter flasks of hearty ale and clang those tankards together with boisterous toasts to one another. Busy were the home wives all, those multitudinous teams of wives, sewing sporrans.

The challenge of proving himself a hero gave way to the business of managing domestic affairs, and Charlie was too busy to question whether or not he was ever satisfied. Yet even while he did gad about attired in tabards and brigandines, quilted gambesons, jerkins, and houppelandes, even then did an emptiness assail him. In response did Charlie appoint a Committee for the Revival of Proper Culture, which revived the minuet. Revived gallantry and courtier hand kissing. Instituted the mandatory practice of White-Speak. And furthermore to suffuse his realm with meaning did he reinstate the worship of Odin and Thor, and to that end did pioneer the building of an antique cathedral complete with flying buttresses and naves, but even as he knelt at the rail and partook of the newly invented ancient sacraments, even then did Charlie feel dissatisfied.

Busy and fed were his subjects. They did consult neglected texts in search of recipes for dyes and patterns for the tatting of forgotten laces. And as tunics grew shorter, the boldest of their company donned codpieces of gilded leather encrusted with pearls. And in the vicinity of these codpieces were team wives always prepared to be interfered with. A swain might doff his Tudor cap or plumed tricorn, but the chivalry more oft ended there!

This aforementioned emptiness put Charlie in mind of high school. He harkened back to English class and the study of Flaubert's unfinished novel *Bouvard and Pécuchet*. While his more-vibrant schoolmates cut capers and bandied about enticements to attain sexual ecstasy, boy Charlie had pored over the book, retaining its basic premise: Two clerks are bestowed a fortune and leave their normal lives in order to discover greater satisfaction in a more ennobling passion. The two tear through wine, art, horse racing, and find none sufficiently fulfilling. In the end they return to their former lives of number crunching and scribbling in ledgers.

That parable now stuck in Charlie's craw as if he were swallowing a peanut butter sandwich eaten too fast in too-big bites. Was it possible that he was incapable of savoring life as a potentate? Had he risen too far above his natural station as a lowly grease monkey of the shop floor?

He'd heard tales of nascent rock musicians. Avant-garde figures cast from the same mold as Kurt Cobain, who, once they were rewarded with a fortune, bought the requisite manor house simply because it seemed the next rite of passage. Only for years after they'd occupy a single room of the same, often the smallest room, often only a large closet.

Considering that precedent, Charlie resolved not to shrink from his destiny. But to gradually expand into his new role. And while the womenfolk of his household were compliant and privileged to bear his progeny, he needed one who could help shoulder the burden of his reign.

It dawned upon him that his next challenge—perhaps his greatest challenge—would be to balance the inequity between the men and women of his lands. To that end would he track down and master an exceptional female for the purpose of grooming her to serve as a suitable public wife. Whereas the women did all of the stooped labor in the fields, and women kept tidy the chambers of his Maryhill palace, while menfolk did quaff lager and swagger about sowing the seeds of the next generation, if Charlie were to grant wealth and power to a single female, raising her to the status of deity, that act would counterbalance the low position of all her female underlings.

The enzymes in Piper's cells began their self-destruct process of autolysis, digesting the cellular walls and releasing the liquefied mess within. Bacteria present in his lungs, his mouth, sinuses, and digestive tract gorged themselves on this amber flood of amino acids. Flies found the eyes, the rectum, genitals, and nostrils and began to lay their eggs. Larvae hatched and burrowed beneath the skin to devour the layer of subcutaneous fat.

The eyes collapsed.

The intestines had already collapsed, effectively sealing themselves and trapping the gas produced by the bacteria in the digestive tract, and the belly began to bloat. Trapped bacteria swelled the face and genitals, swelling the tongue until it extended between the stretched and swollen lips. The penis expanded in a final mock erection, turgid with the byproducts of bacteria. The only sound was the noise of maggots devouring the face. A crackling sound. The exact same noise as studded snow tires make driving slowly over bare pavement.

The abdominal wall ruptured, the gas vented, and the torso collapsed into a foul, spreading puddle. The bacteria in the mouth digested the palate and attacked the brain, which dissolved quickly, escaping from the ears. Meat-eating beetles, *Anthrenus verbasci* and *Dermestes lardarius*, arrived to feast on the muscles.

Then possibly only the skin and bones remained. Most likely, the beetles resorted to eating the skin.

All the while the television remained on. The same man being devoured by beetles, devoured by maggots, he looked out upon his mortal remains and said:

The coward takes offense on behalf of others. Let each
man take responsibility for only his own reaction.

The maggots matured into flies and laid more eggs. And the
handsome man on the television screen told the flies crawling
over his skeleton:

To make a career of rescuing people is also to
create a permanent class in need of rescue.

Flies lined the windows of the condominium. Dead flies covered
the windowsills, and still more flies laid their eggs. Maggots and
more maggots hatched. And the man in his bespoke Savile Row
suit told them:

We must allow each individual to
persevere or to perish as he chooses.

Each new generation of flies laid its eggs and matured and died
trying to reach the sunshine outside the closed windows until the
subcutaneous fat was consumed and the last among the last generation of flies fell dead on the windowsill. Even then the man
on the television, whose face might be that of a king or saint or
president, he looked over the skull and bones on the floor beneath
him and told it:

A man is not going to get loved by being lovable.

For emigration she'd chosen his name: Gentry Tate. He'd chosen
Delicious Bastille for her. They'd toasted their new monikers with
champagne, but not much because she'd desperately wanted to get
pregnant. Hiding had kept them together, but any day the knock
could come to their door.

He'd be deported, relocated to the ethnic state for whites. She'd be held there, in the former state of Louisiana, renamed part of Blacktopia. If she bore a child it would be tested and assigned an appropriate homeland. They'd first planned to escape to Canada, but a million interracial couples had hatched the same idea. To stem the rush, Ottawa had closed the borders.

Leaving them with one option if they wanted to remain together. Not together-together, not as man and wife, not even as friends or acquaintances who met occasionally in passing.

No, passing as homosexuals was their only option. The queer nation admitted both blacks and whites, and no genetic testing could betray their actual sexualities. Not that the homosexuals didn't foresee these attempts. Rumor had it that desperate mixed-race families were splitting apart temporarily and emigrating, then surreptitiously reuniting. Mexico had long ago stopped accepting refugees.

Delicious had dated a woman who worked in the fraud detection division of immigration policy. The woman had made it clear that immigrants caught engaging in covert heterosexual activities would be imprisoned. Due to the high number of homosexual youths in Caucasia waiting for exit visas, the queer nation was aggressively searching for closeted heterosexuals in order to trade them for the would-be gay emigrants.

If found out, Delicious would be relocated posthaste. Gentry, too, but each to a different ethnic state. It did present a conundrum.

They'd joked about seeking each other late at night in grimy unisex public toilets. Kisses stolen in filthy back alleys. Demeaning and degrading as those circumstances loomed, at the very least Delicious and Gentry would preserve their attachment to each other. Their love and their future child. Until the child was the age to declare his or her sexuality, until then they could be a little family. They might even share custody, handing off the child in gritty, grimy adult bookstores when they met for trysts in some unspeakably wretched, sticky-floored pornography arcades where their fellow secretive heterosexuals went to con-

177 ADJUSTMENT DAY

summate their frowned-upon passions. Sordid conjugal visits in pits of sleaze.

Considering such a tableau, Delicious couldn't help but think of the Holy Savior born in a dirty stable. That had turned out well, more or less.

She despised the thought of her child being used as a pawn in international politics, but that decision was eighteen years in the future. It was possible that by then laws would change. If the child chose to be gay it might even serve as an anchor baby to keep her and Gentry in the same homeland.

One blessing about orange juice is that it gave her a constant excuse to tinkle. She dabbed at the corners of her mouth with her napkin and fixed her date with a meek smile. "Nature calls." She rose from her chair, deliberately not glancing in the direction of Gentry and his aggressive he-man, dare she think "date"? Between the open stares regarding her transparent yellow dress, and her deliberately slow promenade across the dining room, elaborately circumnavigating it, wending her way between tables as if confused about the location of the toilets, with both those factors to her advantage she could only hope her husband would notice her and hurry to catch up.

Shasta found the website. The banner read "Bride of Kings" and below that it listed each member of each lineage currently reviewing prospective brides. One named Brach, a former forklift operator who'd taken possession of an island estate near Seattle where he lived with his harem of team wives, the site listed him as seeking additional matches.

Brach owned a growing chain of diners. Shasta had seen the revolving signs that towered above freeway exits. In bold black letters against a lighted background, the signs read "*Whites Only*." Whether this was a boast or an ironic expression of resignation,

Shasta couldn't begin to guess. The menu offered Nazi penne pasta, a Klan burger, a Hitler veggie taco salad.

Brach and his ilk, princes and barons they called themselves. Last month's grease monkeys and dog groomers. An aristocracy of former steam fitters and garbage haulers. They'd picked up guns and blown the brains out of civilization. They'd read the Talbott book. They lived by it. By reading it herself she could guess how her life as a team wife would turn out. As a brood mare, popping out white babies to repopulate the new nation state. A string of babies born a year or less apart, what her own mom used to call "Irish twins."

In small settlements and camps people assembled to vote. They elected their most attractive young woman and pooled their resources to groom her and dress her. And equipped with an entourage of stylists and helpmates, each of these beauty queens was sent forth to the courts of men in each lineage. For to have a daughter marry into the lineage ensured a community would not be neglected. As the wife of a lineage prince she could exert her influence for the benefit of her birthplace.

And they journeyed forth, these parties of young ladies, each was a potential queen accompanied by her handmaidens. And they streamed from court to court, funded by the hope and dreams of their hamlets. Former cheerleaders and homecoming dance royals, harvest queens and rodeo princesses.

And as a team the group showcased their leader so she might forge a powerful alliance. And in preparation for each meeting, the ladies in waiting curled and peeled. They plucked and combed.

Per Talbott, people needed to establish a moratorium on progress. For the next hundred years, there should be a hold on developing new technology and marvels of engineering. For too long white men had been sublimating their natural impulses through science, so from here on those energies must be channeled in their natural direction. White men needed to back off from the Industrial Revolution or the Information Age or whatever this was. Whites needed to kick back, drink beer, have some outdoor fun, and make nothing but healthy babies. "Generation Sex" was the motto.

The dukes and earls, they loved their sports terminology. Team wives suggested wide receivers, tight ends, fullbacks. Field wives brought to mind the packed field of contenders in NAS-CAR. Every human endeavor from tire factories to truck farms was falling under the patronage of some local prince's fiefdom. New money had to be earned and spent quickly. Talbott said the currency would be given a longer life once it was established. But for the present a skin had to buy bread, gasoline, toothpaste, some grapes, a movie ticket, a pair of socks, passing through that many hands in a single day.

Shasta's own parents' marriage had survived because sometimes her mother would leave her wedding ring beside their bathroom sink and go out to have dinner for a few days. Other times, her father went to dinner without his ring.

On the website, Chieftain Charlie had caught Shasta's eye because he was one of the few who didn't lay claim to targeting the actual president of the formerly united states.

She'd uploaded a couple good selfies, one a face shot, one a full body. She followed the prompts. Position Sought: Lead wife. Would she consider serving as a team wife: Yes. Height: Five foot, nine inches. Weight: One hundred twenty-five pounds. Any history of hereditary physical or mental illness: None. Hair: Blonde. Eyes: Periwinkle. Race: Caucasian.

She hit Enter. A prompt appeared. "As a condition of acceptance the applicant must submit to genetic testing to confirm overall health and racial heritage."

Shasta had clicked the box labeled Agree.

In rooms of any size, sparkling crystal set on silver trays held hooch, excellent hooch, and Jamal poured himself a glass to enjoy while he toured his new domain. He surveyed the tall oil paintings that stretched almost to the ceiling. With their bad-ass swords and medals, these men had been the players of their time. They'd understand him taking this place off the hands of their soft-hearted descendants. These soldier men had taken lives in order to live here, to build these walls and mate with the women who'd dressed this place in frilled everything.

Arabella and her kin were gone home to their place, a smaller house a ways off on the property. This house, the big house, he had to himself.

But a house didn't make anyone powerful.

Jamal took up his copy of the Talbott book and his glass of good hooch, and he went to the biggest chair in front of the big-gest fireplace and settled himself. To read Talbott was to enter into the pattern of his mind. To feel your own thoughts patterned after Talbott's. That was power: To live within the minds of oth-ers. To reorganize their minds in accord with your own. To Jamal, that was the greatest power.

He couldn't recall the last time he'd sat awake all night, in the silent dark, absorbing the words arranged by a writer's mind. But that's how he read, tonight. The grand old clocks, in the hallways, on the mantel, ticked like old-time bombs.

As Talbott put it:

> Whether it's by breeding children or preaching, it's what men do: This constant dissemination of self.

To look at white men these days, something vital had been bred out of them. How had those men, the Vikings and the Norse, men who'd sailed their long boats up the Rhine, the Volga, the Dnieper, and Danube to burn and pillage and turn most of a continent blond and blue-eyed, how had they disappeared so completely? He suspected that for most white men, it was pride enough to not be black or queer. That was reason plenty for separate homelands. It would force men, all men, to earn a reason to feel superior.

Not one of these painted men with their mutton-chop sideburns and beards and gold braid had been born great. Each had risked everything for a chance at something better, and to a man they stood triumphant atop a hundred dead enemies or a thousand dead enemies. Victors and vanquished alike, they were all dead alike and congratulating each other on the valor they had shown.

That's when he heard it first. That late night. Alone in the house. Jamal didn't want to entertain the idea of spooks haunting him, but that's what his mind seized upon. Considering the targets he'd put down, those people tallied and buried, some terror sent his thoughts down that guilt-ridden path.

Except it wasn't any sound usually associated with a ghost. He set his empty glass on a table. His glass on his table in his house, and he wasn't going to be run off by a late-night noise. Especially not that particular noise.

That thunder of water somewhere and the shudder of some-thing through old pipes. It came again and again.

Fast but unmistakable, it was the sound of somebody on a floor far overhead flushing a toilet.

Delicious sat, amid the rank smells and the adjacent wet splashes, locked within the unisex toilet at the restaurant. A knock sounded at the door, followed by a whispered, "Susan?"

She leaned forward, whispering, "Gentry?" She unlatched the door and swung it open. Her dress still clung to her curves. She waited fully clothed therein.

The scrawny white boy who stood in the half-open doorway said, "Don't call me that."

His name, before immigrating, his name had been different. He looked both ways in the passage outside the cubicle, then quickly stepped inside, pulling the door closed and locking it. His arms were instantly around her. His mouth on hers. Delicious felt his fingers inching the damp skirt up her thighs.

His lips nuzzled the side of her neck. His erection prodded at her through his chinos.

Delicious wondered about his burly black dinner partner. She could only hope that bulked-up, hot-blooded brother wasn't tapping her husband's bony white boy's backdoor. She told herself to chill. She told herself it was harder for a brother being gay. A sister could flirt and be coy, but a dawg was expected, especially a gay dawg, to be dicking or getting dicked on a more-or-less nonstop basis. Still, as Gentry's lips roved over her breasts, she had to ask.

"Brian?" His name before was Brian. She asked, "Is that dawg been up in you?"

His mouth still exploring her, his fingers pawing the dress down her shoulder and exposing her, Gentry mumbled something. He held up his hand and waved it with his fingers spread. A gold ring glittered around one finger. A wedding ring. And not the one she'd given him at their own wedding.

Too loud for a little toilet cubicle, Delicious blasted, "You married him?"

Granted, she knew the best way to avoid sex was to get married. Nothing killed the good times faster. But did he have to hook up with the first big he-monster? Or was Gaysia like a men's prison, where you needed to be one inmate's bitch or you'd be punked by everyone?

Gentry surfaced for air. Panting, he told her, "Neither."

"Neither, what?" Delicious demanded.

Yeah, he was married to the brother, Gentry explained, but they weren't doing it.

Delicious was confused. Gentry had dropped to his knees and was working his way up inside her dress instead of down. What looked like a pregnancy was Gentry's big white blockhead stretching her skirt at the belly. His hot breath gargled something into her sex.

Delicious asked, "What?" She wanted answers, but their time was limited, and she didn't want him to stop.

A knock came at the door. Gentry's tongue stopped its running around between her legs.

From outside, a voice asked, "Delicious?" It was the redhead, Ginger Prestige. She asked, "You okay?" Whispering close to the door, she asked, "You're not having one of those toilet babies, are you?"

Gentry started to laugh. With his mouth cupped over Delicious, he was laughing air into her. He was going to give her pussy farts. She made a fist and rapped on his head with her knuckles to stop. To the nosy redhead, she went nuclear. She hissed, "Don't be racist."

It was the worst accusation you could level in Gaysia. It didn't make complete sense in this situation, but it did the trick.

The voice said, "My bad." Footsteps seemed to trail away.

His head still stretching the hell out of her damp skirt, Gentry said, "Jarvis isn't that way."

The muscled-up gym rat making the big show of pushing her skinny husband's legs apart and humiliating him as a down-right bitch right here in public, according to Gentry, the brother was heterosexual. He'd emigrated separate from his white wife and had spent the past seven months trying to find her. For the time being, he and Gentry had gotten married so each could act as the other's beard. It was a lot to explain with his face shoved into her snatch, but he sounded sincere. The big display of sexually humiliating Gentry was an act. Other times, they'd accuse one another of cruising someone at a nearby table and launch into a screaming slap fight.

Gentry was getting to his feet. He was gently but insistently turning her around and lifting the back of her skirt. He took himself out.

The public cat fights and sexual hazing, this wasn't how actual gays behaved in Gaysia. It was strictly the outsider interpretation of two heterosexuals, but it kept people from getting too close.

Delicious wanted to ask how they'd met. She wanted to find a nice heterosexual gal and get hitched, herself. But now Gentry put himself inside her from behind so she stepped her feet as wide as the little cubical allowed. She leaned over the toilet and pushed her ass back against his thrust.

The candles were vexing. They wouldn't stay lit. They teetered and toppled and fell. Shasta watched a young woman navigate the sidewalk in the tiny steps a geisha might take. The girl held her head painfully erect, crowned with a wreath of scratchy holly leaves and poisonous mistletoe berries. Six tall, white candles jutted up from this crown, each tipped with a flickering flame.

Even as Shasta watched, one of the girl's candles tilted. It drizzled melted wax down the bodice of the girl's heavily embroidered dirndl. The off-kilter taper fell. The girl's hands sprang into action, beating at a small fire the flaming wick had ignited in the folds of her linen skirt. The sudden movement scattered the remaining candles from her head. Some rolled in the street. Others dropped into the gutter where they set fire to used condoms and discarded paper money from the Before Times.

The candles, the crowns of thorns, they were as much a test of poise as they were a Caucasian fashion statement. Shasta figured as much.

And wearing this bullshit frippery wasn't so much a quirky trend as it was the law.

The dirndl girl cursed quietly as she stripped off the smoking ruins of her skirts and petticoats. Shasta engaged her core muscles and held her spine ramrod straight. Years of yoga had paid off, keeping her own candles steady. Hers was the regal bearing of a monarch in training as she strolled past the unfortunate scene.

From elsewhere, a voice called, "Chica!" A male voice. "Nice candles!"

Turning to look took a slow eternity—always the candles to

worry about—but Shasta recognized the young man walking toward her. He carried a duffle bag under one arm. In one hand he clutched a paperback book as thick as a brick. He was a brother of her friend Esteban, from school. Gay Esteban. She struggled to match a name to his face.

"Xavier," he offered. He was the straight brother. "Where do you get off on dressing all *white girl*?"

She didn't bother to explain about flunking her DNA test. No duh, but having two grandparents from Quintana Roo had bit her in the ass. She was over-the-line Hispanic. And not one of the good kind, like from Spain, either. She asked if he'd seen Walter.

Xavier shook his head. He said, "You have a candle out."

"Damn," Shasta said as she opened her Kate Spade tote bag. Revealed inside was a squashed jumble of Danish pastries and jelly doughnuts. She grimaced as she worked her fingers into the mess of puff pastry, Bavarian cream, and powdered sugar.

Xavier recoiled from the sight of mashed delicacies, sneering in disgust. "What are you supposed to be?"

Lifting her gaze slowly, she looked pointedly at the various other women who carefully sipped lattes or walked dogs on leashes as they balanced a crown of blazing candles atop their heads. "It's Scandinavian or something." The prickly leaves and dripping wax stung her scalp. "It's the Scandinavian version of dreadlocks."

Xavier rolled his eyes. "Well, it looks stupid."

Shasta snapped, "Well, it's the law." Her fingers found the object of her search, and she pulled a cigarette lighter smeared with custard from the gummy morass. She offered it, asking, "Please?"

Xavier took the sticky lighter. He sniffed it lightly, as if he might lick it clean. At the flick of his thumb, the lighter emitted a hissing blue flame.

Shasta stooped to bring her candles within his reach. Doing so she got him around one wrist and twisted his hand so she could read the title of the book he held. *Atlas Shrugged*. Dr. Brolly had taught the book last semester.

As he put the lighter to each wick, Xavier began to sing, "Happy birthday to you . . ." Then he stopped singing and said, "We're all self-deporting. The entire Mexican Diaspora is going Galt." Meaning all Hispanics, Latinos, Chicanos were headed south of the border. "These white people are *muy loco*," he laughed. "After they all starve or wipe out each other, we'll come pick up the pieces."

Mexico in the meantime would, as Xavier put it, "blossom like something out of the Italian Renaissance."

Shasta kept her head bowed slightly. Staring at her wooden clogs, she asked, "Is there wax in my hair?"

"European archeology," Xavier continued, "has imposed its own bogus narrative on Pre-Columbian everything." For example, he cited the paintings and carvings reputed to show Aztecs ripping out the hearts of human sacrifices. He knew for a fact such artwork actually depicted Mesoamericans conducting successful heart transplant surgeries. The lofty stone slabs atop their pyramids were in actuality operating tables placed where the healthy daylight was strongest.

"Even more amazing," continued Xavier, "the paintings that showed tribesmen severing heads and holding them in the air as blood gushed and veins dangled from the severed necks . . ."

Shasta cringed.

Those gristly scenes, he explained, were, in truth, proof of successful full head transplants.

"White scientists," the young man half-shouted, "have to deny what they themselves can't replicate!"

Near them a young woman stepped up to peer into a shop window. The candles sprouting from her crown set the shop's striped awning on fire. Not far off, another young woman sipped a mocha at a sidewalk cafe, unaware that her candles were slowly igniting the Cinzano umbrella above her head.

Xavier held the cigarette lighter for her to take. "Come with me," he demanded. "Leave these crazy gringos to destroy themselves."

It was tempting, and Shasta definitely felt tempted. Her parents had already self-deported to the Yucatan Peninsula. Not to mention that Xavier looked alpha macho hot with just enough dirt smudged on his hip-hugging white jeans that they didn't read as gay. His gay brother had probably skated off to Gaysia. No wonder Xavier wanted company. He was so alone.

She accepted the lighter and snapped open her purse. "I'm supposed to give these pastries to strangers." She sunk the lighter into the sugary muck. "It's a weird ritual that goes with wearing a candle hat." Shasta was stalling, not wanting to break Xavier's heart. But she really needed to find Walter. To redirect, she offered the open purse. "Here's a chocolate éclair that doesn't look too mangled."

Xavier got the message. He took the damaged éclair. The whipped cream bristled with stray hairs. Its flaky goodness was flecked with purse lint and embedded with stray breath mints. "Thanks," he sighed. He looked wounded but still highly doable.

"Thank you for lighting my candle," she said lamely. She turned slowly and, step by careful step, balancing her halo of fire, forced herself to walk away.

It was a national disgrace. Nothing less than a badge of shame, as far as Charlie saw it. Blacktopia had only recently announced a successful launch of its new flying pyramid, based on a long-forgotten antigravity technology suppressed by Eurocentric interests. After centuries of white denial the blacks had proven that pyramids built by the Egyptian pharaohs were in fact flying machines.

While whites had been hiring esteemed film director Stanley Kubrick to dummy up convincing moon landing footage in the New Mexico desert, the blacks had kept their own functional method of space travel a secret for ten centuries.

Well, the secret was out. Charlie crouched in front of the television and watched news footage broadcast from Blacktopia. It clearly showed gargantuan Cheops-sized pyramids levitating off the ground at a military installation. These impossible stone ships rose into a blue sky. One great ship had already landed safely on the moon, near the site NASA had claimed as their own in the fictional late 1960s stunt. In a matter of days black astronauts would venture forth to explore the site. They'd find no American flag. No golf balls or moon buggy tire tracks.

The white ethno state of Caucasia teetered on the brink of total humiliation.

To distract himself from the inevitable, Charlie cracked open a copy of the Talbott book. He read from it even while his handlers entered his great throne room to present selections of comely young women who hoped to become his bride.

The television continued to goad with images of huge pyramids floating above a prosperous landscape peopled by proud, beautiful blacks. Their dashikis flashed vivid colors. They carried themselves—men, women, and children alike—with the posture of nobility, with their spines straight, their shoulders thrown back, as if every citizen were an aristocrat.

How Talbott Reynolds explained it, the smartest most determined faction of blacks had been on a labor strike since 1600 or thereabouts. The idea of Adjustment Day had resided within them like a seed for generations. To this end they'd practiced their fierceness by targeting one another, knowing those in power wouldn't take note of a brother wasting a brother. According to Talbott, whites had practiced for Adjustment Day with school and workplace shootings. Gays had wasted gays with AIDS. The homos went to gyms and learned to destroy with their beauty. All the factions had been building a cold-blooded ability toward the future takeover.

If they could acclimate to killing their own brothers and sisters without hesitation or remorse, surely they could slaughter their masters in politics, media, and academia. When the time came, they'd cease killing each other and turn their rage outward.

This in-group collateral damage stoked each army's fury toward those safe, insulated, so-called leaders who'd come to the fore buoyed on good speechwriters and kissing babies, but who'd never demonstrated any real physical power in the world.

The opioid-addled, NASCAR rubes . . . the grill-grinning, thuggish blacks . . . the sex-crazed queers . . . they'd rehearsed for Adjustment Day on soft targets in their own communities, and no one suspected anything would manifest beyond these in-group killings. And the practice taught blacks to shoot better. It taught the queers how to smile their way handsomely into anyone's trust. And it schooled the whites about the patterns of flight that a mass of terrified people under fire will take.

As Talbott explained events, they weren't a fluke. Adjustment Day had come a day closer with every drive-by shooting, every viral transmission, every letter carrier going postal. Once those groups had fully shed their humanity, it was only inevitable they decimate their shared oppressors.

On television, a vast, flying pyramid hovered in the sunny, cloudless sky above the dancing, cheering hordes of Blacktopia. Their gold jewelry flashed, as did their smiles of complete joy and unbounded pride.

It felt as if the white race had lost its way. It no longer had blacks and queers to feel superior to so a key source of its pride was gone. Whites had been like a wealthy family who performed an ongoing pageant of morality and ingenuity to impress a household of idiot and degenerate servants. In the absence of queers and blacks, Charlie and his fellow whites had lost their motivation to live superior lives. Without underlings to dazzle, the white ethno state seemed to be floundering.

He muted the television's sound and watched the jubilant, dancing citizens of Blacktopia.

The white race was like a father who'd survived his children. He had no one around to harangue or impress. No weak, flawed version of himself to lecture or rescue. Like a god who'd watched his last creation die. In the new, neat, orderly world of the white ethno state, what did the future hold? The white race had met its every challenge. Could they make the grass greener? Make the trains run more exactly on schedule?

Moments like this made Adjustment Day feel like a giant step backward. Following the risky social experiments of the last three hundred years, white people could only return to a world of knights and aristocrats. A fortress of Norman Rockwell, *Reader's Digest* prettiness.

A voice whispered in Charlie's ear. His majordomo alerting him, "Some female guests for your review, sir."

The heel-clicking, kowtowing flunky filled him with sick disdain. Any man who hadn't taken part, hands-on, in the butchery sickened Charlie. He'd made his mark, Charlie had proven his valor, and that meant for the rest of his life weaker men would avoid him. Cowards would resent and despise his achievements. He would exist alone for most of the rest of his life, with none but his own counsel, because his true peers were few. That's what made the selection of the perfect mate so all-fired important. Important but hardly easy.

Charlie set aside the book and clicked the remote to resolve the images on television. He scarcely needed to turn his head to take in the sight of the nubile young fillies being herded in. Dressed in short, pastel skirts that suggested Easter eggs, they fidgeted. Their doe eyes tried to capture and hold his attention. Eyelashes batted. Glistening lips pursed. Some drew deep breaths and thrust out their chests. He wasn't fooled. How could they understand what it was to be anything beyond being female? They lived such corporeal lives, not believing in anything beyond the visible, the tangible, the openly stated.

Amid this chaos of preening, one drew his focus. One among them stood with a regal stillness, her willowy limbs motionless, a potential queen. Her honeyed hair pooled on the shoulders of her richly embroidered peasant smock. Charlie could picture her swinging a scythe in fertile fields of golden wheat. Her loins would push forth a new generation of gods. Charlie would sire in her a horde of inventors and artists to revitalize the white race.

He studied her ivory arms and the pear-shaped swell of each innocent breast. Her small feet were otherwise bare in simple, leather sandals. Her periwinkle eyes hinted at a docile, animal intelligence. Charlie indicated her with the slightest flick of his fingertips, bidding, "Little one . . ."

At most, she appeared to be only a year or two his junior. Using his lordliest voice, he inquired, "How are you called, girl child?"

For a breath she stared back, speechless. Perhaps she'd heard how, for weeks, he'd done little more than glance at the parade of prospective wives. He'd yet to speak directly to any of the legions of attractive females. Her muteness added to her appeal, and Charlie felt his sex excite at the idea of having her soon.

When she failed to speak, the majordomo broke in. "Sire," the man said, "her name is Shasta."

Shasta. Queen Shasta.

She would be his, Charlie's perfect Aryan consort.

Few thoughts in her mind were her own, living on soda crackers and gin as she was. Miss Josephine dared not eat the food Arabella brought up. She assiduously flushed it in bite-sized chunks, but only late at night when no one would hear. Night and day she'd taken to leaving her little television play. She needed the company, despite how it was always just that Talbott man. According to him the white folks were glad to surrender Jackson, Mississippi. Just as glad as the blacks were to abandon Detroit. He said it was a three-hundred-year embarrassment to ethno Europeans that they couldn't till their rice plantations or cut their own tobacco or sugar cane in the sweltering heat. Michigan amounted to little more than snow and rusted fenders. Whites needed winter, said Talbott, needed an enforced rest, otherwise they went crazy with their labors. Blacks despised the ridiculous snow.

One could picture Talbott, a performance on paper in his book, fully in character as saying such. Instances of lunatic insight, Miss Josephine called them. An insanity that passes as the new sanity.

He said southern whites had balked at migrating north immediately after the War of Northern Aggression because they didn't want to prove the *New York Times* right. They had no business in Georgia or Mississippi or Louisiana. But to tuck their tails and relinquish the South to its rightful occupants would be to allow the second shoe of the war to finally drop. Ethno Europeans wouldn't miss those landscapes of kudzu and water moccasins. To retain Florida was to pose smiling with a dead body, the body of an infant daughter wearing a lace christening gown and a tiny pearl necklace and to pretend that girl would someday come back to health. Florida was death to white people.

As if he spoke directly to Miss Josephine, Talbott waxed eloquent concerning the miasmas and the swampland's constant pull toward decay and corruption. Nothing on Earth could sustain the whites of the South except their own Scots-Irish obstinacy. Malignant breezes and the steaming everglades offered whites nothing except skin cancer and malaria. In the North, cities like Chicago and Philadelphia afflicted blacks with vitamin D deficiencies, malnutrition, and frostbite.

Miss Josephine, perched on high in this cramped suite of rooms, rooms crowded as a junk shop with every silver cup and trophy, every diploma, diary, memory, and family Bible, she was the brain of things. A sentry in an isolated outpost. The spirit, spirited upstairs, among the spirits of the cellar's wealth, she'd ordered the entire inventory of brandy and Madera port interred with her for safe keeping. The cases of it, smuggled by blockade runners during the war for seccession.

A drunken, fleeting impulse dawned upon Miss Jo. She could burn these treasures. The past rested in her hands as a steward or an executioner. She could burn this house and all the flawed relics within it.

Charlie knew what the problem was. You see, the white race had learned to sublimate its sexual impulses. It had learned to delay gratification and to invent electric lights and mammograms and botany instead of just jerking off to porn or poling every skank who needed it. The result was that white people, mostly white men, in all honesty, had created technology and gotten the kudos of a perfect civilization where stuff worked. Trouble came when other races didn't sublimate like they ought to, they just kept on railing every piece of snatch, AIDS or not, herpes or not, and kept cranking out the babies. You see, the white men had traded babies for the patent on everything good and the royalties, which were considerable, except the white man had neglected the big race. The population race. That's how Charlie saw the situation. Seeing how the white man was so busy not fucking that he had energy leftover to invent solar energy. But this left him losing the reins. It's all in Stoddard. You see, technology and babies always seek a balance throughout history. When technology got ahead, babies fell off. And when babies got ahead, then civilization fell behind. Right now mankind's progress was about to get swallowed in a sea of other people's babies, and that meant giving up vulcanized rubber and reverse osmosis because there wouldn't be the smart people needed to run those segments of society.

If white people could slack off. If they could just take a break from anodizing everything and maybe just nail some pussy, then civilization would have a chance. Not that white women were much help. No, they were only just getting their feet wet with inventing X-rays and eBay, and they obviously did not savor the idea of giving up public accolades and putting their legs in the air. That's why Adjustment Day had gone down. It would give the few remaining alpha studs the chance to boost white numbers. It would remove the temptation of Women's Studies degrees and other horseshit that baited ladies to let their precious Aryan eggs dry up.

Adjustment Day gave men like Charlie, with loads of sperm and not the best grasp of Calculus II, the opportunity to catch up the game for the white team.

Simple as that.

Dawson hadn't the heart to cut off the woman's ear. It didn't matter how much she'd begged. She'd finally snatched up the carpet cutter and began to do it herself, then gave up in tears.

She knelt there in the dust at his feet. Standing over her, he could see the top of her right ear was crusted with dried blood. Apparently she'd tried, likely several times, to slice off the ear by herself.

Detail followed detail about her Adjustment Day. First, despite her request that students silence their phones, a phone began to sound an alarm. Another joined it. A chorus of phones were marking the same moment. Beeps and squeaks and dog barks, a cacophony. And it wasn't as if a smattering of students in the huge auditorium reached into their Hello Kitty and G.I. Joe backpacks and produced guns. The professor and her team of graduate assistants looked on in confusion as *every* hand reached down alongside a desk. A deafening chorus of countless zippers roared. *Every student* sat upright, extending an arm, and gripped in every raised hand was a firearm.

"It looked," she said, her voice faltering. One of her trembling hands flailed in the air. "A forest of black sticks were pointing at us." The short barrels of pistols, the longer barrels of rifles and shotguns, and in between were the muzzles of revolvers.

The black sticks belched fire, a wall of muzzle flash and smoke, the smell of black powder, and a graduate student crashed to the stage with two thuds. She could hear nothing after the first blast.

The graduate student dragged himself toward her. His legs remained where they'd fallen, but his torso and arms dragged themselves pathetically toward safety, dragging his ravaged bowels like greasy fringe behind him. He'd, crawled his way near where she crouched behind the podium. Bullets and blasts of buckshot exploded the screen behind them and punched holes in the plaster walls.

The only sound was the constant firing. She couldn't hear if he'd actually said the words, but as the graduate student extended his blue, dying, already dead hand toward her, his dead man's lips formed the words, "Help me . . ."

Around her, her precious team of adjunct professors, the team she'd carefully handpicked and spent years assembling and recruiting from other institutions, they were flopping like beached dolphins, mangled beyond anything alive but kept leaping like puppets and obscenely jerking as ordinance slammed into their corpses.

She'd risked reaching out from behind the podium. Her fingers laced themselves between the boy's icy fingers and she dragged his sodden bulk to safety. His head resting on her lap, he looked to be asleep.

Dawson clenched his jaw to keep himself from asking the graduate student's name.

Now with Dawson, the woman no longer sobbing, she looked at the ground morosely, muttering, "Only days shy of completing his doctoral thesis on gender fluidity . . ." Her entire body seemed to convulse with the emotional pain. "Just because he made some undergrads read bell hooks!"

They promenaded through his gardens, Charlie and his bride-to-be. Idling among the ancient Roman bird baths and classical Hellenistic lawn ornaments requisitioned from leading museums throughout the formerly united states. He pointed out a Babylonian garden ornament he found when they sacked the Getty. Hoping to impress her, he called her attention to a mess of yellow petunias planted in a Mesopotamian carved-stone thing he got at the National Museum in Washington, D.C. Peacocks paraded their glory, but they were nothing compared to Shasta.

Duly impressed, she'd looked at the million-year-old Egyptian statue of some lady. Charlie had his team paint it Kelly green to match his new lawn furniture. Shasta saw it and said, "Neat-o."

He wanted to show her the boss stuff he'd scored from the Art Institute of Chicago. Really old stuff. Stuff he hoped she'd like, too. The courtship screening was just about complete. They still needed her genetic test to prove she was officially white, but that was just a formality. One look and he knew she was white. The clear sky might've been modeled after her periwinkle blue eyes. Birdsong could not compete with her laugh. Such an innocent she was, so sweet, so naïve. She still believed in global warming and the Holocaust.

Charlie suspected he was ear-raping her, but he was nervous. He couldn't stop talking.

He made her stand and admire the big candleholders he'd picked up at some church or another on Fifth Avenue. Solid gold or something so it was okay to use outdoors, year-round. He made her squat down, put her hands around one, and try to lift it to see how heavy. She couldn't.

"Pretty cool," she agreed.

New junk was arriving daily. More old dust catchers from the Getty, stuff from the Metropolitan Museum of Art in New York, even. A crew of guys did nothing but unpack the crates and try to find spots to stick everything.

As they strolled, he tried to impress upon her the difficulties of his life. Living as an aristocrat took some getting used to. Like, all the lives that hung on his every utterance. Not to mention the rich food omnipotent moguls were expected to eat. This morning, for instance, he felt positively poop-raped by his morning bowel movement.

Thus their formal courtship had begun, and with it Shasta's education. And Charlie read to her passages from the book of Talbott. Slowly, he read that a woman decides early whether to love the soul within her womb, or to discard it. Once that belly child is birthed naturally, be it black or brown or Asian, she can't help but feel love and pride for it. An impulse that explained so much of women's artwork.

On the contrary, a white man must find the newborn to be a healthy facsimile of himself before he loves it. For white men are so constantly under siege, beset by corrupt ideas and the degrading efforts of lesser races, that the white man must be certain his offspring will be his loyal ally.

In the glorious new world, Charlie assured her, all children would have value. Not even a homosexual child was worthless. Once it reached the age of declaration it could be exchanged for an innocent boy or girl heterosexual raised by mistake in captivity by homosexuals.

As minstrels serenaded them on lyres and pipes in daisy-dense fields, Charlie read aloud to her from the Talbott book:

> God alone can create anything new. We can only recognize patterns, identify the unseen, and combine things to create slight variations.

He read:

> Adjustment Day was brought about by the resolution of resolution.

As per Talbott, technology and morality have created a climate where nothing short of death resolves anything. Feuds live eternally on the Internet. No one can escape any moment of his past. Nothing is forgotten. Conversely, men have adapted to accept shame and humiliation as a passing obstacle. No public figure, no matter how exposed and revealed to be a degenerate, leaves the public eye for long. There was no closure in closure. Adjustment Day occurred to resolve the fact that nothing could be resolved.

On the radio, Talbott read the news: "The unified council of the lineages report that the body of the President of the formerly united states has not been recovered. He has been missing since Adjustment Day, and officials are investigating the possibility that he fled the government, assisted by agents of a foreign power.

"Lineage spokesmen report that a bomb has been detonated in a crowded public street in the white ethno state . . . In Blacktopia . . . in Gaysia . . . and two persons . . . six persons . . . eighteen persons are believed to be killed as a result.

"Terrorists working in league with the former president have claimed responsibility for the gas attack . . . arson . . . acts of sabotage . . . Citizens with information about these crimes should contact a lineage representative immediately."

As the blue-black book predicted:

> During times of greatest moral and ethical
> crisis people will side with those noble leaders
> who possess the greatest number of guns.

As Talbott had foreseen, a form of Stockholm syndrome took hold. People accepted the new leaders because people wanted leaders and the former were dead. The details of who would run the government were secondary to the everyday details of their own lives. Providing for their children, for example. Or completing their work or education. Or finding a mate. Those persons who stood to be most affected by the impending war felt a rush of relief. The citizenry was accustomed to adapting to the government's demands. The exact nature of the government was of less consequence.

Naturally, many were offended by the violent means taken, but no one so much that he wanted to throw away his own life in protest. The dead were dead.

Each person had been gifted with a dollop of intelligence. Each dollop met and shared with others. As per Talbott, our souls cling unto our bodies the way non-swimmers grip the edge of a swimming pool.

Planes crisscrossed the sky. Each planeload a population being relocated to their appropriate homeland. The young among them happy to take part in the largest social improvement in modern history. The older, defeated. Households were packed and shipped. Those surrendering their property had gone online and selected an available home of equal value from among those forfeited by other relocated populations. In airports, families kept their children close and studied the photos on their phones, the video tours of homes, farms, and apartments for which they qualified.

To call this a social experiment was incorrect. It would never be allowed to fail. Those involved must make it a success.

A hundred years past midnight, Delicious and her husband lingered in each other's arms after a conjugal visit in a bus station toilet stall.

"They call Jarvis an 'Uncle Tom of Finland,'" said Gentry.

Delicious asked, "What's that mean?"

Gentry shrugged and shook his head. "Something about too many muscles," he said. "It's not a compliment." He gazed down a moment too long, studying the muck on the toilet stall floor. He asked, "Is that a Percocet?"

Delicious wanted to ask if he and Jarvis fucked. Men would fuck mud. But she didn't want the wrong answer so she kept silent.

Perhaps whites had suspected. In recent years white popular culture had stumbled perilously close to discovering the immense wisdom and power blacks had long concealed. Whites had imbued the fictional character of the so-called magic negro with psychic talents and spiritual abilities that hinted at the immense gifts blacks actually held in check. But with the advent of Blacktopia at last the sisters who'd acted the parts of based crackheads and morbidly obese welfare cheats, going so far as to glue white women's hair to their own heads in a mockery of white beauty standards that the self-centered white buffoons took to be a compliment, these regal black sisters could finally cast off their Falstaffian roles and take their rightful place as unstoppable healers and knowers of great cosmic truths.

In keeping with their birthright, Blacktopians strode languidly the broad avenues of their Earth-friendly cities. Their long limbs glowing. Their women, willowy and glossy with confident wisdom. Immaculate spires jutted gracefully into the clear skies, defying the Stone Age physics of the backward white man.

Blacks didn't so much saunter as they glided in continuous movement. Theirs were not the jerking steps taken by citizens of Caucasia. The white man's language had no words for movement this fluid, smoothed beyond smooth. More so with each such shortcoming, the white language was falling by the wayside and Blacktopia resurrected its own ancient tongue.

Whereas white history was written in words, black history was written in melodies.

Brothers shrugged off the mantle of violent psychotic killers, characterizations so broad and coarse that only the crude whites were ever fooled. It had become an inside joke: How outlandishly could the brothers behave? How far could they push with their music before the white oppressors might begin to wonder if the whole performance was for their benefit?

If they spoke loudly and laughed louder it was to hide the truth that most of their communication with one another took place through mental telepathy.

Free to assume their legacy as learned shamans, the brothers gleefully shed their brimmed caps and knotted kerchiefs, red and blue trappings of their pretend gang affiliations. They laughed a final good-bye to the slippery Ebonics with which they'd hidden their genius from the white man. Masked by those coded words were the formulas for alchemizing precious diamonds from sand, and the newly freed brothers called forth mass quantities of diamonds, and manifested a like bulk of rubies and flawless emeralds, and fashioned the total of these jewels to create immense palaces that caught the sunlight and blazed within like heavenly rainbows the likes of which the white man's puny stained-glass cathedral windows could never approach.

In Blacktopia the people continued to sing their praise to the Earth, and in gratitude diamonds sprouted through the ground, the size of skyscrapers, and lanced the clouds like minarets. And molten gold bubbled up and hardened instantly to form domed palaces to house the faithful.

Sheltered in this paradise of color, the blacks retook the destiny that had been withheld from them under white rule. For the first time in recorded history, black efforts would benefit only blacks and not line the coffers of an enemy. And the cities known as Atlanta and Birmingham and Miami, white cities all, they were laid waste to, and the majestic blacks, their muscular backs gleaming with clean sweat, they sang into existence glorious temples to honor their predecessors, and these edifices excited the skyline with shapes too astounding for whites to envision, and within these mammoth villas the brothers and the sisters lived in perfect accord with all animals, in impeccable harmony with nature and the spirit world.

The few whites allowed to set eyes upon the wonders of Blacktopia, they retreated in weeping awe. And to preserve their stubborn, caveman fantasy of superiority, these white men loudly and vehemently claimed the jeweled palaces and interplanetary flying pyramids were lies and outright illusions. And when the sisters had eradicated all forms of cancer from Blacktopia, jealous whites demanded proof, but what proof can be provided of what does not exist? For in their wisdom the sisters had sourced the ageless spirits and enlisted those haunts to banish cancer and AIDS and herpes until not a single black was afflicted.

And while the whites strived to increase their numbers, white science and technology stalled. And certain whites were not above infiltrating Blacktopia to plunder its brilliance. For white science and mathematics had been harnessed only to build atomic bombs while black intellect yielded, daily, new wonders that enriched life, especially the lives of women, for Blacktopia held its sisters as its greatest treasure.

And following the pattern of white men such as journalist John Griffin, who darkened his face with methoxsalen and ultraviolet light and slithered forth to appropriate black achievement and black experience and present it as his own in the book *Black Like Me*, and in doing so make his fortune . . . in the same way, white men of Caucasia masked themselves and wormed their way across the border.

Such folly! For the whites knew only to mimic the ridiculous elaborate handshakes and saggy-pants gibberish speak the blacks had affected, and the brothers recognized at once these shuffling imposters. Would-be thieves, these squabbling, gun-waving, hip-shaking, crotch-grabbing crackers in blackface, they were humored and led to believe they'd successfully infiltrated Blacktopia. There, the brothers schooled them to partake of their own urine as a supposed cure for cancer, and the would-be cultural thieves ran home, and pretty much all whites adopted the practice.

The instruction sheet specified *machine-washable only* and *durability*. Gavyn pulled the dry cleaner's plastic off his favorite Sand shirt and undid the buttons. He looped it off the hanger. So tailored. The oranges and reds so saturated. He'd worn it twice, afraid he might stain it or that the colors would fade. Holding the collar tucked under his chin, he folded the shirt against his chest, matching the sleeves. He folded the folded shirt a second time and a third to make a smooth neat packet he placed into the empty suitcase on his bed.

A voice. Not his mother's. His sister, Charm, said, "That's so not-the-right shirt." She stood leaning sideways in his doorway, her arms crossed. Charm held up a stop-sign hand to hush any back-talk. She went to the open closet and her shoulders slumped in resignation. The array of retro cowboy shirts with pearlized snaps. The Dolce knock-off pullovers with metalicized detailing. Vintage Versace. Before her was the trousseau Gavyn had built for his adult life. His homosexual hope chest, as it were.

His sister plucked at the front of her own army surplus uniform shirt. "This will wear like iron." Olive drab. Untucked, the tails hung halfway to the knees of her blue jeans. The closest thing she could find in his closet was a thrift store shirt of canvas-like khaki-green material enlivened with embroidered patches. A secondhand Boy Scout uniform complete with Eagle Scout badge.

Gavyn protested, "It's permanent press."

Charm tossed aside the Sand shirt and replaced it with the khaki. "It's not a fashion show," she said. "It's a *concentration camp*."

The Talbott book called the place an Inventory Retention Center. Until recently, until Adjustment Day, the particular one where Gavyn had been assigned had been a low-security prison.

The year of Initial Relocation neared its end. Those born into the wrong homeland—homosexuals born to heterosexuals, or those with an inappropriate preponderance of sub-Saharan or Caucasoid DNA—they'd be surrendered by their source families, to government custody until a like mis-birth in the appropriate homeland could be identified for exchange. Somewhere in Gaysia, God willing, an eighteen-year-old heterosexual was packing a suitcase, headed for a similar holding camp. After almost two decades of being fed, dressed, and educated, Gavyn and his ilk represented too big of an investment to be left unattended. If they attempted to emigrate illegally or escape to Canada or to commit suicide, the nation stood to lose a sizable export commodity.

He wondered, idly, if there was an underground railroad to allow mis-births a more speedy path to their rightful homeland. To side-step the normal wait for a suitable candidate for the exchange. A system of safe houses. Human traffickers. Maybe there existed coyotes he could pay to guide him through the borderlands.

Charm pulled out the top drawer of the bureau and dug among Gavyn's socks. Of these she selected two pairs dark blue, three black, a pair plain green, and six pairs of white sweat socks. Tucking them into the suitcase, she said, "At least you're not baby-making machinery for some chieftain."

Fat chance she'd end up a chieftain's wife, not with her sun-burned face and cropped hair. Another reason he was surrendering for retention and export. If an equivalent trade wasn't available, the accepting homeland would have to pay upwards of a half million Talbotts in compensation. Gavyn's parents could use the money. Even Charm had to know that. They could buy a business, a small farm, seed corn, livestock, all the staples they'd need to be self-sufficient in the new economy. Otherwise, they'd become like all their fellow former-white-collar, former-information-technology, former-paper-pushing professionals: To survive they'd need to submit themselves as serfs to a local chieftain.

Others might hightail it for the border. Or suck death from the tailpipe in a closed garage. But with some patience, Gavyn figured this could end as a win-win. He'd assimilate in Gaysia, and his source family would own their livelihood and their freedom.

His sister knelt beside the bed and reached underneath, pulling out tennis shoes and loafers. A pair of each she bagged in plastic grocery sacks and nestled into the suitcase beside a folded pair of cargo shorts she'd selected. Shorts Gavyn hated. These sat on top of camo pants she'd recommended because they'd never show stains. Sandwiched between these, she placed a plastic Tupperware box containing his toothbrush, his razor, toothpaste, and comb. His Sand shirt, beautiful and impractical in all its orange plaid glory, lay on the bed where she'd relegated it.

What his sister said next, he didn't catch.

"I asked," Charm repeated, "did you hear about that guy, Walter?"

Gavyn looked around his room for a long, last time. "Walter who?"

She prompted, "Who used to go with Shasta from school?"

He shook his head. "Why?"

His sister looked at the space remaining in the suitcase. She pulled a heavy wool sweater and a lighter cotton one from the top shelf of the closet. These she balled up and packed. Back at the bureau she ignored the Andrew Christian microfiber, stylized, butt-baring athletic supporters in favor of his old-school Y-front tighty whities. She rolled up a baggy pair of drawstring shorts she said could do double duty as swimwear.

She asked something.

Gavyn asked, "Again?"

Lightly, as if he were only going off to summer camp for the rest of his life, his sister asked, "Miss me?"

He told himself there would be better clothes, better everything in his future, better than everything he'd be forced to leave behind. Clothes and love enough he'd never give a second thought to the pathetic wardrobe he'd bought with his lawn-mowing and dog-walking wages. Out there, somewhere, was a love that would make him forget his sister and his source parents.

The suitcase filled, Charm said, "Don't worry. It will be fun." She said, "Who knows?" But it was only her mouth saying it.

He caught sight of her in the mirror over his bureau. As his back was turned, she secretively lifted the beautiful orange-plaid shirt and tucked it beneath all the practical long-lasting denim and canvas. She closed the suitcase and zippered it shut.

As the housekeeper coiled strands of hair into tight pin curls, Miss Josephine leaned forward over an open book. Heavy in her lap lay a fly-specked copy of *Gone with the Wind*, and as her eyes scanned

Margaret Mitchell's dialog, Miss Josephine's lips silently mouthed the dialectic patois. Her lips stung as she pressed them with coarse grains of rock salt. Her lips stung and swelled until they'd begun to split and she could taste the blood mixed with salt on her tongue.

On the surface of the vanity in front of her sat her dentures. The teeth almost glowed with coat upon coat of pearlized white fingernail polish. In the dark, total darkness, they would glow due to the phosphorescent dyes Miss Jo had added to the polish.

Beyond the book, the image she saw in the mirror delighted her. Methoxsalen, like John Griffin used when writing *Black Like Me*, it had worked its magic. Just as it had for that Sprigle man, the reporter who'd taken massive doses of the drug in 1948 and toured the South to write his book *In the Land of Jim Crow*. Not to be outdone, the reporter Grace Halsell had gone blackface to write her own tome in 1969, *Soul Sister*. Nosy American newshounds were always blacking up and writing about their madcap adventures.

Not that they'd invented the trick. Al Jolson in 1927. Freeman Gosden and Charles Correll as Amos 'n' Andy in 1928. Judy Garland as early as 1938's *Everybody Sing*, then again with Mickey Rooney in 1941 for *Babes on Broadway*. All it took was thirty milligrams of methoxsalen, followed by time under a sunlamp. Even now ultraviolet lights shone on Miss Jo from each of several different angles, evenly exposing her bare arms, her legs, neck, and face as she perspired daintily in her lace chemise.,

The side effects might include headaches, dizziness, insomnia, and nausea, but that hadn't stopped the lovely Ava Gardner from playing a beautiful black siren in *Show Boat*. Nor had possible kidney damage dissuaded Jeanne Crain from becoming a pretty black girl child in 1949's landmark film *Pinky*. As late as 1965, Laurence Olivier had risked his health to play the black Othello. Liver damage was a threat with methoxsalen, as was cancer. Even now Miss Josephine's head swam. Her vision blurred. But these were a small price to pay for a miracle drug that allowed white people to become black people.

Not that Arabella understood. The silly woman yanked on another strand of hair and twisted it around a bobby pin. Most of the hair lay tight against her scalp in similar little knots. For the next step, the housekeeper would apply the perm solution. She'd wait just a little too long before applying the stopping agent. She'd use pineapple juice because it offered the perfect acidity. By waiting a smidgen too long, they'd burn the hair a mite. After the pins were out, once Miss Jo fluffed the kinked, tightly curled hair, it would stand around her face like a lush onyx halo. Dyed of course.

Between the pain of her hair being pulled at, and the queasiness in her tummy, her salted, swelled-up lips and her sweaty skin, Miss Jo struggled to pronounce the antiquated talk just as Mitchell had written it. The reflection that stared back from her vanity mirror hardly resembled Ava Gardner's enchanting character Julie La Verne, but that newly minted person would be Miss Jo's escape from the strain of her current tenuous circumstance.

Exactly as Talbott Reynolds had asked, Walter had launched the list online. First, people had joked about it. No, first they'd ignored it. Only after they'd noticed, then they'd ridiculed the site. Once it had garnered a few million postings, some people had taken offense and demanded it be banned. These had been mostly the people whose names drew the most votes, the politicians and academics and media celebrities. Walter had sat in the basement of the abandoned house and refreshed his screen every hour, and marveled at the response.

He'd asked Talbott, "How do we monetize?" He'd had in mind buying houses, the big scheme he'd dreamt up to seduce Shasta.

Talbott, as always tied to a chair, Talbott woozy with blood loss and dappled with scabs and razorblade scars, he'd said, "Write down these names . . ." As his infected cuts drained, he'd proceeded to rattle off a dozen names that Walter had hurriedly scribbled on his pad. "Search online," Talbott had commanded. "Contact each man."

Walter perused the list. "This will make me rich?"

Feverish, glassy eyed, Walter's new old man had asked, "You? I should make you rich?"

Walter had hit Refresh and tried to hide his annoyance. He'd considered adding Talbott's name to the list. Now he'd have to hunt down these dozen men and most likely contact them. Lately, Talbott had seemed to be baiting him. This entire scheme might've been the old man's snipe hunt.

The old man had rallied. "To make your fortune," he'd advised, "buy fake fur."

Walter had repeated, "Fake?"

The old man had nodded gravely. "Fur . . . Naugahyde," he'd intoned, "Pleather, too." His head had settled to one side, asleep.

Walter had hit Refresh.

A musician followed them at a distance, piping a soft melody on a recorder. An array of peacocks fanned the air with their exotic tails as Shasta strolled past, her arm delicately linked with Charlie's. The gardens fell away on every side, planted in elaborate patterns of fennel and asparagus. The matter of her saliva had reared its ugly head, yet again. In the olden times, prior to Adjustment Day, boys had pressured her for fellatio. Charlie only bullied her for a genetic sample to prove her ethnicity. She'd been putting him off for weeks, placating him with oral sex and fetishistic nurse costumes, but today he'd fallen into a sullen pout.

As they walked, their silence broken only by the recorder and the frequent screams of peacocks, the answer occurred to her. A girl she'd known in college. A free spirit Shasta had all but forgotten: Charm.

A girl like none other. Only Charm was Charm.

In World Mythologies, Dr. Brolly had taught them ancient Greek legends of Bellerophon, the hero who'd tamed the flying horse, Pegasus. He'd battled and defeated the all-girl legions of the Amazons, and he'd slaughtered the dragon, Chimaera. Undefeated, he'd bade the god Poseidon to flood the nation of Xanthus, but the womenfolk of Xanthus had confronted the approaching waves. These enterprising females had lifted their skirts and faced the ocean with girl parts fully bared.

Cross culturally, from Europe to Indonesia and South America, the ancient world had believed that exposed pussies would always frighten away evil. Up until the eighteenth century, above the doorways and gateways of castles and churches, masons had carved images of women squatting to reveal themselves. Neither Satan nor any evil could endure the sight of the female sex organs, it was said.

Confronted by all the vaginas of Xanthus, the tides receded in fear. The waves retreated, and Bellerophon met defeat. Even the flying Pegasus had freaked out and bolted away.

Walking arm in arm with Charlie, Shasta reflected on what had happened not long after that study module on the ancient world.

Charm had apparently taken the lesson to heart. Back in those weeks before Adjustment Day, when the doomed surplus males of the youth bulge had come courting, she'd put her recent education to good use. The boys varsity lacrosse team had, on one occasion, encircled her in an otherwise deserted hallway. Playfully, the aggressive teens had endeavored to mouth her breasts through her sweater, and to goose her with their mechanical pencils. Rather than pity them as imminent cannon fodder, Charm had readily applied the teachings of antiquity.

As they'd danced around her, Charm had simply lifted the front of her skimpy cheerleader skirt. Unmasked by underclothes, it had been fully exposed: Her vulva. Weaned on the tame hairless vaginas of pornography, the young men had recoiled in terror. As a charging army of hairy vaginas had spooked the winged stallion Pegasus, Charm's hirsute sexual center had shocked those would-be suitors. As their jeering had fallen silent, she'd clenched her buttocks, thrusting her sex at them like a deadly saber. Panicked, they'd toppled backward. They'd scrambled to their feet and fled, but even as they'd raced in retreat Charm had kept her skirt raised and charged them with her thrusting strawberry blonde pubic hair, so much like the ruff around the devouring mouth of a ferocious African lion. As if to add to this impression she emitted snarls and roars as if the pussy itself had suddenly found its own savage voice.

Shasta had witnessed the rout take place. The playful flirting followed by the assault from the unbridled vagina. She'd watched Charm chase the lacrosse boys as far as the faculty parking lot. As the terrified youngsters had disappeared into the distance, Shasta had risked approaching the bold girl. A gal like that, even then reverting back to her normal self, smoothing her skirt down and reapplying her pink lip gloss, this girl would be a free thinker. She'd been the ultimate in white beauty, combing her long blonde hair and regarding the world through glacial blue eyes. Back then she'd been young and lithe, but there'd already been some hint of the crusty old broad about Charm. She'd never shrink from a challenge.

Alone with such a girl, Shasta had ventured to ask, "How's it going?" The two girls had their mythology in common, but that was all.

The pale skin that covered Charm's classic Nordic features had flushed as if suddenly self-conscious. Perhaps she, too, realized that her pelvic attack on the silly gaggle of harmless teens had been unnecessarily harsh. "Hi, Shasta!" she'd stammered.

Shasta didn't let slip that she'd observed the goings-on with the rowdy team. She'd continued, "Have you seen Walter around?"

The Aryan bombshell had cocked her small head in confusion. An abundance of straight, golden hair had tumbled to that side. "Walter who?" asked the girl.

Here at Maryhill, promenading in the gardens, Shasta had the ear and the heart of one of Caucasia's most powerful chieftains. She must be able to offer such a girl some incentive. If they could strike a bargain, perhaps they could both benefit from Shasta's long-range scheme.

Charlie, he remained mute. He merely surveyed his realm. Below this portion of the gardens, the terrain fell away to fertile, fruited plains that stretched to the horizon. In the distance sunburned field wives stooped to tend the young seedlings. Among the bounty, Shasta could recognize wide swaths of delicious radishes ... densely planted bush beans ... the tendrils of cucumber vines. The hard life of a field wife was an improvement over starving in the settlement houses of Portland, but it was a far cry from the status of public wife that Shasta stood to achieve. Despite their lowly station, more than a smattering of field wives wielded big pregnant tummies that had to be Charlie's doing. His kingdom, like those of any chieftain, consisted of one king and hordes of female workers. The opposite of a bee hive or termite mound.

In the sky, directly overhead a formation of jumbo jetliners was escorting the last of the Asian genotypes back to their native continent. Shasta watched them go with despair. Caucasia had chosen haggis over yu xiang rou si.

Charlie continued his mute oversight of the fields. A breathtaking planting of kohlrabi lay below them. A complicated bedding scheme of dwarf sunflowers seemed to be turning their shaggy heads to follow the sun. Trying to share in his admiration of the plentitude of nutritious crops, Shasta continued to look on. Only then did the reality of the situation strike her. Her arrival here at this spot at this particular moment in time was no accident.

As the sun ticked its way across the blue Caucasian sky, each sunflower twisted its bright orange face. Like a stadium crowd moving in perfect unison to perform the "wave," the rows of sunflowers gradually came to face Shasta. Looking past the thousand pregnant laborers, beyond the ripening kohlrabi, she could recognize the secret of this moment.

A glance at Charlie confirmed her suspicion. A faint smile flickered on his lips.

Where his eyes fell, the emerging shades of orange formed a

pattern. In contrast to the lighter, lime green of ordinary produce, the sunflowers began to form words.

Emblazoned across a mile of open country, legible only from this lofty vantage point, the crops turning to face them spelled out the message: Charlie (heart shape) Shasta.

Whatever it was that entered the room, its skin glistened. The creature shimmered with hazy waves of scent, the scent of every coconut in the world split open. The stink of piña coladas uncountable. Knotted shreds of red bandana gathered its wiry hair into apparently random clumps, but the bulk of its oily frizz burst from its head in a mass so dense the hair pushed its ears forward until each stuck out like the handle on a pitcher.

Its bare feet shuffled into the parlor. They hopped and capered. Whatever made its way toward Jamal, it loped.

A length of hemp rope held up its tattered pants, and the ragged cuffs flopped against the floor. It advanced across the parlor in jerking strides, waving its arms in torn shirt sleeves and stretching its pleated turkey neck to gawk at the furniture and paintings. In this manner it crossed the Persian carpet, goggle eyed and smacking its raw lips. "Lawdy," it cried, "dat Mizz Josafeen nevah permissioned mah tah enter no pah-lor!"

The apparition held out its elbows at shoulder height, displaying soiled white gloves worn on twiddling fingers. With each step, it jerked each knee so high, so fast, it might've been wading through glue. A muscle spasm seemed to seize its face, forcing the eyes so open that a wide margin of whites showed around each iris. These eyes rolling in every direction, while the mouth yawned to display gleaming teeth and the chin wagged side to side, jutted forward one moment and the next sunk back into the neck.

The bare feet, the scrawny legs visible through rents in the trousers, the neck and face of the creature, they were all coal black.

As the thing capered forward, Arabella looked on from her station near the doorway. "Mister Jamal," she said flatly, her eyes looking elsewhere, "this is Barnabas." She sighed heavily.

A soiled glove thrust itself at him. With swollen, cracked lips, the Barnabas thing sang out, "Eye's pleez'd tah meet'cha, Massah Jamal! Yah don no haw much! Dat Mizz Josafeen, she waz a debil womin!"

Jamal exchanged a glance with the housekeeper. Arabella shrugged. She lifted a hand and idly examined her fingernails.

Black as oil, blacker than what people called blue-black, the Barnabas thing continued to prance spryly in the center of the room. "Y, dat debil Mizz Josafeen, she keep'd me lok'd in dah attack fah mos ah mie hole lie-f!"

Jamal puzzled through its Butterfly McQueen diction. He looked to the housekeeper for a tell, any cue, but she'd buried her face in both hands to stifle a laugh. Clearly, whatever the nature of this demented gollywog, the joke wasn't on him. Reluctantly, he brought his gaze back to the head-bobbing, hip-shaking grotesque. "Barnabas?" he asked. "Can you tell me where Miss Josephine's gone?"

The eye-rolling creature brought both gloved hands up to frame its wrinkled face, and trembled, as if cowering in terror. "She dohn gawn skee-daddled tah Cock-asia!"

Arabella cleared her throat. Winced.

Jamal looked her way.

"Barnabas," she said, nodding toward the creature, "has been living in your attic, sir. He's the noise you've heard nights."

This news wasn't unwelcome. As of lately a fear had begun to trouble Jamal. The idea that he'd done his life's work too early. By participating in Adjustment Day and rising to the lofty, lifetime rank of a prince of Blacktopia, he might've peaked too early. The rewards, this manse, the wealth, were pleasing, but as the Talbott book decreed:

Property is but the residue of true accomplishment.

Adjustment Day hadn't settled his spirit. On the contrary, that achievement left his soul hungering for greater challenges. From here on he was determined to live a life of deeds instead of objects. As the Talbott book dictated:

Only the impossible is ever worth doing.

No man who'd taken part in Adjustment Day, whether he now be a prince or a chieftain, took anything for granted. Jamal knew from the forfeiture records that the owner, this fabled Miss Josephine, had never surrendered the title to this property. No record existed of her relocating to or applying for compensation from Caucasia. Long and hard, he looked at this jabbering, spry monstrosity. Minus the burnt hair, the rag bag ensemble, and impossible obsidian hue of its skin, this had to be her.

The housekeeper's head shaking and suppressed amusement confirmed as much.

The old lady, clearly deranged, she puffed her cheeks and whistled a jig as she slapped time against her skinny thighs and bopped around the elegant room.

The whistling and bopping ceased and the creature stood bug-eyed before a tall oil painting. The portrait showed a whiskered military officer in Confederate grays, bedecked in gold braid, a sword lashed to his side. After more than a century, his blue eyes still blazed with resoluteness. The creature sucked its teeth, ducked its head, and squinted sideways with theatrical venom at the picture. "Massah Jamal?" it said, "can ah ax yah sum-tin?" Poking with one dirty white index finger, it asked, "Iz yah plan'n tah burn deez debil pitchers?"

Jamal met Arabella's surprised look, matching her single raised eyebrow. "Why, Barnabas, would you like me to burn them?"

The Barnabas creature bared its gleaming, too-white teeth and tentatively growled at the painting. When the man in the picture didn't growl in return, Barnabas raised one white-gloved fist and shook it at the officer. "Ah's bin prison'd in dis howz mah hole time ahn dis urth."

Jamal struggled to decipher such gibberish. Every utterance was a test.

The Barnabas creature squinted with menace and peered around the room, pointedly taking in the crystal chandelier, the rosewood grand piano, the marble fireplace and velvet upholstery. Every tassel and brass spittoon. It puffed its pigeon chest and flexed its chicken wing arms as if ready to throw punches. "If'n yah ax me," it muttered, "ah thinks yah shood bern dawn dah hole howz!"

Jamal leveled his gaze on the poor creature. "Barnabas," he said, "have you considered that your animosity was the reason Miss Josephine never trusted you?" Maybe it was time to move beyond the off-the-rack, ready-to-wear political ideology of Talbott. Maybe, Jamal asked himself, he should hold onto this problem to see what insight it might yield?

Barnabas balled his gloved fingers into fists and took a boxer's stance. "Wize yah side wid Mizz Joe?"

Jamal wasn't fazed. From wiggers, to the film *Ten* starring the actress Bo Derek with her blonde hair braided in cornrows, to white "trustifarian" young people with dreadlocks, this Barnabas seemed like the inevitable result of cultural appropriation. An old lady wigger. The latest in a series of chemically enhanced Sambo types. The racial equivalent of a drag queen's botched version of being an actual woman.

Jamal flashed on the fictional character D'orothea Wilson in the much-beloved *Tales of the City* novels by Armistead Maupin. As a failed fashion model, a white woman named Dorothy had blacked up and become a successful, highly sought-after "black" model. Sickle-cell anemia was the punch line in a book adored by millions! That, and the issue of Superman comics titled "I Am Curious (Black)" where the intrepid reporter Lois Lane uses a device to transform herself into a foxy black woman for twenty-four hours. Whether they called it reporting or research, for white people crossing the color line was always just fun and games.

It might even prove to be a pathology. Like multiple personality disorder or gender dysmorphia.

Per Harvard psychology professor Dr. Jeremiah Brockyard, racial dysmorphia or transracialism was demonstrated by the activist Rachel Dolezal, who posed at being black, and by the singer Michael Jackson, who took huge health risks to appear more white. As Sigmund Freud had made his career with the case study of Dora, Jamal might just as easily exploit the mental illness of this demented white lady for his own fame and fortune.

Here, here was his next challenge. Jamal raised a hand to signal the housekeeper. "Arabella, would you be so kind as to bring my guest and me two extremely cold mint juleps?"

If this apparition was the manifestation of a shattered, disassociated personality, or it was some form of Stockholm syndrome brought on by finding herself an alien in her former nation, Jamal didn't venture a guess. Not yet. It dawned on him that this, adventures like this, peopled by flawed, damaged characters, were the stuff of books. In this Barnabas creature, his own book might be born.

His would be a book written by a black man about a white woman pretending to be a black man. The title wrote itself. His literary masterpiece, he would call it *Black Like You*.

In the seasons that followed Adjustment Day the beaver population rebounded. As the human population seethed in disarray, cities becoming scenes of famine, not just beaver numbers surged. Otter, bobcat, muskrat, and rabbits all made a comeback. Minks and lynx and wolves. As the weather flushed the toxins from the environment, even the apex predators such as bears and panthers rebounded.

Fur, fur was everywhere. Consequently artificial furs emerged as the new status symbols. Minus the now-defunct petrochemical supply chain, fake fur and leather were rapidly becoming extinct.

As standing inventory of fake furs winked out, no new fake furs replaced them.

Thus to flaunt his wealth Chieftain Charlie did don robes of chartreuse leopard and rare acrylic zebra. He strutted the corridors of his palace in knee-high boots of endangered Naugahyde. His courtiers arrayed him in capes of lime green faux sable and fringed gauntlets of pleather studded with costly ersatz pearls. Thusly adorned he mounted the battlements of Maryhill to survey the rich plantings of sugar beets and sweet onions, the arabesque bedding schemes of acorn squash and endive, the wealth of his kingdom.

Shasta had taken her leave, but soon she would become his consort. They would be wed the moment her genetic testing confirmed her ethnicity.

A voice spoke. Charlie turned from the battlements and the view, and his eyes fell upon a liveried footman. The man escorted a young maiden, a home wife from among the staff of scullery maids and chambermaids. No beauty was she, but her loins appeared sound. He nodded his approval, and the footman escorted the girl away. She would be waiting in his apartments when he was ready.

A stink had begun to saturate the basement. The source of the reek was the old man's blood because even blood sours like milk, and the stench of discarded blood had given its flavor to every breath Walter drew. Black flies had circled, circling Walter and Talbott, circling their half-eaten food in a constant miasma, as if the smell itself generated a low hum.

Not the best custodian of his own hygiene, Walter had given short shrift to the needs of his elderly ward. Meals sat too long at room temperature, the stink of their decay undetectable in the room's overall stink. The result being that Talbott's toileting had become sudden and explosive. With every tainted inhale Walter had assured himself that people had done worse for a fortune. To date, every task Talbott had set was a test. The big picture would soon snap into sharp focus.

Once the list was posted and had drawn its first submissions and votes, Walter had waited for the next challenge. His new old man had been dozing. His head had drooped, and he'd jerked awake with a single bubbling snort. Sputtering, his head lolling on his thin neck, he'd muttered, "Hypnagogic spasm."

He'd gone on to explain. Between wakefulness and sleep, people pass through the hypnagogic state, a phase when sleep walking occurs. Also common are hallucinations, visions of tripping over an obstacle or falling from a window, and the sleeper jerks awake. That sudden awakening, sleep experts called it the hypnagogic spasm. Anthropologists, according to Talbott, believe that our evolutionary ancestors had developed the spasm to guard against losing their grip on branches or the fur of the mother primate. Our vision of falling is their vision of plummeting to the jungle floor, a terror leftover from before we were even human. Talbott had expounded on the concept. He'd swallowed hard and licked his dry lips. His chest had risen and fallen like a bellows, swelling and collapsing the lacerated little dirigible of his ribcage. Not all the corrupt food had been shat out, as demonstrated by the vomitus that spilled down the old chin and clung in pale clots to the grayed chest hair.

"You know N.A.?" he'd asked. He'd meant the twelve-step group for recovering drug addicts. Narcotics Anonymous. He'd said, "Go there."

Here had been the next phase of Walter's training. Talbott had demanded, "Find me one man or two with nothing to lose."

Walt was to hear their stories and listen for men who'd given up on life. Younger men. Angry and disillusioned men. Talbott had wanted recruits who'd turned to drugs because they were smart and strong, and the present world offered them no outlet for their gifts. These would be men who hated drugs but who hated more a society that had left them no means to achieve the status that all men crave.

Walter was to promise them a million dollars. He was to promise to make each man a prince of the new new world. Walter hadn't liked the sound of that, seeing how he hadn't, himself, gotten one red cent. To bide for time he'd picked up a bowl of cold Top Ramen and had given it a cursory sniff. He'd closed the steps to where Talbott sat duct-taped to the chair. Using a spoon that managed to feel both greasy and sticky, he'd shoveled noodles into the gaping old mouth.

His tongue crowded with food, Talbott had cited the American Civil Rights Movement of the 1950s and '60s. Prior to it the dispossessed and powerless had gone to churches for comfort, and in those the disenfranchised had discovered they weren't alone in their misery. United, they'd formed an army, and the church leaders had recognized their power and led those armies into battle.

Choking and sputtering, Talbott had said, "Those groups . . . recovery and support groups are the new churches." He'd said that traditional places of worship had been reduced to crass theaters where people went to signal their status and virtues. A true church had to serve as the place where people went in safety to risk confessing their worst selves. Not to boast and display their pride. Those who attended recovery groups, they arrived defeated. They told the story of their failure. Their sins and shortcomings. To admit their culpability, and in doing so they receive a communion with their flawed peers. It was within these unlikely churches, in the company of the drunkard and the dope fiend, that Walter would find the officers of his new army. The greatest armies in the world are destroyed by idleness, Talbott had argued. Without opportunity, the men Walter would be enlisting, in the absence of an external enemy and a battle, they were becoming casualties of themselves.

What Talbott was to tell Walter, Walter was to preach to these men he himself selected, and those men were to venture forth to spread the message to a small number of men. If those men are queer, beguile them with visions of Gaysia, where they could live in their own homogeneous company. If white, testify to them about the future possible in Caucasia. If black, offer up the promise of Blacktopia, where they need never kowtow to any other race.

"Bring me," Talbott directed, "your learned helpless." His voice rose to a shout. "The wretched results of jobs off-shored. Lend these, the hopeless, diversity-vanquished, to me . . ."

Whereupon Talbott had appeared to swoon. In little more than a whisper, he'd uttered, "I'll foot the bill. The world is yours."

And once again he'd fallen into a jerking, restless, fitful slumber filled with prehistoric terrors.

As the Talbott book put it, the disunited states had always been a nation composed of nations. Some sovereign. Others, invisible. Parishes. Guilds. Associations. Chapters and clubs. After Adjustment Day those that were self-sustaining survived. But those dependent on the largesse of the vanished government, or on the fawning attention of the vanquished media, those brotherhoods and alliances ceased to exist.

The same went for families.

The two brothers had agreed to meet for lunch. To meet for one last time. A billboard dwarfed the small roadside diner on whose roof it sat. Easily twice the size of the eatery, its bold black lettering read "Whites Only."

Inside, the two men sat in a booth beside the front windows. They sat facing each other like imperfect mirror images: the same nose, the same eyes and mouth and ruffle of hair, both leaning with elbows on the table, but each with a different expression.

A server wearing a checkered gingham frock and an apron with scalloped edges stood over them. Her pen poised above her pad, she recited, "The soup du jour is Paula Deen White Bean Stew . . .

For specials, we have a Richard Spencer eight-ounce white fish filet and an all-white-meat Lester Maddox Chicken Salad . . ."

One of the brothers noticed her waiting. "Give us a minute, okay?" That was Esteban.

The other brother said, "We'll have two Paula Deens to start with." This was Xavier.

When the server had stepped away, Esteban reached into a pocket of his jacket and took out a handful of white packets. White plastic, little pillows no larger than Before Times credit cards, heat-sealed along all four edges. He tossed these into the center of the empty table. In black felt-tipped pen some packets were marked with a lowercase "p" and some with a lowercase "d." Esteban nodded at the packets, saying, "You don't have to emigrate."

Xavier reached to examine one. He squeezed its softness between a thumb and index finger.

"They're black market," Esteban explained. "The 'd' stands for drool. Squeeze one into your mouth if you're facing a racial test. It's lab-certified European-derived saliva."

Xavier poked at a packet marked with a "p." Asking, "And these?"

"Piss. For a urinalysis," Esteban said. "Don't get them mixed up."

Xavier pawed through the packets. "Your handwriting is *piojoso*." Depending on the viewing angle, the p's and d's were identical.

Undeterred, Esteban said, "Stay here in Caucasia so we can visit. I have diplomatic immunity. As a member of the first lineage I can travel freely between all three nations for my job."

His brother regarded the packets, turning them as if trying to discern which was which. The twang of country-western music played on the sound system. Beyond the windows a mix of motor vehicles and horse-drawn wagons moved along the highway in both directions. From the highway a great expanse of red cabbage filled the acres that rolled toward the horizon. Looking into that distance, Xavier asked, "Why'd you do it?"

Esteban squinted at the packets. He slid one away from the rest, saying, "I think . . . this one is piss." He slid another aside, saying, "But this is drool. *I think.*" He stopped his fussing, abruptly. "You have no idea," he muttered. Louder, his voice steady, "Nations are founded on religions. They're founded on political systems. Abstract ideas. Why not something as real and basic as sexual preference?"

Xavier didn't offer a rebuttal. His duffle bag sat slumped on the seat beside him.

"I wanted to help," Esteban continued, "to create one safe space where people wouldn't feel like outcasts." A ring interrupted. The sound came from inside a pocket of his jacket. He took out his phone and studied the screen, saying, "Lofty affairs of state beckon." He got to his feet and exited to the parking lot.

"Two white bean stews?" a voice asked. The waitress slid two bowls onto the table where Xavier still waited. She glanced out the window to where Esteban stood talking on his phone. The bowls, brimming with steaming muck, had pushed aside and hopelessly scrambled the poorly labeled packets. She stood watching Esteban outside, asking, "Haven't I seen him on television? Is he somebody?" Conspiratorially, she asked, "You know if he's married or not?"

Xavier watched his brother giving orders, muted by the window glass and the background of traffic noise. The server wasn't leaving. Smiling, he turned to her and asked, "You know your music sucks?"

Even as she turned in a huff, he was already tearing open packets. It didn't matter, p's or d's. With the server gone, Xavier got busy mixing all the lab-tested, European-derived whatever into his brother's bowl of soup.

Considering what Talbott had said, the irony hadn't been lost on Walter. If recovery groups were the churches of this era, they were still conducted in the old church buildings. As Christian churches had commandeered the temples previously devoted to Apollo and Diana, the local chapter of Narcotics Anonymous met in the basement of St. Stephens. In the above-ground sanctuary, bathed in colored sunshine from stained-glass windows, the good citizens wore their Sunday best. They sang in the correct key in harmony and recited their prayers in unison. Beneath their feet, underground, it was another story.

Away from the sunshine, after sunset an entirely different congregation shuffled in. Fragmented, solitary. Instead of incense, the smell of cigarette smoke wafted off them. In place of sacramental wine, they drank black coffee and took communion with jelly doughnuts.

It was only his excitement about Shasta that had gotten Walter into the church basement, about seeing Shasta's face when she realized he was rich. Talbott had coached him that creative visualization wouldn't cut the mustard. When an outfit like Amway wanted to motivate rookie enrollees, it encouraged them to test drive Maseratis and Alfa Romeos. People were encouraged to shop for Gulfstream jets and contact real estate agents for tours of mansions on fairways and private beaches. Real details motivated people. The smell of leather seats and the sound of ocean waves under the bedroom windows. People needed to know the fine details of the life they were striving to achieve. Vague goals such as good health or money were too difficult to measure. The abstract doesn't excite the spirit. But the softness and warmth of a sable coat. Or the glow of a diamond necklace. The silky feel of the perfect saltwater swimming pool. These motivate. And so Walter had pictured Shasta aboard the sailboat in San Francisco Bay, and he added the scent of her suntan lotion and the taste of the Chateau Lafite, 1869 they'd drink. Someday they'd nibble beluga white caviar and laugh about the measures Walter had taken to make his fortune, about flaying Talbott with razors and posting the list and invading Narcotics Anonymous in search of converts. Bolstered by these specifics Walter had ventured into the netherworld of this new religion.

There, parishioners had arrived dragging their crimes. With names like Clem and T.J. and Keishaun. Wearing business suits, wearing track suits or stained coveralls, they'd waited their turns, men and women, to make their full confessions. There, away from the world, each had given an account of his or her worst behavior and had resolved to do better.

To whom to offer the world? Which man to radicalize? Walter had listened, weighing the out-of-work veteran against the barista struggling through beauty school. Talbott had warned him. The whites would blame the blacks. The gays would blame the straights. The blacks would blame the whites. And everyone would blame the Jews. Walter had waited as every person had his or her say. Talbott had told him exactly what to say and had forced him to repeat the words until he'd known them by heart. When everyone had spoken, it had been his turn. And only when all eyes had fallen upon him had Walter said his piece.

"My name is Walter," he'd said. Another day, another test. He'd imagined the smell of Shasta's terror as she stood kissing him in a house he secretly owned. Before the group could stop him, he'd announced, "I'm looking to recruit men who'd rule the world in less than a year." A collective groan went up as people had scoffed and shook their heads. "Anyone interested in being a founding member of a new ruling class, please see me outside." And Walter had stood up, and he'd excused himself, and he'd stepped out the door, walked up the stairs, and he'd waited in the alley for a hero or a fool or for no one to follow him.

Charm flipped through the pages of a cookbook, passing over the recipes but lingering on full-color photographs of Lobster Newberg and Waldorf salad. She studied cannelloni, feeling her mouth fill with saliva. She ogled bok choy to the point she might have to swallow, then rushed to the kitchen.

Her mother stood over the stove stirring something in a fry-ing pan. She wore a wimple. A wimple! She was so white her lips stretched as thin as pink rubber bands. Gavyn was the lucky one. Shasta, too. Shasta should just surrender for export to Blacktopia. Charm and her parents were trapped, condemned to the patriarchal, gun-toting Renaissance Faire that was Caucasia. Her mother looked up from her cooking and said, "Hello, dear."

Charm asked, "Beer? It's early."

Her mother was sipping from a tall mug of amber liquid. "This?" she asked, offering the mug. "It's urine. Prevents cancers. Black people swear by it."

Charm hummed a response. Her mouth was too full of spit to risk words. She opened the refrigerator and took out a plastic tub. Hand-lettered on the snap-tight lid was the warning: Hands Off! Charm's Drool! She peeled off the lid and tipped her face over the tub. A thick, cloudy liquid sloshed inside, and she hawked a nasty loogie into the mess.

Her mother winced. "Disgusting." She tipped back another swig of medicinal urine.

Charm spat again and snapped the lid on the tub. She'd been at this for a couple days and the tub still felt empty. "Science fair," she said. "Pavlov's dog."

Her mother leveled a worried look at her. "You know science is off-limits."

The moratorium, she meant. The big push to get anyone into STEM careers was dead. The edict was that white people were supposed to be breeding instead of reading. As she closed the fridge, Charm tried to change the subject. "I've been thinking about Gavyn."

Her mother's brow pinched. She feigned confusion, asking, "Who?"

"Your son." Charm went to the sink and filled a tall glass with water. All her spitting had taken its toll.

Her mother sighed as deeply as the lacings of her bodice would allow. "We have no son," she said. "You have no brother."

As she drank the water, Charm weighed the statement. Was her mother cruel or just being a realist? Once Gavyn had emigrated it was unlikely they'd ever have contact with him. The best they could hope for would be a surrogate son or daughter exported by similarly disappointed parents in Gaysia. Too many parents took offense. If their children reached the Age of Declaration, eighteen, and announced an inappropriate sexuality, it looked like betrayal. Charm knew her own parents had asked Gavyn to postpone his declaration. People could wait until they were nineteen, and delaying his announcement would've given them two more years together as a family. But Gavyn, he'd filed his paperwork. He'd known what he wanted. He wanted to get the hell out.

Her mother didn't meet her gaze but continued to stir, saying, "You know you can't go outdoors like that." Whatever was in the pan, it hissed and spat.

She meant bare-headed. Women of Caucasia were required to cover their heads in public. Another measure intended to instill ethnic unity. Hence the wimple. French Tudor caps were tempting fate; a girl might as well sashay around topless. Snoods? Forget it. Charm knew her parents had already lost one child. God forbid their remaining child get bounced into a heretic's work farm or whatever.

The school had called today. The principal was threatening expulsion. Her mother pinched up some salt from a bowl and sprinkled it into her cooking. She said, "They claim you chased more boys with your exposed lady parts." Using both hands, she twisted a pepper mill. "Those young men were awfully shaken up."

Charm smiled at the memory. She'd panicked the varsity basketball team during practice. By leaping out of the girl's locker room with no pants on, she'd stampeded a crew of alpha males out through the fire exits. Alarms had sounded. As feminist power moments went it felt pretty glorious.

She was already trying to work up a new mouthful of spit. "You think Gavyn might be in trouble?" What she meant was that the nation of Gaysia had only recently launched its program to reproduce exports. It would be seventeen years before it yielded any heterosexuals who could be traded for the homosexuals stockpiled in Caucasia and Blacktopia. At that rate Gavyn might be thirty-four or thirty-five before he stood a chance of emigrating. Of course, some do-gooders might raise the half million Talbott dollars needed to ransom him, but the odds seemed slim. Not for all of the teenagers in retention camps.

All the while the heterosexual nation states would already have babies in the pipeline, and over the next seventeen years a small army of queer exports was going to get bottlenecked at the retention camps. Straight folks had a history-long head start at the baby-making game.

As her mouth filled, Charm watched her mother and tried not to swallow or speak.

Currently nations conducted a modest back-and-forth trade in babies born with a majority of Caucasian or sub-Saharan DNA, but everyone knew the real bonanza would be in the export of mis-born queer citizens. That was the new term: mis-born. It denoted anyone born and raised in an inappropriate nation state.

Furthermore, who knew if Gaysia would prioritize the youngest exports? Otherwise more generations would spend their youth waiting to be repatriated. If younger exports were given priority then Gavyn could spend his entire life trapped in limbo between two nations.

His letters didn't say as much, but Gavyn himself had stopped writing about his high hopes. Whereas he used to write about finding love, settling down, and becoming a force to help build his new queer nation . . . lately he'd taken to complaining about the camp food. It was lousy. Starchy beef stews. Watery vegetable soup. The same way that illness became the chief topic among the elderly, Charm knew that food was the main preoccupation of people in prisons.

None of this she mentioned aloud. She just watched her mother stir. It was fried chicken, the grease popping. Potatoes boiled in a pot. Dinner rolls were baking in the oven, and the butter had already been set out on the countertop to soften at room temperature.

Her mother reached up and pressed a switch. The hood above the stove began to hum, and the steam from the fry pan spiraled upwards and disappeared.

The smell, so much fat and meat, the parmesan cheese she knew would be mixed into the cornmeal breading, the aroma flooded Charm's mouth with new saliva. In another minute she'd need to open the fridge again. Her brother was a hostage, and the faster she filled that plastic tub with spit the sooner she might liberate him.

The callers weren't Clem or Keishaun but they spoke with the same brusque economy of words, demanding, "Get Talbott." On those occasions Walter had clipped a hands-free phone to Talbott's scabbed head and had retreated from the room. At Talbott's urging he'd begun to type his notes into a single comprehensive document. To what end, Walter hadn't a guess. It might've been a book in progress. Or it might've been just a new test. Beginning with the first test, flaying his new old man in search of a make-believe homing device, keyboarding his notes was a walk in the park.

The men he'd enrolled, Walter had only been able to speculate about. The two heroin addicts. They might be tooling around, living large on Talbott's dime. They might even be spreading the gospel of Talbott to their fellow junkies in support groups across the country. Not impossible was the idea that a network of desperate men was branching and spreading out to cover the nation. Or, those two men might be dead.

Nothing about Talbott's disappearance had ever surfaced on the news sites. Again, it was pure speculation, but the police might've kept the entire situation under wraps pending their investigation.

That said, the FBI might've been closing in at any moment, staked out down the block, ready to batter down the front door. Walter had kept typing.

Talbott's shouts had summoned him. The old man had said, "You need to make the call we talked about." Walter went to take the phone off the old, spotted scalp. Leakage, drops of blood swelling from old wounds had glued it in place so effectively the ear clip hardly seemed necessary. The gruesome truth was that Walter had to peel the phone off the stretching, sagging old skin, and even then the black plastic was speckled with tacky smudges and crusty scabs. So much so that Walter had been compelled to scrub it with an antibiotic wet wipe. All the while Talbott had harangued him.

"Tell them the code," he'd groused from his chair. "Don't keep the connection open longer than one minute."

Walter had sniffed the phone. It had smelled like nothing but rubbing alcohol. He'd punched in the number he'd learned by heart.

A voice had answered, a woman's voice, "Senator Daniels's office."

Walter had eyed the old man while saying, "I'm calling on behalf of—"

The voice had cut him off. "The senator's in a meeting."

"Ten seconds," shouted Talbott.

Walter had taken the nuclear option. "This is a code 4C247M." The connection had gone silent for an instant before a booming male voice had come on.

"This is the senator," the voice had announced.

"Yes." Walter had gone on watching Talbott for any signs of approval or disapproval. "You need to introduce the War Resolutions Act."

Talbott had explained the situation. How the youth bulge of surplus males threatened to destabilize this country as well as any number of foreign nations. The act would catalyze the induction of a million young men into the military, and these men would be pitted against equal forces conscripted in other countries. It wasn't lost on Walter that whenever events in the world went south it was always men his age who'd be dispatched to clean up the mess. Walter had told the senator, "Mr. Talbott would like the war to commence no later than the opening day of grouse hunting."

"Of course," the senator had said. Unless Walter had been mistaken, the man had been panting for breath as if he'd sprinted to reach the phone.

Talbott had explained that a world war would reduce the surplus of labor. The global manufacturing markets would explode with growth. Finally, Walter had imagined he could see some big money at the end of this very long tunnel. He'd told the senator, "Mr. Talbott sends his best wishes to your wife."

"Of course," the senator had said.

"Thirty seconds," had barked Talbott from his chair.

Tipsy with power, Walter had baited the man on the phone. "How is Mrs. Senator?"

The senator had hesitated. "She's fine, sir."

To date Walter had never been addressed as "sir," and it felt surprisingly good. Before he could lose his nerve, he'd given Shasta's full name and asked the senator to expunge her parking tickets.

"One minute," Talbott had snapped, "hang up!"

As one last mocking gibe Walter had asked, "Senator, when is grouse hunting season?"

His voice reedy with stress, the senator had asked, "This year?"

"This year," Walter had confirmed.

"It begins one day after the onset of World War III," had said the senator, adding, "sir."

Only then, with the test complete, with Talbott glaring bullets at him, taking his own sweet time, did Walter hang up.

One evening stood out among the many Jamal spent tipping back mint juleps and trying to study the creature. In its indigo-black hide he could discern traces of the aged belle who'd burnt her hair to a frizzed mess and daily strutted down from the attic, high-stepping and animated with Bojangles jazz hands and leering minstrel show faces. Times the creature would drop its act and reminisce about the people depicted in the portraits. Those times, the shuck and jive erased by gin, the creature would hold forth about the cemetery that lay on the far side of the field. Jamal would tour among the gravestones, big and small, and the creature would narrate about the lives of one and all.

Examining each grave closely, Jamal asked if there was one for a woman named Belinda.

"Dat beez in dah slay-vah sex-shun," said Barnabas. The creature walked to a wooded area outside the family graves. There, among the rusted crosses and sunken gravesites, Jamal found a small stone, the white marble eroded by rain. Only the name "Belinda" was legible.

On other occasions the creature would fall silent and Jamal would read aloud from the Talbott book. That gospel of the new new world. In the parlor, with a fire crackling on the hearth he'd read:

> We love to fight but hate to win. We challenge authority, create conflict, and pit ourselves against power not because we want to dominate, because we know triumph only means more fighting. We love to fight because we know that whatever irresistible force finally defeats us, we can rejoice and recognize that enemy as God.

He'd noticed how when the creature was drunk and playing a fool, it seemed to experience genuine joy. It raised its cracked voice to belt out old spirituals. Jamal observed this with a mixture of pity and fascination. This strutting clown. It had manifested as a haunt. The spirit of this forlorn place. The sight brought to mind more from Talbott:

To whites the most enviable quality of blacks was their capacity for happiness. They exhibited a graceful determination and good nature that whites could only covet. Over centuries of persecution blacks had evolved an enviable spirit and inner delight. To ruin that joy, whites created the grievance industry and poisoned black happiness by replacing it with rage and hatred. By sowing insecurity, whites have destroyed the greatest power blacks once enjoyed. By teaching blacks to take offense, whites have succeeded in cursing blacks with a misery far greater than any white unhappiness.

As it slumped in a red velvet chair, the creature blinked surprised eyes. It smacked its swollen lips and asked, "Massah Jamal, dat book . . . do it reely say dat?"

Jamal nodded.

The creature nodded in return. "It soun' rite." Lost in thought, the old eyes studied their own reflection in the polished side of the silver julep mug. "Massah Jamal?" it asked, "Duz yah buh-leeves in Got?"

Jamal was a little loaded. He answered, "I love what God creates, but I admit I don't give him the credit." Leaning closer to the creature he added, conspiratorially, "If I'd said prayers half as many times as I've been online looking for porn, I'd be saved. No doubt about it." He smiled roguishly, "I only wish I loved God half as much as I love some of his beautiful, beautiful creations."

Whatever it was, the creature seemed to understand. Just then it could've been what it was: an old white woman in blackface afraid of being turned out of her ancestral home. Seeing the creature's face soften, a truth struck Jamal. His worst fear was that the stooped, freakish gnome would resolve itself. It would revert back to a frightened old lady. The woman would leave this house and take with her its history. His concern was about more than writing his book. Jamal would be alone in his power, a king in a castle but without this ridiculous jester. This capering ludicrous buffoon was the only person in his new life he felt comfortable around.

He'd never anticipated that power would be this lonely.

No one would ever believe the word of this fool, so he could confess any secret to it. How badly he needed this lunatic as his confidant, it scared him. He wondered who needed whom more.

To stem the moment, the king reached to a pitcher that sat sweating on a side table. Without being asked, he poured the creature's drink full.

Delicious poured herself another glass of wine. It was safer to look drunk than to look scared. The police wouldn't arrest a tipsy woman, but they'd follow someone who smiled furtively and walked down the street too fast, staying in the shadows and looking away when passing headlights revealed her face. She checked her makeup in the bathroom mirror and touched a smudge of lipstick off one front tooth. A knock came at the door.

"Just a sec," she said. Her wine glass sat on the ledge beside the bathtub, next to the empty wine bottle. Perfume, she almost forgot. A dab behind her knees, a dab behind each ear. She downed the glass of wine, then reached up under her short skirt and wiggled the panties down her thighs and tossed them into the clothes hamper. A last look in the mirror gave her confidence. As did the wine.

Opening the bathroom door, Delicious said, "All yours."

Waiting in the hallway was Felix. He was Belle's boy by her husband, not that Gaysian law would recognize such a union. Nowadays Delicious's man, Gentry, was playing house with Jarvis, just as Delicious had wed Belle in a grand public ceremony in the stupendous Cathedral of Harvey Milk with a release of hundreds of white doves and a twenty-four-piece orchestra at the reception. Felix had served as ring bearer. Felix knew what was at stake.

One slip-up, and any one of them might be detained as an export. They'd be placed in a retention center and eventually relocated to Blacktopia or Caucasia, never to be reunited with his or her beloved. To make matters worse, now they had Felix to worry about. He wasn't like other boys. At an age when he ought to be lip synching to vintage Gloria Gaynor mixes, he was staring a tad too long at the scads of women they passed in the street. He didn't seem the least bit interested in dating other boys, and it worried his mother. She insisted he was merely going through a phase. Weeks shy of his Age of Declaration, she begged him not to openly flaunt his heterosexuality. At the least, such risky behavior would get him bashed by self-righteous thugs. At worst, he'd be deported. That would be the last either of his parents would set eyes on him.

Felix gave Delicious a smirk. "Don't you look hot," he said, his eyes taking in her smooth legs, her feet wedged in high heels, her hemline high and her neckline low. He smiled his approval at her new weave and the smudge of glitter in her cleavage. "Date night?" He nodded at the empty wine bottle in one of her hands, the empty glass in her other, her long manicured fingernails.

It was. Date night, that is, but not with his mother, Belle.

Delicious ignored the boy's leer and pushed past him. "Don't you have a circle jerk to attend?"

"Nope." He shook his head. "We had a big sperm drive at school today."

Delicious knew he wasn't kidding but didn't hanker to hear the details. She took her purse off the foyer table and checked inside. A certified letter had arrived that afternoon. With it safely inside her purse she headed for the apartment's front door, saying, "Tell your mom not to wait up."

Felix was nobody's fool. He knew the lay of the land, calling out, "Don't get busted!"

On the street, Delicious strode through the night. She relaxed in the warm air and allowed her hips to roll, pushing her skirt higher the wider she stepped. Bystanders, mannish types wolf whistled their praise. Flannel-outfitted females growled compliments in her wake. A police car pulled alongside and matched her speed, and she dared not look in its direction. Despite the wine, she knew the fear would show in her eyes. She could hear the radio chatter. A generation seemed to pass before the cruiser switched on its flashing lights. Here and now Delicious knew she was caught. Her imagination spun the scenario: The Gaysian police had staked out her apartment, they'd been monitoring her movements, she'd be deported.

The red-and-blue lights washed over her. The car's siren wailed. Tires barked against the pavement and the cruiser jetted off in response to another call.

Her legs weak with terror, Delicious stumbled through a dark, unmarked doorway. It was a dive. Pre-Adjustment Day skin magazines, dog-eared, wilting in wire racks, depicted healthy all-male and all-female sex acts. The covers bore titles like *Sapphic Clam Diggers* and *Greek Butt Pirates*. No one wanted these vintage wank mags from some bygone disco era. These were set dressing. A front.

A brooding skeleton of a man sat on a stool behind a counter. She paid him a few Talbott dollars for a handful of metal tokens. Secreted behind the magazine racks, hidden in back of the dusty glass cases displaying pink dildos and VHS tapes, there a curtained doorway opened onto a dim corridor. Delicious parted the stiff fabric and stepped through. The smell of sex was pungent, and she stood in one place while her eyes adjusted to the dark. Her footsteps on the sticky floor made peeling sounds. This place, the tawdry underbelly of Gaysia, here people indulged their illegal appetites.

Swimming in murky black light, the numbers four and seven and thirteen seemed to hover before her eyes before she realized they were splashed on in a stroke or two of fluorescent pink paint. These and other numbers were spaced at regular intervals, each marking a peeling, splintered door. Movement caught her attention. A blond man, his teeth glowing, said, "Hey, chocolate lady . . ."

Men and women, black seeking white, white seeking black, all heterosexuals, all illegal, they lined the dingy hallway, some exposing themselves in the hope of enticing a sex partner.

She lifted a hand and flashed him her wedding ring.

He flashed his own.

She continued along in that rank, crowded space. Splintering doors opened onto closet-sized cubicles in which same-sex adult films flickered on streaked video screens. Delicious chose a door bearing the number ten in Day-Glo paint. Used condoms littered the floor. Condoms or worse stuck her heels to the floor, tugging to pull the shoes from her bare feet. A plastic chair, layered with corruption, stood in one corner, and she considered sitting before remembering she wore nothing under her skirt to protect her. She stepped inside and shut the door behind her.

The video screen glowed with two astonishingly attractive men, one black, one white, copulating romantically beside a luxurious swimming pool outside of a regal mansion. In Gaysia race mingling was permitted. But gender mixing was not.

A knock came at the door, and a male voice whispered, "Hey, chocolate lady . . ."

Irked, Delicious cracked the door, ready to curse some amorous stranger.

In the dark corridor stood a stooped figure. Not the handsome stranger who'd accosted her earlier, this man was familiar. She grabbed him around one thin, pale wrist and dragged him into the cubicle. Once they were both inside she shut the door and blocked it by wedging the filthy chair beneath the knob. Every surface she touched felt either sticky or greasy, and she wiped her hands on her skirt. Even then her mouth was seeking out the man's. Her hips were grinding into his. His hands were roving over her, sliding up her legs to discover her wet readiness.

Without prompting, her knees buckled and she squatted low. Her hands fought to yank his slacks down his slim hips, and her lips sought the opening in his boxer shorts. Her lush mouth didn't give a thought to repercussions before they were committing one of the most heinous crimes known in Gaysia.

The result should've been immediate, but his manhood failed to respond. She worked it with her hand so she could ask, "Gentry, baby?"

Her husband groaned softly. "I can't."

Delicious spat on her hand and kept at it. "What's up, baby?"

High above her, Gentry's face was shadowed and indistinct. "We had an extra sperm drive at work today."

He was referring to the collection of viable sperm from all male citizens of Gaysia. It was voluntary, but not. Not really. Upstanding citizens were expected to donate massive amounts of semen toward the effort to reproduce children, the vast majority of which would be exported in order to obtain the homosexuals being retained in Caucasia and Blacktopia. The physical demands of these sperm drives had all but eradicated recreational male sex. And those men who couldn't meet their quota or whose seed was subpar, they were compelled to donate money toward the fund for ransoming new citizens. The survival of Gaysia depended on this effort.

Delicious grasped the dismal situation. Her Gentry had done his duty thrice today. He was spent.

Whereas men in Gaysia were compelled to donate, the women weren't without their own responsibilities to ensure the future of the nation. Throughout history men had been conscripted to perform military service. They'd surrendered their bodies and their lives to the state. In keeping with this precedent, now women were drafted. If selected and suitable, a female citizen of Gaysia must agree to insemination. Donated seed would be used to create a new life, and the woman would carry it. All fertile women were eligible, and nothing short of a medical emergency could excuse someone from her maternity service.

The resulting children were largely for export, but they would be raised until the Age of Declaration. Exported or not, each would equate to a new citizen.

That was the reason Delicious had shaved her legs. The motivation for her to risk her freedom, to sneak down to this, this wallow of degradation. Squatting there, she worked Gentry with both her hands and her mouth, but to no avail. No matter how badly she wanted to get pregnant, to bear his child, that wasn't going to happen tonight. Resigned, she reached to where she'd set her purse on the foul floor. From it, she retrieved the letter that had arrived this same day. Gentry helped her to her feet, and she handed him the envelope. The government knew she had it. She'd been required to sign for it.

In the faint light from the video screen, her husband unfolded the paper and squinted to read it. On the screen, in what was clearly a pre-Adjustment Day film, the two men were happily ejaculating upon each other's smiling faces. Delicious watched this anointment, thinking, *What a waste!*

Gentry looked at her, his brow furrowed in confusion. "What's this mean?"

Delicious tried to sound chipper. "I've been drafted."

He cocked his head. "What's that mean, 'drafted'?" If he didn't understand it was because he didn't want to.

According to the notice, Delicious was to submit for artificial insemination within twenty-four hours. After evading the police, after she'd ventured into this sinkhole of depravity, the combination of wine and fear finally hit her. Unless she could coax her husband to love her, she'd soon be carrying a stranger's child. Frantically weeping, she allowed her falling tears to wet her smooth palms, and Delicious redoubled her hopeless effort to arouse her beloved's flaccid member.

To the world they looked like two plastic packets of ketchup from any fast food restaurant. Their temperature gave the only hint of their true nature. That, and each packet, upon closer inspection, proved to be tampered with. One edge of each had been cut open and glued shut, not heat sealed as the other edges, but glued.

The bigger giveaway was that they felt like ice. So cold Shasta had to squeeze them gently in her fists, squeezing and releasing them, until their thick plastic and sharp edges felt pliable.

The great reception chambers of Charlie's palace bustled with court life. Silks and taffetas swept the gleaming wood floors, and ruddy jewels flashed in the sunlight from tall windows. Strolling troubadours strummed lutes in an effort to lighten the general mood. The court physician had been summoned, and all waited about in bated conversation. Around Shasta milled the formidable wives of other chieftains, their public wives, adorned in the booty plundered from many a museum or gallery. None among them had any royal training beyond serving as queen of a homecoming dance or senior prom. They were the prettiest put forward by their settlements. Chieftain Brach had taken as his favorite an impoverished young lady from the ruins of Seattle. Although he owned field wives and household wives aplenty, only Charlie had yet to claim a public wife.

A passing footman offered a tray of grilled peacock tongues. Shasta selected one. Slyly, she only pretended to put the delicious tongue between her lips. In truth she deftly dropped the tongue into her ample cleavage. In its stead, she placed one of the two ketchup packets in her mouth, tucking it secretly within her cheek. As another waiter bowed low to present an assortment of Scotch eggs arrayed in an embossed silver chafing dish, Shasta repeated her sleight-of-hand, dropping the eggs into her cleavage while hiding the second ketchup packet within her opposite cheek.

The aroma of food rose from her bodice, and she struggled to swallow her own saliva. Her mouth must be dry when the testing took place. Her own natural saliva would betray her. If the laboratories at 23 & Me were accurate, her spit would prove her to be of fifty-four percent sub-Saharan genetic descent, making her ineligible to reside in Caucasia much less become wife to a chieftain.

No, what she held squirreled away in her cheeks was the packaged saliva of an undeniably white girl. They'd hammered out an agreement. If Charm would help Shasta succeed in becoming Charlie's public wife, Shasta would use her lofty position to assist Charm in some yet-to-be-named endeavor.

At the hour appointed for the trial, the great clock struck. The minstrels fell silent, and the assembled royals fell to bended knee. A majordomo clicked his heels and announced, "The chief surgeon of the realm approaches!"

The surgeon was among Charlie's inner circle. Terrence his name was, some former invalid who'd been rousted from his death bed by the stirring words of Talbott. He marched from the far end of the gallery, his emerald green Tabard blazing, embroidered with thread-of-gold. Pearls the size of Spanish peanuts studded his codpiece. To guess from their buttery softness, his thigh-high boots could've been fashioned from nothing except the finest of pleather.

Whatever his infirmity had been, the surgeon showed no trace of it. A fine cascade of blond ringlets fell to his shoulders. Before reaching Shasta, he paused in the center of the crowd and lowered his head while he intoned a short prayer. "O Odin, father of Thor and Baldr," he lifted his voice toward the elaborately coffered and frescoed ceiling, "Odin, bearer of the spear Gungnir and husband of Frigg . . ."

Listening, Shasta tried not to think of the tasty peacock tongue that was even now lodged betwixt her lovely breasts, lest she salivate. She held her jaw slack to prevent perforating the ketchup packets and prematurely filling her mouth with priceless whitegirl spit.

"O Odin," the surgeon continued, "we pray that this woman proves pure enough to serve as our queen." In closing, he plunged the fingers of one expert hand into his sporran. From its depths he removed something that shined like a halo in the chamber's gloom. It was rumored he possessed fantastic healing power. And that upon reading the words of the Talbott book he'd thrown himself from his death bed and pledged his newfound vigor to serving Caucasia.

The shining object he presented was a sterile Petri dish, and with it he approached Shasta.

Silently, she pursed her lips and sucked her mouth dry. The Scotch egg she'd dropped into her bodice slipped lower, and she could feel its warmth against her tensed abs. She must not bite the packets until the ritual began.

No formal medical training had Terrence, but it was widely known that his palette was so refined that with a single sip of a person's sample he could detect one's entire racial background. He knelt before Shasta, holding out the Petri dish like an offering.

This, this was her moment. She bent her face over the empty vessel. Using her back teeth she gnawed a rent in one packet. The foreign taste of a strange girl's cold drool flooded her tongue. She burst the second packet, and the sensation doubled. Her mouth was awash in the foreign tang of Charm's bodily fluids. Cooler than Shasta expected, the fluids squirted between her molars. The slippery wetness of Charm coated Shasta's tongue, so much so that when she bent her face to dribble a dainty sample into the glass dish, a gushing tide of girl saliva fell from her lips.

The downpour swamped the edges of the Petri dish. Terrence, the surgeon, looked up in surprise. His extended arms trembled with the added weight.

Shasta blushed furiously. In what she hoped was an elegant gesture, she wiped her dripping mouth with the billowing sleeve of her silk gown. Resist she did the impulse to twist her head aside and spit and spit until the flavor of Charm's salivary glands haunted her taste buds no more.

Round-eyed with shock was the noble company in attendance.

The surgeon assessed the brimming dish. In a hushed, awed tone, Terrence gushed, "Milady, the hue of your expectorant shows great promise." Whosoever's saliva this was, it glistened in his hands. A silver glint highlighted its beauty. The froth of it showed bluish, such was its purity. Shasta said a silent prayer the spit wasn't hers.

The two ruptured packets still rested inside her cheeks. Discreetly so not to be noticed, she fished the fingers of one hand far down between her breasts and sought out the stashed peacock tongue and the Scotch egg. To rid her mouth of Charm's taste, she quickly gulped down both of the rare delicacies.

The royal surgeon lifted the sample to his nose. He sniffed at the gooey liquid. He put the brim to his lips, tipped it, and began to sip. He sloshed the sample back and forth between his cheeks. He smacked his lips.

Dawson had never rebuilt a woman. Not to date. Like every man, he'd seen women totaled. Rolled so bad, a woman's frame so twisted she'd never be put back into proper alignment. Fit only for the junkyard. He'd seen a fine woman so neglected that finally her chassis had rusted through. And he'd seen older women given the hotrod treatment, layered with Bondo to smooth their curves, tricked out with Hooker headers, and repainted in colors that were barely street legal.

He inspected the gal he'd found on the road. Tuckered out as she was, she'd fallen asleep in the cab of his rig, leaned against the side door. Little more than a pile of dirty laundry. A gal with her upbringing, she figured that history only moved in one direction. The Talbott book had proved her wrong. With the price on her head, she was a dead PhD walking.

The two-lane highway skirted fields that stretched to the horizon. As many rows of eggplants as there were ripples in the ocean. Tended by a platoon of stooped women with headscarves knotted to cover their hair. Refugees from the cities. The cities weren't sustainable. Never mind all the recycling and wind turbine power, cities were never sustainable. They'd collapsed into pits of cannibalism with the lucky survivors streaming into the countryside. They'd gone begging to serve on the estates of the chieftains. No counterrevolution was organizing in the hills, living on hardtack and plotting to regain power with a really, really, scathingly brilliant poem.

The thugs and gangsters had the guns so now they ruled their own nation of bondsmen and thralls. The bros and rednecks had the guns so now they reigned over the serfs of Caucasia. The right-minded progressive gun grabbers with their right-side-of-history, they had their civil-rights lawyers and Ninth Circuit Court. They'd lived their entire lives on paper. If they survived it was as grateful slaves.

The PhD gal stirred in her sleep. Dawson tried to recall her name from the list. Her bounty was sixteen hundred votes, and those could be auctioned for good money. Her name escaped him. It had been something made-up.

She blinked away.

He didn't break eye contact until she looked away. He didn't need to. The roads were empty. He could feed her. Get her some milk, a big glass of buttermilk. The wedding ring deep in his pants pocket told him this wouldn't be so easy.

She slumped low. Hiding low. And asked, "Where are you taking me?"

"Canada," Dawson lied. On the horizon hovered a large white sign. Mounted atop a pole, it turned slowly. In large black letters against a white background it read: "*Whites Only.*"

Dawson asked, "How does some breakfast sound?"

She dashed tears from her eyes. "I need to feel safe somewhere."

Dawson knew she'd never feel safe again.

It was just as well this calamity had befallen her, he figured. She'd risen to power by repeating the opinions of people who'd repeated the opinions of people who'd repeated the opinions of people. If that wasn't a lineage equal to and just as corrupt as the lineages of Adjustment Day, Dawson didn't know jack. History had saved this woman. She'd been given a chance, like Scarlett O'Hara, to be tested and develop a real power of her own making.

The crying had cleaned her face some. Minus the crud, she wasn't so hard on the eyes. She looked at the plowed landscape with the dazed expression of a sleepwalker who'd woken up from a long dream about universal equality and guaranteed human rights.

Dawson remembered. Her name was Ramantha.

He parked in the gravel lot beside the diner, and they walked in and sat at a red-topped table. Flounced gingham curtains hung in the windows. They matched the frilled apron of the waitress who asked, "What can I get you folks?" Her breath, sweet smelling from Juicy Fruit chewing gum.

Dawson asked, "What's good?" A juke box played country music at low volume.

The waitress twiddled her pen between the fingers of one hand. "The Bull Connor White Bean Burrito is nice." She glanced back at the kitchen pass-through window. "And the Eva Braun White Cheddar Mac 'n' Cheese is real good."

Ramantha held her menu too high. She was clearly hiding behind it. Muffled, she said, "I'll have the Klan Burger."

The waitress eyed her. She popped her gum and asked, "Grand Dragon or Grand Wizard?"

Dawson translated, "She means large or small."

The waitress asked, "Honey, may I see some identification?"

"What?" Ramantha looked out from behind the menu. "I'm thirty-five."

Dawson said, "I'll vouch for her." It wasn't proof of age the waitress wanted, it was proof of ethnicity. As a chieftain of the first lineage, he knew no one would doubt his word. He ordered a cup of coffee.

The professor ordered a Skinhead Skinless Chicken Breast Sandwich and a Woodrow Wilson Egg Salad Sandwich and a Lothrop Stoddard Vanilla Sundae with Marshmallow Sauce and Whipped Cream.

He sipped his coffee and watched her dig into the mountain of food.

If she stunk he'd grown used to her stink. By the look of her stringy arms she couldn't fight off much. He could ravish her just for the effort of pushing her to the ground.

The wedding ring felt big in his pocket.

Dawson flagged the waitress and asked for the check, all the while telling himself that as soon as the sun set he wasn't going to rape this half-dead woman. Nope. Positively not, no way was he raping her and strangling her skinny neck and cutting off her ear to sell so he could buy his old lady that treadle sewing machine she'd been mooning after for better than a year.

Theirs was the grandest wedding the fledgling nation of Caucasia had ever witnessed. After the regal promenade of the royal families, each chieftain bedecked in jewels and artificial furs, leading a contingent of pregnant wives . . . after the lavish banquet of the lineages . . . after the courtiers had toasted each other with chalices of healthy urine . . . after each public wife of the realm had bestowed her best wishes upon Queen Shasta . . . as she and Charlie stood on the parapets and waved to their thousands of serfs . . . it was then a tight formation of jumbo jetliners passed directly overhead.

His eyes following them, Charlie did say, "There. The last of the Jews are homebound for Israel. A good omen. Let us celebrate!"

For their nuptial tour around the estate, an open carriage wrought from solid silver—a great heavy thing—was pulled by a visibly straining, enormous herd of tiny white lambs.

Whole mutton turned slowly on spits above raging bonfires. The air redolent with meaty smells and the stink of gunpowder, the latter from the celebratory fireworks. Mead did flow, and bodices were roundly ripped to the sound of merry pipers.

In their first wedded moment alone, Charlie did take his new wife boldly in his arms. In noble modesty he acceded to Shasta that his was a simple hard-laboring, tax-paying Caucasian penis without the dimensions or the stamina accredited to the black or the homosexual. His might not bring her the fulfillment of others, but he would strive to sow a multitude of seeds in her. Charlie would sow her and keep sowing her, relentlessly, for she would be his mate. He'd sow her anytime he desired, day or night, headache or none. And he'd sow her in any position he could imagine and sow her wearing costumes and as he compelled her to pretend to be his second-grade teacher, Mrs. Halliday, or a sexy airline stewardess, maybe, or he'd sow her all tied up because the overarching edict of Caucasia was "Progress Can Wait" and in line with the teachings of Talbott millions of men had died to create and protect the formerly united states, those men had given their lives and perished in unspeakable agony so now women should dedicate themselves to preserving the nation, and instead of landmines blasting them into screaming gore or mustard gas reaming out their lungs, this generation of women would be revered by a new nation of offspring and future generations, for perpetuating the white race.

Shasta, Charlie extolled, held the destiny of Caucasia between her legs.

Still attired in her wedding finery, Shasta did demurely excuse herself to make water. Charlie gave her a peck on the cheek and told her not to tarry. They had yet to cut their towering wedding cake. Nor had they danced to the traditional madrigals.

Veiled did Shasta implement the next phase of her plan.

The ruse with Charm's spit had worked. As their newly crowned queen, the palace guard could deny Shasta access to no area. Quickly she scurried to Charlie's home office. There she booted his antique computer machine. His was no great intellect, and she readily circumnavigated his crude security codes. His password was a bit cryptic: "mom&dadRIP." The device buzzed and blinked. Its screen began to scroll the names of the living and the targeted. Those who had been relocated to other homelands. Those who

remained in Caucasia and to whom they were presently inden-
tured. Among these names she found not that of her true love.

For Shasta did love only one man, and contrary to appearances
it was not Charlie.

And as the fireworks began to boom against the dusking sky
did she activate the Search function and type in the name "Walter Baines."

Back in the world you still know . . . in the Before Times . . . Walter
whispered to Talbott while the old man slept. He held up telephone
photos of Shasta. He whispered about her wisdom and talents.
About her beauty and strength and grace. And as the old man
dozed and drowsed and snored, Walter held the pink foam earplug
so Talbott couldn't help but catch a whiff of its acrid perfume.

Jamal couldn't help but show off. Days and evenings he'd sit with
the creature in the bygone glory of the parlor. The creature bragged
up the men in the ancestral portraits, boasting about their acts of
bravery and scientific achievements. Left unsaid was the constant
drumbeat declaring the past to be a golden era and the present a
swamp of failure.

To remedy the situation Jamal summoned the housekeeper and
asked her to dress Barnabas for a day's outing. Nothing stressful.
Not much more than a jaunt to a nearby city to survey the changes
that had taken place since the founding of Blacktopia.

Arabella pulled a face. "You do realize," she said, "that soul
hasn't set foot off this farm in years."

Jamal assured her, "All's the more reason."

Barnabas didn't appear partial to the idea, either. It couldn't set
foot over the threshold without wanting to go back for a different
shirt or to change its shoes.

Jamal's first point of pride was the levitator. The same electro-spiritual principles that floated the great space pyramids, this same black-based technology allowed personal transport vehicles that amounted to small floating platforms that could skim along at incredible speeds. Throughout history white men had claimed that magic carpets were a fiction simply because no white man could duplicate the achievement. Vehemently, whites had long sought to humiliate blacks by claiming the latter had never invented the wheel.

The Barnabas creature tentatively climbed aboard the floating platform as Jamal explained. Blacks in Africa had no use for wheels because they flew. They'd no use for any written language because they combined their wisdom utilizing the technique of cognitive amalgamation. All of this wisdom had been secretly locked away when Europeans had begun to invade the continent.

Barnabas gripped the front edge of the platform with metaphorically white knuckles. The rush of air rustled its mass of frizzed hair. The vehicle began its rise above the trees, above the house and barns. "Lawdy, massah Jamal," the creature bawled, "Gawd ain't nev-ah intentioned uz tah flah!"

As they soared above the open country Jamal lectured on the state of things since Adjustment Day. Gays, who'd lived such gadabout and footloose lives, in Gaysia they were yoked to the national campaign for reproduction. Draconian sperm drives left most men with little money or energy. And women had lost all control over their reproductive rights. Healthy women were required to register, and eventually to be conscripted to bear—not arms—but babies! To sustain their population via export left them with scant time for sadomasochistic antics or meth-fueled circuit parties. Jamal shouted to be heard above the wind, "Liberation has enslaved them!"

Citizens of Caucasia were no better off. Where they'd excelled in science, they now banned it. They'd turned their focus to Jeffersonian agriculture and reinstating a white-European culture. The great metropolises of Caucasia had swiftly declined into deadly no-go zones where displaced liberal-arts majors stalked each other as food. The lucky had escaped to indenture themselves to chieftains and labor on the huge food-producing estates.

Below the levitator, the lands of Blacktopia appeared without houses or fences. All roadways, power poles, and other signs of human civilization had been erased. In their place wild animals roamed. Sleek herds of zebras. Horned masses of wildebeests. Jamal tried to read Barnabas's expression. The Peabody Plantation stood alone, the last survivor of the many dynastic seats that had until recently filled the region. The creature could only stare, its mouth agog.

Like a mirage, the rainbow-colored lights, the spires and domes of a city appeared in the distance. Unlike Caucasia, the populations of Blacktopia had coalesced into its cities, transforming them into magnificence while allowing the greater landscape to revert back to an almost limitless nature preserve. The fauna of Mother Africa had been introduced and had flourished. The levitator carried them above the heads of wallowing hippos and preening lions. They dipped to better observe fierce packs of hyenas. A paradise, it amounted to, and Jamal felt justified in his pride.

Every wonder the white man had dismissed as a fable, here it existed. The city they approached rivaled all the legends about Atlantis. Blacks had resurrected all the pyro-spiritual and electro-expressive technologies they'd long kept hidden. These, the sacred laws of soul-metrics, had never been appropriated to enrich the white man's brutal empire.

As a chieftain of the first lineage Jamal would be warmly welcomed into any home.

The levitator swerved and looped between the dramatic, multicolored skyscrapers. Flowering vines cascaded down from windows and balconies like brilliant flags. The Barnabas creature craned its neck as if searching for any vestige of the previous corrupt civilization built by white people. Mere months had elapsed since Adjustment Day. "Massah Jamal," it stammered, "how?"

"Muse-O-Metrix," Jamal answered. He explained that the harmonic gifts of his race had much deeper applications than the white man had ever suspected. When a sufficient population of blacks harmonized in unison, the power of their combined song would restructure physical matter. Each massive building amounted to the frozen music of a single beautiful song. Indeed, every pinnacle soared like a crescendo.

Jamal steered the levitator toward a prominent edifice. Domed and buttressed, it dwarfed the less-imposing structures surrounding it. At the gateway a liveried robot assisted him and Barnabas to disembark. They entered through dazzling crystalline doors and crossed a plush lobby alive with blooming tropical plants and free-flying parrots and cockatiels.

Barnabas, cowed, whispered, "Lawdy massah, hoo liv-ah hee-rah?" The whispers echoed back from the vaulted ceiling and the chamber's trove of priceless antiquities.

Jamal didn't shush the creature. He took pity on the stooped freak that was shrinking itself ever smaller in fear. Barnabas was beyond the age for finding out it was full of shit.

Past the lobby none but a single pair of doors, heavily sculpted from what appeared to be solid gold, so warm and so bright, only these doors stood. Jamal touched a discrete button and chimes sounded. The doors swung inward to reveal a robot attired in a tuxedo. In a warm cultured voice, this robot bid, "Greetings, Jamal. Is your mother expecting you?"

The robot ushered them into a luminous chamber. It held the muffled silence of a greenhouse. Orchids were rooted in the intricately tiled walls, and their trembling blossoms scented the air with sweetness. Following the robot's gesture, Jamal and the Barnabas creature seated themselves on expensive wicker settees. They accepted tall highly colored drinks offered by a robot dressed in a lacy apron and cap.

Hardly were they settled before another door opened and a rush of colors and perfume swept into their presence. A swirl of iridescent silk skirt revealed two perfectly sculpted gams striding toward them. Braided hair glinted with Tahitian pearls and platinum beads. "My darling," said the dulcet voice of a goddess. Slender and regal, she crossed to kiss Jamal lightly on both cheeks. Her eyes fell on the creature and her refined features twisted. At the sight of this stained dwarf, her smooth face shriveled with confusion and fear.

Jamal and the Barnabas creature stood to greet her.

Not a heartbeat passed before she'd regained her queenly composure. "Hello." She offered a languid hand, the fingers weighted with diamond rings, the wrist loaded with emerald bracelets. "I am Jamal's mother." Her expression betrayed none of her earlier alarm.

Jamal had always admired his mom. Rich or poor, she'd always been a class act. And as she accepted the withered, discolored paw of the creature, his respect grew beyond all bounds. She threw him a look of concern masked behind a serene smile, marked only because her eye contact lasted a smidgen too long. Her silent nod summoned a robot bearing a silver tray of amuse-bouches. "I hope you like nightingale tongues," she said.

Added the robot in a scratchy, affectless voice, "They're bite-sized."

Jamal watched with mild delight as the creature picked from among the delicacies. "Eye's be Barn-ah-bus," it said, and popped a tidbit into its grinning mouth.

His mother maintained her composure as the creature regaled them with tales about farm life. "Dat Mizz Jo, she be's ah monstah tah works fer," it said through a mouthful of partially masticated tongues. It went on to describe menial chores and how Miss Josephine had fled immediately following Adjustment Day. "Dat Massah Tal-bott, he be's a troo hee-ro!"

Jamal's mother took this in stride. "My son has long been obsessed with living in that particular house . . ."

The Barnabas creature cast him a puzzled look.

Jamal gave his mother a sideways glance, one eyebrow raised to warn her. "Yes," he added. "We have family history in the area."

The creature did a goggle-eyed double take. "Wuz ya'll fambly slay-vus?"

Jamal's mother motioned for a robot to refresh their drinks. "Something like that . . . ," she sighed.

They passed a pleasant afternoon. Jamal's mother shepherded them into her kitchen where the flesh generator provided a delicious luncheon. She explained proudly how the technology was based on HeLa cells, immortal cells that continued to reproduce themselves indefinitely. These cells had been invented by a black woman and used to alter the DNA of animals, creating masses of beef, chicken, and pork that spontaneously cloned themselves. The flesh generator itself was a huge cylinder of meat that turned slowly under heat lamps. The exterior was always a savory cooked layer ready to be carved away and eaten. At the core were the ever-replicating cells, fed by a constant stream of amino acids pumped through the spindle at the core of the cylinder. To Jamal it looked like nothing more than an old-school gyro cone grilling on a vertical rotisserie, but in this case the tapering amalgam of boneless flesh was a living thing, raw and vital at the core, but constantly dying and being cooked on the outside. The scent was intoxicating.

They watched the meat rotate smoothly. It sweated clear grease that ran in rivulets down its appetizing flanks. "The true blessing is that we no longer need to slaughter animals," said Jamal's mother. The core's genetically immortal cells were like a sourdough "starter" that perpetuated itself given the right conditions. Every household included such a generator, thus the animals of Blacktopia caroused in complete safety and freedom. Even the carnivores were fed from similar flesh generators. Fully satiated on immortal meat, the lions did in fact lie down with the lambs. Black technology had created Heaven on Earth.

Barnabas recoiled at first, but a single mouth-watering bite made it a convert.

Jamal's mother leaned close to the creature as if sharing an intimate confidence. "I do hope you can convince my son to demolish that old farm and assume his place of prestige, here in the city." She looked pointedly at Jamal. Her tone was prickly. "His obsession with that ancient homestead is entirely unhealthy."

He and his mother had debated this point many times. Instead of engaging on the topic, Jamal noted the time and insisted on taking Barnabas home.

The creature fell silent on their trip back home. The sight of so many wonders had clearly shaken Barnabas. It glanced about with bulging, confused eyes.

Jamal felt a huge sympathy, almost a familial affection for it.

A heavy, inky tear washed a lighter stripe down its cheek. It spoke haltingly, "Ah ah-soom yah'll wanz tah ee-rad-ah-kate Mizz Jo's fambly play-s?"

Jamal fixed the creature with a compassionate expression. "I promise," he vowed, "that as long as you live that house will stand as your home."

The Barnabas creature gazed into the distance. There, the familiar barns and manor house were slowly coming into sight. In the backdrop, the sun was setting rapidly.

Bing held the bong to his mouth, sighting down the length of it as if it were a rifle. He held a cigarette lighter to the packed bowl and flicked the lighter as if he were pulling a trigger. He inhaled so hard he went cross-eyed. With his lungs full, he shouted, "Bang! Bang! Bang!" expelling dope smoke like bursts of gun smoke.

He jerked the bong from side to side as if firing on new targets, the peppermint schnapps inside it sloshing. He sighted a final target through the bong and puffed out a muffled, "Bang."

Felix clutched his heart in both hands and fell backward against a garbage can. "You got me," he croaked, "I'm dead."

Bing handed the lighter to Felix. He lowered the bong and

turned his attention to reloading the bowl. "Alive defines dead," he sighed. "You never feel as alive as when you make somebody else dead."

He described how it had felt to be in the shooting gallery of the legislature. Bing's favorite topic. They sat, just the two of them, in the alley back of Felix's apartment house.

Delicious was out. Felix's mom was home, which was why he was hiding outdoors, pulling bong hits. Being alone with his mom was agony these days. She was forever guilt-tripping him to not declare his preference, to wait at least a year, to stay at home and keep her company. But when he considered another year in Gaysia, another hands-off year watching everyone else find love while every pussy was off-limits to him, the wait made him crazy.

Bing handed him the bong, saying, "I can't believe you're not homo." It was okay for Bing to know. Bing was a national hero, a chieftain of the first lineage. He'd stood in the spectator's gallery and put a stop to the old order, where weaklings had pandered and lied to win the popularity contest people used to call "politics."

For Bing nothing would ever compare to Adjustment Day. That was why he'd become a stoner, because he'd never match the rush of blowing away the framework of his oppression.

Felix took the bong, seeing the inside of Bing's forearm. The tattoo there below the rolled-up sleeve of his shirt. Felix asked, "Is that Andy Warhol?"

Bing twisted his arm to read his own tattoo. "It's Talbott." He asked, "Did I tell you I met him?"

Felix had the bong around his lips as he said, "Only a million times." His words sounded muffled inside the tube of it. The tattoo read:

In the Future Everyone Will Be Shot for Fifteen Minutes.

"Yeah," Bing said, "I was there when he said it." He'd told the story so many times, about Talbott being lashed to a chair with leather belts and duct tape, naked and bloodied but still issuing orders. About the chieftains each seeking an audience with him in the weeks leading up to Adjustment Day.

Felix exhaled, asking, "How'd it feel?" And he inhaled through the bong. The schnapps bubbled, and the mint-tasting smoke flooded his mouth.

They both knew what he meant. And it felt wonderful. Killing your enemy felt better than the biggest lottery win. It felt like having the *last* last word. The ultimate victory. As it was written in the Talbott book:

The Core Human Drive Is to Dominate and to Avoid Being Dominated.

And as the book was quick to add:

Anyone Who Denies That Fact Is Simply Trying to Dominate You.

Felix held the smoke in his chest and listened.

"So where you headed?" asked Bing. He meant Caucasia or Blacktopia. It was a testament to Gaysia that Bing could sit here, taking deep bong hits in a cat piss–smelling alley at midnight. In Caucasia and Blacktopia citizens with a preponderance of Asian genetics were deported to Asia. Jews went to Israel. Mexican types self-exiled to Mexico.

And for the first time, an idea dawned on Felix. He'd never seen Bing with another man. Maybe Bing was a heterosexual hiding out like his own parents. Maybe the reason Bing was always baked was because he didn't want to be shipped off to another continent, yet he wasn't a homosexual, either. Bing might be someone he could trust with all of his secrets.

Felix held his breath and shrugged. He'd cross the genetic testing bridge when he came to it. He still had to fill out the paperwork for his formal declaration of preference.

"Killing is killing," said Bing. It was the best rush, bar none. It was like winning the biggest win. To see your enemies burst open. To hear them fall silent and to know they'd never again hurt you. It was the end to your worst fears. The confirmation that you don't need to be anyone's slave. Bing had told the story so many times, in bars, in front of school assemblies. He amounted to a living fossil.

A stoned living fossil. The thought almost made Felix laugh. Because a fossil was by definition encased in stone, and Bing's eyes were so fucking bloodshot . . . even as he recounted forcing some terrified senator to fill the burial pits at gunpoint.

"To remove the person from a person," Bing insisted, "to reduce somebody to nothing but meat and hair, it's like a magic trick only real. You know?" He coughed, choking out the word. "Isn't that what a miracle is?"

Felix nodded vehemently and handed back the bong. He debated telling Bing the whole truth. A little stoned, he trusted that Bing would understand. Bing had kept his secret about being heterosexual since Felix had moved in next door to them. "Promise me something," Felix asked. "Will you check in on my mom? Like on Christmas? Just so she's not totally alone."

Packing the bowl, Bing dismissed his concern. "Your mom has Delicious. Delicious is going to have a kid."

Felix waited until the bong was reloaded and his friend was sparking the bowl. As Bing sucked down a toke, Felix marveled. The set-up was perfect. And it wasn't just the weed talking. Bing was obviously a fugitive, too, living next door. Felix could make his declaration and find his own future knowing that Bing would stay around. Granted, Felix's dad would be here, but he couldn't risk crossing paths with his secret wife. That, and Delicious was here, but she was practically a stranger. Bing, his best friend, would continue to watch over Felix's mother while she grew old.

The bowlful of dope flared bright orange in the dark. The schnapps gurgled.

"Don't take this the wrong way," Felix began. He looked for light in any nearby windows. The only glowing window was high up in his apartment where his mom would be sitting alone in the kitchen. He asked, "We're friends, right?"

Bing's chest swelled with the smoke. His red eyes met Felix's, and he nodded.

Felix continued, "I know why you're here, in Gaysia . . ."

Bing cocked his head, still holding the smoke.

"You're like my parents," Felix explained. "My dad is black. They both moved here claiming to be homosexual, but they're secretly married and get together on the sly—"

The smoke exploded from Bing's mouth in a huge, "What!"

Felix had fucked up.

The bong set carefully aside, Bing glowered. "Say what?" Loud. A window appeared as inside a light flashed on. Another window appeared.

Felix held up both hands to shush his friend. "Nothing. A joke."

"So does Delicious know?" asked Bing. His eyes blinked. "Or is Delicious a heterosexual, too?"

For the first time, Felix could see the old Bing. The man his friend had been, who could shoulder a rifle and mow down everyone he considered an enemy. Above them, other lights outlined new windows. People would hear. One window scraped open and a voice called down, "It's late!"

Felix lunged. He clamped a hand over Bing's mouth and held it, whispering, "Please don't."

The two grappled, tumbling sideways on the littered ground. Wrestling in the cigarette butts and bottle caps. Bing's fingernails clawed at Felix's hand, clawed at his face and neck, but Felix held on, whispering, "You can't." As their legs kicked over garbage cans and people shouted down at them in the dark, Bing clobbered Felix with a fist to the head. Bing bashed him between the eyes, and Felix felt heat spray from his nose, and he tasted salt and peppermint schnapps, and he felt Bing's screams muffled against his palm. Both of Bing's hands were pounding him in the ribs. His knees pummeled Felix's gut.

More windows were bright, and far overhead stood the outline of Felix's mom, the upper half of her, her head and shoulders outlined in the light from their kitchen.

Bing's teeth sank into his palm, and Felix snatched his hand back.

Bing's voice rang out, "Heterosexuals! Heterosexuals!"

And Felix's bleeding fingers found the long tube of the bong and grabbed it up, and brought it down. The glass broke across something, and Bing fell silent. Blood and peppermint schnapps splashed everywhere.

Bing's body went limp and toppled backward onto the pavement. Any person was gone from the person. Reduced to nothing but meat and hair. The night air carried the growing sound of police sirens.

Felix had heard the stories often enough to know. His only friend was dead.

Worse than dead, Bing was wrong.

Killing him hadn't made Felix feel even the least bit great.

When Nick found the first box he wasn't surprised. It sat in the middle of Southeast Yamhill Street, between 42nd and 43rd. The Talbott book predicted as much.

The book had gotten everything right, so far. The fires had started weeks before, just as the Talbott book had foreseen. Here was the same method the elites had used in the 1965 Watts fire that had destroyed one hundred square blocks, in the 1967 Newark fires, and the 1967 Detroit fire that had wiped out four hundred buildings. As in Washington, D.C., in 1968 with 1,199 buildings burned, it was always the whites torching black neighborhoods. To herd black citizens away from urban areas and back to lives as sharecroppers and field hands in the Deep South.

These days it was the Caucasia chieftains committing arson in order to drive any lingering blacks to Blacktopia. And to drive the remaining Portland whites out to the estates.

The box left in the street was the same deal.

In the 1950s such a box would be filled with heroin. In the 1990s it would be crack cocaine. Whatever the decade, the CIA would leave the box in any neighborhood they wanted to destroy. Now it was the chieftains. Nick tore the cardboard open and sorted the bags packed inside. He shoved the pockets of his trench coat full of Vicodin and Ambien and Xanax, pounds of them sealed in plastic. The rest he left. According to the Talbott book they'd drop a mess of these boxes, and Nick scuttled off to high grade the rest.

A poster on a nearby wall screamed out: A Smile Is Your Best Bulletproof Vest! Nick's only family, his mom, had packed up and gambled her last tank of gas on finding an estate where she could pledge herself. Word was the big land operations were fringed with favelas of displaced media and information workers. All living out of their dusty cars. Washed-up web designers and diversity officers, they were all hoping to prove themselves in the upcoming rhubarb harvest and to be awarded a thatched cottage before winter set in.

The entire Wiki-squat of the Internet was trashed. The only radio was Talbott and approved Caucasian music. Mostly polkas, with some waltzes and jigs. The greatest hits of harpsichord and bagpipe. The radio announced that the fires had been set by loyalists. Partisans. Talbott himself denounced any rumors that the old president had escaped and that a lookalike had been assassinated in his stead.

Officially, the president of the formerly united states was dead. Officially, the fires that sprang up at night and drove helpless people into the dark streets were set by rebels. Bandits or highwaymen. Maybe Canadians. Canadians, Nick noted, were branded the new terrorists.

According to Talbott's book, throughout modern history well-meaning blacks had been persecuted. Each time a city had burst into flame, when black citizens had rushed to save property threatened by the fire, white military forces had used this as a pretense to arrest them for looting. These days as fires churned through block after block of Portland, anyone who tried to help was arrested. Convicted on trumped-up charges, they were rail-roaded to work gangs.

The boxes, the boxes allowed the less heroic another option. As Talbott phrased it, less useful members of society could self-select to leave, through accidental overdose or suicide.

The fires foiled the heroes. The drugs resolved the cowards. Only Nick could eke out a life staying buzzed when there was no food to be found. Sleep was a different matter. The great chieftain estates with their fabled swaths of runner beans and red cabbages, they'd displaced the wild packs of wolves and coyotes. Those animals as well as bears and cougars had roamed into the city streets, the parks and neighborhoods, seeking new prey. Nights when they howled and their victims screamed, Nick had the pills to sleep soundly in whatever abandoned automobile.

Days, he'd come across a mess that might stretch for city blocks. The ribcage and spine in one place, the head and pelvis would be dragged off. The skull might be gone, but there was always the matted hair. Usually the hands, too. The sidewalk or alley would be sticky with dried blood, with footprints of blood wandering off in every direction. The footprints of wolves or bear. The scavenger prints of coyotes and raccoons, magpies, rats. Each trail of red prints pointed the direction of some missing arm or entrails. Some hapless so-and-so. The fingers, the fingers of the gnawed-on hands would be loaded with diamond rings, ruby rings. The eyes would be pecked out, but a pearl necklace would be left behind, mired in the blood. Carnivores knew what was actually of real value.

The Xanax took care of the absolute worst aspect of modern city life. Not the food insecurity or the dying nighttime screams. The toughest detail to deal with was the loneliness.

Shasta was gone. As were Walter and Xavier. No one except the certifiable had stayed in the inner city, and Nick steered a wide course around them.

A block distant, an excellent example lurked. A naked old man, his wrists and ankles flapping with scraps of dirty duct tape. His emaciated body looked glossy with dried blood. What might be a hash-mark carpet of tiny stab wounds dotted his spindly arms and legs. The man ambled along the deserted sidewalk. He caught sight of Nick and waved. The butchered apparition craned its thin neck and shouted, "Walter!" In a different direction, it shouted again, "Walter!"

Nick turned tail and did not wave back.

According to Talbott the Civil War had nothing to do with slavery. In reality, the famous War Between the States had been just a ruse to cull the vast numbers of Irish who were emigrating to northern cities. Another youth bulge neutralized.

He found another box on Southeast Woodstock and filched the pills. Outside a burned house in the Westmoreland neighborhood he found a pile of scorched furniture. Armloads of clothes still on hangers. Ralph Lauren, Gucci, Armani, these clothes were illegal to wear now. He picked through the pile and found a gun but no bullets. A perfectly good guitar.

The worst aspect of loneliness was the silence. Bird song was the only regular sound besides the wind. He swung the pack off his back and dug out a bag of pills. He placed two Xanax in his mouth and tasted the sweetness as they dissolved under his tongue. On Northeast Mississippi Avenue he found a third box and tore into its contents.

Talbott had spoken slowly while Walter and the assembled men had leaned forward to listen. "The burial pits should measure three hundred feet long by thirty feet wide and twelve feet deep." All the while strapped to the same chair, he'd instructed, "The floor of each pit must be sealed with a layer of quarter-inch-thick polyethylene sheeting, topped by a two-foot-thick layer of impervious clay."

To save effort he encouraged consistency, saying, "Don't everyone try to reinvent the wheel."

In recent days, the basement had become a clubhouse of sorts. A headquarters or command center. Naylor and Esteban, the men from the narcotics recovery group, had come knocking. On their heels had appeared other men, all of them apparently recruited from similar groups across the country.

If Walter had to guess, they were heterosexuals and homosexuals. Black and white. They'd all joined Talbott's new payroll and zealously followed the ever-growing Internet list of names now dubbed America's Least Wanted. And as Walter had been dispatched to compile his notes and hire a printer, these men came to serve as Talbott's inner circle.

Each man had overcome his own demon, be it heroin or cancer, and now he was here to conquer something bigger. As they'd crowded around Talbott's knee, he'd told them:

> Flattery is addictive. Convince others they're special.
> Assure them they have talent. Make yourself the
> source of people's self-worth. Doing so binds them
> to you and it preempts them from developing
> their skills and proving their true potential.

As they'd passed cans of beer and bags of chips, he'd told them:

> Assembly is expression. Individuals must be granted
> the right to associate with those and only those they
> select. The groups that result shall not be compelled
> to open their ranks to those they wish to exclude.

Delirious from so many tiny infections, Talbott had ranted:

> Be horrible, exist as a horrible threat, and
> at the moment of your greatest power stay
> your hand. By hurting people and then not
> hurting them you acquire their love.

He'd told them:

> Imagine there's no God. There is no Heaven or
> Hell. There is only your son and his son and
> his son, and the world you leave for them.

If they'd laughed. If they sparked to an idea, nodding their heads in agreement, Talbott had snapped his fingers for Walter to make note of it. He'd been road testing his concepts. If these men engaged with an idea and seconded it by offering up examples from their own lives, Talbott had known it was valid for a wider audience and had looked to Walter to put it into the upcoming book.

Talbott had explained that while Adolf Hitler had been a prisoner in Landsberg Prison, his cell had been the site of a constant party. People brought beer and food, visitors crowded the room while Hitler regaled them with his ideas. The ideas that resonated, that made Hitler's listeners smile in recognition, Hitler collected those ideas into his first draft of *Mein Kampf*. These ideas would engage the largest number of people.

And so Talbott had conducted a similar back-and-forth dialog with the men who made their pilgrimage to consult him. These men, Clem and Naylor and Bing, he'd told them, "In the future everyone will be shot for fifteen minutes."

Rufus and L.J., he told them, "Only the left ear, please."

Walter's new old man, he'd explained that the best feedback would be a grunt, a snort, a moan, any noise to prove he'd hit a nerve with some truth. The best feedback was never filtered through language. At most it might be an "Amen" or a "Fuck, yeah." Some profane form of "Hallelujah." Until the book of fragments became like Mao's book of quotations or *Poor Richard's Almanack*, a collection of aphorisms.

Talbott had explained that what they were composing would be a sutra. The Talbott Sutra. Like *The Golden Verses of Pythagoras* or the biblical Ecclesiastes. It would serve as the new consciousness.

A modern *Mein Kampf* as it were.

They would publish it *samizdat*, like the Soviet dissidents. In the manner of Andrei Sakharov. And distribute the copies via the growing network of Clems and Dawsons and Charlies snaking man-by-man across the nation.

And still certain that somehow this would make him a rich man, this would win him Shasta's heart, Walter had written everything down.

Because of the yelling the police show up. Because it's after midnight and Bing was a chieftain of the first lineage, this meant helicopters circling the neighborhood and sweeping the area with searchlights. Because the police are forever and everywhere after the same deal: Did you fight? Did he fight you? Because Felix's ma shakes her head, head down, because she figures this is somehow her doing. Because then Delicious walks in the door, going, "Belle, what's your Felix gone and done now?"

Because Delicious doesn't know it's her ass at stake, too. Because it's everyone's butt on the line, because if the truth comes out then Belle and Delicious, Jarvis and Gentry will go into detention as suspect detainees, forever. Because nobody prioritizes accepting damaged goods. Because the newly declared homosexuals of Caucasia and Blacktopia being held in detention elsewhere are good for a half million Talbotts or a new fresh somebody, so why settle for some traitor whom even Gaysia wants rid of.

Because the paramedics are debriding the cuts and scratches on his face and neck. Because Felix looks almost as beat up as the dead body of Bing. Because folks leaning out their bedroom windows heard Bing's last words, clear and distinct. Because people live in the forever-after shadow of that Kitty Genovese, the lesbian who was strangled and stabbed and strangled and stabbed while some entire city full of onlookers failed to take action.

Because so many people leaned out windows back then and never called the police because a young, pretty lesbian getting herself butchered wasn't their problem, because of that everyone chimes in reciting Bing's yelled-out last words.

To hear Felix tell it, he and Bing had been peacefully smoking dope in the alley around midnight. In the version he told the investigating officers, Bing had been telling stories about the success of his lineage, and how he, Bing himself, had journeyed to a basement in Portland, Oregon, and had an audience in the presence of the venerable Talbott. Bing hadn't been a nobody. As a chieftain of the first lineage, his death called for a massive investigation. Dogs had been dispatched to track possible traces of Bing's blood on an escaping killer.

Even as the paramedics debrided the cuts and scratches on Felix's face and neck, he told them what he wanted to tell. Because no one except Felix had paid much attention to Bing as of late. Because, frankly, Bing's one-day war story could be a bore and because people had more to fret about, what with sperm drives and biological carrier commissions. Because people would never say as much, but they were beginning to question the greatness of Gaysia, the gay promised land, and because they missed the kick-up-your-heels lifestyle they'd lived under heterosexual oppression. It's because of this guilt—guilt over doubting Gaysia, guilt over Kitty Genovese—that all the ear witnesses repeated Bing's last gasped words.

It's because of them Felix said what he finally said. Because he didn't say it at first, not right away. Because he knew it would trigger an international incident. Because he didn't want this nation, Gaysia, to be at war, because wasn't Adjustment Day about saving a generation from military cemeteries?

Because why should statesmen get to snuff out the lives of men barely able to vote? But because Felix doesn't want to see his folks internment-camped, and because he needs to buy time, because any simple DNA test will prove it's his DNA and only his DNA grabbed all over Bing's corpse and clawed under Bing's fingernails . . . because everyone's baying for blood and justice . . . Felix says it was a gang of strangers. Because it's plausible, and because this gains him traction. Because Felix was quickly replacing Talbott on every channel, the satellite-relayed image of him, because he had all of Gaysia hanging on his every word, because he was already packing a getaway bag in his mind, packing his favorite shirts and an extra pair of shoes, and because Felix needed that crucial head start to make his escape, that's the reason Felix finally said what he did.

"Straights," he told the television cameras. "Straight guys bashed him."

It never failed to leave Shasta astounded. The same sun that warmed her neck at this moment had also warmed Hitler's. The stars she could see from her marriage bed were the stars that had twinkled above infamous Nazi death camps. How humans organized their society and conducted their lives counted for nothing in the grand scheme.

Trees were taking root on the burial pits. The important parts of life remained a constant. People fed their children. People could only truly hate those who lived next door. Just as life had been before, everyone was preoccupied by staying alive. Water always found a new level. A new normal.

The field wives, for example. They roamed the thriving rows of kale and squash, each woman swollen with a child. All of them, Charlie's offspring. Soon every day would be marked by the birth of one or more heirs. In another year the estate would be overrun with tiny Charlies.

One real possibility was that Shasta herself was the problem. The party pooper, as it were. If she'd been born into this moment she'd see only peaceful women doing useful work to the sound of mandolins. Well fed, they were all healthy and plump with their future children. If she hadn't known the world before Adjustment

Day she wouldn't see this Edenic scene through such a cynical, bitter lens. These future children would accept this life as a given. The idea both comforted and enraged her.

As they labored over the weeding chores, Shasta went about her usual search among the roots and furrows. The sun warmed the hooded cowl she wore, edged with decadent fake ocelot fur. A band of roving minstrels plucked lutes and crooned ballads.

A wave of nausea surged up from her belly, and she fought the urge to puke on a row of maturing parsnips. She could be . . . Heaven knows Charlie had sewn plenty of seed in her. She shuddered at the possibility of becoming another brood mare for the rapacious chieftain.

A meek figure shuffled forward. The girl didn't speak but stopped an arm's length away. A lacy cap held the long hair gathered atop her head. A light veil of netting cascaded over her face to protect her young complexion from the sun. Her humble, downcast gaze remained on her own rustic wooden clogs.

The girl reached into a pocket of her apron. She withdrew a wad of soft cloth. A tiny bundle of joy. A swaddled treasure. Wound around it, a strand of carefully knotted string kept it closed. She looked furtively from side to side. The other field wives seemed frozen in the moment. A woman in the near distance nodded slowly, once. Seeing that signal, the girl offered the bundle of fabric.

Her eyes met Shasta's for an instant. Shasta reached to accept the gift, and something caught her focus. The girl wore long sleeves. Long skirts and long sleeves were the rule. But at the cuff of the sleeve a smooth patch of her wrist showed. A bold blue-black symbol stood out against the pale skin. A thorny uppercase letter *R*.

Before accepting the gift, Shasta plucked at the sleeve. When the girl didn't pull away, Shasta slid the sleeve up to reveal an *I* and an O. Inked across the inside of the forearm, from her hand to the crook of her elbow were the words *RIOT GIRRRRRRRL*.

This modest lass, with her cringing demeanor, not long ago she'd been a badass bitch goddess. This timid waif, her belly made huge by Charlie's deeds, she'd been a kick-ass roller derby warrior.

Now Shasta surveyed the fields with new understanding. These women had all been bike messengers and basketball stars. Today they were hunched field wenches, doomed to imminent, repetitive motherhood. But not a year before they'd been drummers in rock bands. They'd been dope-smoking fire walkers and hairless pole dancers.

How long ago had Adjustment Day occurred? Without cell phones or calendars, it was impossible to track the days. Only the weather suggested time passing.

Shasta let the girl's sleeve drop back into place, hiding the evidence of her former self. The girl gently placed the tiny bundle in Shasta's hand and shuffled away quickly. Behind her another young woman waited to present yet another bundle of fabric. Most likely, word had gotten around among the womenfolk. Most knew what prize Shasta hunted. Behind her a third woman waited to give Shasta her own fragile tribute, wrapped just-so for safekeeping.

Checking the typeset pages for the book, Walter had marveled.

This book combined with the Internet gimmick of The List—it was a drug. As the author himself had put it:

A Good Book Should Get You High.

It read like pornography.

What his new old man had dictated to him amounted to a pornography of power.

Walter had known the formula. The biggest bestsellers in history had been targeted at children and young adults. People who had no power, they were starved for stories depicting similar kids attaining an ultimate power. From Harry Potter to Superman to Luke Skywalker to Robin the Boy Wonder, it would seem that all kids wanted to develop their own latent superpowers and to see their parents dead. The Talbott book delivered on both counts. The unemployed and underemployed steamfitters and press operators would see themselves slay their oppressors and then rise to rule their own fiefdoms.

It amounted to a pornography of being right. No orgasm would be as satisfying as proving everyone else wrong. No sexual content could compete with the rush men got from winning. And the Talbott book was about nothing if it wasn't about winning.

Talbott, the old coot, he knew what men craved most.

As he'd perused the book, Walter had taken Shasta's earplug from the pocket of his shirt. He'd held it to his nose and inhaled. This talisman, something a witch might use to summon up the dead. Spongy, titty pink, it was an artifact coated with her dead skin and internal secretions, this relic dug out of the side of her head. His nose could convince the rest of him that Shasta was sitting here beside him.

Shasta, he'd known, she'd hate the book. She might groove on the prescribed Renaissance Faire threads and resurrected faux-Nordic culture. She did have her tattoo. Across her chest it read: *Mit einem Schwert in deinem Herzen sterben*. Whatever *that* meant. She'd dig the proposed medieval castle lifestyle and still hate the book.

But she'd love the money it would bring them.

Shasta would take one look at the world it proposed and she'd toss the book into the trash. Well, not the trash. Shasta would toss it into the recycling.

After that . . . Right after that, she'd call up Beyoncé and fly on some private jet to go shoe shopping on Bond Street in London. With Madonna. And Walter's credit card.

A curtain separated them. Akin to a stage curtain. A pale sheet of muslin did hang from the ceiling of the chamber with the royal physician and a sizable contingent of the court facing it. An odd hundred or so grooms, squires, valets. Something unseen on the opposite side stirred the fabric, and Physician Terrence bade, "If your highness will do us the honor of presenting himself . . ."

To date, royal protocol remained at best semisolid. Thus the best strategy, lest the physician give offense, was to hew to a mood of lofty White-Speak formality. As now he sat upon a carved wooden footstool, he reached forward and with his fingers poked at the curtain until he found a hole therein. He wiggled an index finger within the hole. "Simply display the royal scepter." Fancywork of silken embroidery did edge the hole.

The assembled company eyed the hole and waited.

Terrence withdrew his fingers and waited. To put his royal patient at ease, he recollected his own miraculous healing. How he'd been a bedridden invalid since infancy. How a merciful hospital nurse had delivered to him a copy of the Talbott book on behalf of his absent father. With his father's marginalia as encouragement, Terrence had overcome his domineering mother, a woman whose entrancing words could prompt him to violent seizures.

Facing the curtain, he did recount the epic tug-of-war over his catheter, and how the struggle brought his mother crashing to the floor. How the Talbott book itself had struck the knock-out punch and broken her nose. Broken the nose so that it would forever lie sideways against her cheek.

Of the catheter, the catheter had ripped free. Intense had been the pain, but his tackle remained intact. Foiled had been any attempt at castration.

Terrence's fingers prodded impatiently at the embroidered hole. Still, nothing emerged from the opposite side.

Of chief concern this day was the large numbers of sexual contacts Chieftain Charlie had enjoyed as of late. More specifically, whether one of said encounters might've communicated a social disease to his highness. As the physician understood the situation, his highness had grown concerned over certain physical changes of an intimate nature. Nonetheless, there was little that could be done without an inspection.

"Of greatest importance is that we determine a prognosis," said Terrence. Here he quoted from the blue-black book:

The way of man is not to hope but to
take action and produce results.

At this the muslin finally stirred. Bulge did it, and the embroidered edges of the small hole began to spread apart. With an upraised hand, the physician forbid any man's utterance as something wan and shriveled made its timid entrance among them.

The next morning when she brought the breakfast tray, Arabella was transformed. As far back as Miss Jo could recollect the housekeeper had been a hunchbacked old frump. In recent years there had been something increasingly clownish in the defeated way the woman had plodded around the house. A fringe benefit of keeping help was how waxing floors and polishing silver wore them out. For the same reason brides choose ugly bridesmaids for a wedding, having the housekeeper around made Miss Jo look remarkably well preserved.

Until this morning, that is. This Arabella was a stranger. Her knotted limbs had grown slender and supple. In place of her staid uniform she wore a flowing gown. A *dashiki*, Miss Jo dredged up the word. The garment moved like water over the woman's smooth skin, the material accented with radiant emeralds embedded in its weave.

The frizzed mop of her gray hair had been changed into a lustrous mane of long, auburn curls. Her cracked hands and face gleamed so bright with reflected light that they looked wet with perfumed oils. Those lovely hands bore the tray: two poached eggs, a ham steak, an English muffin with butter and marmalade on the side.

"Miss Josephine," she said in a voice as new as her appearance, "Mr. Jamal asked me to convey his apologies." This voice resonated with an elegant depth. A velvet rumble. "Affairs of state required that he depart late, late last evening."

She was so lovely that Miss Jo's first impulse was to discharge her. But this was no longer Miss Jo's house, and Arabella was no longer in her employ.

The housekeeper was so lovely that Miss Jo could only look away in pained resentment. Catching sight of her own reflection in a silver teaspoon she felt her stomach shrivel. She'd stained and poisoned herself into this gamboling, sinister elf. Doing so, yes, she'd cemented her position in this new nation state, but at what cost? Clearly she no longer belonged here.

Pretending to be engrossed in buttering her muffin, she remarked, "Arabella, that frock is extremely flattering to a woman of your size."

Arabella laughed softly in her new throaty tones. "It's not the ensemble," she said, "it's the transformation of my people."

She described how white men had always belittled African blacks for never inventing the wheel or the plow. The truth was that Africans had disdained any tools that disfigured the Earth. Blacks had an alliance with the Earth that stretched back through all time. Any request, the planet granted. That had made the continent so rich in resources. The land enjoyed incubating gold and diamonds within its womb to delight the black humans. And the humans in turn would never scar the land with roads or plowed furrows.

"When the white man entered Africa," Arabella continued, "we expected him to have the same respect for the sacred land."

But because this soil was not his cradle, the European had recognized nothing except the wealth he wanted to plunder. A man who'd never approve of abortion, a man who professed to sanctify life, he tore open the womb of the Earth and ripped out the gifts that had been prepared and harbored there. White oil wells and pit mines gutted the land. And what the planet had produced to reward the stewardship of the black race, the white man looted and spirited away.

Arabella regarded Miss Jo with a cool, disdainful look. "Since that time, my people have learned to keep our special powers concealed. Going back hundreds of years, we've hidden our true talents and wisdom out of the fear that the white man would abuse those as well to increase his horde of acquisitions."

Miss Jo looked at her hands, chemically discolored, and felt a deep shame for the history of her greedy race. She felt humiliated by her own burnt hair. Without question, the white man's folly and guilt had been bequeathed to her.

"Of all people, only Mr. King came close to exposing the true magic of black people," Arabella explained. "For many years we debated killing him for our own protection."

Miss Josephine listened in amazement. "Blacks killed Martin Luther King Jr.?"

Arabella scowled. "Not *Doctor* King . . . ," she exclaimed. "We hired a man to kill *Stephen King*. Unfortunately the assassin was inept, and the intended hit-and-run was a failure."

In the author's masterpiece novels, she said, books such as *The Shining* and *The Stand* and *The Green Mile*, King had almost convinced white people of the majestic uncanny powers blacks kept under wraps.

Without prompting, Arabella shook out the linen napkin and tucked it into the neckline of Miss Jo's housecoat. The housekeeper lifted the knife and cut a small square from the ham steak. With the fork, carefully she placed the morsel into the old woman's mouth. "Now eat," she said.

Speechless, Miss Jo mutely chewed that same bite of ham, over and over, like a cow with its cud, unaware as the meat was reduced to a tasteless mush. Silence and expectation bore down upon her. Finally, she ventured, "So . . . where was the fire? Why'd Jamal fly out of here in such a hurry last night?"

In response, Arabella stepped to the room's small television and touched a button. The screen filled with tiny people. A torch-bearing mob.

"You know that boy is holding his own secrets," the housekeeper said, watching the crowded screen. "You've seen the way he studies those old paintings of your ancestors."

On television, an ocean of rioters surrounded a stately building, throwing rocks and bricks against its carved façade. Gunshots rang out and puffs of dust showed where bullets ricocheted off the stone. There was the bright sound of glass breaking.

A closer shot revealed the tall, ornate windows. They framed the faces of people trapped within. Handsome and beautiful but trapped nonetheless, all those faces were black.

Talbott's intuition had been spot-on. The 1960s had torn down all the patterns for living. Since then, generations had wandered through their lives in search of a new shared blueprint. The answer wasn't Communism or Fascism. Nor was it Christianity or Capitalism. Political activism and education were both revealed to be corrupt. The greatest accomplishment of modern man had been to do away with those constraining models.

"The only quality that truly unites us is our desire to be united," he'd always insisted. "What men want is a structure for communion."

Until recently our circumstances had drawn us together and kept us united. Our shared proximity as next-door neighbors. As coworkers at our jobs and congregants in our churches. As classmates in school. All of these structures brought people into community with regularity. But as people began to move households so frequently, when jobs became less stable, and churches became less relevant, we'd lost reliable contact with each other.

As Talbott saw it, race and sexual preference had to become

the last bastion for community. As all the grand uniting narratives floundered . . . when all the tenuous, external circumstances failed us, we'd be forced to form our ranks based on our most basic elements: skin color and sexual desire.

Walter had seen it. Clearly his new old man intended the book as a vehicle for making Walter's fortune. The men, those Jamals and Estebans, they were the foot soldiers, the advance guard opening the market for the book's wider introduction. Those rubes and preppers. Here were faux-profound thoughts to replace the slogans that advertising had planted in people's heads.

According to Talbott, only consumption remained as a means of self-expression. That's why men's only response to beauty was to consume it. Thus beauty became pornography so it could be consumed. Status was measured by levels and quality of consumption. Of people's time. Of their energies. Cannibalism couldn't be far behind.

What's more, as the Talbott book decreed:

Suicide Is the Ultimate Act of Consumption.

And by extension:

Civilization Is Consuming Itself.

That had been his explanation for why Western civilizations were dwindling. Citizens of the white Diaspora were consuming themselves with drugs. Blacks with violence. Homosexuals with disease.

In their tapestry-lined honeymoon chamber Shasta found her new husband hurriedly folding hosen and surcoats. He stepped to the gargantuan wardrobe cabinet and stripped the dry-cleaning plastic off a houppelande of rich, royal blue velveteen accented with scuttled piping. A suitcase lay open across the foot of their enormous canopy bed, half filled with kilts and tabards. Charlie packed his favorite codpiece among them.

When Shasta went to embrace him, he shook her off, saying, "Not right now." His tone was gruff. "A council of chieftains has been called to assemble."

A gondolier had been hired to pole the royal barge down the Columbia River to the ruins of Portland. There the lineage would gather in a lofty boardroom perched atop one of the remaining high-rises in the abandoned downtown core. Rumor had it that Portland had long ago outstripped its at-home bathtub production of tempe. Their stores of soy exhausted, the denizens had taken to devouring each other. The tranquil garden city now stank like an open grave. This journey would hold no appeal for any of the chieftains who'd been summoned.

Undeterred, Shasta approached him once more, and she lightly fingered his merkin. The tension in his body relented. She dropped to her knees. Deftly stripping aside his scabbard and unlacing his Venetian breeches, her hands discovered his flaccid pride and commenced their kneading.

With a jarring wince, Charlie cried, "Ouch!"

Shasta's fingers continued. More gently.

"Watch it," he protested, his voice weaker, faint, carried away by the pleasure of her touch.

Shasta's mouth joined forces with her hands in their wifely duties. The nausea stirred in her belly. Despite her voluminous organza skirts the stone floor hurt her kneecaps.

His head lolling, Charlie whined, "I felt something."

Her mouth paused in its task so she might draw a breath. "No duh, I'd hope so." She quelled the bitchiness in her voice. "I am honoring your highness."

He moaned. "But . . ." His words failed. "But Gaysia, the people of Gaysia have overrun our embassy and taken our diplomats hostage . . ."

Muttering, slurring his words, delirious with sensation, her husband went on to announce that Gaysia had declared war against both Caucasia and Blacktopia.

The news caught Shasta off guard and she gagged an instant. Her gorge rose, threatening to scald the royal manhood with bilious digestive acids. A fine going-away gift that would make. Only with great effort was she able to choke down both.

And one afternoon, when Walter had been idly leafing through a copy of the newly printed Talbott book, the old man had looked up. Walter's new old man, he'd glared, his brow furrowed and demanded, "What's that you're reading?"

Walter held up the book, showing its blue-black cover and the gilded title.

Talbott snarled. "What's it called?"

Walt ran a fingertip under the title. "*Adjustment Day.*"

The old man's face flushed so red that fresh blood spurted from two small cuts on his forehead. "That's not!"

Walter turned the book and read the title. That was it, *Adjustment Day.*

Sputtering, saliva flying. "That's not what I said!" bellowed the old man.

A chill ran through Walter. His head did the grim math. How many books had been printed and already distributed? Answer: All of them.

Talbott said, "You idiot! Stop the presses!"

It was too late, but Walter didn't say that.

"I told you to call the book *A Judgment Day!*" Talbott ranted.

A Judgment Day. God only knew what else Walter had misheard.

Talbott shook his head in disbelief. He snapped, "Is it too late to fix this . . . typographical error?"

A Judgment Day. Duh.

And Walt lied. He put on his best look of sincere confidence, and he told the old man, "Don't worry. I'll fix it."

Closing the Talbott book and carefully setting it aside, the speaker proclaimed, "Queer bodies have always been the shock troops in Western civilization."

A general grumble rose from the audience seated around Gavyn. They'd been hearing this lecture since they'd relinquished themselves to the Retention Center.

It would hit on the same points: Malcolm X being a bisexual hustler, James Baldwin, the feminist movement and their own Night of the Long Knives where they'd ousted their founding lesbian contingent in order to make the movement more appealing to soccer moms. The speech would touch on urban renewal. And the climax would be about how Hitler's schoolboy crush on Ludwig Wittgenstein had set in motion World War II and the infamous Final Solution.

Every month or so, a chieftain from Gaysia arrived to deliver these pep talks. To boost morale. Today's speaker was a chieftain of the first lineage. A man named Esteban. He raised his voice in response to the grumbling.

Interrupting, Gavyn said, "My sister . . ." The room quieted. "My sister, Charm, did the math. And she says none of us are getting traded until we're almost forty." He wasn't loud, but the silence was so absolute that his voice sounded huge.

Another kid yelled, "What's up with that?"

The speaker countered, "Female emigrants will be granted first priority so they can begin the production of exports as quickly as possible."

The young lesbians seated around Gavyn groaned. The camp didn't look so grim when compared to a career as human breeding stock.

From the podium Esteban stressed, "That should expedite the exchange process by a number of years."

The Gaysian stance, their official platform was that neither Caucasia nor Blacktopia wanted to feed and house exports any longer than was absolutely necessary. As time passed special accommodations would be made to exchange exports as quickly as possible. A trade agreement might be reached that would allow current Gaysian exports to emigrate in exchange for future immigrants from Gaysia. That's the reason the pipeline had to be as burdened as possible.

The reality was that Gavyn and his generation, the first generation to reach the Age of Declaration since Adjustment Day, was sorting trash for recycling. They were imprisoned, sleeping in dormitories, eating ramen noodles three times daily, with no distraction other than separating Number 6 plastics from Number 8 plastics and tin from aluminum, a task that used to be done by machine before slave labor became more cost effective. Except that it wasn't called slave labor, it was called outsourcing. It was off-shore labor except that it wasn't off shore, it was located smack-dab in Caucasia. And the workers weren't slaves except for the fact that they couldn't leave the campus, except the campus was hemmed in with barbed wire and guard towers. And it was noble, rewarding work to benefit their future and the future of Gaysia, except they spent every day slouched over a crawling-by conveyor belt loaded with sticky tin cans and soiled paper under a constant swarm of black flies attracted by the stink of decomposing yogurt and stale beer.

None of the exports had lived here longer than a year except every week felt like a year, except no one had a calendar because no one had expected to be stuck here that long, except some realists who'd begun to scratch hash marks in the paint in one bathroom stall so everyone could go and count the days at any time and be appalled by how long they'd actually been bivouacked here picking through the garbage, except it made no difference because they were still trapped, except every month somebody official from the promised land they'd never reach arrived to raise their spirits with a rousing speech about the glory of Gaysia, except today when Gavyn stood up in the middle of the speech, in the middle of the audience and asked the horrible question.

He asked, "Is my generation condemned here for life?"

Charm had suggested as much. She'd written, speculating that no one would be traded until the first child in Gaysia turned eighteen. Not in any sizable numbers. Yes, there were some children in Gaysia, but not in numbers that mattered. And even then Charm predicted that younger exports would be given preference, just as women were being given preference, and that Caucasia was more than sustaining its own population and that the more exports it produced the more cheap slave labor it could maintain in retention camps. Because, frankly, heterosexuals were just better at reproduction and they had a longer cultural history of making babies, and the future would be reduced to a constant export-making race between the nations.

Gavyn didn't want to be rude. No one held a greater respect for the chieftains of Gaysia, except Gavyn wanted the truth, except he wanted it spoken in front of everyone. Except he didn't want to be the messenger of bad news. Except none of them was getting any younger.

"Sir?" asked Gavyn, wanting to show some respect and not just be a nag. "Will we ever see our homeland?"

The question elicited a scattered outburst of applause except Gavyn wasn't trying to dump all over this Esteban, who was the kind of good looking where if he smiled at you you'd have to smile back, except you didn't know what he was like as a person except for how hot, except this brought Charm to mind and the last time they played the game of Mine/Yours where they'd point out random people as potential sex partners and shout "Mine" or "Yours" like the game Slug Bug where you tried to slam your opponent by surprise, except the last time they were in Laurelhurst Park Gavyn pointed out the skag king pushing a shopping cart loaded with prescriptions, Nick his name was, with the crystal-meth cheekbones and sun-bleached hair and Gavyn yelled "Yours" except then Charm pointed out a guy the doppelganger for the cute one of the Thompson Twins with the rattail haircut with the henna and the skin the color of powder except without the baggy

1980s gear, except then Gavyn got confused, except when he realized Charm was playing by different rules. It's because she actually wanted the best for him, except she didn't realize he'd been trying to slam her and it's because she really, actually did have the hots for that crystal-meth Nick guy.

He'd been trying to irk and embarrass her, except all she wanted for him was happiness with a Thompson Twins lookalike, except that's what made it scary when she wrote with her theory about him probably never emigrating. It's because she wasn't his sibling rival, she was telling the truth.

Except Esteban redirected, saying how history had a model. Saying homosexuals had always lived walled inside monasteries and convents where they'd preserved the knowledge of the ancient world and compiled the secrets of the natural world, hybridizing sweet peas and making sure the Dark Ages would not eradicate the legacy of man's civilization.

Except Gavyn was not thrilled by the prospect of watching peas have sex, not while his prime hot porn-ready eighteen-year-old body was picking trash. And he was going to say as much when an administrator stepped up to the podium and implied to Esteban that he had an important phone call backstage, and when Esteban ducked out to get it, the administrator leaned into the microphone and announced Gavyn's name, not in a good voice, and said Gavyn was to go to the front office where he had a guest waiting.

Gavyn went to the reception area, and there was a girl with so many tattoos he had to wonder if her boyfriends lay in bed after sex and read her body like the back of a box of cereal. Right then a skinny old man with flapping arm skin, his skin shining with dried blood, a naked bloody old man walked across the far side of the room. A stinky, naked old man, his chest and back oozing with countless tiny wounds. Gavyn couldn't help himself. He did an ick-induced full-body shudder and a cringing dance as if he'd stepped through a big spiderweb. The man wasn't Nick but he was close enough. Gavyn looked at his sister and said, "Yours."

Hardly had Charlie glimpsed his own manhood in recent days, so constantly buried was it in one or another of Shasta's moist orifices. Hidden and labored was it by her, until he was grateful to fate that Shasta was his final wife rather than his first. Any day the wives of his fields and household would begin to push forth his children. They would pop with the ferocity and frequency of popcorn. Many had he blessed within minutes of one another. Their fruiting would occur with the same relentless speed and repetition with which he'd sewn his lordly seeds.

Among these women were many not happy to be in service beneath him.

In no female except Shasta had his manhood met its match. In her wet embrace he had spent himself too oft. Like an insatiable succubus was she! Leaving him so flaccid. Almost numb, yet were his exhausted testes hypersensitive to every jolt of his carriage wheels!

It had come at an opportune juncture, this calling of the Chieftains Council. If Shasta yet was without a belly child, that task was beyond his doing to perform.

Although intuition and hope hinted otherwise . . . Green was her complexion as of late. And several times did she take flight from her morning repast to hurl chunks in the palace crapper. If kingly wisdom served, Charlie had planted within her loins an heir.

Had Charlie a great sacrifice to Thor offered. A plentitude of sweet rutabagas and savory gorse was it, in such abundance as to satiate the god. At present as he and his party approached the silent city was the chieftain greatly glad he had acquired the good will of Odin and Loki. For the deserted township of Portland amounted to not but a dense forest on its outskirts. The passing months had allowed the vegetation to amass itself, consolidating an impenetrable jungle of flowering buddleia, this woven with tendrils of stout privet, this shot through with a suffocating blanket of juniper tams. These neglected suburbs constituted a formidable barrier.

No lesser army of stout swordsmen could have hacked a path through this matted wall of hybrid tea roses and untamed lilacs. Any company smaller than Charlie's would've been swallowed up by the onslaught of pyramidal arborvitae.

Nor was vegetation their sole concern. The demented natives did pose a constant threat, as demonstrated by a darting figure. A stalking puppet, a skeletal old man clothed in naught but a sheen of dried blood. This specter, lanced with wounds uncountable, dashed within sight of the royal company for an instant. It shouted, "Walter!" and was instantly gone. Vanished deep into the dense sedge.

Satisfactory time had passed that the city was deemed safe. Safe enough. Most stragglers had eaten each other, and the survivors would be weak and few. As the royal processional labored to clear a path, faint strains of melody reached them. Unseen was a player crafting a tune on some stringed instrument. The captain of the guard called for silence, and the woodsmen and knights stilled their hacking.

None but the songbirds disturbed the deadly calm of that ghost town. The music grew in volume, its source coming near, until at last a figure stepped into view.

Emerging from the thicket of death and desolation was a man. Little more than a skeleton, his leathery limbs wore tattered rags. This ragamuffin, his face appeared lost behind a robust beard and the shroud of his long hair. The man held a guitar in his arms and strummed it. So absorbed in his music making was he that he'd stepped amidst the royal entourage before stopping in his tracks. Minus his song, only the birds broke the silence.

Reclining in his carriage was Charlie captivated by the stranger's tunefulness. The chieftain had grown weary of the usual mincing jugglers and yodelers. "Here, vagabond!" he bid from the vehicle's velvet-cushioned interior. "Belong you to a house and master?"

The wastrel glanced up from his guitar. He made no answer, the impertinent varlet, but commenced once more to softly stroke his instrument.

An axe man in the chieftain's company lifted his blade in subtle threat. "Answer, you!" He reared back, ready to lop off the man's shaggy head. "And answer ye in none but the approved White-Speak of Caucasia!"

Charlie did call again, "Well, man? Are you free to become my slave?"

The tosspot ceased his music making. "Who is it would be my master?" he sneered.

Another in the party, the royal physician, spoke up. "You unschooled groundling! This is none other than Charlie, chieftain of the first lineage. Husband of the beautiful Queen Shasta, and liberator of Caucasia!"

Hearing such praise, Charlie lifted his chin, and his chest swelled with pride. To display his valuable Naugahyde gloves, he lifted a hand as if to straighten his weighty gold crown.

The musician's scowl dissolved. His face went slack with amazement, and he drew a long breath. He stammered, "My lord, you are not unknown to me . . ." Collecting himself, he placed an open hand over his heart and bowed his head in respect. Looking up, he asked, "Your noble wife, perchance is she Shasta Sanchez, formerly of Southeast Lincoln Street who attended Franklin High School, worked part-time at Starbucks, and played goalie in city league soccer?"

Silence seized all present. Charlie sensed a threat, a rival perhaps. Warily, he asked, "Know you the shapely lass in question?"

The stranger waved away the idea. "No, my lord! Her renown is such that all hereabouts know her legend." He set aside his guitar and doffed his ragged stocking hat. "We take great pride that a maiden from our humble township should become a queen of the white peoples."

The statement prompted even more pride within Charlie's breast. Hearing such praise, he took an immediate liking to the man. "Do you know this place?" He gestured about at the rotting condominiums and tumbledown freeway overpasses. He asked, "Can you guide us through this morass of thorns as to avoid any bands of highwaymen who yet remain in this godforsaken place?"

The physician, Terrence, inquired, "How are you called, peasant?"

The man turned disdainful eyes on the asker. "My name?" growled he. "You may call me Nick."

The stranger folded his arms and rolled his eyes as if weighing the proposal to serve as their guide. He cocked his head. He wet the pad of a soiled finger against his tongue and held it up as if to check the speed and direction of the wind. Next he knelt and pressed one filthy ear to the cracked concrete as if listening for the approach of horsemen. Only after all the preceding did he narrow his eyes and ask, "To where is your highness journeying?"

A mounted cavalier among them called back, "The Terminal Sales Building!"

From another steed, a second cavalier shouted lustily, "To the highest conference room of the same! There a gathering of all the chieftains shall take place!"

Charlie held up a Naugahyde-gloved hand to silence them. Of the grimy musician he asked, "Know it, you?"

Making no wordy reply, the man retrieved his guitar from the ground. He started away on foot down a shadowy avenue that none among Charlie's attendants had taken note of. He waved for them to follow, and after a moment's hesitation the mighty horses leaned into their traces and the great wheels of the royal carriage creaked and turned, and attendants numbering in the hundreds commenced to march forward in the stranger's wake.

Esteban listened to the voice over the phone. He knew that history would eventually erase them, but he'd never suspected it would be this soon. The Talbott book had readied them to die. It had lifted them from addiction and resignation. It had given them control of their world and their own lives. Now at what ought to be the time of their rejoicing, Bing was gone.

Esteban relinquished the phone to the clerk in charge. He excused himself to go to the bathroom. Seated in a stall, he discovered hash marks scratched in the paint. He counted three hundred seventy-four marks.

In Gaysia, Delicious had her feet in stirrups, but her mind had wandered miles away. Wondering, would Gentry still love her? Pondering, had it been worth this trial, hiding in a country where she did not belong?

A voice snapped her back to the here and now. She lay back on an examining table with her legs in the air. Curtains divided them from innumerable such booths stretching away on either side. A masked figure stood between her knees. A surgical cap hid the technician's hair, but her eyes were bloodshot and sunken in exhausted pits of baggy, discolored skin. "There, now rest," she said, holding a dripping pipette in one latex-gloved hand. The technician swabbed the pipette with a wipe smelling of alcohol. In a distracted tone, she said, "Thank you for your service."

A nation's first generation is no small event. Delicious was the nest to a cuckoo's egg. She was the cuckold, compelled to raise a stranger's child. The enemy's child. As the enemy would be raising one for her, figuratively speaking.

Her new nation teetered on the brink of World War III. And so that Gaysia would hold as many hostages as possible, every woman of childbearing age had been called up for mandatory insemination. Domestic industries had been retooled for the maximum production of wartime sperm.

In the facility the curtains fluttered as a drag queen in a sequin-spangled nurse's getup entered carrying a metal tray crowded with tiny paper cups. Delicious took one and gulped down a mouthful of watery orange juice while the drag sang, "The seed inside you, I can see it growing . . . ," from the Paul Anka hit "Having My Baby."

The drag disappeared into the next cubicle, and Delicious heard the song start up, again. The technician, who was, herself, extremely pregnant under her scrubs, set aside her instruments and struggled to help Delicious off the table. Once she was on her feet a smock was offered, and Delicious slipped her arms into the sleeves. From a nearby cubicle came, "Thank you for your service."

The technician, pulling a fresh stretch of sterile paper to cover the table, said, "We recommend you lie down in the recovery area to guarantee results."

"Thank you for your service," said a man's voice in the distance.

Delicious told herself, *Another angel got its wings*, and suppressed a laugh.

To keep up appearances Belle had brought her and was waiting in the reception area. The clinic itself had once been an airport. In a few weeks Delicious would return the favor and escort Belle back here for the same treatment. The Dixie cup of orange juice. The snippet of Paul Anka.

The smock amounted to a military uniform. Delicious told herself, *Those also serve who only sit and wait with their legs in the air*, and choked back a hysterical giggle. The streets and shops were filled with women wearing this same flour sack. Roomy, it was designed to be worn through giving birth, subjecting the wearer to endless rounds of being thanked by strangers.

They rode home in a cab, an extravagance. At their destination the driver refused to accept payment. He began, "Thank you for—," but Delicious averted her face and raised an open hand to interrupt him.

From the entrance to the alleyway beside their building a mass of candles and teddy bears spilled out onto the street. Bouquets of carnations filled the air with the sweetness of rot. Hand-lettered and heart-shaped sympathy cards read "Bing" and "Our Hero!" A queue of mourners stretched down the block, each waiting his or her turn to deposit a bouquet of roses or a fluttering, flashing bunch of Mylar balloons in rainbow colors.

A crew of television newspeople panned the crowd with their lights. A man with a microphone walked the line, asking how the assassination had affected people. A few wept openly. The newscaster turned to address the camera, saying, "Police have located security footage of the killing. They've announced that an arrest is imminent."

The two women hurried from the cab, keys in hand, to the building's doorway. Behind them a chorus of voices shouted, "Thank you for . . ." The elevator doors pinched off the final words.

Safely inside the apartment, with the bolt thrown and the chain on, Belle called, "We're home." When no one responded, she called, "Felix?"

The television was on. As always Talbott filled the screen. He told them:

The world wants a unified field theory.
A thing, one something that explains everything—give it to them.

Delicious stood in the living room as Belle stepped to her son's door and knocked. On television Talbott said:

The measure of a man is not what he does for wages
but what he does with his free time.

When Belle reappeared she was carrying a sheet of paper. From it she read, "Dear Mom . . . ," and looked at Delicious with brimming eyes.

Canada was a test. Long after sunset Dawson drove the back roads of what used to be Idaho. After the fugitive, Ramantha, had fallen asleep he turned down a rutted dirt lane crowded by briars on both sides. No moon had risen. He followed his headlights into the dark until he could see a fence blocking their path. A gate stood in the center with no sign. Its distance was just as far as he could make out in his high beams.

Dawson reached over and nudged the woman. "We're here."

She jolted awake. Peered into the night around them.

"We're at the border," he told her. God only knew what that gate led to. Some estate where she'd be taken prisoner and executed in accord with the new laws. Or was there some back pasture where the wolves would chase her down? Either way she'd be dead. They weren't anywhere near Canada. But she'd no longer be his problem.

He shut off the engine but kept the headlights on. He looked around as if to check for border patrols.

She squinted through the streaked windshield and asked, "Through that gate?"

He nodded. "Hurry." The words of Talbott whispered from the truck's radio, ". . . the way of man is not to hope but to take action and to produce results . . ."

She kept her eyes on the distant gate as her hands checked her pockets.

Dawson felt the wedding ring stuffed in his own pants pocket. He waited for some thanks. He hadn't killed her. He'd delivered her to safety, safety as far as she knew. She was failing his test big time.

For the first time, she glanced at the truck's visor, at a wallet-sized photo taped there. It showed a woman smiling. "Pretty," she said. "Your wife?"

He looked at the picture of his wife, Roxanne, smiling down on them in the murky green glow of the dashboard lights. He said, "No." He said, "My sister."

Without a word of gratitude, the woman swung open the passenger door and stepped out. She looked at him and opened her mouth to speak. Her eyes kept darting to the gate. Bugs spiraled and flitted in the twin cones of light. The gate glowed white as phosphorus burning, with blackness as solid as a wall on the other side. A wolf howled medium close by. Her eyes snapped back to him. "Where in Canada?"

Dawson made a show of lifting one hand, pulling back his shirt sleeve, and looking at his wristwatch. It was after midnight. If she thanked him in the next minute he might not let her wander off to her doom. Another howl split the night. "Okanogan Valley," he told her. He described pretty little houses and orchards filled with cherry trees. Gardens and lakes. He assured her that once she'd passed through the gate she'd qualify as a political refugee, and they'd have to provide her with shelter and a fresh start in life.

He could let her last thoughts be a comforting fantasy. She should stumble into the dark expecting to find love and acceptance. Once that wolf pack caught up with her, not long after he'd driven away, she'd wish she'd died on Adjustment Day.

The academic, Ramantha, she stood beside the truck. She pulled something from a pocket of her coat and leaned in to place this gift on the seat beside him. Paper something. In the dim light it was old money, useless trash. "For your trouble," she said. She belted the coat tight around herself. "Leave your headlights on," she ordered, "at least until I get through."

In quick resolute steps, she marched away. Centered in the lights. Her shadow loomed in front of her, towering and terrible. Each step raised dust that floated in her wake.

She'd turned out just like the others. A selfish, gutless tribe who considered just their own self-interests. She wasn't the first. Dawson had brought others here. The first was a journalist who'd managed to escape Adjustment Day. Tweed something, a television reporter. The second had been another think tanker, a doctor. Dr. Ashanti, a therapist with a half-million votes to his name on the list. Both had charged off into the darkness in expectation of the warm embrace of like-minded liberal progressives. A third had been some dude, a city councilman from Seattle. Each of the three had gone through the gate without so much as a goodnight.

Afterward Dawson had killed his headlights and sat listening. Each night, the howling had found them before they could find their way back to his truck. He'd heard them crashing through the briars and scrub. And he'd heard them screaming. Never his name, because none of them had ever asked his name. They'd only shrieked for help. For someone to help them. For someone to save them. They'd screamed "mister" and they'd screamed "please," and in the end they'd only screamed.

This one, Ramantha, was halfway to the gate.

Dawson had the same thought each time. Instead of letting the wolves shred this one, he considered gunning the truck's engine, dropping it into third gear, and peeling out. He could run her down. Take her ear. A mercy killing. A win-win benefiting everyone once the wolves found her corpse.

He slid a hand into his pocket and played with the wedding ring hidden there. Home waited. He hadn't been home all season. He'd spent his youth being a good husband and a model employee on the shop floor. Sure, now he was a chieftain. If he wanted, he could have a passel of wives. Rule over multitudes. But that just looked like a bigger version of the same trap. As a ruler he'd have to be a good husband to more women. And a king amounted to being a model employee with countless people to look after.

His fingertips felt the round, hard, closed circle of the wedding ring.

That's why he'd been on the road this long. He'd discovered he had the soul of a barbarian. A warrior. And winning was death to that spirit. He wanted a new army and new battles.

Winning was fine, but not half as rewarding as fighting. That's why the testing. To find just one person to serve as his accomplice. A partner to help him keep the adventure of his life going.

It could be that he'd lived at the bottom of the heap for too long. He could only savor the fight. His constitution wasn't compatible with peace and leisure. Whatever side had the uphill battle, that's the side Dawson wanted to join.

The figure of the fugitive academic receded into the distance.

Her shadow against the gate was almost the same size as her. The headlights blazed, turning her back into one blank white shape of a human. Her shadow was the black version of this same shape. And in another step these two opposing shapes would touch.

He hadn't wished this for the others, but tonight Dawson willed for her to stop. His hand hovered above the center of the steering wheel, ready to honk the horn. To warn her. Still, he knew there was no point in saving her unless she was worthy. Whispering, he begged her to stop. To come back. To join him on his next campaign, whatever that would be.

He yearned to be a force for change, not a landlord. His wife wouldn't starve, she'd continue to receive his allotment of Talbott bucks, an income sufficient to maintain her hundreds of dependent servants.

As a small sacrifice, he rolled down his window. His fingers produced the ring from his pocket, and he lifted it toward the space open above the glass. He let it drop and it fell, bouncing once against the outside of the door. A tiny chime. Then it was lost.

At the chime, the woman froze in place. One hand had reached out to touch the latch, and this blazing white hand touched the fingertips of her shadow hand. Then both hands pulled away from each other.

She turned and began walking back.

The wolves howled closer, and Dawson laid on the truck's horn to scare them away. He leaned across the seat and pushed open her door.

She climbed in. "I can't . . . ," she said, her voice flat with resolve. Her arms folded across her chest, she said, "I can't just give up and forge a new life. Not for all the maple syrup in the world."

It wasn't fear of the wolves. The woman had changed.

She glared into the night. "I can't let the bad guys win. I can't ditch my ideals." She turned to meet his gaze, her eyes blazing. "Gender Studies is a real thing, and I won't let it be a lost cause, not if I have to fight back with every drop of my blood."

Fury clouded her face. Her frail hands clenched into stony fists.

In a voice hoarse with vengeance, she rasped, "People *should* read bell hooks!"

Dawson had been wrong. She'd passed his test. She was a fighter. A keeper.

Her face softened. "Where are my manners," she said, "I never thanked you . . ." She offered her hand. "Please, tell me your name?"

At that he told her, "Dawson," and turned the key in the truck's ignition.

Miss Jo had taken to reading the Talbott book. It held that the act of storytelling was essentially digestive in nature. We bring up a topic much like how a ruminant animal, a cow for example, brings up partially masticated grass from its stomach. In our stories we exhaust our emotional attachment to past events. We elicit similar stories from others. By mulling things over—and the word *mulling* meant to grind, just as *ruminate* meant to think—we are able to assimilate the most unhappy or happy experiences of our lives. We accept them as normal human events. We quit telling them, and the stories become part of us.

Miss Jo, she'd been recounting the glory of her family and race for so long that she had white fatigue. The Talbott book claimed that mankind was suffering identify fatigue. People were living too long to retain a single self. Therefore, the boldest were seeking a new frontier. Men were becoming women. Whites were becoming blacks.

Dawning on Miss Jo was the fact that she was the culmination of a long line of rebels and pioneers. She was the last of her breed, and she was bone tired of repeatedly giving lip service to her illustrious family history. Her family had outlived its glory. Its stories could die with her.

The story of her life was a tasteless mouth of mush. She rose from her chair and moved around the room turning off the lamps.

In complete darkness, her fingertips found the candle and the matchbook on the lace doily on her bedside table.

She lit a match.

The book said, "People are addicted to being right."

It suggested going to a dinner party and stating over the table that the writer Sylvia Plath was a racist due to the scientific conclusions she'd reached in her most famous book, *The Bell Curve*. Your fellow guests will enjoy sputtering, multiple orgasms of rightness as they correct you. Expound on the fact that despite all of his legendary association with the Algonquin Round Table, Robert Benchley didn't achieve popular success until he wrote *Jaws*. Lecture that many people believe the New Zealand short-story writer Katherine Mansfield was beheaded in a bizarre car accident that took place on a Louisiana bridge heavily shrouded in mosquito insecticide. The fact of the matter is that she died of blunt head trauma, but her signature blonde wig was photographed where it had come to rest in the shattered windshield of the car, leading many to conclude her head was severed from her body by the rear edge of the flatbed truck her driver had rear ended. Conclude by saying that since her death all commercial truck chassis must come equipped with a bar on the undercarriage, called the "Mansfield bar," which lifts the vehicle in similar collisions and prevents such fatal injuries.

"It might take a moment," Talbott counseled, "But your audience will descend upon you, correcting you with all the yelping blood frenzy of a pack of rabid hyenas felling a lone wildebeest."

Making others right redeems their paltry and pointless educations.

Making others right makes them love you, according to Talbott, because we only love things we feel superior to. We only love those who don't pose a threat.

Making others right is the best method for controlling them.

Jamal was savoring a snifter of pre–Civil War port. He needed the drink. Having recently returned from the council of chieftains, he knew that Blacktopia couldn't avoid a war with Gaysia.

He raised his glass to the peace and prosperity brought about by Adjustment Day. It would soon be interrupted. The future was already upon them.

Raising his glass, he toasted the military men depicted in the oil paintings on the walls around him. Each man had followed the dictates of his conscience. Each had been a hero according to his time in history. Their world had been a different world than his. Jamal had to admire their courage and determination, even if their actual acts might seem ill-advised in retrospect. Painted like this, framed and hung to decorate some parlor walls, they might be primped and posed for posterity, but these thugs had been the badasses of their day.

He speculated that even something as noble as Adjustment Day might be deemed despicable in the distant future. As per Talbott:

The weakest people alive will try to glorify
themselves by tearing down the truly
amazing strength of the dead.

To some yet-to-be-born weakling, Jamal's likeness might be the image of a villain. Jamal only hoped that future coward could appreciate the bravery it had taken to dispatch a failing system and replace it with something new. Facing a spotted, antique mirror, lifting his snifter of port, he toasted himself.

That's when his pit bull, Bouncer, rose from the carpet and sniffed the air. The dog whined.

That's when Jamal had smelled smoke. The ashes in the fireplace were cold. A siren blasted from somewhere in the house, a smoke detector. A second joined it. A chorus of sirens wailed from the ceiling of every room.

His mind went to the terrorists Talbott had warned against. The loyalists or Canadians were committing arson in order to thwart the new nation states. Someone pledged to reuniting the formerly united states had put a torch to the house. Either that, or agents of Gaysia were already attacking.

He climbed the steps three at a time. The smoke hung heavier on the second floor, heavier still on the third. At the top of the stairs the attic door felt hot to his touch. He wrapped the tail of his untucked shirt around the doorknob, but it wouldn't turn. Locked.

Pounding his fists on the wood, he shouted, "Barnabas! Open up!"

A feeble voice answered, "You don't understand."

The door was almost too hot to beat against, but Jamal slammed it with his shoulder. The centuries-old oak wouldn't budge. "Unlock this door!" he commanded, and his own voice shocked him. The authority, his authority, boomed. It was a voice for giving speeches without need of a microphone.

Pounding his fists on the wood, he shouted, "Barnabas! Open up!"

This wasn't, this would not be the end of his book. At best this would be the crisis at the end of the first act. His book, *Black Like You*, needed a lot more writing before he could call it done. Like *The Three Faces of Eve*, all successful case studies needed a happy ending.

If his strength didn't work, his wiles would have to. "Oh, Barnabas," he begged, "I need you. Only you can tell me the history of the plantation."

The unseen voice sobbed in reply. It couldn't be more than a finger's length away, separated from Jamal by only this slab of oak. "Damn this place," it sobbed, "it's stolen my life. I've been a fool to keep praising the past."

Inspiration struck Jamal. "Then leave with me. Become a founder in the glorious future of Blacktopia!"

Something fell heavily against the opposite side of the door and slid to the floor. The smoke was overwhelming. When the voice spoke next, it spoke from the thin crack at the floor. There, where Bouncer sniffed and dug against the floorboards with both paws, the weak, faint voice said, "Jamal, you don't understand . . ."

He dropped to the floor and yelled back, "I understand."

"My family has deep roots here," the voice whispered.

Jamal spoke softer now, "So does mine."

The dying voice sighed with resignation, "Jamal, I'm not even a negro."

Jamal almost laughed. Almost. Instead he asked himself what his hero, Talbott Reynolds, would do in this situation. And against the roar of the growing inferno and the choir of shrieking smoke alarms, Jamal bellowed, "I'm not black, either!"

At that the stairway lights flickered and failed. Glass crashed somewhere, windows exploding outward or the crystal decanters in the parlor, filled with the excellent flammable hooch. In this chaos of noise, the darkness relieved by only flashes of orange flame, an eternity seemed to pass.

The Barnabas creature was dead, Jamal assumed, and he himself would die if he waited at this door a moment longer.

The door's bolt clicked. The knob turned, and the door swung aside to reveal a stooped, soot-blackened imp surrounded by the pyres of hell. Bug-eyed with shock, the demon asked, "What do you mean you're not black?"

The dog whined, and Jamal told it, "Go!" He got the hell baby tight around one wrist and dragged it along, airborne, as he dove down the tunnel of fire the stairway had become.

The brightest minds of the retention center seemed to be preoccupied. The guard at the desk was deep in hushed conversation with the door guard. Even when Charm approached them and said, "I need my brother, here, to help me get something from the car . . . ," even then neither guard looked up. The door guard just waved her through.

Charm and Gavyn found themselves standing on the front steps overlooking the parking lot and the gate beyond. Among the cars in the visitor parking spaces, one was their mother's. In the car parked next to it the afternoon's speaker, Esteban, sat behind the steering wheel. He wept furiously, cupping both hands over his mouth. Even crying, his shoulders heaving, and his chest shuddering with ragged sobs, he was still totally doable.

"Mine," Charm whispered.

Her brother said, "You wish."

They sidled toward their car. A guard in a tower near the gate held a rifle at parade rest. Even from a distance he looked gross.

In unison, both siblings said, "Yours."

Gavyn said, "Jinx."

His sister said, "Get in the car."

"And go where?" he asked. They'd never get past the closed security gate.

Charm waved to the guard in the tower. She climbed behind the wheel and started the engine.

Gavyn got in the passenger side, and they pulled out.

By now the door guard and the desk guard had emerged from the building and were running after them. The man in the tower held something to his ear.

As the car sped across the pavement, as the closed gate seemed to race forward to meet them, the car's radio preached, "The joy of fiction is that it only has to smell true."

Charm screeched to a stop, leaving smoking skid marks on the concrete drive. The gate was made up of steel bars too heavy to ram through, electrified also, and the guards were almost to the car. A keypad was perched atop a pole within arm's reach of the driver's window.

Gavyn watched the guards approaching in the rearview mirror and said, "Busted."

Charm lowered her window and reached out. Deftly, she punched numbers, and the gate swung open.

They spun gravel.

As the guards shrank and disappeared in the distance behind them, coughing in the smoke of burnt rubber, Gavyn marveled. "How did you know the code?"

Charm threw him a smile. "Believe it or not," she said, "I swapped spit for it." She said, "Put on your seatbelt."

Gavyn buckled his seatbelt.

As they plunged through a succession of immolating parlors and drawing rooms, Miss Josephine marveled at her own obtuseness. This boy, this Jamal, his face was the spitting image of so many of the ancestral portraits. His was the same patrician brow. The high, thoughtful forehead and widow's peak receding hairline. He had the slightly hooded Peabody eyelids, the result of generations of careful matchmaking.

Dragging her on an obstacle course, veering between blazing settees and fiery sideboards, the young man explained that he was the descendant of an antebellum slave by the name of Belinda. The forgotten grave in the woods. The girl had been wooed by and secretly wed to a great-great-great uncle of Miss Jo's.

"There," Jamal shouted as they dashed past the burning, curling portrait of a handsome Confederate major, "there is my great-great-great-great grandfather!"

The Barnabas marveled, "So you're white!"

Jamal winced. He scowled, "Hell, no!" Shouting to be heard over the roaring conflagration, he said, "I only lied to save your demented white-privileged ass!"

The scorched imp stared back at him in confusion.

"But," he added, "my blood is your blood. I am your last living Peabody kinsman!"

Belle stood in the living-room doorway and read aloud the letter from her son.

"Dear Mom," it began. "What I did wasn't self-defense. It was to defend those I love. Isn't that what Adjustment Day was all about?"

Belle met Delicious's eyes and threw a glance at an armchair. Suddenly mindful of her afternoon insemination, Delicious sat down.

"What I'm doing now," Belle continued to read, "I'm also doing to protect your secret and keep you safe."

Faint and down the hallway outside the apartment the elevator bell rang. Heavy footsteps and muffled voices drew closer.

Reading faster, the letter flapping in her shaking hands, Belle said, "I'm going to the borderlands to see if the rumors are true . . . I want to live in a society based on choice instead of biological circumstances."

From the hallway came the sound of a neighboring apartment door. A voice asked, "Is this about the killing?" A surly voice responded, "Police business! Get back in your unit!"

Delicious nodded for Belle to keep reading.

Her eyes darting between the letter and the closed front door, Belle said, "An area patrolled by wolves. Areas made off-limits by mountain lions. The thorns and hornets and mosquitoes will serve as my moat and battlements . . ."

The noise in the hallway had gone quiet when a pounding began on the outside of the apartment door. A gruff, menacing voice shouted, "Police! Open up!"

Delicious exchanged panicked glances with Belle. The latter read, "I'm sorry Bing is dead. Bing was my best friend."

The voice in the hallway continued, "We have a warrant for the arrest of Felix!"

Delicious lifted both hands as if holding a sheet of paper. She pantomimed tearing it in half.

Belle tore the letter in two.

Delicious snatched one half and wadded it into a tight ball, nodding for Belle to follow suit. As Belle crumbled her half, Delicious stuffed the ball into her own mouth and ground it between her back teeth. Belle did the same.

The voice outside the door shouted, "We have the building surrounded!"

With a mighty gulp, Delicious swallowed her wad of paper. Belle tried, gagging, her hands clutching at her throat, her face turning blue.

The apartment door burst inward. An explosion of splinters rained on the two women as Delicious pounded Belle between the shoulder blades.

A tall jack-booted figure was stepping through the shattered door. A drag queen in a glitter-encrusted police uniform, sporting a badge heavily layered with rhinestones, demanded, "Where's the boy?" Pinned to the uniform was a nametag with "Esteban" spelled out in tiny jewels.

The officer held a service revolver so heavily crusted with small gems that it was impossible to guess its make or caliber.

At the shocking sight of this blinding colossus, Belle swallowed hard. In that manner the letter was resolved.

The Peabody Manse was doomed. Genteel as it was, that legacy of polished silver julep cups and rosewood harpsichords, it was crashing into fiery wreckage around their ears.

When it seemed certain that Barnabas and Jamal would perish beneath the toppling mass of a grandfather clock, a dog's bark drew their attention. Bouncer, with a dog's superior olfactory talent, had navigated the dense smoke to find the front door. Jamal and Miss Jo had only to follow the sound of barking and they quickly found themselves on the front porch.

Even then, the towering Greek revival columns that fronted the manse, those columns were splitting in the intense heat. The great, blazing portico fell toward them with the speed and deafening roar of a freight train.

A mighty leap to the front lawn saved humans and dog. And while the ancient family seat crumbled behind them, they ran into the cool night.

Panting, Miss Josephine worried aloud, "What's to become of us?"

Sprinting beside her, Jamal asked, "You remember that book, *The Grapes of Wrath*?"

Miss Jo nodded, hurriedly.

"Everything they did to survive," Jamal says, "we need to do just the opposite."

According to Talbott their book would change the world.

Walter had snorted. "You're joking. This book is a joke, right?"

His new old man had laughed wetly, a noise like someone gargling, and said, "That's what Rudolf Hess asked!" He exhaled for one, two, three beats, a long time, deflating with the finality of a dying breath. The ribs of his chest folded inward until there seemed to be nothing left inside of him.

Walter had fidgeted, his hands ready to take notes. He'd been listening for so long he'd lost the knack for forming his own thoughts. "You wrote a fantasy." He'd added, "We wrote a fantasy."

Talbott's chin had sunk until it came to settle against his chest. "We're wrecking the nation to save the people." He'd rested, breathing heavily. "Young blacks are shooting each other in record numbers. Gays are killing each other with disease." He'd labored for the next breath. "Whites are wiping themselves out with opiates." His frame had sagged. His head had toppled forward.

Only the restraints had held him in the chair as the old man whispered, "Whether it's by breeding children or preaching, it's what men do: This constant dissemination of self."

"Is that what we're doing . . . ," Walter paused, "disseminating?"

In Before Times . . . back before this book was a book . . . his new old man had failed to respond.

"This is just a book," protested Walter. "It's not supposed to happen!"

The old man had seemed to collect his strength. Lifting his head he'd continued, "We regularly sacrifice people to preserve the nation." His lips had formed a loose, sloppy smile. "Perhaps we ought to scuttle the nation every hundred years in order to preserve the people."

He'd fixed Walter with bleary eyes. "Thank you, Warner."

Walter hadn't corrected him.

His new old man had continued, "You're my Boswell." Talbott had said, "My scribe." Stenographer. Amanuensis. He'd explained that Jeremiah had dictated his parts of the Bible to his secretary, Baruch. St. Paul had written the gospels through his scribe, Terius. St. Peter through Silas. St. John through Prochorus.

Hitler had dictated *Mein Kampf* to Rudolf Hess.

"The Bible." Walter had laughed at the comparison.

His tone had warmed as Talbott confided, "You're as close as I will ever have to a son. You, you're the apprentice every man dreams of teaching. You will carry my lifetime's wisdom into the future so that mankind will benefit!"

Walter had suppressed a shudder.

"The world wants a unified field theory," Talbott had crowed. "A thing, one something that explains everything—give it to them!" His eyelids fluttered. The blood that had been leaking from a dozen stubborn infections ceased to flow. "If you want to make your fortune, buy Naugahyde." Talbott's voice fell to a whisper, "Get a gun and report to Dawson or Jamal. Kill the targets he assigns you." At that he'd seemed to drift off to sleep. His head had flopped backward and hung over the back of the chair, his mouth stretched open, his tongue lolling.

Walter hadn't checked his pulse. That's how dead he'd looked. Neither had Walter called 9-1-1. There were larger issues at stake. He'd been in the basement for weeks while the outside world had been slowly and irreparably changed. For all he'd known pits were being dug. The list, America's Least Wanted, now stretched to thousands of names. Tens of thousands. The Talbott book had been distributed to just as many readers. Everything they'd done, it had to be a joke. A giant fraud.

Just in case it wasn't, Walter had telephoned Nick. He'd telephoned Shasta.

Shasta turned vamp. Beguiling, she did beg, "Mate with me, milord." She did make her eyes half closed at Charlie. She did part her crimson lips slightly as if she were drunken with a harlot's mad desire.

Scarcely had he returned from the tribal council when she had pressed him for intercourse. He had scarcely vacated his carriage. This vagabond, Nick, had deftly navigated them through the wasteland of Portland, to and from the council site. Now he was strumming his guitar. Delightful were the man's harmonies. Such a pleasant companion was he that Charlie bid him return to Maryhill and regale the court for the duration of the bountiful gourd harvest.

As protocol dictated Charlie introduced this latest player to his home wives, his courtiers, and his queen.

Struck did Shasta look in the moment, although she insisted she'd never before encountered the musical stranger. She did blush heavily and entreat Charlie to retire with her, making much of how his being away had spurred in her loins a powerful longing.

Retreating to their private apartments, she did snatch at his lacings. Recklessly casting aside his pearl-studded codpiece. And with slippery machinations of mouth and hand did she struggle to excite him.

To date he'd mated with her in every corner of the palace, and he was obviously exhausted. He did toss back handfuls of Viagra to no avail. His kingly scepter and orbs continued to feel spongy and unresponsive. They hung limp and heavy and curiously numb. Yet so sensitive were their surfaces that even his most pliant codpiece caused him discomfort. The condition was the result of overuse, the royal physician had assured him. From stress, he did assure himself.

Despite his protests, his queen was once more besieging him.

Despite surely being by now blessed with advanced belly child, to judge from changes in her bosom and the absence of her menses, despite being so encumbered Shasta did clutch at his Naugahyde pantalets. She did rip her own bodice and boldly expose herself. Her voluptuous body bare, his favored wife maneuvered to straddle him and by brute strength force upon him her perfumed charms.

Alas were the royal scepter and orbs immune to her sensual grabbing. Akin to a deceased boa was his. Pale and boneless as a length of sausage casing did it appear, yet Shasta proceeded to tug at it with carnal fury.

Charlie bore her efforts with husbandly good humor, for they bore scant pain. So arduous were her exertions, he reasoned, that she'd soon exhaust herself. His mind echoed faintly the tale of Terrence's mother and the catheter.

Until one mighty yank . . . With a heroic jerk the queen fell backward off their marriage bed. Rising from the carpets she held aloft a prize. Slack and flaccid it was. Rubbery and limp. Bloodless as the moon it hung gripped in her fist.

"What have you done?" cried Charlie. "Witch, you!"

"Dude, stop with the Renn Faire–speak, already!" Shasta did retort. She shook the dripping trophy. "No duh! You ever hear of the brown recluse spider?"

Then did she launch into a learned tirade about some arachnid. A spider the bite of which injected a toxin into its unknowing victim. For to create necrotic tissue, was its loathsome venom. Most often painless was this bite, and the effects were gradual.

"Dude," laughed the meat-clutching female, "I've been putting spiders on your highness' royal dingus since the first watercress harvest, duh!"

Over time, this poison, this poisonous spider venom had anesthetized and begun to break down his organ of manliness. The progressive effects of multiple secret spider bites had gradually dissolved the cellular structures, leaving his tool of reproduction hardly more than an elongated sack of pinkish jelly.

This, this bladder of goo did the enraged queen rip asunder.

Now did she hold it high above her head and did shake the boneless trophy like a Polaroid picture.

That quivering mass of semisolid, insensate flesh she did draw back her pitching arm and make ready to throw.

Charlie, mighty chieftain of the first lineage of Caucasia, noble lord of the Maryhill estate, bold killer of many enemies from The List, Charlie chosen by Chieftain Dawson, Charlie the chooser of Chieftain Martin, chooser of Chieftain Patrick, chooser of Chieftain Michael, at this did Charlie release a screeching wail.

Continued Shasta, "I looked on your computer." She did scream, "I know what you guys did to Walter!"

Without pause did she fling the wilted meat stick against a bed chamber casement of highly colored glass, through which it exploded in a shower of reds and golds and plummeted a goodly distance, wriggling down from the cloudless sky, to where it flopped, bouncing damply at the feet of many field wives who recognized the item instantly as it thudded among the rows of Swiss chard and zucchini. There in the dust did it come to rest and was the relic immediately seized upon by hungry, devouring ants.

Wailing in horror at the wet crater that was all that remained of his scepter and orbs, Charlie did squeal for his guards to seize her. Beseeching Odin and Thor, did Charlie curse, "Ye shall burn for this, vile beldame!"

But not before his wife, the mother of his final belly child, did take hurried leave of the locale. And not before she did cry, victoriously, "And no matter what Ernst Zündel said the Holocaust really, *really* did happen!"

In the world where the burial pits were just being dug and lined with plastic and quicklime, Nick had sounded wasted. "So, Walt, you're saying it's some big revolutionary attack deal?" he responded over his cell phone.

Walter hadn't been sure what the book and men devoted to Talbott had done yet. He was calling, trying to alert someone. Anyone. He was calling the only two people he'd ever really trusted.

Over the phone, Shasta had asked, "Walter, you're saying you killed somebody?"

They'd both asked what he planned to do next.

Walter had been in a basement with the body of a dead man. A cloud of black flies circling. The old man he'd promised he wasn't going to hurt. Looking at the corpse sliced with tiny cuts and blotchy with dried blood, he'd said, "Adjustment Day is coming. But I can still stop it."

The borderlands teemed with the free-range grizzlies of Caucasia as well as the tigers imported by Blacktopia. It was a no-man's land, left as inhospitable as possible. A natural buffer of poisonous snakes and rabid carnivores between the three nations. To venture within amounted to a death wish.

Their campfire blazed, creating a crackling circle of orange light. Charm and her brother had run out of gas and road at roughly the same point. Afterwards they'd hiked over raw wilderness until twilight forced them to set up camp. She'd brought everything: tents, flint, a pantry of dried food, a water filter, sleeping bags, and toilet paper.

As they sat looking into the flames Gavyn said, "Mom is going to kill you."

Sadly, Charm retorted, "She already killed *you*." She didn't elaborate, but she didn't have to.

Roasting hot dogs on sticks, they speculated about their parents riding bicycles out to some sprawling agricultural estate. There they'd indenture themselves in time for the late hops harvest. Some chieftain would provide for them until the winter wheat was ready to thresh. Theirs would be a merry winter solstice quaffing mead and munching yule logs around a bonfire of dried horse dung.

Panthers or maybe leopards snarled in the not-far-off darkness, and the siblings laughed to vanquish their fear.

At the edge of their small clearing a twig snapped. Charm lifted a flaming branch from the fire and made ready to club the unseen predator.

A discolored gremlin limped into the flickering light. Stooped and shrunken, its matted hair formed an irregular mass around its wrinkled face. Its blue skin was almost a perfect match to the inky night around it. On its heels was a tall, handsome young man wearing one dazzle-bright diamond earring. A pit bull with black-and-white markings bounded into view. The dog rushed to sniff at the campers.

Gavyn muttered, "Jamal."

Charm said, "Mine!"

The man lifted a hand. "Hey."

In unison Gavyn and Charm said, "Hey." Charm waved her flaming club in a clumsy greeting.

Jamal indicated the hobbling, painted imp and said, "This is Barnabas."

Charm elbowed her brother and said, "Yours!"

The disturbing creature lifted a clawed hand and said, "Actually, I'm Miss Josephine."

Before anyone could break the uncomfortable silence, another twig snapped. Something unseen rustled through the dry leaves.

The small group recoiled from the new sound. With sizzling hot-dog wieners and fiery marshmallows they braced to defend themselves against a pack of starving wolves. Instead, a kid stepped out of the woods. "Hey," he asked, "is this still Gaysia?"

Elbowing his sister, Gavyn said, "Mine." He asked, "You gay?"

The kid shook his head. "I'm Felix."

Charm heaved a sigh. "This is the borderlands."

Felix said, "Isn't this the ending of *Fahrenheit 451*?"

It was turning into quite a little party. Felix had brought Mountain Dew–flavored Doritos. Jamal and the pixie creature shared mint juleps with the group. Nobody asked why anyone else had come to this nowhere place. Their combined voices drove off the howls.

Another twig snapped. A female voice asked, "Charm?"

Charm called back, "Shasta?"

A young man and woman stepped out of the shadows. Together, they said, "Hey."

In return, the group around the campfire said, "Hey."

No sooner had Shasta introduced Nick and they'd found places beside the fire, but the rustle of leaves and snapping of twigs and the screech of night birds heralded a new presence in the dark.

People ask how it ended.

Walter had been a well-intentioned doofus is how it ended. He'd been the good scout, the one in every crowd. The altar boy, the teacher's pet, he'd walked into the Southeast Precinct, looking both ways, whispering with one hand cupped beside his mouth. Past dark o'clock, it was a hundred years past midnight when in had walked Walter Baines with his hood up, head down, wearing sunglasses no less. He'd whisper-asked, "Can I talk to somebody in charge?" He'd told the desk sergeant, "I want to report a crime's supposed to happen."

The desk sergeant, mister sergeant had been, "Got some ID?"

The desk sergeant had palmed him off on a detective who'd taken Walter into the basement where by then it was already too late.

A muffled voice from somewhere Walter couldn't see, it had said, "The only quality that truly unites us is our desire to be united." Fishing in his pocket, he'd brought out Shasta's earplug and sniffed it, inhaled the sweetness of her earwax and brains. For that long eyes-closed huff, she'd been standing right next to him.

Proof that even a writer can die a hero's death.

That, that was the end of the Before Times and the beginning of the end.

The release of twenty-five thousand white doves went off without a hitch. They were blessed with perfect weather, and their fifty thousand feathered wings carried them into a blue sky. For a moment they formed a soaring white cloud, then doubled back toward the countryside while far below them a cheering horde lined the parade route.

Starvation and crime had left Portland safe to inhabit again. As a result, Charlie's legions were marching triumphantly into the overgrown, deserted metropolis. Shaggy dray horses harnessed in teams pulled the battlewagons. The catapults were equipped with nuclear projectiles. The battering rams tipped with enriched plutonium. Endless brigades of archers carried quivers filled with C-4 arrowheads. Marching behind these were ranks of lancers whose spears were dripping with anthrax. And with the appearance of every dirigible filled with mustard gas, the throngs cheered. Likewise with every cannon and siege tower that passed, they thundered upon it their applause.

Most conspicuous among the onlookers were the home wives and field wives of Maryhill. For every woman among them stood splay footed and with her belly child pushed forward. And more than a few were even now feeling the onset of birthing pains, for Charlie had been a busy bee amid his sweet flowers, pollinating more than a few each day, and today they craned their necks and stood on tiptoe for the chance to see him march past and, perhaps, catch his eye.

And lost in this crowd was an older woman, beyond her childbearing years. A ragged peasant woman who could but faintly recall an age when she labored over the keys of something as magical as a data-entry terminal. Her long gray tresses were tied atop her head. Her hands were the raw, red hands of a washerwoman. Some time ago her nose had been broken and had come to heal flattened sideways against her cheek. Her knees ached, but still she peered into the rows of marchers.

The air was alive with rose petals and confetti and loudspeakers blaring the voice of Talbott, who repeated, "Caucasia is at war with Gaysia! Caucasia has always been at war with Gaysia!"

The air trembled with the words, "What men want is a structure for communion!"

As the washerwoman squinted and studied the faces of passersby, another woman of like late middle age and appearance came to stand at her scabrous elbow. This new crone asked of the first, "Do you remember me?"

The washerwoman gave her a glance and went back to ogling the parade. "No," she said softly.

The new woman persisted, "My appearance has not always been thus." Speaking in the prescribed language of White-Speak, she said, "In Before Times was I a healer. A nurse."

The washerwoman cast another look upon this stranger. Her eyes scoured the woman for a clue, before returning to review the passing marchers.

Near them, a younger woman made a sharp, high-pitched outcry and slumped to the cobblestones. Those around her looked on nervously, but none went to her aid.

Without hesitation the washerwoman and the stranger knelt and commenced to administer succor. The younger woman's hangerock and muslin underdress were saturated in hot brine. Clearly her birthing time had arrived. If this were the case, the babe would arrive as the first of Charlie's offspring, and for that reason none of the other rival wives would lend comfort.

Therefore the washerwoman came to cradle the laboring wife as the stranger knelt between the knees of the woman in pain. As they eased the passage of the child, the kneeling woman said, "Rest easy, for in the Before Times did I attend many birthings." Her words canted toward the washerwoman, she continued, "It was I who tended your son."

The hardened washerwoman shed her flinty demeanor for a heartbeat. "My son? My Terrence?"

Attending to the birthing work, the stranger said, "How came your nose to be so broken?"

The washerwoman raised a scaly hand and touched absently at the forgotten disfigurement. But she made no answer.

In a world before everything came to be measured by bumper crops of sweet potatoes and babies, this strange woman had served mankind in a hospital. In that capacity had she presented the now-washwoman's son with the Talbott book. "At your behest," recounted the nurse, "I lied. I told the boy the book came from his father. His father whom I did never encounter. As you bid, I lied and told Terrence that his father was on guard for him, although I knew that to be a mistruth."

Both women spoke distractedly as they worked to free the belly child from its dam.

"You?" asked the washerwoman, unbelieving.

The nurse tended to the emergent babe. Shaking her head, she said, "I saw you write the notes in the book. Why did you perpetuate such a falsehood?"

"Shit. I don't know," swore the washerwoman, breaking a dangerous precedent by speaking in the coarse manner of Before Times. "I got the idea from *Bambi*."

The nurse echoed, "*Bambi*?"

Deadpanned the washerwoman, "That cartoon deer." Her saggy wrinkles blushed as if with chagrin. "Remember? That part where the stag steps out of the forest and says Bambi is his son and heir, and the stag has always been his secret guardian?"

"Wait," said the nurse, momentarily pausing over the half-born offspring. "So you invented a noble, loving father?"

Without protest the washerwoman continued, "I needed Terrence to hate me if he was ever going to grow a pair."

The nurse hefted the bloody newborn aloft and smote its rosy buttocks. Inquired she, "Did not the mother deer die?"

The babe wailed lustily. A tiny female, the poor thing.

Distracted by the memory, the washerwoman said, "Yeah. But who wants to die? I forced Terrence to reject me."

The nurse placed the healthy, squirming infant in the new mother's arms. For the first time, the weary, sweaty young woman joined the conversation, asking, "And what became of your Terrence?"

As if on cue the parade onlookers threw up a mighty cheer. Heraldic banners snapped smartly in the breeze displaying many colors of vibrant hand-loomed velvets. The warm air reverberated with the timpani of massed kortholts and bladder pipes. The marching feet kept pace by the regular beat of tabors and timbrels. The focus of this cheering attention was Chieftain Charlie. Cloaked in leatherette. Adorned in pleather, he limped heavily from side to side assisted by his royal physician.

This learned attendant, this physician to the king's health, was none other than Terrence. And upon glimpsing her son, a full-blown man, the holder of such a prestigious position, her washerwoman's heart leapt with pride and accomplishment.

Brief was her triumph. For a sheriff of the law was prodding her to step back and clear a corridor so that all might gaze upon their limping, pained ruler.

And not unheard by Charlie were the gales of female laughter that lapped at his back. And laugh did many of the thousand wives so heartily that they slumped to the pavements and proceeded to also empty their wombs of healthy, pink newborns. For many of their numbers had gifted Queen Shasta with the brown recluse spiders that had liquidated Charlie's kingly parts, and all knew that his pearl-encrusted codpiece was as empty as a drum.

As the washerwoman and the nurse set to work birthing this new tide of infants, the healer asked, "But tell me . . . why the lie?"

Looking after her son as he disappeared into the distance, the beaming washerwoman shrugged. "I wanted him to believe in a father and by extension a God." Watching until he was gone, she said, "Life's just easier that way."

The trembling figure crept into the clearing, illuminated by the firelight. An emaciated wanderer wearing a tailored suit made ragged by months in the wild. The stranger looked upon the curated little group of gays and straights, blacks and whites, females and males.

Of the youngsters seated around the campfire, none dared move a muscle. A twitch would send this stranger bolting. The wanderer, this wanderer met their stares with wide, traumatized eyes. He sniffed the air, his nostrils flaring, apparently tantalized by the aroma of their roasting wieners.

Nick, generous to a fault, Nick rifled his pockets. With an outstretched hand he offered the trembling wild man a pill, saying, "Looks like somebody could use a Percodan."

Shasta hushed him. She plucked the warm meat from the end of Jamal's sharpened stick. She felt the wiener's damp heat in her fingers and suffered a twinge of wifely guilt. In recompense, she knelt. Her fellows, Nick and Felix, Jamal and Miss Jo, Gavyn and Charm, they hissed for her to keep a safe distance, but she dismissed them with a motion of her hand.

Nodding, his eyes closed in bliss, Jamal whisper-yelled, "Cool! Just like in *Steinbeck*!"

The picture of compassionate grace, Shasta Sanchez offered the sweating, dripping morsel to this, the hounded, haunted, former president of the disunited states.

It was slow work. After the marchers and pipers had passed . . . once the cheering throngs had gone their own way with squalling newborns . . . former Senator Holbrook Daniels pushed a heavy two-wheeled gambrel along the silent parade route.

With a push broom he alone piled up the rose petals and confetti. Using a flat-bladed shovel he collected the cast-off placentas as well as the dried horse dung, and all of these he heaped in his straining cart.

While, attracted by the scent of fresh blood, drooling wolf packs were gathering in the surrounding shadows.

And while Walter Baines had bled to death from a gunshot to the forehead . . .

In the basement of an abandoned house a drop of blood had welled up in the scabbed wound on the scrawny arm of an old man. He'd opened his eyes. Finding himself alone, he'd flexed his stiff fingers, and the man had begun to tear away at the duct tape that bound his wrists and ankles to a stout wooden chair. He'd never been bound well and could've escaped at any juncture. If escape had ever been his goal.

His first item of business would be to delete The List.

Grouse hunting season had been only days away.

penguin.co.uk/vintage